Unanimous Praise for the Great
Contemporary Romances from the
"Fabulous"*
JAYNE ANN KRENTZ

WILDEST HEARTS

"The phenomenal Jayne Ann Krentz once again delivers one of her patented storytelling gems. . . . Another guaranteed top-notch read!"
—*Romantic Times*

FAMILY MAN

"In her own saucy, upbeat style, Krentz turns this eccentric family and pair of mismatched lovers (so everyone tells them) into an entertaining story. . . . Her fans will eat it up."
—*Publishers Weekly*

"I love Jayne's writing . . . this book is no exception. . . . Set in Jayne's home turf—the beautiful Pacific Northwest—and filled with quirky secondary characters, this book's a winner."
—*Heart to Heart*

PERFECT PARTNERS

"With bold style and a wicked sense of humor Krentz tells the story of Letty Thornquist. . . . Toss in a gaggle of vividly drawn minor characters . . . and it adds up to entertaining contemporary romance. . . . She's in top form."
—*Publishers Weekly*

"[A] totally entertaining . . . compelling novel filled with finely crafted characters . . . exceptional reading."
—*Romantic Times*

*Romantic Times

SWEET FORTUNE

"Passion, humor, and dimensional characters involved in believable relationships add up to a fast-moving, well-developed story. . . . Jessie and Hatch . . . were made for each other."
— *Rendezvous*

"The inimitable Jayne Ann Krentz is back, wheeling and dealing in corporate boardrooms for our reading pleasure. . . . Always a consistent delight, Ms. Krentz has penned another winner."
— *Rave Reviews*

THE GOLDEN CHANCE

"If you're in the market for irresistible romance and high-powered corporate intrigue, run, do not walk, to the nearest bookstore and pick up this splendid novel by the fabulous Jayne Ann Krentz."
— *Romantic Times*

"Philadelphia Fox is one of the feistiest, most memorable heroines in years. *The Golden Chance* is Jayne Ann Krentz at her very best. Pure entertainment."
— Susan Elizabeth Phillips,
author of *Fancy Pants* and *Hot Shot*

"Jayne Ann Krentz has taken the powerful themes of family loyalty, the struggle for power, and sex, and woven them into a suspenseful and satisfying story that strikes a deep, human chord."
— Patricia Matthews,
author of *Oasis* and *Sapphire*

SILVER LININGS

"The Krentz mark of excellence is more than evident in the snappy dialogue, steamy sensuality, and vivid characterization. Don't miss this outstanding romantic adventure."
—*Romantic Times*

"Wonderful characters, a great plot with lots of action, and a fine romance with lots of sparks—what more could you ask for?"
—*Rendezvous*

AWARD-WINNING JAYNE ANN KRENTZ

FROM *ROMANTIC TIMES:*

- 1991 CAREER ACHIEVEMENT AWARD IN CONTEMPORARY ROMANCE
- 1991 CAREER ACHIEVEMENT AWARD IN HISTORICAL ROMANCE
- 1991 REVIEWER'S CHOICE AWARD FOR BEST CONTEMPORARY ROMANTIC SUSPENSE
- 1989, 1990, 1991 REVIEWER'S CHOICE AWARD FOR HISTORICAL ROMANCE

FROM B. DALTON BOOKSELLER:

- 1991 BESTSELLING REGENCY ROMANCE
- 1990 GREATEST ANNUAL INCREASE FOR CONTEMPORARY ROMANCE

FROM *AFFAIRE DE COEUR:*

- 1988 BEST CONTEMPORARY ROMANCE AWARD
- 1988 SILVER PEN and FAVORITE AUTHOR AWARD

Books by Jayne Ann Krentz

The Golden Chance
Silver Linings
Sweet Fortune
Perfect Partners
Family Man
Wildest Hearts
Hidden Talent
Grand Passion
Trust Me
Absolutely, Positively
Deep Waters

Writing as Jayne Castle

Amaryllis
Zinnia

Published by POCKET BOOKS

For orders other than by individual consumers, Pocket Books grants a discount on the purchase of **10 or more** copies of single titles for special markets or premium use. For further details, please write to the Vice-President of Special Markets, Pocket Books, 1633 Broadway, New York, NY 10019-6785, 8th Floor.

For information on how individual consumers can place orders, please write to Mail Order Department, Simon & Schuster Inc., 200 Old Tappan Road, Old Tappan, NJ 07675.

JAYNE
Hidden
ANN
Talents
KRENTZ

POCKET BOOKS

New York London Toronto Sydney Tokyo Singapore

This book is a work of fiction. Names, characters, places and
incidents are either the product of the author's imagination or are
used fictitiously. Any resemblance to actual events or locales or
persons, living or dead, is entirely coincidental.

An *Original* Publication of POCKET BOOKS

POCKET BOOKS, a division of Simon & Schuster Inc.
1230 Avenue of the Americas, New York, NY 10020

Copyright © 1993 by Jayne Ann Krentz

ISBN: 0-671-01965-1

First Pocket Books printing October 1993

10 9 8 7

POCKET and colophon are registered trademarks of
Simon & Schuster Inc.

Cover art by Tom Hallman

Printed in the U.S.A.

Hidden Talents

Prologue

SHE SAT UNMOVING AT THE EDGE OF THE CRYSTAL CLEAR hot spring pool. The silvery vapor that hovered over the warm water twisted and curled in on itself, drawing her deeper into the trance. She gazed down into the liquid's fathomless depths and waited. Slowly the vision took shape.

Sunlight, warm and golden, poured into the white room. Somewhere in the distance a waltz was playing. She held the infants cradled in her arms and watched the closed door. Soon it would open and he would come to her.

The door opened.

A man walked into the white, sunlit room.

He smiled at her.

"Damn," Serenity said. "Wrong man."

1

I THINK YOU SHOULD KNOW THAT SOMEONE IS TRYING TO blackmail me," she said.

Her name was Serenity Makepeace, and until thirty seconds ago Caleb Ventress had been giving serious consideration to having an affair with her.

He had not mentioned the idea to Serenity because he had not yet finished assessing the situation. Never had he been more profoundly grateful for his natural inclination toward calm deliberation than he was at that particular moment.

Caleb never made a move without first thinking through all aspects of a problem. He applied the time-tested method to his personal as well as his business affairs. He knew better than anyone else that his habit of approaching everything with an unemotional, logical detachment was one of the chief factors responsible for his phenomenal financial success.

To date, his relationship with Serenity had been limited to a handful of meetings in his office, three working lunches, and two business dinners. He hadn't even kissed her. He'd planned to take that step tonight.

It had been a near thing, Caleb realized. A strange, cold feeling twisted through his gut as he acknowledged the close brush with disaster. What really bothered him was the uneasy feeling that Serenity Makepeace had the potential for making him ignore his own rules.

She was unlike any other woman he had ever known. She fascinated him. If he had lived in another time and place, an era during which people routinely believed in superstitious nonsense, for example, he would have wondered if she had put some kind of spell on him.

She sat there now, on the other side of his desk, ostensibly in his world, but somehow not quite of it. It was as if she had dropped into his reality from some alternate universe.

Serenity Makepeace had eyes the color of a peacock's tail, and a wild, fiery red mane that today was only partially controlled by a black ribbon tied at her nape.

There was a fey quality about her that stirred the hair on the back of Caleb's neck. The odd little griffin pendant she wore somehow accented her aura of otherworldliness. She possessed an ethereal air that almost convinced him that she had been meant to dance in moonlit meadows at midnight rather than conduct business negotiations in a high-rise office.

He sincerely hoped that she was better at dancing in the moonlight than she was at dealing with business matters. He'd had to guide her every step of the way through their recent contract discussions. The problem wasn't her lack of intelligence; she had a disconcertingly healthy amount of that quality. The difficulty was her lack of experience.

Serenity managed a tiny grocery store in a small mountain community called Witt's End. From what Caleb could discern, the store catered to an eccentric clientele of misfits and nonconformists, artsy-craftsy types and social dropouts. Serenity knew a lot about whole-grain bread, beans, and tofu, but she knew virtually nothing about sophisticated business practices.

That was where he came in, Caleb reminded himself. Serenity wanted to expand her small grocery into a mail order catalog operation. She needed a start-up consultant.

Caleb was one of the best start-up consultants in the Pacific Northwest; perhaps the best. He was very good at what he did.

The Witt's End by Mail project had been very different from Caleb's usual ventures. For one thing, he wasn't accustomed to working with people who were as unsophisticated about business as Serenity obviously was. His usual clients were high-powered corporate executives who sent their lawyers to work out the terms of the contracts. He rarely, if ever, consulted with small, independent businesses the size of Witt's End Grocery. The owners of such firms couldn't afford him. Serenity was no exception. She couldn't pay his usual fees, either.

The only reason Caleb had taken Serenity on as a client in the first place was because she had caught his attention and piqued his admittedly jaded professional interest. He had been bored with his own highly successful career and with life in general for longer than he cared to remember.

He recalled Serenity's initial letter of inquiry quite clearly. The scope of her plans had amused him.

Dear Mr. Ventress:

Allow me to introduce myself. My name is Serenity Makepeace and I need your help to save my hometown, Witt's End, Washington.

You have probably never heard of Witt's End. It's located in the Cascade mountains, approximately an hour and a half drive from Seattle. It is home to a variety of artists, craftspeople, and others who need an environment that accepts and nurtures independent spirits who choose unconventional lifestyles.

I am well aware that I cannot afford your usual consulting fees, but I am prepared to offer you a share of the future profits.

My goal is to create a viable mail order business, an offshoot of my grocery store, that will provide an outlet for the unusual products of our local residents. I'm appealing to you, Mr. Ventress, because my community cannot survive much longer unless it is given a solid economic base.

I am aware that this project is probably very small and insignificant compared to the consulting projects you normally handle, but I urge you to take on the task. I'm told that you're very good at this kind of thing.

I am committed to saving my community. I

believe that the world needs places like Witt's End, Washington, Mr. Ventress. They are the last frontier towns, the only communities left that are suited to those who do not fit in well with the modern urban landscape.

In a sense we all need places like Witt's End. And Witt's End needs you, Mr. Ventress.

Sincerely,
Serenity Makepeace

On a whim, Caleb had invited Serenity for an interview. The day she had walked through the door three weeks ago, looking completely wrong in a conservative gray suit and matching one-inch heels, he knew he would be signing a contract with her.

He had taken Serenity by the hand, and she had followed his experienced lead with charming naiveté. If he'd really been trying to take advantage of her, he could have tied her up six ways from Sunday and she would never have had a clue. Instead, five minutes ago she had signed on the bottom line of what he considered a reasonably fair contract.

Of course, he had given himself a very large, very flexible escape clause, and left her with only one carefully controlled exit out of the deal; an exit that she would probably need a lawyer to find. Business was business, after all, and a contract was a contract. When it came to this part of his life, Caleb made it a habit to do things on his own terms or not at all.

His escape route was spelled out in section six of the contract. All he had to do was exercise it.

Caleb did not take his eyes off of Serenity as he absorbed the body blow she had just dealt him.

7

"What did you say?" he asked. There was virtually no chance that he had misunderstood her, but he had to make certain.

Serenity cleared her throat delicately. "I said someone is trying to blackmail me."

A dark rage ignited somewhere deep inside Caleb. It had been so long since he had last felt such a powerful emotion that he almost failed to recognize the hot anger for what it was. For an instant it threatened to overwhelm him.

"Damn it to hell." Caleb made no effort to tone down the savage edge that etched his words.

Serenity tilted her head to one side and studied him with a perplexed but very steady gaze. "Is something wrong?"

That was taking the element of charming naiveté a little too far, he thought in disgust. He wondered what he had ever seen in her. No one would have labeled her beautiful, he decided, making a desperate attempt to regain the cold, detached objectivity he had cultivated all of his life. Attractive, yes. Interesting, certainly. Amusing, even. But not beautiful.

Serenity's intelligent face was expressive and vivid. He had to admit that there was a natural elegance to her high cheekbones. He also conceded that there was something about her full mouth that made him think of sultry nights and damp, tangled sheets, even though this year October was proving to be cool and crisp in Seattle.

No, she was not beautiful, but he had been riveted by her from the first moment she had walked into his office. He had wanted her.

God help him, he still wanted her.

"Under the circumstances, that's a rather idiotic question, don't you think?" Caleb muttered.

"I'm sorry," Serenity said politely. "I realize this has probably come as a surprise to you. It certainly has to me."

Caleb spread his fingers flat across the gleaming surface of his glass-and-steel desk. "Why would anyone blackmail you, Miss Makepeace?"

"I'm not sure." Her red brows drew together in a serious, considering expression. "It was the strangest thing. The pictures were addressed to me at my hotel this morning. There was a note with them that said copies would be sent to you if I didn't break off my business dealings with Ventress Ventures immediately."

"Pictures?" Caleb's insides tightened. *Please, don't let it be what I think it's going to be.* "Of you?"

Serenity blushed but did not look away. "Yes."

"With someone?" Caleb made himself ask very carefully. Maybe it wouldn't be so bad. Maybe they were photos of her with a past lover. She was twenty-eight years old, he reminded himself. She was bound to have had a few affairs. He could handle that. He'd had a few of his own. Not many, but a few.

"No. The pictures are of me alone. They were taken about six months ago."

Caleb set his back teeth. "What, exactly, are you doing in these photos?"

"Nothing much. I'm just sort of lying around in most of them."

"Just sort of lying around." Caleb picked up a pen and tapped it very, very gently against the glass desktop. *Ting, ting, ting.* The noise grated on his ears.

"What makes the pictures suitable for blackmail purposes, Ms. Makepeace?"

"That's just the point. I don't think they are suitable for blackmail." Her lovely mouth curved ruefully. "But someone apparently believes that they're potentially damning. At least in your eyes."

"Why do you think someone might have that impression?"

Serenity shrugged with graceful nonchalance. The airy motion made her look even more out of place in the prim little gray suit. "I'm not exactly sure why anyone would think of them as blackmail material. I suppose it's because I'm not wearing much in any of them."

"Just how much are you wearing in the pictures?"

She touched the little griffin that hung from the chain around her throat. It was obvious that the pendant had originally been finished with an imitation gold overlay. The cheap veneer had since worn off in several places, allowing the inexpensive metal underneath to show through on the wings of the beast. "Mostly I'm just wearing this."

"Nude photos. Christ." Caleb threw down the pen and got to his feet. He shoved his hands into the pockets of his expensively tailored trousers and paced to the window.

Was this what it had been like for his family all those years ago? he wondered. He brushed the fleeting thought aside. He knew very well that the old scandal had been a thousand times worse for his grandfather and the rest of the proud Ventress clan. After all, his father, Gordon Ventress, had been married when the photos of his mistress, Crystal Brooke, had been sent to Caleb's grandfather, Roland.

Crystal Brooke had been the stage name of the part-time model, would-be starlet, and full-time hustler who had gotten her bright red claws into the wealthy up-and-coming young politician from Ventress Valley, Washington.

Caleb had never known his mother Crystal, but he had been told a great deal about her during his youth. Her specialty had been nude spread shots for the sort of men's magazines that were not generally purchased because of the high quality of the articles.

When the evidence of his son's affair with Crystal Brooke had reached Roland Ventress, the ensuing explosion had rocked the conservative farm town of Ventress Valley. Toughened by years of ranching, a stint in the military, and a streak of gritty stubbornness that ran in the family, Roland had flatly refused to pay the blackmail demand.

The anonymous blackmailer had promptly sent the pictures to the *Ventress Valley News*. The editor of the town's only newspaper had been feuding with Roland Ventress at the time. He had gleefully printed a photo of Crystal that had been carefully cropped to make it suitable for a small-town paper. The accompanying editorial had fulminated against the declining morals and abysmal ethics of young Gordon Ventress. It had questioned his suitability for a seat in the state legislature.

The resulting scandal had ripped the family apart. Gordon's elegant, young wife, Patricia, raised in an old-money, East Coast family, had done her duty up to a point. She had bravely stood by her husband until word came that Crystal Brooke had a baby son. Gordon freely admitted to being the father.

The news that her husband had a child by his

mistress proved to be too much for Patricia. Not even the sturdy notions of wifely fortitude and family loyalty that had been handed down to her by several generations of stalwart New England forebears could sustain her. She agreed to a divorce, the first in the history of the Ventress family.

After a stormy confrontation with Roland, Gordon had gone back to Los Angeles to be with Crystal. He vowed to marry her as soon as his divorce was final, but that weekend he and his mistress had both died in a fiery car crash.

The only survivor had been their three-month-old son, Caleb.

Roland Ventress had followed in the proud tradition of the Ventress family. He had done his duty by his unwanted heir. With the glaring exception of Caleb's father, the Ventresses always did their duty.

Roland went to Los Angeles to bury his only son and claim his grandson. He had grudgingly handled the arrangements for Crystal Brooke's burial also, simply because no one else had stepped forward to do it.

Roland had brought the infant Caleb home to Ventress Valley and informed his grieving wife, Mary, and the rest of the family, which consisted of his nephew Franklin and his niece Phyllis, that in spite of the scandal, the Ventresses would uphold their responsibilities to the boy. Caleb was, after all, Roland's only hope for the future.

Caleb had been dutifully raised and dutifully educated. He had been instructed in the duties and responsibilities that were expected of a Ventress.

And he had never been allowed to forget for one

moment that he was the result of the scandalous affair that had brought disaster on the Ventress clan.

If it hadn't been for Caleb, everyone agreed, the scandal could have been dealt with eventually. Perhaps Crystal Brooke could have been bought off. Perhaps Gordon would have come to his senses and dropped his little bleached-blond mistress.

If it hadn't been for Caleb, everything would have been all right.

But Caleb existed.

The indomitable Roland came to terms with that fact. He had then set out to ensure that the bad blood the boy had inherited from his mother was not allowed to surface.

As for Caleb, he knew now that he had wasted most of his youth trying to satisfy a grandfather who viewed even the smallest of failures as evidence that Crystal Brooke's genes had not been successfully stamped out.

Looking back on it, Caleb knew that for the most part, things had been all right during the early years, when his grandmother had still been alive. Stricken as she was by her loss, Mary Ventress had eventually recovered sufficiently from her grief to refocus her natural maternal affections toward her grandson.

Mary had learned to love Caleb although she had never successfully concealed her hatred of the woman who had borne him. Whenever Caleb thought of his grandmother, he could not help but recall the sadness that had always been there, just beneath the surface. He had always known that somehow he was responsible for that deep anguish in Mary Ventress.

After her death eight years later, Roland had taken over the task of raising Caleb. Franklin and Phyllis had pitched in to help with the job. Both had been as concerned as Roland that young Caleb not be allowed to repeat his father's mistake.

Caleb was well aware that he had been paying for the cheap photos of his mother all of his life. He understood the realities of blackmail better than anyone else.

If there was one thing guaranteed to awaken the beast within him, it was blackmail. If there was one type of woman with whom he had vowed never to get involved, it was the sort who could be blackmailed because of sleazy nude photos, photos such as those that had been taken of his mother.

The realization that he had been planning to start an affair with Serenity Makepeace made Caleb want to smash the heavy glass top of his desk into a million glittering shards.

"Who took the pictures?" Caleb forced himself to speak in a remote, neutral tone. It wasn't easy. He wasn't accustomed to dealing with such fierce anger. But he'd had years of practice controlling all his emotions, and he'd gotten very good at that kind of thing.

He was good at a lot of things, he reflected bitterly.

Serenity looked momentarily confused by his question. "What do you mean? A photographer took the pictures, of course."

"What was the name of the photographer? Who was he working for?"

"Oh, I see what you mean," Serenity said. "His name is Ambrose Asterley. And he wasn't working for anyone, unfortunately. His career has been in the doldrums for years. At one time he was considered very good, though."

"Is that right?"

Serenity apparently missed the sarcasm. "Oh, yes. He actually worked in L.A. Hollywood, you know. That was years ago, however. I'm told he was on the way to the top. But poor Ambrose has a drinking problem. It's ruined his life."

She had posed naked for a cheap, washed-up drunk of a photographer. Caleb's hand closed into a fist. The pictures had no doubt been barely good enough for the raunchiest of the skin magazines. "I see."

"Ambrose has been doing a little better since he moved to Witt's End a few years ago," Serenity assured him earnestly. "He's made a couple of small sales, but he hasn't been able to get his career back on track. I felt sorry for him."

"That's why you posed for him? Because you felt sorry for him?"

"Yes. And because, whatever else one can say about Ambrose, there's no denying that he's a very gifted artist."

"Damn it to hell." Caleb stared down at Fourth Avenue, which lay twenty floors below his office window. Everything and everyone down there on the street seemed to be a long way off, just as most things did in his life these days. He preferred it this way. It made things simpler. At least it had until recently.

His carefully controlled emotional distance had initially been as a means of protecting himself from the silent accusation he had seen in the eyes of his grandparents and everyone else in the family. But lately it seemed to him that the detached, clinically remote feeling he had relied on for years was unaccountably growing stronger.

There were times recently when he felt as if he were

starting to dematerialize. Ordinary life went on as usual around him, but he was only going through the motions, pretending he was part of what was happening, but knowing that in reality he was not really a participant, just an observer. Nothing touched him, and he was not sure that he could touch anything in turn.

It was as if he were becoming a ghost.

But Serenity Makepeace had reached out and grabbed him in some manner that Caleb was helpless to explain.

Emotions, strong, exciting, dangerous emotions, had begun to reemerge deep within him the day she walked into his office. The first thing he had felt was raw, energizing desire. It made him feel alive as nothing else had in ages.

Now he was experiencing rage.

He should have known that Serenity was too good to be true.

"Those photos must be very interesting, Ms. Makepeace," Caleb said. He thought of the old photos and newspaper clippings that were locked away in the little jewelry box that had belonged to his mother. Damning photos. The stuff of blackmail.

The jewelry box, a gaudy case encrusted with large, fake gems, was the only thing he had inherited from Crystal Brooke. Roland Ventress had given it to him on his eighteenth birthday along with yet another solemn warning not to make the same mistakes his father had made.

Caleb had opened the jewelry case only once. It had remained closed and hidden away ever since.

"Ambrose may have a drinking problem, but he's a talented photographer," Serenity said with what would have been touching loyalty under other circumstances. "The shots he took of me would be considered art by most people."

"Nude photos of you just sort of *lying* around? Give me a break. We're not talking about art, we're talking about the kind of shots that get published in cheap men's magazines."

"That's not true." She was clearly shocked by his uncompromising attitude. "The pictures were never published at all, but if they had been, I assure you it wouldn't have been in a tacky men's magazine. Ambrose's work is much too good for that kind of format. He deserves to be hung in the best galleries."

"He deserves to be hung, all right," Caleb muttered. "Look, you can drop the artistic outrage. I know exactly what kind of pictures Ambrose Asterley takes."

"You do?" She brightened. "Don't tell me you've actually seen his work?"

"Let's just say I'm familiar with the style. It's obvious that he has a talent for producing the kind of photos that can be used for blackmail."

"But these pictures aren't like that," she protested. "I'm trying to explain."

"I don't want any more of your damned explanations."

There was a moment of startled silence behind him as his words went home.

"So whoever sent the note was right," Serenity said slowly. "You don't approve of nude art photography. Does this mean you'll want to break off our business arrangements?"

"I'm going to have to think about it."

"I see."

He sensed her withdrawal, and the rage within him grew stronger. She was the cause of this, not him. "Tell me, Serenity, what other talents do you possess? Do you act as well as model?"

"I beg your pardon?"

"I was just wondering if, by any chance, you've made a few films with Ambrose Asterley or some of his colleagues."

"Films?"

"You know the sort I mean. The kind that get shown in X-rated theaters. The kind that are displayed in the adults-only section of the video stores."

"Good grief." Serenity was obviously affronted. "What are you accusing me of?"

"I'm not accusing you of anything." Caleb swung around and met her offended gaze. "You're the one who announced that she was being blackmailed because of a bunch of nude photos. I just wondered how wide-ranging your talents actually are."

"You think I'm some sort of porn film star?" Serenity leaped to her feet. She clutched her small briefcase to her like a shield. "That's ridiculous. Look at me. Do I look like a woman who could make a living that way?"

He studied her slender, delicate frame dispassionately. He was well aware that she lacked the plastic breasts and the aggressive sexuality that one associated with the models who graced the pages of cheap magazines and soft-porn films.

But there was a disturbing sensuality about Serenity that heated Caleb's blood whenever he was in the same room with her. It was an earthy, elemental thing that defied explanation. It was all too easy for him to envision her lying sleek and naked in some grassy meadow, her eyes full of feminine mischief, her mouth parted in invitation.

A jolting thought went through Caleb. A photo that actually succeeded in capturing Serenity's ethereal sensuality probably would be a work of art.

But those weren't the sort of pictures that got shot by a seedy, drunken has-been of a photographer who had once worked in L.A.

Caleb sucked in his breath. He could not stomach the thought that Serenity had posed for the kind of photos that could be used for blackmail purposes; photos like those that had destroyed his parents thirty-four years ago. He lashed out with the fury of a wounded beast.

"No, you probably wouldn't be much of a success as a porn star," Caleb said. "I suppose it's no surprise that Asterley failed to sell the pictures he took of you. You haven't got what it takes, have you?"

The blood rose into Serenity's cheeks. "I told you, Ambrose Asterley is an artist."

"You can call him anything you like."

"You don't understand."

"I understand very well, Serenity. It's simple when you get right down to the bottom of it. A few months ago you posed for some trashy photos, and now someone is trying to use them to blackmail you. I believe that about sums up the whole mess."

"The blackmail attempt can only succeed if you allow it to do so," she said quickly. "Caleb, don't you care that someone is trying to stop us from revitalizing Witt's End?"

"I don't really give a damn if somebody wants to halt the march of progress in Witt's End. From what you've told me about the inhabitants, your blackmailer could be any one of those misfit refugees from mainstream society that you've got living there. The point is, this isn't my problem. It's yours."

"It doesn't have to be a problem at all." Serenity gave him a pleading look. "I only told you about the pictures because I thought you should know about them. I certainly don't intend to let anyone blackmail me into dropping my plans for Witt's End."

"Bravo for you. I wish you the best of luck."

"Look, I'll find out who sent the photos and talk to him or her. I'm sure that whoever made the threat acted out of a fear of change. I can reassure the person that things will remain very much the same in Witt's End even if I do get the mail order business up and running."

"You're going to try to reason with a blackmailer?" Caleb asked, amazed at her naiveté.

"Why not? I know everyone in town." Serenity sighed. "It may have been Blade, although I can't imagine how he got hold of the photos."

Caleb scowled. "Blade? You mean that weird survivalist you told me about? The one who keeps a herd of rottweilers and drives around with AK-47s hung on his gun rack?"

"I don't think they're AK-47s," Serenity said doubtfully.

"What difference does it make? The guy's a nut case."

"Blade's okay. You just have to get to know him. He makes wonderful herbed vinegars. I think they'll sell very well in my catalog."

"The man sounds like a dangerous, freaked-out, paranoid idiot. You said yourself that he's convinced that some clandestine government organization is plotting to take over the country."

"It may not have been Blade," Serenity said in a gentling voice that implied she was accustomed to dealing with temperamental types. "It could just as easily have been someone else."

Caleb discovered that he did not like being soothed and calmed as if he were a restless stallion. "Look, there's no need to deal with the issue of who sent the pictures until I decide whether or not to continue as your business consultant."

Serenity's fair skin turned even paler, highlighting the sprinkling of freckles on her nose and cheeks. She searched his face. "I can't believe you'd quit because of this."

Caleb's brows rose. "Anyone who knows me will tell you that I've always maintained certain standards in my business dealings. I don't intend to lower those standards now."

Serenity looked as if he'd just poured ice water on her. For the first time anger flashed in her eyes. "This is incredible. I had no idea you were such an arrogant, self-righteous prig."

Caleb folded his arms across his chest. "I had no idea you were the type of woman who posed nude for fifth-rate photographers."

"How dare you say such things. You know nothing about me or the pictures." Serenity took two steps back toward the door. "Do you know something? I actually liked you, Caleb. I thought you were nice."

"Nice?" Damn it to hell, Caleb thought. For some reason that was the last straw. "You thought I was *nice?*"

"Well, yes." Serenity's brilliant eyes filled with uncertainty. "You seemed so interested in my ideas for Witt's End. So helpful. I thought you were as concerned about the future of the community as I am."

"Witt's End can rot for all I care." For once in his life, Caleb did not stop to think about his next actions. He started toward Serenity with grim intent.

For nearly a month he had been suffering the torments of unsatisfied desire. He had consoled himself with his burgeoning plans for an affair, confident that Serenity was as attracted to him as he was to her. Now it was all coming apart and that knowledge clawed at his insides.

Serenity stood her ground, briefcase hugged protectively to her breasts. "Just what do you think you're doing?"

"Correcting a false impression." Caleb came to a halt in front of her. He lifted his hands, gripped her shoulders and jerked her close. "I wouldn't want you to go away thinking I'm a nice guy, Ms. Makepeace."

He took her mouth, crushing her soft, full lips beneath his own. The anger and the despair boiling within him was instantly channeled into the kiss. He felt Serenity tremble under the onslaught, but she did not try to pull away.

For a few seconds she stood stiffly within his rough embrace. She seemed more startled than frightened. Caleb knew he was destroying something important, something he had wanted very much to protect. The realization drove him to do a thorough job of it. He was, after all, a very thorough man.

His fingers tightened around Serenity's shoulders.

He could feel her teeth as he dragged his mouth across hers. It was the first time he had kised her, and it would no doubt be the last. The anguished rage within him transformed itself into a fierce passion that shook him to the very center of his being.

He tried to drown himself in the taste of Serenity, tried to fix the imprint of her against his body so that he could take out the memory of it five, ten, or twenty years hence and examine it.

Caleb deepened the kiss, easing Serenity's lips apart. He was ravenous for her. At any moment she would wrench herself out of his grasp and out of his life. This was all he was ever going to get.

Something very heavy crashed down onto the highly polished toes of Caleb's shoes. He winced. Serenity had dropped her briefcase.

Dazed by the torrent of emotions pouring through him, Caleb lifted his mouth from hers. He had to let her go.

"Not, not yet." Serenity wrapped her arms around his neck and pulled his lips back down on hers.

Before Caleb realized what she intended, Serenity was kissing him back with a heady intensity that sent shock waves through him and drove out all thoughts of the past or of the future. *She wanted him.* In that moment it was suddenly all that mattered.

Caleb lowered his hands to her small waist and started to lift her up against his heavily aroused body.

"That's enough." Serenity tore her mouth free and removed her arms from around his neck. She leaned back and pushed against his chest.

"Let me go, Caleb. I've changed my mind. You're not very nice at all." Her eyes glowed with anger and

23

passion. "You've ruined everything. *Everything*. How could you do this? I thought we understood each other. I thought we could trust each other."

He could not seem to breathe. "Damn it, Serenity."

"I said, let go of me." She tugged at his hands.

Caleb released her. Serenity reached down, scooped up her briefcase and ran for the door. She opened it and bolted through the opening into the outer office. Caleb's secretary, Mrs. Hotten, looked up, startled.

"Serenity, wait." Caleb started forward.

"I wouldn't wait one single minute for you, Caleb Ventress." Serenity whirled around to face him.

"What are you going to do?" he demanded.

"First, I'm going to track down the blackmailer. And then I'm going to find myself another business consultant. One who doesn't feel that he has to maintain such impeccable standards."

Serenity swung around again and stalked past Mrs. Hotten's desk. She wrenched open the outer door and vanished into the hall.

She was leaving.

Acting on blind instinct rather than logic, Caleb followed her.

The phone rang shrilly on Mrs. Hotten's desk. She snatched up the receiver. "Ventress Ventures." She paused for a few short seconds. "Yes, Mrs. Tarrant. He's right here. Please hold."

Caleb gained the entrance and looked out into the hall. It was too late to catch Serenity. The elevator doors were already closing on her. "Damn."

"Mr. Ventress?" Mrs. Hotten cleared her throat anxiously. "It's your aunt."

Caleb closed his eyes for an instant and took a deep,

steadying breath. The family was calling. Mrs. Hotten knew that he was always available to any member of the Ventress clan.

The sense of detached calm slowly returned. He was once more a remote, untouchable ghost in a realm where there were no dangerous emotions, no burning passions, no uncontrollable desires. He was safe. He was in control. Nothing could reach him here in this place where he was spending more and more of his time.

"I'll take the call in my office."

"Yes, sir."

There was an odd expression in Mrs. Hotten's normally placid, efficient, middle-aged gaze. Caleb had never seen that look before. Belatedly he realized it was sympathy.

Annoyed, Caleb ignored her to walk back into his inner sanctum.

He leaned across the desk and picked up the phone. "Good afternoon, Aunt Phyllis. Is there something I can do for you?" As always when he spoke to any of the family, he kept his voice deliberate and very, very polite.

"Good afternoon, Caleb." Phyllis's brisk, no-nonsense voice came crisply over the line. "I called to make certain you haven't forgotten the annual Ventress Valley Charity Drive. It's that time of year, I'm afraid, and we Ventresses must do our part."

She was fifty-nine years old, and she had made a career out of sitting on the boards of every major charity in Ventress Valley. As one of Gordon Ventress's cousins, she was not technically Caleb's aunt, but he had always addressed her by that title. In a similar fashion, he had always called his father's other cousin, Franklin, uncle.

"I haven't forgotten, Aunt Phyllis. I'll make the usual family contribution."

"Yes, of course. The community depends upon us, you know.'

"I know."

The Ventresses had been one of the most influential families in Ventress valley for four generations. As the heir apparent to Roland's lands and fortune, Caleb had taken control of the Ventress investments, most of which had originally been in land, but now were carefully diversified, soon after he had graduated from college. The family income had promptly doubled and then tripled under his management.

Roland still interfered whenever he felt the urge, of course. He would never really retire, and everyone knew it. But more often than not these days he was content to oversee his Arabian stud farm and leave the family finances to Caleb. Franklin and Phyllis never failed to make their opinions on financial matters known, and their offspring occasionally offered advice. But for all practical purposes, Caleb was in charge of the Ventress inheritance.

No one had ever actually thanked Caleb or shown any particular sign of gratitude for his efforts on their behalf. The entire family simply took it for granted that Caleb was merely doing what was expected of him.

"Well, then, that takes care of that," Phyllis said. "Now, when shall we expect you on Saturday?"

"I'm not certain. Probably around noon." Saturday was Roland Ventress's eighty-second birthday. Caleb had never missed a single one of his grandfather's annual celebrations since the day he had been brought home to Ventress Valley. Caleb made it a point to be very faithful to all family rituals.

"Very well, we'll expect you at noon." Phyllis hesitated. "Last week you mentioned you might bring a guest."

"I've changed my mind."

"I see. Does this mean that lovely Miss Learson won't be coming with you?"

"I'm no longer seeing Miss Learson."

The affair had ended three months ago by mutual agreement and with no hard feelings on either side. Susan Learson was the daughter of a successful California industrialist. She was poised, sophisticated, and charming, but Caleb had made it clear from the outset that he was not thinking of marriage.

Susan had been satisfied with the arrangement for nearly a year. Through Caleb she had met a variety of interesting and eligible men, and eventually fell in love with one of them, the CEO of a mid-sized Seattle company. She was planning to be married at Christmas. Caleb wished her well.

He had missed Susan for a time after the relationship had ended, and he thought of her now with a sense of remote affection. He knew his grandfather and the rest of the family missed her a lot more than he did. Roland was desperate to see Caleb married, desperate to know that the family would continue into another generation.

Caleb knew that the old man was beginning to wonder if his grandson's failure to find a suitable wife was more than just bad luck. He was starting to view it as a subtle form of revenge on Caleb's part, or proof, perhaps, that Crystal Brooke's bad blood had finally surfaced.

Caleb had not bothered to disabuse Roland of that notion, because he was not altogether certain it wasn't true. The only thing he was sure of was that a wife would demand more of him than any ghost had to give.

There was a distinct pause as Phyllis digested the fact that Susan Learson had gone the way of the small, select handful of other women who had been involved with Caleb over the years.

"It's unfortunate that you're no longer seeing her." Phyllis's tone was laced with censure. "Your grandfather was quite taken with her."

"I know."

"She reminded me a bit of Patricia, your father's wife. Excellent family. Good breeding. Miss Learson would have made you a very suitable wife."

"No doubt." *If I was looking for a wife, which I'm not.*

"What happened between the two of you?" Phyllis demanded, sounding exasperated. "I thought you liked her."

"I did. I do. But it's over."

"I'm sorry to hear that. Your grandfather won't be pleased."

Caleb had had enough of blackmail ploys for one day. "That won't exactly be a new experience for him, will it? Good-bye, Aunt Phyllis."

He hung up the phone and gazed thoughtfully at the receiver.

It seemed to him that his whole life had been

shaped by blackmail. Hell, he was a pro at dealing with it.

Something told him that Serenity Makepeace was not.

She'd left his office determined to find the blackmailer who had destroyed her hopes and dreams for Witt's End.

She was no doubt headed for trouble, and, like it or not, she was still officially his client. They had both signed that damned contract.

Caleb picked up the phone and then slowly replaced the receiver. It was not his way to do anything without giving it a lot of thought beforehand.

He made himself contemplate the matter for another half hour. Then he slowly and deliberately dialed the hotel where Serenity stayed when she came to Seattle to meet with him.

The front desk clerk was brief and to the point. "I'm sorry, sir," he said, not sounding sorry at all. "She just checked out."

2

THE FOLLOWING MORNING SERENITY LEFT HER COTTAGE to set off through the soggy, mist-shrouded forest. She was headed for Ambrose's cabin. She wanted a few answers to some very specific questions.

She had not paid him a visit last night after returning to Witt's End because she hadn't trusted her strange, unhappy mood. This morning she was calmer, but a frustrated anger was still burning within her.

She didn't know which annoyed her the most, that Caleb Ventress had not turned out to be the man she'd thought he was, or that she'd misjudged him so completely.

Serenity hated the rare occasions when her perception of others turned out to be faulty. She was accustomed to trusting her instincts.

But she should have known better than to trust her own judgment when she dealt with a man from the mainstream establishment world, she reminded herself. She'd never really understood that world, nor had she adapted well to it during the period she'd lived in it.

She had been born and raised in Witt's End. The tiny mountain community might strike outsiders as odd, but as far as Serenity was concerned, it was home. It was the place where she belonged. The community sheltered her and raised her when there had been no one else to take her in. She intended to give back to Witt's End what it had given her: a future.

Now it looked like she'd have to accomplish that goal without the assistance of Ventress Ventures.

She stuffed her gloved hands into the pockets of her beaded, fringed jacket and tried to examine her emotions from an intellectual viewpoint. Maybe this was how a woman scorned always felt, she thought as she forged a path through the dripping trees.

A woman scorned. She shuddered at the thought.

For the first time, Serenity realized just how much she'd been attracted to Caleb. She could not deny that she'd responded instantly and unconditionally to him in a way that she had never responded to any man. She wrinkled her nose in disgust. She must have been out of her mind to get so carried away by a man who was obviously so wrong for her.

But she knew that she had begun to fantasize about having a committed relationship with Caleb. It probably couldn't have lasted forever, of course. After all, she was from Witt's End and he was from the outside world, but perhaps they could have shared some portion of the future together.

And, if they had both been very lucky, they might

have found something that resembled what Julius Makepeace, the man whose surname she bore, had found with his friend, Bethanne.

Serenity smiled briefly, thinking of the postcard that had been waiting for her when she got home last night.

Dear Serenity:
   Having a wonderful time. Marriage is great. Should have done this years ago.
                    Love, Julius and Bethanne

The card had been postmarked Mazatlan, Mexico. Julius and Bethanne were on their honeymoon. After fifteen years of living together, they had decided the time had come to marry. Two weeks ago Witt's End had pulled out all the stops to give the couple a wedding celebration worthy of the event. Even Ambrose had come to the party. He had actually condescended to take a few pictures of the bride and groom, all the while making it clear that wedding photos were beneath him.

Serenity paused briefly to get her bearings amid the trees. An eerie silence enveloped the woods this morning. The fog blanketing the mountains last night had grown heavier after dawn.

She ducked beneath the low branches of a damp fir. It would have been stupid to have let herself get involved with a rigid, conservative, hidebound traditionalist like Caleb. The man probably wore pin-striped underwear.

Serenity scowled. Something was wrong with that analysis, and she knew it. In her present foul mood it was tempting to categorize Caleb as inflexible, unyielding, and narrow-minded. But she sensed that was far from the whole picture.

Her first impression of him had been deeply disturbing in its intensity. Prepared for a middle-aged corporate type with soft hands, a soft jawline, and the beginnings of a soft paunch, she'd been totally unprepared to find herself dealing with a wild beast trapped in a gleaming, stainless steel and glass cage.

Caleb had reminded her of the griffin that hung from the chain she wore around her neck. Intriguing, different, and powerful. Not quite real, perhaps. Possibly dangerous.

It was his eyes, gray and filled with a cool, detached watchfulness, that first alerted Serenity to the fact that she was not dealing with a typical member of the mainstream business establishment.

The rest of Caleb had been as disconcerting as his eyes. While it was certainly true that he didn't have the wings of an eagle or the tail of a lion, she saw a certain, mysterious, griffin–like quality about him. Caleb had risen from behind his desk that first day, a tall, lean, startlingly graceful man. His hair was as dark as a night in the forest, and his features as bold and uncompromising as the mountains around her. His voice had been deep but virtually devoid of any discernable emotion other than a cool civility.

The remote, distant quality that emanated from him was initially quite chilling. He had appeared completely self-contained. He projected the image of a man who needed no one, relied on no one, trusted no one.

Oddly enough, the very strength of that image made

Serenity realize that whatever was going on inside Caleb, it was neither calm nor unemotional. No man cultivated such profound self-control unless he had something very fierce and powerful inside himself that needed to be controlled.

She'd found herself inexplicably drawn to what she knew her friend Zone would describe as the masculine force in Caleb. It fascinated her, intrigued her, and seemed to resonate perfectly with an element deep within her that Zone would label the feminine force. This morning Serenity could still feel echoes of the excitement that had flashed through her when Caleb kissed her in his office. She hadn't experienced anything like those feelings before.

Too bad Caleb had turned out to be a stiff-necked, straitlaced, sanctimonious prude, she thought now. Shaking off the memories, she walked a little faster.

The cold fog wove its tendrils around her, making her more aware of the chill in the air. In another couple of weeks the first snows would arrive in the mountains. Witt's End would be snugly tucked up for the winter.

Serenity huddled deeper into her jacket, wishing she'd never written that letter to the president of Ventress Ventures last month. She should have sought start-up help for her new business from another source.

But even if the abrupt termination of her arrangement with Caleb had been for the best, she was outraged at the reason. Her mouth tightened. She still could not bring herself to believe that Ambrose, a neighbor and friend, had actually tried to blackmail her. It made no sense.

The whole thing had seemed ludicrous yesterday morning, when she opened the envelope in her Seattle hotel room. Not for one moment had she dreamed that Caleb would take the threat seriously.

He had a nerve, she thought. He was a businessman, after all, a member of corporate America. Who was he to throw stones? He probably consulted for companies that dumped toxic waste into rivers. Maybe he had a wife whom he had never bothered to mention, too. Serenity winced.

She grabbed a branch that was in her path and shoved it aside.

A sudden tingle of awareness made her pause. She glanced to the left and saw a dark shadow materialize in the fog. A small frisson of uneasiness went through her. She swung around to face the creature that coalesced in front of her.

The beast fixed her with a steady gaze as it padded slowly toward her. The studded steel collar around its neck glinted evilly in the gray light.

Serenity relaxed. "Oh, hello, Styx. Where's your buddy?"

Another rottweiller trotted forward out of the fog. He was wearing a studded steel collar similar to his companion's.

"There you are, Charon. How's it going, pal?"

The black-and-tan dogs made no sound as they approached. When they reached Serenity, they lifted their massive heads for a pat. Serenity scratched the animals behind their ears. "What are you guys doing, running around in the fog? You should be lying in front of a nice, warm fire. Where's Blade?"

"Right here, Serenity."

Serenity turned her head at the sound of the familiar raspy drawl. The man everyone in Witt's End knew only as Blade emerged from the mists.

He was built very much like his rottweilers; big, heavily muscled, with huge shoulders and a barrel chest. He had a large, square-jawed face, eyes the color of blue steel, and virtually no neck. Beneath his fatigue cap, his hair was cropped very close to his skull.

Serenity assumed Blade was approximately fifty, but it was difficult to be certain. He had never volunteered any information about his age. In Witt's End there was an unwritten rule against asking questions about a person's past unless you were invited to do so.

Blade was dressed, as usual, in camouflage gear and a pair of thick-soled, military-style boots. A variety of lethal-looking knives and assorted implements were suspended from the webbed belt slung low around his waist.

"I see you're making your rounds, Blade." Yesterday on the long drive home to Witt's End, Serenity had tried to envision Blade as a blackmailer. She'd abandoned the attempt almost as soon as she'd begun. She'd known Blade all of her life. He was too direct to bother with blackmail, and much too concerned with his endless conspiracy theories. Besides, he was a member of the family, one of the people who had raised her since infancy.

"Checkin' things out," Blade allowed.

"In the daytime?" Serenity raised her brows. Blade usually slept during the daylight hours and did his endless sentry rounds at night.

"Some unusual activity on the road last night.

Heard a car drive off near here real late. Didn't get a look at it because of the fog."

"Probably just someone on his way home from visiting a friend. Jessie, perhaps."

"Maybe. Maybe not. Got a feeling there's somethin' about to happen. Zone agrees with me. Figure I'd better watch for the point man."

"Point man?"

"There'll be one. Always is before a well-planned operation. He'll move in to do a recon job. Then he'll signal the others to go ahead with the assault."

"Yes, of course. The point man."

Blade regarded her with the same unwinking stare the rottweilers used. "What are you doing back here? You're supposed to be in Seattle workin' on your new business plans."

"I came back a day early," Serenity said.

Blade's eyes narrowed. "Everything goin' accordin' to schedule?"

"No." Serenity looked down at Charon, who was rubbing his head against her hand. "Things didn't work out."

"Does that mean you won't be openin' up that mail order shop for local stuff, after all?"

"No, it doesn't. I plan to go ahead with the catalog business, Blade, but it looks like I'll have to find another start-up consultant. Mr. Ventress decided I wasn't a suitable client. Apparently, I didn't meet his high standards."

Blade was silent for a long time while he considered that information. "He give you a bad time?"

"Ah, no," Serenity said hastily. "No, he didn't. It was just a business decision on his part."

"You want me to go see him? Talk to him for you?"

Serenity could imagine all too clearly what Blade's notion of a conversation with Caleb would be like. She would no doubt wind up being sued. Still, it was sweet of Blade to make the offer. She was touched. Blade never left Witt's End if he could avoid it. He didn't function well in the outside world.

"No, really, it's okay, Blade. The decision was mutual. I decided I don't particularly care to do business with Mr. Ventress any more than he wants to do business with me."

"You're sure?"

"I'm sure." Serenity smiled with rueful affection. "But thanks, anyway."

"Where you headed?"

"I'm going to Ambrose's cabin. I want to talk to him."

Blade nodded once. "Right. Sure you won't get lost in this fog?"

"It's not that bad. I'll be all right."

"Guess me and the dogs better be movin' along, then." Blade studied the gray mist with a speculative gleam in his steel-blue eyes. "Just don't like the feel of things today."

"I understand. But don't you think it's a little too foggy for a successful clandestine operation?"

"Can't be too careful." Blade summoned the silent rottweilers with a movement of his hand. "No tellin' when they'll make their move."

"True."

He touched the peaked bill of his cap. "Have a nice day."

"Thanks. You, too." Serenity stood with her hands tucked into her pockets and watched as Blade and the rottweilers disappeared into the gray mists. When they were gone, she turned and started once more toward Ambrose's cabin.

It occurred to her that it would have been interesting to see the expression on Caleb's face had Blade actually turned up to confront him in his office. She sighed with regret, knowing that there was nothing to be gained from dreams of revenge. She had to think about the future. There were new plans to be made. For starters, she would have to find a new consultant.

A few minutes later Serenity emerged from the trees into the small clearing that surrounded Ambrose's log cabin. She studied the windows curiously and wondered why there were no lights showing. On a foggy day like this, it would be quite dark inside the cabin.

There was no sign of smoke from the chimney, either, she noticed. She hoped Ambrose had not passed out drunk, as he was occasionally prone to do. She had a few questions to ask him, and she wanted some answers.

She determinedly approached the front steps of the cabin. The deal with Caleb had been shot down in flames and there was no saving it, but she intended to find out who had pulled the trigger.

She could not believe that Ambrose had been the person behind the blackmail scheme, but of one thing she was certain: whoever had sent her those photos had to have gotten them from him. Ambrose was the man who possessed the negatives and the only person, so far as she knew, who had a set of the pictures.

Serenity climbed the steps to Ambrose's door and knocked loudly. There was no immediate response.

"Ambrose, I know you're in there. Open the door. I want to talk to you."

The answering silence began to make her uneasy.

"Ambrose?"

Serenity tried the doorknob. It turned readily enough, as did most doorknobs in Witt's End. Nobody bothered to lock their doors in this neck of the woods. There had never been any need to take such precautions.

She opened the cabin door cautiously and peered into the gloom.

The sense of wrongness hit her in a cold wave. Serenity stood very still on the threshold.

"Ambrose, are you in here?"

She took one step into the living room and reached out to snap on the light switch on the cabin wall. In the dim glow of a weak lamp, she surveyed Ambrose's quarters with a quick, worried glance. The air was stale, she noted absently. It smelled of old wood smoke from the fireplace. The ashes on the hearth were cold.

Newspapers were stacked everywhere, as usual. Ambrose was a news junkie. He subscribed to every major daily paper from Seattle, Portland, and Los Angeles. In addition to the papers, there was a wide variety of photography equipment lying around the room. Cameras, lenses, and light meters occupied most of the available space. Ambrose had a passion for the hardware of his art. Unfortunately, it was a passion he could ill afford. At one time or another everyone in Witt's End had loaned him money to buy a new camera or a fancy lens.

A couple of unwashed coffee cups stood on the scarred pine table in front of the sagging couch. The ashtray near the cups contained several cigarette butts and small piles of ashes. Ambrose did a lot of coffee and cigarettes when he was trying to avoid alcohol.

Serenity went toward the hallway that led to the kitchen.

"Ambrose?"

Still no response. She noticed that the door that opened onto the basement stairs was closed. She wondered if Ambrose was working downstairs. His was one of the few basements in Witt's End. It was where he did his darkroom work and where he filed his meticulously maintained collection of photos, negatives, and business records.

Serenity peeked into the kitchen and noted that it was empty. She went to the basement door and knocked. If Ambrose were doing darkroom work, he wouldn't want the door opened without warning.

Again there was no response.

"I'm going to open the basement door, Ambrose."

After another beat of silence, she did so.

The basement was enveloped in darkness. The odor of alcohol was so strong she nearly choked. Serenity found the switch on the wall.

The first thing she saw when the light came on was what looked like a pile of old clothes at the bottom of the stairs.

And then she saw the hand that was partially covered by a jacket sleeve. And a pair of boots.

"*Ambrose*. My God, Ambrose."

For an instant Serenity was paralyzed with horror. A ghastly tightness gripped her chest, cutting off her breath. She managed to break free of the spell and go slowly down the staircase. Tears welled up in her eyes.

Ambrose Asterley would have no more chances to

make the big time in the cutthroat world of commercial photography.

"Got rip-roaring drunk and fell down the stairs, poor bastard." Quinton Priestly drove his battered van slowly through the fog along the narrow paved road that led to Serenity's cottage. "I suppose it was inevitable. Ambrose was the self-destructive type. Everyone knew it. Too bad you had to be the one who walked in and found him."

"If I hadn't gone to his place today, he might not have been found for days." Serenity clasped her gloved hands on her lap and stared sadly out through the dirty windshield of Quinton's van. The mist had lifted slightly, but now the long shadows of early evening were bringing a deeper darkness to the mountains. "I hope he didn't suffer too long."

Quinton had been the first person she had called after dialing the emergency number to summon the sheriff and a medical aid car to Ambrose's cabin. She had known it would probably take nearly an hour for the authorities in Bullington to arrive, and she had no wish to wait alone.

As the owner of the only bookshop and brewery in Witt's End, Quinton was the town's resident philosopher. In his early fifties, he was thin and wiry, with fathomless dark eyes and a bushy beard that was rapidly going gray.

Quinton had studied philosophy and mathematics at a prestigious private college before leaving the establishment world behind to concentrate on developing his own philosophical system. During his early years in Witt's End he had actually written and published four slender volumes. The books, taken together, detailed a comprehensive, carefully crafted philosophical theory derived from mathematics, which had succeeded in creating a small cult following among the intellectual elite at major universities.

His goal accomplished, Quinton had turned to other projects, namely the creation of a bookstore and a brewery. As he had once explained to Serenity, running a bookshop paid better than writing, and the quest to brew the world's finest beer was a far more certain route to philosophical enlightenment than the traditional, academic approach.

"The medics said Ambrose broke his neck in the fall and probably died instantly." Quinton slowed the van for the turn into Serenity's driveway. "Don't dwell on it. There was nothing you could have done. Life is a series of lines linking points on an endless number of mathematical planes. We all exist on different points of the planes at different times. Sometimes those points are momentarily connected through the planes by a straight line, and sometimes they aren't."

As usual, Serenity had no idea what Quinton was talking about. It didn't concern her. No one in Witt's End claimed to be able to understand Quinton when he went into his philosophical mode.

"Jessie took the news better than I thought she would," Serenity remarked. "I was worried about her reaction."

Jessie Blanchard was an artist, a longtime resident of Witt's End who'd conducted an on-again, off-again affair with Ambrose for the past three years. Lately the affair had been in an off phase, as far as Serenity knew, but she also knew that Jessie cared very much about Ambrose.

"I don't think she was really surprised," Quinton said. "Her artistic eye allows her to see beneath the surface of life to the second layer of reality. She knew that Ambrose was a deeply troubled soul."

"Yes, I suppose she did."

Quinton glanced at her. "What with one thing and another, we haven't had a chance to talk about how things went in Seattle. How come you returned ahead of schedule?"

"As they say in business circles, Mr. Ventress and I were unable to reach a mutual agreement."

Quinton frowned. "What happened?"

"It's a long story. I don't feel like going into it at the moment. I'll tell you all about it later, I promise."

"Whenever it feels right." Quinton turned into Serenity's driveway. "Looks like you've got company. Who do you know who owns a green Jaguar?"

"No one." Serenity watched curiously as the sleek vehicle emerged from the swirling gray mists. It was parked next to her own red four-wheel-drive Jeep.

"Maybe a lost tourist who stopped to ask for directions." Quinton brought the van to a halt and switched off the ignition. "I'll come in with you. Make sure everything's okay."

"Thanks. I appreciate it."

"Can't be too careful these days," Quinton said as he cracked open the van door. "Even here in Witt's End. The vectors of angles on other planes sometimes reach into our plane of existence."

"Uh-huh." Serenity opened the door on her side and jumped down from the high perch. She went around the front of the van. Quinton fell into step beside her and together they walked toward her front door.

Quinton eyed the empty passenger seat of the Jaguar. "Whoever it is apparently felt free to walk straight into your place. Maybe it's time you started locking your door, Serenity."

"It must be someone I know." Serenity hurried up the steps with Quinton right behind her.

The front door of the cottage swung open just as she reached the top step. Caleb Ventress stood there looking as if he had every right to occupy her home.

It was the first time Serenity had seen him dressed in anything other than a formal suit and tie. Caleb was wearing black, neatly creased trousers, and a dark green, long-sleeved shirt that almost matched the Jaguar. His emotionless gray gaze swept over Serenity and then settled intently on Quinton.

Serenity came to an abrupt halt, her mouth open in astonishment. "What are you doing here?"

"I came to see you." Caleb did not take his eyes off Quinton.

"Do you know this man, Serenity?" Quinton asked quietly.

"I know him," she said. In spite of everything, a small flame of hope flickered to life within her. Perhaps Caleb had changed his mind, she thought. Perhaps once he'd had a chance to calm down, he realized that the blackmail attempt had been a trivial matter after all and that he'd completely overreacted. "This is Caleb Ventress, the business consultant I've been dealing with in Seattle. Caleb, this is Quinton Priestly. He's a friend of mine."

"Priestly." Caleb held out his hand with a cool, deliberate air, as if he didn't expect Quinton to observe the formalities and didn't really care one way or the other. It was a minimally polite gesture, nothing more.

Quinton shook the proffered hand once and released it immediately. "So you're Ventress."

"Yes."

"You're very much of the outside world, aren't you? A man who has absorbed the steel and concrete of that other universe into his bones. A man who has not touched other planes of existence in a long time, if ever."

Caleb's brows rose. "It was a long drive from Seattle, if that's what you mean."

Quinton gave Serenity a sidelong glance. "Do you want me to hang around for a while?"

Serenity shook her head. "It's okay, Quinton. I can deal with this."

"All right. But remember, merely because two points appear on the same plane at the same time, it does not necessarily mean that they are intended to connect with each other. Sometimes one is just passing through one level of reality to the next."

"I'll keep that in mind," Serenity promised.

Quinton nodded brusquely at Caleb and went back down the steps.

Caleb watched him leave. "Does he always talk like that?"

"Yes."

"What were you doing with him?"

"A friend of ours died last night," Serenity said quietly. "I found his body a few hours ago. Quinton helped me deal with the authorities and all the rest that goes with a death."

"Hell. I'm sorry about that." Caleb looked at her. "Close friend?"

"You could say that. Everyone here in Witt's End is a close friend." Serenity walked past him into the small living room. The walls were lined with books, as were most of the other walls in her cottage.

Some of the volumes were left over from her youth. Until the day she left home for college, Serenity had never been inside a formal classroom. Julius, together with the rest of the residents of Witt's End, had home-schooled her. They had done such a good job that she had aced the college entrance exams.

Much of the rest of Serenity's personal library was comprised of relics of her short-lived career as an instructor in Sociology at the small college in Bullington. Her teaching days and her unfinished Ph.D. all seemed very far away now.

"Who was he?" Caleb asked quietly.

"His name was Ambrose Asterley," Serenity said. She held her breath, wondering what Caleb's reaction would be. "You probably recall the name. He's the photographer who took those nude pictures of me."

Caleb let the front door close slowly. There was calm speculation in his eyes as he turned to watch Serenity shrug off her beaded, fringed jacket. "How did he die?"

Serenity lifted her chin. She confronted Caleb with her legs braced and her hands shoved into the deep pockets of the long, hand-knitted turquoise tunic she wore over white leggings. "It looks like he got drunk and fell down a flight of stairs. I believe I mentioned that Ambrose had a drinking problem."

"Yes, you mentioned it. You went to see him today?"

"Yes."

"Why?"

"I would have thought that was obvious. I've always considered Ambrose a friend. But friends don't try to blackmail each other. I wanted to know if he was the one who had sent me the pictures or if he gave those pictures to someone else who used them to wreck my business arrangement with you."

"Damn. I knew you'd try something like that," Caleb muttered.

Serenity blinked back tears. "I never got any answers. Ambrose was dead when I arrived." She spun around and walked into the kitchen.

"Serenity."

"Why did you drive all the way up here today, Caleb?" She kept her back to him as she filled a teakettle at the sink.

"I didn't like the idea of you attempting to track down a blackmailer on your own."

"Why should you care what I do?"

Caleb came to stand in the doorway of the tiny kitchen. "Dealing with blackmailers can be dangerous."

"So what? It's none of your business." Serenity dashed the dampness away from her eyes with the sleeve of her tunic. She put the kettle onto the stove and switched on the burner. "I told you, poor Ambrose is gone. He can't give anyone any answers."

"You said yourself that the blackmailer might have been someone other than Ambrose."

"That's true." Serenity slid him a quick glance. "But as you so succinctly put it yesterday, it's my problem, not yours."

"Unfortunately, according to the terms of that contract you signed in my office, that's not the case. I told you, I've got standards. You're a client, Serenity, and I have never yet abandoned a client. I don't intend to start now."

Serenity stared at him. The flicker of hope within her died. Caleb was here because of his precious, inviolable business standards, not because he felt anything for her. "Forget it. I don't want your help. Not in this blackmail thing or anything else."

"You don't have a hell of a lot of choice. I'm not about to let you ruin my reputation."

She widened her eyes in sheer amazement. "Your *reputation.*"

"That contract you signed is iron-clad. I should know, I wrote it. Unless I choose to let you out of it early, you're stuck with paying my extremely high fees."

"You weren't going to charge me any fees," she said. "You were going to take a cut of the profits instead."

"You obviously didn't read clause number ten very closely," Caleb said smoothly. "It provides for full payment of my standard fees in the event that you cancel the project before completion. Be reasonable, Serenity, I can't see you wanting to pay all that money and not get something for it."

"I don't intend to pay you a dime."

"I can line up a whole team of lawyers who will see to it that you do." Caleb's mouth curved in a faint smile that did not alter the detached watchfulness in his eyes. "Like it or not, it looks like we're going to be partners."

3

SERENITY STARED AT CALEB. "FOR A MAN WHO DOESN'T approve of blackmail, you're very good at it."

Caleb's jaw tightened but his gaze never wavered. If anything, his expression grew more forbidding. "This isn't blackmail. It's business."

"Is that all you ever think about? Business?" How could she have been so wrong about this man? Serenity wondered. She'd actually gained the impression somewhere along the line that the two of them had something in common, that their inner voices spoke to each other, that they somehow understood each other, silently yearned for each other.

Obviously her normally astute powers of intuition had become confused and disoriented in the fog caused by the attraction she had felt for Caleb. She suddenly realized that this was her first brush with real passion, the kind that involved body and soul.

50

"No, business is not the only thing I think about," Caleb said evenly. "But it's definitely high on my list of priorities."

"I can see that." The kettle shrilled. Serenity picked up a spoon, opened a canister and began to ladle tea into a pot. "Some of us have other priorities."

"Are you telling me that getting a viable mail order business going here in Witt's End isn't still high on your priority list?"

"I'll find another way to get it up and running. I don't need your help."

"You're going to get my help whether you want it or not." Caleb's smile was humorless. "As long as you're paying for it, you might as well take advantage of the opportunity."

"What opportunity? The opportunity to work with someone who thinks I'm pond scum because I once posed nude for a professional photographer?"

"No, Serenity," Caleb said with cool patience. "I think you should take advantage of the opportunity to work with the man who is arguably one of the best, if not the best, start-up consultant in the Northwest."

Serenity widened her eyes. "And so refreshingly modest, too." She yanked the kettle off the stove and poured boiling water over the tea leaves in the pot.

"Take it easy." Caleb's tone softened as he watched her wield the kettle. "I know you're upset. You've obviously been through a traumatic experience today, what with finding Asterley's body and all. When you've had a chance to calm down, we'll talk about future plans."

"Don't hold your breath. I might not calm down for a long, long time."

"I'll wait." Caleb's brows rose as he watched her prepare the tea. "Mind if I have some? It was a long trip."

Serenity hesitated. The temptation to refuse him a cup of tea was almost overwhelming. But that would be petty and spiteful, she told herself. "All right." She reached reluctantly into the cupboard and took down another mug, one fashioned in the shape of a bright yellow flower.

"I don't use milk or sugar," Caleb said helpfully.

"I didn't ask." She shoved the flower mug into his hand.

"I know. But I'm sure you would have sooner or later." Caleb examined the beautifully worked pottery mug he was holding. "An example of local craftsmanship?"

"Zone makes them in her spare time."

"Who's Zone?"

"She works for me as an assistant at Witt's End Grocery."

"I like her style." Caleb ran a long finger over the abstract petals of the mug. "Clever and whimsical. But it's got a sharp, crisp, modern edginess to it."

Serenity was surprised by his perception. "That's a good description of her work."

"It'll sell."

"I beg your pardon?"

Caleb looked up from the mug. "I said, it will sell. We'll put her mugs in your catalog. Assuming, of course, that Zone can produce a sufficient quantity in a reliable time frame."

"I'm sure she can." She hesitated. "How do you know her mugs will work in the catalog?"

"It's my business to know that kind of thing. I have

a feel for it. It's one of the reasons I'm so good at my job."

"Have you ever sold mugs?"

He shrugged. "Not until now. Trust me, Serenity, these will work."

"If you say so." Enthusiasm surged through her. He liked Zone's beautiful mugs. He thought they would sell. Serenity could hardly wait to tell her assistant the good news. Zone would be thrilled. Serenity had to struggle hard not to betray her excitement.

Caleb sipped tea thoughtfully. "I don't think you're pond scum, you know."

"Yes, you do." She started toward the doorway where he stood blocking her path. "But I don't particularly care what you think. I should have known better than to get involved with a man like you in the first place."

Caleb waited until the last possible moment before moving out of her way. "A man like me? What the hell is that supposed to mean?"

"Arrogant, elitist, rigid, self-righteous, and inflexible." Serenity was intensely aware of the heat and strength in him as she brushed through the doorway. He was much too close. She hurried into the living room and sank down into the corner of the over-stuffed sofa.

"That's quite a list."

"Is it? Let's be honest here. How would you characterize me?"

He considered her question as he seated himself in the room's single armchair. "Naive, gullible, too trusting, emotional, and completely inexperienced in modern business practices."

"You may have a point," Serenity said. "I must

53

possess a host of those sterling attributes or I wouldn't have misjudged you so completely."

"Believe it or not, I didn't intend for this conversation to degenerate into a slinging match."

"What did you expect it to degenerate into, what with me being so emotional and all?"

"I'd like to talk business," Caleb said calmly.

Serenity pursed her lips. "I doubt that we can do that now that we've discovered we have nothing in common." She would not let him see how much his condescending words offended her, she vowed silently. And she definitely would not let him see that at least some of the barbs had struck deep.

No, make that all of the barbs, she thought glumly. She had been naive. She had been too trusting. She had also been emotional, and she was certainly inexperienced in dealing with men like Caleb.

"Try to keep this situation in perspective, Serenity." Caleb's voice grew darker and deeper. "This is just business."

"According to you, business is not my forte."

He drew a deep breath. "Look, you need me if you're going to proceed with your big plans to get a mail order operation going here in Witt's End. Admit it."

"Maybe I'll try opening the new business without the aid of a fancy start-up consultant," Serenity mused. "Lord knows that every time I get involved with men from your world I wind up getting burned." She shook her head in disgust. "You'd think I'd have learned my lesson by now."

"Men from my world? What is this? You make it sound like I come from outer space."

"You might as well have come from Mars as far as

I'm concerned." Serenity curled her legs under her and took a swallow of tea.

"Damn it, I'm not some kind of freak."

The savage edge in his voice startled her. It was almost as if, deep down, Caleb believed he might actually be some kind of freak. An unwelcome sense of empathy tingled inside Serenity. She knew that feeling of being different, of not belonging, of being an outsider. She had felt it often enough during her years at Bullington College.

"Look, there's no getting around the fact that you and I come from different worlds," she said. "For the record, I tried living in your world once upon a time. It was a disaster."

Caleb frowned. "What do you mean, you tried living in my world?"

Serenity lifted one shoulder in a small shrug. "Believe it or not, there was a time when I couldn't wait to see Witt's End in my rearview mirror. I was seventeen and ready to take on the world. I started with Bullington."

The corner of Caleb's mouth twitched. "Bullington is only thirty miles away."

"It was a start. In any event, for me it might as well have been the other side of the world."

"I can see how being raised here in Witt's End might not give you a truly cosmopolitan background," Caleb said dryly.

"Life is different here," she agreed quietly. "At any rate, I enrolled in Bullington College, and after I graduated I worked there for a while as an instructor in the sociology department. For a time I lived on campus. I wanted to be normal, you see."

"Normal?" Caleb gave her a quizzical look.

"I guess all kids rebel against the lifestyle and upbringing they experience in their childhood. Kids raised in conventional, middle-class households want to be free. They want to break the rules."

"What did you want?"

"Me?" Serenity grimaced. "Believe it or not, I wanted rules. I was raised without structure and routine, so naturally I longed for a world where people did things on time. A place where you could count on a certain degree of orderliness. A place where people planned for the future instead of just going with the flow. I thought I wanted to live in an environment where people worked regular hours instead of waiting for inspiration to strike."

"I see."

"I wanted a savings account," Serenity continued, amused as always by her own youthful ambitions. "I wanted a car mechanic who didn't try to fix a broken water pump with a meditation mantra. I wanted a fulfilling, successful career in academia complete with retirement benefits."

"What did you find?"

"I found out that savings accounts pay very low interest rates, that car mechanics who don't chant mantras are not any better than those who do, that the academic career ladder is very slippery, and that no one can count on retirement benefits anymore."

Caleb sipped his tea. "You learned a lot."

"Uh-huh. And the lesson that I learned best is that I don't fit into the so-called normal world. Oh, I can pass for a short period of time, but I can't live there very happily for any extended period. I was born into an eccentric, frontier society, and that's where I'll always feel most comfortable."

"You think you fit in here at Witt's End?" Caleb asked.

"It's home. People know me here. They understand me and accept me for what I am. Here in Witt's End, we're very tolerant of each other's eccentricities."

"Is that a fact?"

Serenity set her back teeth. "Believe it or not, no one around here would blink an eye at the notion of someone posing nude for an artist. Happens all the time."

Caleb placed his cup very carefully on the beautifully polished end table that Julius Makepeace had built by hand. "But you need someone from my world to help you get your business ideas off the ground, don't you?"

"I thought I did." Serenity narrowed her eyes. "Now, I'm not so sure."

"Believe me," Caleb said, "you need me. Left to your own devices, you're going to lose every dime you sink into Witt's End by Mail."

Enough was enough. "I'm not stupid. Inexperienced, maybe, but definitely not stupid."

Caleb looked at her, mildly amazed. "I agree. But you do lack experience in the mail order business. You've got a lot to learn, lady."

"And you're going to teach me?"

"Looks like it."

"Whether or not I want to take the course, is that it?"

Caleb stretched his legs out in front of him, leaned back in his chair and regarded her from beneath half-lowered lids. "Like I said a few minutes ago, I've got a reputation for maintaining certain standards. I don't intend to let you ruin my track record."

A flicker of deep uncertainty went through Serenity. She suddenly had a strong hunch that Caleb was not telling her the truth about his motives. But she could not imagine any other explanation for his presence here in Witt's End.

"Something's missing in this equation," she finally said. "It occurs to me that I'm ignoring the financial aspect."

"What financial aspect?"

"Maybe you're willing to overlook my notorious past in favor of the future profits you expect to make as a silent partner in Witt's End by Mail. Is that it?"

Caleb's mouth tightened. "What do you think?"

"I think that with motives like that, you've got a lot of nerve looking down on me simply because I once posed nude. Definitely a case of the pot calling the kettle black."

"You're welcome to think what you like about my motives," Caleb said in a voice that dripped shards of ice. "But for your information, the profits I expect to make off your mail order business aren't going to amount to enough to make my accountants even blink."

"Hah. I'll bet some sneaky start-up consultant once said that to L.L. Bean."

"Why don't we just agree to disagree on that point," Caleb suggested. "Let's try coming at this relationship from a fresh angle."

"We don't have a relationship," Serenity said quickly.

"No?"

"No." Serenity flushed at the memory of the kiss in Caleb's office. She knew by the look in his eyes that he was recalling it, too. "I'll admit that at one point I thought we might be able to have one, but I realize now that I was mistaken. You and I, well, we aren't—"

"You misunderstood me," Caleb said smoothly. "I wasn't talking about a personal relationship. I was referring to our business relationship."

"Oh." Serenity's cheeks burned.

"I suggest you stop thinking about this arrangement in personal terms and start thinking in business terms."

"Is this lesson one?"

"It is."

He was lying, Serenity realized. She sensed that for all his talk about keeping matters on a businesslike basis, Caleb was here for some very personal reasons. Perhaps his reputation really was that important to him, although it was hard for her to understand how losing one small client in Witt's End, Washington, could harm him professionally.

On the other hand, she thought, Caleb was imbued with a glacial pride. He was the kind of man for whom standards and a reputation were no doubt extremely personal things. He probably didn't give a damn about what others might think, but she sensed that he cared passionately about not violating his own code.

"Let me see if I've got this right," Serenity said. "The bottom line here is that you're willing to put serious pressure on me to accept you as my consultant just so that you can tell yourself that you haven't lowered your professional standards. Is that it?"

Caleb hesitated. "Let's just say that's a practical way of looking at the situation."

Serenity shrugged. "Okay, you win. Go out and build me a mail order empire."

Caleb didn't move from the chair. "It won't be easy, you know."

"Nonsense. For a man of your abilities, I'm sure it will be a piece of cake. You'll probably have everything up and running by next Tuesday. Call me when you've finished."

"It's a cooperative venture, Serenity."

"You'll have to excuse me, I'm not feeling terribly cooperative at the moment. And I've got a lot of other things on my mind. It isn't every day that I stumble across a neighbor's dead body."

"A neighbor who took pictures that were later used to blackmail you," Caleb pointed out grimly. "The guy couldn't have been much of a friend."

"I considered Ambrose a friend," Serenity said quietly. "And that's the way I prefer to remember him."

"Regardless of the fact that he might have been the one behind the blackmail attempt?"

"If Ambrose was the blackmailer, he must have had his reasons. He was probably driven to it by desperation."

"Desperation for what?" Caleb demanded. "Hell, I don't believe this. You're inventing excuses for a blackmailer?"

"We don't know that he was the blackmailer."

"Okay, let's pursue that avenue of inquiry. Who else had access to those photos?"

Serenity sighed. The logic was inescapable. "No one, as far as I know. I can't see Ambrose giving them to anyone else. There was no reason for him to do so."

"The blackmailer wanted you to call off your business discussions with me," Caleb said. "Who would want to see your plans shot down?"

"I don't know." Serenity was getting impatient with the inquisition. The man was like a locomotive. Once

60

he started moving, it was difficult to stop him. "Furthermore, it's none of your affair."

"I disagree. I'm your consultant, remember?"

"I'd prefer to forget."

"I'm not going to let it slip your mind," Caleb said. "But we can talk about some of this stuff later."

"Gee, thanks."

"The first item on my agenda is to find a place to stay tonight. I didn't notice a motel anywhere in Witt's End."

"The closest one is thirty miles back down the road in Bullington," she said helpfully.

"That's going to be a little inconvenient." Caleb glanced out the window. "The fog has gotten worse. I'd have to be crazy to try to drive thirty miles down that mountain road in this soup."

"Don't look at me," Serenity said, alarmed by the direction the conversation seemed to be taking. "I don't do bed and breakfast."

Caleb examined the book-lined living room of the cottage with a considering expression. "I could sleep on your sofa."

"No."

"It's big enough."

"No."

Caleb's brows rose. "Not even for one night?"

"No."

"What's the matter, Serenity? Do I make you nervous?"

"Yes."

"It's all right." His gaze was intent. "I'm not going to jump on top of you."

"I can't be certain of that, can I? After all, you think I'm a slut. No telling what you might do."

"I don't think you're a slut," Caleb said wearily. "I think you're naive. Having gotten to know you during the past three weeks, I can understand how Asterley might have talked you into posing for him. He probably fed you a line of bull about doing it for art."

"How very generous of you," Serenity said. "But I should probably warn you that I don't care for your second opinion of me any more than I cared for your first. You make me sound like a mindless nitwit."

"I'm trying to take a tolerant, open-minded view of the situation," he said tightly.

"Gosh, I'll bet that's really hard for you."

"You're in a hell of a mood, aren't you?"

"Can you blame me? I've had a rough day."

"I know," Caleb said. "Like I said, I'm sorry."

"Tell you what. You can work on your tolerance and practice your new open-minded attitudes while you look for a motel." Serenity glanced pointedly at her watch.

Caleb looked at her. "You're not really going to force me to find my way back down an unfamiliar mountain road in this fog, are you?"

"Well, you certainly aren't staying here." She was determined to stand her ground. Unfortunately, she also knew that he was right. And she did not want the responsibility for his safety on her shoulders. "I suppose you could spend the night at Julius's house. He wouldn't mind."

"Who's Julius?"

"Julius Makepeace. He's my father. Sort of."

"Your *father*." Caleb looked taken aback. "I'm not so sure that's a good idea."

"Don't worry about it." Serenity got to her feet, relieved at having found a reasonable answer to her dilemma. "Julius and Bethanne are out of town."

"Where are they?" Caleb stood up, looking wary.

"On their honeymoon."

"Their honeymoon?"

Serenity plucked the keys to Julius's cabin out of a small ceramic bowl. "It was love at first sight, if you ask me. Bethanne roared into town on a Harley-Davidson one afternoon fifteen years ago. Julius took one look at her and he was a goner. They've been together ever since."

Caleb frowned. "They're finally getting married after being together for fifteen years?"

Serenity shrugged. "Bethanne said it was time."

"Don't you think that's a little odd?"

"Not in Witt's End," Serenity retorted. "How long did your father and mother know each other before they got married?"

"They didn't," Caleb said in a strangely neutral tone. "Get married, that is."

Serenity blinked. "Your parents never married? Neither did mine."

"But you just said that your father finally married this Bethanne person." Caleb paused. "Who arrived in town fifteen years ago. I see what you mean. Bethanne isn't your mother."

"And Julius isn't my father. His name just happens to be on my birth certificate. I think of him more as an uncle. The same way I think of Montrose and Quinton and Blade."

Caleb gave her an unreadable look. "You've got a lot of uncles."

"I've got several aunts, too," Serenity said. "My biological parents are both dead. They died before they could get married. My father died when my mother was still pregnant. He was killed in a military training accident when he was in boot camp. My mother died the day I was born." She touched the little metal griffin at her throat.

"You're adopted?"

"By the town of Witt's End," she said, trying to clarify things for him.

"No offense, but that doesn't sound entirely legal."

"Who cares about details like that? I've got a family, and that's all that matters, isn't it?"

"It depends on your point of view," Caleb said slowly. "I guess we've got something in common. My parents both died when I was three months old. Before they could get married. I was raised in my grandfather's house."

The words hovered in the air between them. Serenity didn't want them to reach out and touch her, but they did. Everything about this man seemed to touch her in one way or another. "I'm sorry. It's strange, isn't it?"

"What's strange?"

"Never having known them. I don't even know what my parents looked like. I don't have any photos of them. Do you have pictures of your parents?"

"Yes." Caleb's eyes were bleak. "I do."

"You're lucky, then."

"Do you really think so?"

Serenity realized she had trodden onto some very dangerous ground. She sought for a way to retreat from whatever it was that had turned Caleb's gaze so cold. "Come on, let's go. Julius's place isn't far from here. We can walk."

She took her jacket down off the hook, slipped into it and opened the front door. The gray fog formed a seemingly impenetrable wall in front of her.

"Got a flashlight handy?" Caleb asked politely. "Night comes early up here in the mountains."

"Of course." She opened a cupboard and rummaged around inside until she found the flashlight. She pulled it out, flicked it on, and started determinedly down the steps into the fog.

"What happens if we get lost?" Caleb fastened his own jacket and pulled the shearling-lined collar up around his neck.

"We'll wander around for a few hours and then we'll succumb to hypothermia," Serenity said blandly. "The good news is that if that happens, we'll miss the invasion."

"What invasion?"

"The one Blade thinks is due any day now."

"Thanks for the early warning."

"Any time." Serenity realized she couldn't even see the vehicles parked in her own driveway. Nevertheless, she strode boldly forward. She was committed to getting Caleb out of her cottage.

"I don't think this is such a good idea," Caleb said behind her. "Maybe we should wait for a while and see if this stuff lifts a little."

"I know my way around Witt's End like the back of my hand." Serenity took another stride forward and collided with the unyielding metal fender of her Jeep. "Oooph."

"How about the way around your own drive?" Caleb came up beside her and took the flashlight from her fingers. "Are you all right?"

She winced. Her knee had taken most of the brunt of the collision. "Yeah, I'm okay, I'm okay."

"I'm glad to hear that. This is as far as we're going for now, however. You may enjoy stumbling around out here in the fog, but I don't intend to maim myself trying to find this other cabin." Caleb took hold of Serenity's arm, turned her around and started back through the mists toward the cottage.

Serenity was ill-tempered in defeat. "I suppose we could eat dinner first and then walk over to Julius's place."

"I thought you'd never ask."

Caleb awoke the next morning from a restless sleep and wondered why the bed was moving. The obvious answer flashed into his head.

Earthquake.

He sat straight up, prepared to rush for the door. The bed swayed more violently, and Caleb belatedly remembered that Julius Makepeace's bed was suspended from the timbered ceiling by four heavy chains. The smallest movement caused it to shudder and sway. He wondered if he'd get seasick.

He sprawled back against the pillows and gazed moodily at the gray dawn light as it filtered through the colorful stained-glass windows of the bedroom.

Tentatively he eased one leg out from beneath the heavy pile of handmade quilts. He drew it back instantly. It was freezing in the Makepeace cabin. Apparently the embers of the fire he had managed to get going in the wood stove last night had died.

The good news was that he was still in Witt's End, not thirty miles away in Bullington.

Steeling himself for the chill, Caleb tossed aside the covers and got out of bed. He grabbed his carryall and headed for the tiny bathroom. Unfortunately, he'd left his robe and probably several other crucially important items behind in Seattle. Normally he packed carefully before a trip.

Of course, he hadn't had a lot of time to prepare for

this scenic jaunt to Witt's End, he reminded himself. The whole thing had been a spur-of-the-moment action for him. Completely out of character.

He wondered if he had lost his mind.

Caleb stalked into the bathroom and turned on the hot water in the shower. He was startled to see that one entire wall of the thing was a plate-glass window. He glanced up and saw a skylight overhead. Apparently Makepeace liked the illusion of bathing in the woods. There was nothing to see but trees outside the window, but Caleb knew he was going to feel awfully exposed when he took his shower.

While he waited for the water to get warm, he briefly glimpsed his own grim, unshaven features in the mirror. He quickly turned away from the image. Lately he had begun avoiding mirrors and other reflective surfaces. They sent a chill down his spine.

He knew it was crazy, but for some reason he was half afraid that one day he would chance to look at a mirror or some other highly polished surface and not see anything at all. He wasn't sure that ghosts could see their own reflections.

He got into the shower and tried to concentrate on a battle plan for the day.

What in the name of hell was he doing here? This wasn't business. It never had been.

In the cold light of dawn he forced himself to confront his real motives. The hot water cascaded over him, warming him as he gazed out into the forest. There was nothing to be gained by lying to himself. He hadn't come to Witt's End because of the unfinished contract, his professional reputation, or the possibility of future profits from a small-time mail order company.

He had come to Witt's End because he wanted Serenity.

And the feeling of being alive that she gave him.

Forty minutes later, freshly shaven and dressed in jeans and a thick wool sweater, Caleb wandered out into the kitchen. It was colder than ever, but he did not want to fool around with the wood stove again. He opened cupboards until he found a canister of home-made granola. There was no milk in the empty refrigerator.

It took several minutes to crunch his way through a bowl full of the dry nut and grain concoction. It was fortunate, he decided, that he had sound, strong teeth. He'd better remember to pick up some milk. His teeth were good but they weren't made out of steel.

While he munched granola, he perused the art work that hung on the walls of the cabin. Most of the carefully framed pictures were lovingly detailed portraits of antique motorcycles. The chrome-plated monsters, gleaming and strangely majestic, had obviously been painted by a talented artist. Caleb peered at the signature on one of the pictures. *Jessie Blanchard.*

The motorcycle paintings were separated by book-cases. Caleb glanced at a few of the spines on the shelves. James Joyce, Proust, and Milton shared space with Kerouac and Ginsberg.

He finished the cereal, rinsed out the bowl, dried it and placed it neatly back in the cupboard. Then he picked up his jacket and went outside.

The fog had faded to gray wisps. Standing on Makepeace's front porch, Caleb could make out Serenity's cottage through a stand of trees. He smiled faintly in spite of his mood, and recalled his first impressions yesterday.

Serenity's cottage looked like something out of an illustration for a fairy tale. Fashioned of logs and natural stone, with a plump chimney and a steeply pitched roof, it had clearly been built by loving hands. It was small and quaint and there was an incredibly welcoming charm about it. The perfect abode for a lady who looked as if she enjoyed dancing in moonlit meadows at midnight. In spite of the chilly reception he had received at the cottage the previous afternoon, he discovered that he couldn't wait to return.

He pulled on his leather gloves and went down the steps. At that moment he would gladly kill for a cup of coffee. He hoped Serenity had some. Tea just wasn't going to cut it on a morning like this.

It didn't take long to reach the cottage. Her Jeep was still parked in the drive next to his Jag, but when he pounded on her front door, there was no response. Caleb twisted the knob, and shook his head in disgust when it turned easily in his hand. The woman really was living in another world. She didn't even bother to lock her door.

"Serenity?"

There was no answer. He closed the door again and went back down the steps. He glanced at the Jeep and realized she couldn't have gone far on foot. It was early, but perhaps she'd walked into the tiny village for coffee.

He couldn't help but notice that she had failed to invite him to join her.

The walk into the heart of Witt's End took less than ten minutes.

The only thing one could say about the small cluster of eccentric, highly original, hand-built structures that comprised downtown Witt's End was that each was unique. There were several odd geometric forms worked in wood and glass and decorated in vivid colors. Caleb spotted a small café next to Witt's End Grocery. The lights were on inside.

The lights were also on inside Witt's End Grocery. Curious, Caleb changed course and walked into Serenity's store. Bells tinkled overhead as he opened the door.

"Serenity? Are you in here?"

A strange apparition garbed in flowing saffron and orange robes emerged from between two aisles. It levitated toward him. He couldn't decide at first if the being who confronted him was male or female. He or she had completely shaved his or her head. There was a ring in his or her nose.

"Serenity is not here." The voice had sepulchral overtones, but it was definitely female.

"Who are you?" Caleb asked.

"I am called Zone."

"I'm Caleb Ventress."

"Caleb Ventress. He who brings danger, turmoil, and confusion."

"Actually, you've got that backward," Caleb said. "I'm a business consultant. My job is to straighten out turmoil and confusion."

"You are the great unknown." Zone lifted her hands toward the ceiling in a ritualistic gesture. The wide sleeves of her robes fell back to reveal a row of silver bracelets on each arm. "Out of the chaos and danger will come change, but there is no sign yet of whether that change will be good or evil."

"I've got a track record that strongly indicates the change will be highly profitable for all concerned. Would you mind telling me where my client is?"

"Client?"

70

"Serenity. You may remember her. She's your employer."

"Serenity has gone."

"Where?"

"To poor Ambrose's cabin. She said there was something she wanted to get," Zone said.

"The negatives," Caleb said under his breath. "Of course. I should have thought of that myself."

"All negative forces are countered by positive forces," Zone intoned. "It is the nature of the universe."

"Sure. Look, could you give me directions to Asterley's cabin?"

"Turmoil and confusion," Zone whispered. "Turmoil and confusion. And great danger. I have seen the warning in the mists. I hoped it was a dream, but now I fear that it was a true vision."

"Let me put it this way," Caleb said patiently. "If you don't give me directions ASAP, you and I will be having a serious conversation about your unemployment benefits or lack thereof."

"Take a right when you leave here. First left outside of town. Ambrose's cabin is at the end of the road."

"Thanks," Caleb said. "You've been very helpful."

4

A DEEP SENSE OF MELANCHOLY SWEPT THROUGH SERENIty as she searched the extensive files stored in Ambrose's basement. The man had had so much talent, she thought. But his artistic gifts had been compromised by a lifelong battle with the bottle and a personality that always got in the way of his relationships with others. The evidence of his repeated failures surrounded her. It consisted of sixteen file cabinets full of unsold photographs.

And the corresponding negatives.

Fortunately, Ambrose had filed by date, usually lumping three or four years' worth of work together. Within that constraint, he filed items alphabetically. She pulled open one of the drawers that contained Ambrose's records for the past three years and started searching for her name. As she expected, the folders were in pristine order.

She found the file labeled *Makepeace, Serenity,* almost immediately. Footsteps sounded on the hardwood floor overhead just as she reached inside the folder. She froze.

"Serenity?"

The sound of her own name was muffled by the thick wooden ceiling of the basement, but there was no mistaking the dark, deep voice. Caleb was upstairs.

Serenity didn't know whether to be relieved or annoyed. That was one of the problems she was having with Caleb lately, she thought. Her emotions seemed all mixed up around him.

"I'm down here. In the basement." She hastily plucked the single large envelope out of the folder, tucked it under her arm and closed the drawer.

Caleb's footsteps echoed as he approached the basement door. A moment later he appeared at the top of the stairs. "I should have figured you'd try something like this. Tell me, just as a matter of idle curiosity, are the laws concerning breaking and entering different here in Witt's End than they are in Seattle?"

"I wouldn't know." Serenity decided that what she was feeling now was definitely annoyance. Extreme annoyance. "I've never compared the legal codes. As a free-spirited child of the universe, I don't feel the need to pay much attention to man-made laws."

"A convenient philosophy." Caleb started down the stairs. "Did you find the photos?"

She gave a start. "How did you know?"

"I may not be a child of the universe, but I'm not an idiot."

She clutched the envelope tightly to her side and

glared at him. "I'm not stealing them, you know. They belong to me. Ambrose once told me that if I ever wanted them, I could have them."

"Did he?" Caleb's gaze went to the large envelope under her arm. "What are you going to do with them?"

"I don't know. Tear them up and throw them away, I suppose." She scowled at him. "They've caused me enough trouble as it is."

"I thought you said they were high art."

"They are art. But they've also proven to be trouble. So I'm going to get rid of them. I certainly don't have any use for them."

A thoughtful expression crossed Caleb's hard face. "You do realize that the fact that you found those photos here implies that Asterley was the blackmailer, after all. It's obvious now that he didn't give or sell those negatives to someone else."

"Yes, I know." Serenity felt another twinge of sadness. "I still can't believe Ambrose would have done something like this. I suppose he must have had his reasons."

"Hell, you'd make excuses for the devil himself." Caleb came to a halt on the bottom step and surveyed the room. He whistled softly. "I see Asterley liked photography equipment. Looks like he only worked with the best."

"Ambrose cared passionately about his work."

"Yeah, sure. A real artist. Come on, let's get out of here."

Serenity smiled coolly. "Surely you don't want to be seen leaving here with me? If we're caught, you might be implicated in my criminal activities."

"As your partner and business consultant, I'll just

have to risk it. Part of the job, you know. Let's go, Serenity."

She was genuinely amused now. "You're really nervous about being down here, aren't you?"

"Is that so strange? Where I come from, people get arrested for doing things like this."

"Relax, Caleb. Ambrose was a friend. He wouldn't mind my being here." Serenity started toward the stairs. "But I'm ready to go now. There's something very depressing about this basement."

She was less than a yard away from where Caleb waited impatiently on the bottom step when she heard the muted sound of an automobile engine.

"Damn it to hell," Caleb muttered. "Someone's out there."

"It's probably just Jessie or someone else from Witt's End," Serenity said, hoping that was the case.

"What if it's one of his relatives come to collect his things? Or the cops? If you don't mind, I'd just as soon not get caught taking stuff from a dead man's house." Caleb went back up the stairs, taking them two at a time, and quickly closed the basement door. Then he returned to the bottom of the steps, reached out, caught hold of Serenity's arm and urged her toward the wall.

"What in the world are you doing?" she gasped.

"Quiet." Caleb flipped the second light switch, which was located at the bottom of the steps. The basement was instantly plunged into total darkness. "Maybe if we get real lucky, whoever it is will simply go away."

"I'm sure it's someone I know," she grumbled.

"Not another word," Caleb breathed in her ear.

Serenity was genuinely nervous now, in spite of her

brave assertion that there was nothing to worry about. She listened as the cabin door was opened in the room above. Footsteps quickly crossed the floor. Whoever it was seemed to know his or her way around, she thought. *A friend of Ambrose's, then. Jessie, perhaps.*

She was about to voice her conclusion to Caleb and tell him that there was no cause for alarm when she heard the footsteps move directly overhead, heading toward the basement door. She groaned silently and nudged Caleb with her elbow. She hoped he realized that there was no place to hide if someone opened the door at the top of the stairs.

"Hell," Caleb muttered. "Guess we'll have to play this by ear. Try for the casual touch. Just an old friend tidying things up or something."

"Honestly, Caleb, you worry too much."

"All of us big-time consultants worry. It's why we're so highly paid."

"I wish you'd stop bringing up the subject of your outrageous fees."

"It's a subject that's very dear to my heart. Here, let me have that." He whisked the envelope she had been holding out from under her arm.

"Caleb, that's mine."

"I'll give it back later." He snapped the wall switch again. The overhead bulb lit up the windowless room. "All right, we're going to take the offensive. Act like we have every reason to be here."

"We do. Sort of."

The door opened at the top of the stairs. A man appeared. "What the hell? Who's down there?"

"Who are you?" Caleb demanded with the sort of natural arrogance that one tended to associate with cops and other authority figures. "This is private property."

The stranger at the top of the stairs gave a visible start. He gazed uncertainly down into the basement.

He appeared to be in his late fifties, thin and wiry, with a narrow, smoker's face and sunken eyes. Dressed in an old sweater and a pair of slacks, he had the restless, twitchy look of someone who ran largely on nervous energy. He was clearly alarmed to see that the basement was occupied. His mouth opened and closed and then opened again.

"Now just a damned minute," he finally said forcefully. "I've got a right to be here."

"Hello," Serenity said brightly. Out of the corner of her eye she noticed that the envelope containing her photos had disappeared inside Caleb's jacket. "Didn't mean to startle you. Are you a member of the family?"

"Family?" The man stared at her. "What family?"

"Ambrose's family," Serenity explained gently. "Sorry if we're intruding. We didn't think he had any close kin. He never mentioned his relations."

"I'm not a relative, I'm a friend." The man hesitated. "I mean, I was a friend. My name's Gallagher Firebrace. I'm a photographer from Seattle. I've known—I mean I knew Ambrose for a long time. Last night a photographer I know in Bullington called me. He told me he'd heard that there'd been an accident. I drove up here to see if there was anything I could do."

"Caleb Ventress," Caleb said easily, as if he was accustomed to being discovered skulking around other people's basements. "This is Serenity Makepeace. She was a friend of Asterley's, too. We just came by to straighten things up a bit."

"I see." Gallagher glanced down at Serenity. "You're right. Ambrose doesn't have any family."

"I wonder who will inherit all this stuff?" Serenity said.

"I have no idea." Gallagher's eyes swept the array of expensive equipment stored in the basement. "He owed me a lot of money."

"Is that right?" Caleb watched him.

"Probably owed money to a lot of people." Gallagher sighed heavily. "He was a hell of a photographer. Too bad he couldn't get his personal life under control. It was the drinking that ruined his business."

"The drinking seems to have ruined everything for Ambrose over the years," Serenity said softly.

"And in the end it finally killed him." Gallagher came slowly down the steps. "No surprise, I guess. Still, he was a pal, a fellow pro in the field, and I had been kind of hoping he'd climbed on the wagon to stay. Well, that's neither here nor there now. I wonder what will become of all his equipment. He spent a fortune on it, you know. A lot of it was my money."

"There's some valuable-looking items in here and in the room above," Caleb observed.

"Ambrose didn't care much for people, but he loved camera equipment," Gallagher said. "Poor, dumb bastard. He was always so certain that if he just bought a new camera or the latest high-tech lighting gadget, he'd finally get his career back on track."

Serenity frowned. "I hadn't thought much about it until now, but Ambrose must have spent a lot of money on equipment over the years."

"Tell me about it," Gallagher said with a rueful smile. "God knows how much I gave him. No telling who else he talked into loaning him a few bucks."

"His friend Jessie probably gave him some," Serenity said. "And I know Julius gave him a little cash from time to time. So did Montrose and Quinton. So did I, for that matter."

"No matter how much anyone gave him, he always seemed to need more," Gallagher said. "Face it, the guy was a mooch. Still, there was something about Ambrose that you had to like, you know?"

"I know," Serenity said. "It was his passion for his work, I think. People responded to it."

"I guess that was it." Gallagher hesitated. "Ambrose had talent. But he got a reputation in Seattle for showing up drunk on one too many shoots, and that was the end of the line for him. He moved up here to Witt's End and more or less fell off the face of the earth as far as the rest of us were concerned. Still, when I heard the news, I had to come up and check it out."

"And maybe help yourself to a few pieces of photo equipment from Asterley's collection?" Caleb suggested. "At a rough estimate, I'd say that Nikon lens over there on top of the last file cabinet is probably worth a thousand, maybe fifteen hundred."

"Now, see here," Gallagher began angrily. "I told you, the guy owed me money. A lot of it. I've got a right to collect one way or another."

"The county sheriff might have a few things to say about that," Caleb said. "If there's no immediate family or heir to claim this cabin and everything in it, the state will step in to handle the property of the deceased."

Gallagher compressed his lips into a thin, disgruntled line. "Yeah, I suppose so."

"Bet on it," Caleb advised. He took Serenity's arm

and started purposefully up the stairs. "I think all of us had better be on our way. Doesn't look like there's much we can do around here."

Serenity looked at Gallagher as she and Caleb reached the top of the stairs. "We'll probably have a wake for Ambrose sometime soon. I'll be glad to phone you and let you know the time and place."

"Thanks, but I've got to go down to Portland for a shoot tomorrow," Gallagher said. "An annual report for a major firm. I'll be busy for several days."

"We understand. Business is business." Caleb turned off the light and closed the basement door. He gave Gallagher a mockingly polite nod. "After you."

Gallagher took one last, frustrated look at the closed basement door and then shrugged. Without a word, he led the way out through the living room and onto the front porch.

"See you around." Gallagher took a package of cigarettes out of his pocket as he went down the steps toward a nondescript green sedan.

"Drive carefully," Serenity called automatically.

Gallagher jerked open the car door. "Shouldn't be any problem. The fog has finally lifted." He got in behind the wheel and slammed the door closed.

Another car, a familiar, aging Chevrolet, pulled into the drive just as Gallagher started his engine and began to back out.

"For a dead man, Asterley is sure getting a lot of callers this morning," Caleb muttered.

"That's Jessie Blanchard," Serenity explained. "She was closer to Ambrose than anyone else."

Jessie, starkly, artistically elegant at the age of forty-nine, got out of her car. She was dressed, as usual, all in black; sweater, jeans, and high boots. She had on a black jacket and she wore an abundance of silver and turquoise rings on her long-fingered hands.

The style, which Jessie had perfected years ago and which never varied, accented her silver and black hair and her exotic bone structure. She turned to glance at the green car as it disappeared down the road. Then she looked at Serenity.

"Who was that?" Jessie asked in her husky voice.

"His name's Gallagher Firebrace. He said he was a friend of Ambrose's," Serenity explained.

"Firebrace." Jessie's brows drew together. "I think Ambrose did mention him from time to time. He's from Seattle, isn't he?"

"Apparently." Serenity went down the steps to give Jessie a quick hug. Jessie looked weary but calm, almost resigned. "Are you okay?"

"I'm doing all right." Jessie gave her a tired smile. "Part of me always knew it would end like this. Poor Ambrose never could stay away from the bottle long enough to get his act together. But lately I really had begun to let myself believe he might actually make it this time. He was trying very hard."

"We all hoped he was going to make it," Serenity said gently.

"Yes." Jessie looked at Caleb. "You must be Serenity's new business consultant. The man who spent the night in Julius's cabin."

Caleb's smile was wry. "That's the thing about small towns, isn't it? Nothing goes unnoticed. I'm Caleb Ventress."

"Too bad Ambrose never got a chance to meet you," Jessie said.

Caleb caught Serenity's eye. "I'd like to have had a few words with him, myself."

Serenity hastened to change the subject. This was neither the time nor the place for Caleb to make accusations of blackmail against Ambrose. "Do you know what will happen to Ambrose's things, Jessie?"

Jessie looked at her in surprise. "He left everything to me."

"Asterley had a will?" Caleb asked sharply.

Jessie nodded. "He went to a lawyer in Bullington last year and had one drawn up. Ambrose was going through a period during which he convinced himself that his talent would never be recognized in his own lifetime."

"So he started hoping for a little posthumous glory, is that it?" Caleb asked.

Jessie sighed. "I'm going to do my best to get his work some critical attention. He certainly deserves it. He really was very talented. I just wish that he . . . well, never mind. It's too late now, isn't it?"

"Did Asterley leave you everything?" Caleb asked. "The cabin and his photo equipment, too?"

"Yes. Once I get Ambrose's place cleared out, I think I'll turn the cabin over to a real estate agent in Bullington. He can either rent it or sell it, I don't particularly care. I suppose I'll try to sell the photo equipment. Maybe I'll put an ad in the Bullington paper."

"Better keep an eye on the equipment until it's sold," Caleb said grimly. "There seems to be a lot of interest in it."

Jessie's eyes widened slightly. "What do you mean?"

"Mr. Firebrace seemed to think he had some kind of claim on it because of the money he says he loaned to Ambrose over the years," Serenity said.

Jessie glanced over her shoulder in the direction Gallagher had disappeared. "Knowing Ambrose, it's entirely possible that he died owing money to quite a few people. If Mr. Firebrace wants to contact me, maybe we can work something out."

"Not unless he can produce some proof that he actually loaned money to Asterley and that it was not repaid," Caleb said flatly. "Make sure Firebrace has a genuine IOU with Asterley's signature on it before you agree to turn over any of the equipment."

Jessie smiled faintly. "You are definitely a businessman, aren't you?"

"It's what I do."

Jessie shrugged. "It shouldn't be an issue. Ambrose was obsessive about the files that pertained to his work. If he borrowed money from Firebrace in order to buy photo equipment, you can bet there'll be a record in one of those file cabinets."

"Speaking of Ambrose's files," Serenity said, "I came by for the negatives of those photos that he took of me last spring. I wasn't sure who would get his things, so I thought I'd better grab them before any of his relatives showed up."

"Right. Did you find them?" Jessie asked.

"Yes."

"Good. They're yours, of course. Ambrose always said you could have them if you wanted them. I'd never send them off to a gallery without your permission."

"A *gallery?*" Caleb looked startled. "I should hope to hell not."

Jessie smiled. "Those photos are definitely some of Ambrose's best work, if you ask me. Have you seen them?"

"No." Caleb slanted a glance at Serenity. "I haven't."

"Have Serenity show them to you," Jessie urged. "You'll see what I mean. Ambrose was brilliant from time to time. Those shots of Serenity were taken during one of his peak periods. He called the series 'Spring.' I think he had plans to portray her as Summer, Fall, and Winter, too, but he never got around to finishing the project."

"For which we can only be grateful," Caleb muttered.

"Caleb doesn't care for artistic photography," Serenity said.

"Is that right?" Jessie gave Caleb an odd look.

"Jessie, if you're okay here alone," Serenity said quickly, "I think we'll be on our way. I've got to get to the store. Let me know if you need any help sorting through Ambrose's stuff."

"I will." Jessie inclined her head toward Caleb. "Nice to meet you. Serenity says you're going to do some great things for our little town."

"That remains to be seen," Serenity said in a forbidding tone. "You know what they say about the best laid plans." She jammed her hands into her jacket pockets and set off down the drive.

"Good-bye, Jessie," Caleb said politely. "I'm sure we'll run into each other again soon."

"I'm sure we will." Jessie went up the steps to the front door of the cabin.

Serenity heard the crunch of gravel behind her as Caleb followed her toward the road. She did not look back. He caught up with her in three long strides. Serenity held out her hand.

"I'll take that envelope, if you don't mind," she said crisply.

Caleb hesitated and then reluctantly reached inside his jacket for the envelope. He pulled it out slowly, but instead of handing it to her, held onto it. "Serenity, I'd like to talk about something."

She snapped her fingers impatiently. "May I please have my pictures?"

"I've been thinking about your photos," Caleb said carefully.

"Is that so? What, exactly, have you been thinking about them?"

"I'd like to see them."

"Over my dead body." Serenity kept her hand outstretched.

Caleb's expression was grim. "All right. If that's the way you want it." He gave her the envelope.

"Thank you." Serenity tucked the envelope under her arm and kept walking.

"Serenity?"

"Yes?"

"Can you envision any circumstances under which you would feel comfortable showing me those pictures?"

"Why would you want to see them?"

"I'm not sure." Caleb kept his eyes on the road ahead.

"Has your prurient interest been aroused?" she asked acidly.

His expression was as unreadable as stone. "What do you think?"

"I don't know what to think. A couple of days ago you were thoroughly outraged when you found out about these photos. Now you say you want to see them."

"Will you just answer my question?" he asked quietly.

She considered it. "You want to know if I can conceive of any circumstances under which I'd feel comfortable showing you the pictures? Well, maybe. Hypothetically speaking, that is."

"What kind of circumstances?"

"Well, *hypothetically* speaking, I might show them to you if I ever felt I could trust you."

"If you felt you could *trust* me." Caleb came to a halt in the middle of the empty road and caught hold of her arm, forcing Serenity to stop, too. "Are you saying you don't trust me? That's a damned insult, lady. I've got a reputation in the business community that is second to none. Ask anyone who's ever dealt with me. Go ahead, ask. No one, but no one, has ever accused me of being untrustworthy."

Serenity was startled by the intensity of his reaction to her remark. She was also irritated. "Oh, I'm sure you're quite *trustworthy* when it comes to your business dealings. Your contracts are apparently airtight and you've probably never been accused of fraud. But I'm talking about being able to trust you on a personal level."

"Damn it, Serenity, I resent that. I do not lie."

"If you resent it so much, you're free to leave Witt's End. No one's trying to keep you here."

Caleb released her. He started forward, his stride angry and dangerous. "You're going to be difficult about this, aren't you?"

"Difficult?" Serenity hurried to catch up with him. "Caleb, I don't understand what's going on here.

What do you expect of me after what's happened between us?"

"Isn't it obvious? I want you to give me another chance."

"You're getting another chance," she shot back. "I can't seem to stop you. According to you, I'm stuck with you as a consultant whether I like it or not."

"I'm not talking about the business side of this thing. I'm talking about the personal side of it."

In spite of her wariness and her deep uncertainty, a thrill of excitement and hope raced through Serenity. She clutched the envelope tightly. "Personal side?"

"Look, let's try for a little honesty on both sides, okay?" Caleb asked quietly. "We're attracted to each other. We both more or less admitted it when I kissed you in my office. You kissed me back, if you'll recall. I know damn well that you want me as much as I want you."

Serenity's insides tightened. "I don't think I want to get involved with a man who would have to concentrate very hard not to think about a few photos of me every time he kissed me."

"I'll admit the news of those photos came as a shock at first, but I've had a chance to calm down. I know you're not—"

"Not what?" She was suddenly very curious.

"I know you're not the kind of woman who would deliberately pose for dirty pictures. I'm sure you believed Asterley when he told you that he wanted you to pose for the sake of art."

"Gosh, Mr. Ventress, your magnanimous attitude is overwhelming. I don't know what to say."

"Say yes." Caleb stopped once more. He searched her face with stark eyes. "Say you'll give me a chance to prove that you can trust me again on a personal level." He paused briefly, as if gathering himself for a plunge into very deep water. "Please."

It was the raw need buried in that single word, *please,* that was Serenity's undoing. She met Caleb's eyes and for the briefest instant thought she glimpsed the trailing wake of some deep, dark emotion that swam just beneath the surface. Once again he had reached out and touched her in some intimate, indefinable way, and she could not resist the contact. She was compelled to touch him, too.

"Okay," she said gently.

Relief flashed in Caleb's expression. That emotion disappeared as swiftly as the other, more mysterious emotion, had. He scowled. "Okay? Is that all you have to say?"

"What else is there to say?" She gave him a misty smile. "Hey, it's no big deal. Witt's End exists for people who want a second chance. It's practically the town motto. I'd be remiss in my civic duty if I didn't give you an opportunity to prove you aren't an arrogant, straitlaced, inflexible, unbending SOB."

"Very decent of you, Ms. Makepeace," he muttered dryly. "Let's make a deal. When you show me the photos, I'll know that you trust me. Fair enough?"

Serenity hesitated briefly and then shrugged. "Deal. But the decision will be mine. Understood?"

"You're a tough negotiator."

"I'm taking lessons from an expert."

Forty minutes later, alone in her tiny office in the back of Witt's End Grocery, Serenity opened the envelope she had taken from Ambrose's files.

She turned it upside down and shook out three

photos. She glanced at the prints without much interest. She'd seen them before. The pictures showed her reclining and sitting on a large boulder next to a stream. The lighting was dramatic and other worldly. The black and white shots didn't worry her.

What worried her was that the negatives were not in the envelope.

5

W

HAT THE HELL DO YOU MEAN, THE NEGATIVES ARE gone?" Caleb planted both hands on top of Serenity's desk and leaned forward in what probably appeared to be a thoroughly intimidating fashion.

Some people would no doubt claim that it was not very nice to intimidate the queen of the butterflies, which was exactly what Serenity looked like this morning. The floaty, gauzy, iridescent-green sliplike thing that she was wearing over a green, high-necked, long-sleeved jumpsuit definitely made her look like butterfly royalty. The chaotic mass of her wild red hair only added to the overall effect. Here in Witt's End, Caleb had noticed, Serenity did not wear beige and gray, as she always had in Seattle.

At the moment he didn't particularly care if he was charged with butterfly intimidation. He was furious. So furious, in fact, that he didn't even give a damn that he was skating on the jagged edge of his temper.

Anger wasn't the only emotion twisting his insides. Serenity's news made him deeply uneasy in a variety of ways. He couldn't believe what he was hearing. No, he corrected himself, he could believe it, all right. He just didn't want to believe it.

"Please don't yell at me." Serenity gripped the arms of her chair and glared at him. "I'm having a difficult day. I don't need you making it worse."

"I'm not yelling. When I yell, you'll know it."

"I'd appreciate it if you'd stop snarling, then."

"I am not snarling, either. Why didn't you tell me earlier that the negatives were missing?"

"Because I had a hunch you'd overreact," Serenity admitted. "I wasn't up to dealing with it."

"You think I'm overreacting? You don't know what overreacting is." Caleb swept aside the pile of business papers he'd been going over for the past two hours.

He straightened and began to prowl the tiny office. The only reason he wasn't actually yelling was because he knew he'd be overheard by Zone and the sprinkling of locals who were shopping at Witt's End Grocery. The closed door that stood between the office and the main part of the store was not very thick.

"I had a feeling this morning that this thing wasn't over," Caleb muttered. "I knew something else was going to go wrong."

Serenity pressed her lips together in a mutinous expression. "Don't worry about it, Caleb. This isn't your problem, it's mine."

So much for their short-lived truce, Caleb thought. "I've already told you, as long as you're a client, your problems are my problems."

"You and your precious business ethics. Nobody's

asking you to go above and beyond the call of duty here. You're the one who's pushing it."

"I'll decide what constitutes above and beyond the call." Caleb reached the wall, swung around and stalked back across the room. He was disgusted to realize that he was pacing. He never paced. He had too much self-control to pace.

A shock of self-awareness jolted him back to a cold, calm acknowledgment of just what was happening. Pacing was clear evidence that he was allowing his emotions to gain the upper hand.

Emotions were dangerous. They left a man vulnerable, weakened him, encouraged him to make mistakes, made him forget his responsibilities, caused him to run off with a platinum-blond centerfold model and to father an illegitimate son who would spend the rest of his life paying for his father's emotional stupidity.

Caleb was discovering that emotions were also what made a man feel alive.

He fought back the confusion within and came to an abrupt halt in the middle of the room. "All right, let's calm down here and think this through in a logical manner."

"I am calm," Serenity said pointedly. "Unlike some people I could mention. Not finding the negatives came as a surprise, that's all. I'm sure there's nothing to worry about."

"The hell there isn't. You've got a set of missing blackmail negatives to worry about."

"Those pictures can't do me any more harm than they've already done. The only thing that really concerns me now is the possibility that maybe Ambrose wasn't the one who tried to blackmail me. Maybe someone else was involved. Damn. I was so hoping this thing was finished."

"Asterley is still the most likely suspect." Caleb forced himself to do what he did best, to unemotionally analyze a situation and reach a reasoned conclusion. "He probably removed the negatives from his files at some point and hid them in a safe place while he conducted his blackmail dealings."

"Why would he do that?"

"Because what he was doing was illegal." Caleb gave her an exasperated glance. "If you'd gone to the cops and those negatives had been discovered in Asterley's possession, the authorities would have nailed him. This way, if he was caught and his files searched, he could always claim that the negatives had been stolen from him and that someone else had done the blackmailing."

"If that's true, there's no telling where he might have hidden those negatives. We'll probably never find them." Serenity exhaled softly. "I suppose it's for the best."

"I'm not so sure about that." Caleb rubbed the back of his neck. "I don't like the fact that those negatives are floating around out there somewhere. Someone else might find them by accident."

He eyed the envelope on top of Serenity's desk with a brooding gaze. The thought of another man drooling over nude photos of Serenity, photos that he himself hadn't been allowed to see, made every muscle in Caleb's body tighten.

"It's not really very likely when you stop to think about it." Serenity sat forward determinedly. "Well, I certainly don't intend to sit around worrying that someone might find the negatives. I've already explained to you that I'm not ashamed of the pictures."

"Is that right? Let me tell you something, you looked damned worried a few minutes ago when you pulled that envelope out of the drawer and told me the negatives were missing." For just a few seconds there she'd actually looked at him as if she needed him, Caleb thought with a surge of satisfaction. Really needed him.

Hope, he was discovering the hard way, was perhaps the cruelest emotion of all.

"As I said, it came as a shock to discover that the negatives weren't in the envelope with the prints," Serenity admitted. "My first thought was that someone else had taken them and used them to blackmail me."

"I know."

"It's not exactly pleasant to think that you might have an enemy."

"I'm well aware of what it's like to have enemies."

"I don't doubt that for a moment," Serenity retorted. "But I grew up believing that even though the outside world considers all of us here in Witt's End a little off the wall, we're neighbors and friends. More than that, we're a family. I've always felt I could count on everyone I know here in town. We're a very close-knit community."

"With the exception of Asterley, that was probably a valid assumption. I think it's also logical to assume that, with Asterley dead, the problem with the pictures is over."

He was pleased with the way that came out. He

sounded cool and dispassionate. In control. The rush of anger and alarm that he had initially experienced when she had told him that the negatives were still missing was receding.

Old habits took hold once more. Caleb deliberately distanced himself from the rage and the primitive sense of protectiveness that had set the adrenaline pumping through him.

He was an expert at stuffing strong emotions into a box, closing the lid and sealing it tight. He'd practiced the trick all of his life. He had learned to operate by remote control with the members of his own family, and he could certainly do it with Serenity.

"I'm sure you're right," she said.

"It's usually best to assume the obvious."

"The obvious?"

"In this case the obvious conclusion is that Asterley was the blackmailer." Caleb held up one hand and ticked off his points as he made them. "He put the negatives in a safe location while he carried out his plans. He died before he could retrieve them. No one is likely to discover them by accident. End of story."

"Okay, you've sold me on your theory." Serenity paused, her peacock eyes still troubled. "The only thing that bothers me about your theory, the thing that has sort of bothered me all along, in fact, is that it was Ambrose who sent me to you in the first place."

Caleb stared at her, dumbfounded. "What did you say?"

Serenity frowned. "Didn't I mention that Ambrose was the one who suggested you as a possible consultant? He gave me your name when I told him I was going to look for a hotshot start-up expert. He suggested I try you first because he'd heard that you were very good."

"No," Caleb said between his teeth. "You did not mention that interesting little fact."

"Oh. Well, I guess it slipped my mind."

He wanted to shake her. Naiveté was one thing. Stupidity was another. "How the hell did Ambrose Asterley, a drunken failure, a washed-up photographer living in a town so small it isn't even on most maps, know about me?"

"You've told me yourself that you're the best in the business. Is it so strange that someone like Ambrose would have heard of you? We're not completely out of touch with world events here in Witt's End. We do get newspapers. And Ambrose read nearly every major paper on the West Coast on a regular basis."

"Newspapers?" Caleb recalled the stacks of aging newsprint that he'd seen piled around the front room of Asterley's cabin.

"That's where Ambrose probably got your name," Serenity explained patiently. "Out of a Seattle newspaper. Has Ventress Ventures ever made the business section?"

"Yes." It was possible, Caleb conceded. Ventress Ventures showed up every now and again in the financial pages of the West Coast papers, and more often in Northwest papers. It was a logical connection.

"But why steer you in my direction and then turn around and blackmail you?" Caleb mused aloud. He broke off suddenly. "Damn."

"What now?"

"Never mind. I think I just answered my own question."

"I'd appreciate it if you'd answer it for me," Serenity grumbled. "Why would Ambrose send me to you and then use blackmail threats to stop me from doing business with you?"

"Because he probably felt that he had things under control that way," Caleb said, thinking quickly. "You told me that he wasn't in favor of change here in Witt's End."

"That's true. Ambrose wasn't in favor of much of anything. He was a very depressed person."

"I assume he knew that you had made up your mind to create Witt's End by Mail?"

"Everyone in town knew that."

"He also probably knew you well enough to realize that he couldn't talk you out of it. Right again?"

"Right."

"So he pretended to help out. He sent you off in a direction he knew he could control. How old did you say Asterley was?"

"Somewhere in his mid-fifties. Why?"

Old enough to have read about the old Ventress scandal when it first broke thirty-four years ago, Caleb thought. His grandfather had told him often enough that the news of Crystal Brooke's affair with Gordon Ventress had been all over the Northwest papers.

It wouldn't have taken much in the way of brains for Asterley to have surmised that even three and a half decades later, a bunch of nude photos and a threat of blackmail would have a strong, exceedingly negative impact on anyone with the last name of Ventress.

"Caleb?"

He looked at Serenity, who was regarding him with a mixture of curiosity and concern. "It's a long story. I won't bore you with it now. Let's just say that I have a hunch your friend Asterley sent you to me because he knew he could kill any deal you made with those photos."

"But how could he know that you'd go off the deep end the way you did over a few pictures that Ambrose himself considered very good art?"

"I didn't go off the deep end."

"Yes, you did. You went nutso at the thought of doing business with me once you heard I'd posed for nude pictures. Admit it."

"I did not go nutso." Caleb leaned over her desk again. "I'm here, aren't I? In spite of those damn photos."

"Well, yes, but you can't deny that you overreacted to them when you first heard about them."

"I never overreact," Caleb said icily.

"That's a matter of opinion. Personally, I suspected from the start that you were a very emotional sort of person, and every move you've made lately has verified my conclusion."

"I swear to God, Serenity, if you don't stop saying things like that, I won't be responsible for my actions."

"See what I mean?" She smiled triumphantly. "Emotional. Don't worry about it. I tend to get a little emotional myself from time to time. The question is, how could Ambrose know you'd have the reaction you did to those photos?"

Caleb took a firm grip on his temper. She was deliberately baiting him, and he was not going to bite again. "I told you, it's a long story." One he had not discussed with anyone outside the family in his entire life, he reflected silently. He certainly didn't intend to start now. Some things were better left buried. The past had caused him enough trouble. "The details aren't important."

"Caleb, what's going on here?" Serenity clasped her hands in front of her on her desk and studied him with sober attention. "What did Ambrose know about you that made him think you'd go bonkers over those photos? How could he possibly know how straitlaced you are? How could he know anything about you at all?"

"Because he read newspapers," Caleb said roughly. He was not straitlaced, he told himself. He had been caught off guard, that was all. Basically he was a reasonable, tolerant man.

"Yes, but what did he read in the newspapers that made him think you'd refuse to do business with me if you found out about the photos?"

"Look, Serenity, I'll go into it later, all right? This isn't the time or the place."

"I'm not so sure." Someone pounded on the office door before Serenity could continue. She broke off with a frown. "Come in."

The door opened and Zone thrust her shaved head around the edge. The earring in her nose gleamed. "That new sales rep from the whole-grain distributor is here. He says he has an appointment."

Serenity glanced at her desk calendar. "He does."

Zone glanced over her shoulder and then lowered her voice to a confidential whisper. "His aura is very weak and tinged with a sort of pale green. I believe that there is great anxiety in him."

"That's because he's worried about keeping us as

clients," Serenity said. "Based on that one conversation I had with him on the phone, I get the feeling he hasn't been very successful in his chosen field. Started out selling computers and lost that job. Went on to shoes and bombed again. Now he's trying to make it in the whole-grain line."

"Ah." Zone's bracelets clanked gently beneath the saffron and orange sleeves of her robes. "I thought I detected a fear of failure in that green aura. He has obviously not learned to align himself with the positive forces of the universe."

"Don't worry," Serenity said briskly. "We'll cheer him up with a large order today."

Caleb scowled. "What is this? You're going to give that sales rep an order just because you're worried about his weak aura?"

"Can you think of a better reason?" Serenity asked innocently. "Besides, I need to lay in supplies. We'll get our first snow before too long. Deliveries will be unpredictable after that." She glanced at Zone. "Show the rep in here, will you, Zone?"

"Of course." Zone gave Caleb a pointed look.

"I was just leaving," Caleb said.

"It's for the best," Zone murmured. "The vibrations were getting very dangerous. I had an unpleasant vision while meditating the other night. And then you showed up. I was starting to become quite concerned."

"Keep on worrying. I meant that I was leaving Serenity's office." Caleb strode past Zone. "Not Witt's End."

"Then we must prepare ourselves for the turmoil and danger which await."

Caleb ignored her. He glanced at the man hovering near the front counter. The sales rep was clutching a cheap, imitation leather briefcase and fidgeting with his badly frayed collar. His tie was too narrow and his pants were made of polyester. His eyes darted about nervously behind the lenses of his horn-rimmed glasses.

"You can go in now," Caleb said. "I'm through."

"Thanks." The sales rep edged around Caleb. "You in natural foods?"

"Tofu."

"Oh, yeah. Tofu." The man looked greatly relieved to learn that he wasn't in direct competition with Caleb. "I'm in whole grains, myself."

"You're lucky. Longer shelf life for your product."

The sales rep brightened for a moment. "Yeah. Hadn't thought of that." He glanced around and then leaned closer. "How was it in there? She a tough sale?"

"Tough as nails," Caleb assured him.

"I was afraid of that." The salesman's Adam's apple bobbed. Sweat broke out on his forehead. "Mind if I ask if you closed your deal with her?"

"I'm still working on it."

"Too bad. Well, here goes nothing." The nervous salesman scurried into Serenity's office and closed the door.

Caleb ignored Zone, who watched him from her station behind the counter. He wandered down the nearest aisle, studying the interesting array of goods stocked on the shelves and stored in large, round, wooden barrels.

He walked past buckwheat noodles, dried beans,

peas, nuts, soy flour, whole wheat bagels and fresh rye bread. The granola in one barrel looked familiar. He was almost certain it was the same kind he'd had for breakfast. He remembered the mental note he had made to buy milk.

The dairy case at the rear of the store contained blue corn tortillas, goat cheese, and tofu in three different textures—soft, medium, and firm. Down another aisle Caleb discovered four different brands of olive oil, what appeared to be an assortment of home-bottled herbed vinegar, and several jars of unsulfured molasses. He frowned thoughtfully at the vinegar bottles.

The bells over the front door jangled cheerfully. A blast of chilly air announced the arrival of a man who looked as if he'd just stepped out of a war movie.

"Good morning, Blade," Zone said with a gentle enthusiasm that surprised Caleb. "I see you can't sleep today. It was a difficult night, wasn't it?"

"The last three nights have been bad," Blade said ominously. He glanced over his shoulder and spoke to two huge rottweilers who were loitering on the sidewalk. "Stay," he ordered.

Caleb watched through the open doorway as the dogs obediently sat. Then he glanced at Blade again and decided that he would have recognized the survivalist anywhere from Serenity's brief description. If the camouflage fatigues and boots hadn't given Blade away, the armament he wore would have been a significant clue. The stuff dripped from him like icicles.

"Did you get any sleep at all?" Zone asked anxiously.

"Plan to sleep a few hours this afternoon." Blade went toward the counter "Doin' sentry duty until then. You?"

Zone shook her head. "Not much. The lines of negative influence were just too powerful."

"Yeah, I know what you mean." Blade leaned one elbow against the counter and stared at Caleb with basilisk eyes. "Been a lot of negative influences around here lately. Kind of makes you wonder, don't it?"

Zone followed his gaze. She narrowed her eyes. "Yes, it does."

"Something wrong?" Caleb asked politely.

"Could be," Blade said.

The front door opened again. Quinton Priestly, bundled up in a thick parka, a scarf tucked under his beard, hurried into the warmth of the store. "Getting cold out there. Won't be long before the first snow. The endless vectors of points on the mathematical planes are mirrored in the microcosm of our seasons. Morning, everyone."

"Good morning," Zone said.

"Mornin'," Blade muttered. He didn't take his eyes off Caleb. "We were just talkin' about all the negative influences around here."

Quinton heaved a sigh. "You refer, of course, to the recent death of a member of our community. Ambrose was a difficult man in many ways, but he was one of us. We'll miss him."

"Some of us will probably miss him more than others," Blade said.

Quinton turned and saw Caleb. "Perhaps you're right."

Caleb walked to the front of the aisle and looked at Zone, Blade, and Quinton in turn. "Do we have a problem here?"

"Seems to me," Blade said, "that what we got here is an amazin' coincidence."

"How's that?" Caleb asked.

"Can't help but notice," Blade said, "that the first death we've had around here in years took place just a few hours before you showed up in town. For all I know, you might have been here right about the time Ambrose bought the farm."

Caleb went very still. "What the hell are you implying?"

"Nothin'." Blade ignored Zone and Quinton, who had both turned startled stares on him. "Just pointin' out a few facts. What with the fog and all, no way of knowin' who was where the night Ambrose died."

Caleb took a step forward.

"Come on, Blade," Quinton said hastily. "Take it easy. Don't get carried away here. We all know Ambrose's death was an accident."

"Yeah?" Blade squinted at Caleb. "All I know for sure is that Ambrose is dead."

"And all I know for certain," Caleb said softly, "is that you are a paranoid son of a bitch."

"Seems to me," Blade said, "that it's possible poor old Ambrose might have just had the bad luck to be your first target."

"My first target?"

"Might be your people are a little smarter than I figured. Instead of usin' a whole commando team, maybe they just sent in a single man to pick us off one by one. A sniper who works alone. You that good, Ventress?"

Zone's face registered serious alarm. Her eyes skittered anxiously from Caleb back to Blade. "Blade, I don't think you should say things like that. I don't like the color of his aura. It's getting very dark."

"Yeah, Blade," Quinton muttered. "Calm down, big guy. Serenity knows Ventress. She wouldn't have invited him here if she didn't think she could trust him."

"Sometimes Serenity's too damn trusting, if you ask me," Blade said. "She's . . . whatchacallit— naive. Yeah. That's the word. Naive."

"I think I've heard enough." It was one thing, Caleb thought, for him to call Serenity naive. It was another for some jerk built like a tank to call her names. "One more word and I'll wrap that tool belt you're wearing around your neck. Assuming I can find your neck, that is."

"Is that a fact?" Blade straightened away from the counter. He braced his booted feet widely apart and centered himself slowly and heavily into a martial arts stance. "Any time you want to try, I'll be waiting."

Caleb studied him curiously. "Where'd you learn your hand-to-hand style? From a kung fu movie?"

"We'll see just how good you are, mister." Blade started forward with a crablike movement.

Caleb reached for one of the jars of vinegar that occupied a nearby shelf.

"Jesus," Quinton whispered.

Zone opened her mouth and screamed. *"Serenity! You'd better get out here fast."*

The office door slammed opened. Serenity scanned the tense expressions of everyone present. "I'm trying to do some business. What on earth is going on out here?"

"I think we're in the middle of a very, very negative force field," Zone whispered.

Quinton threw Serenity an uneasy glance. "Blade's gone a little overboard with his latest conspiracy theory. He's implied that your friend Ventress, here, had something to do with Ambrose's death. Blade thinks he's the point man for a team of commandos."

Serenity's face whitened with shock and then her eyes became brilliant with outrage. "Of all the crazy, idiotic notions. Blade, you're entitled to your conspiracy theories, but you will not implicate my business partner in them. Is that perfectly clear? I won't tolerate it."

Blade's expression turned mulish. "Just how much do you know about this guy?"

Serenity lifted her chin. "Enough to be certain that he is not part of some clandestine operation trying to take over Witt's End. For heaven's sake, Blade, I chose Mr. Ventress, he didn't come looking for me. He didn't have any way of knowing who I was or where I came from until I told him."

"You sure?" Blade asked.

"Of course I'm sure. Ambrose's death was a tragic accident. We all know that. I will not have you making groundless accusations against Mr. Ventress. Kindly apologize to him immediately."

Blade looked abashed, but to Caleb's surprise, he didn't argue with Serenity. He nodded brusquely at Caleb. "Sorry, Ventress. Can't be too careful. You're a stranger around here, and all strangers are dangerous until proven otherwise, as far as I'm concerned."

"I can see that." Caleb glanced at Serenity and saw that she was still tense with anger. It occurred to him that he had never before had anyone jump to his defense. "A man can't afford to take chances."

Blade's eyes gleamed like steel. "That's the pure truth."

There was a short, brittle silence. Everyone seemed to be taking a deep breath.

"You're the one who makes these herbed vinegars, aren't you?" Caleb asked casually. He glanced down at the jar he had picked off the shelf.

"Yeah. That's my stuff." Blade sounded cautious. "Bottle it myself."

"It looks it." Caleb examined the short, squat jar full of vinegar. A spray of rosemary waved gently inside. "Serenity tells me you make a good product. But your packaging is lousy."

"Huh?" Blade started down the aisle at Caleb. "What's that supposed to mean?"

"It means," Caleb said patiently, "that if you want to sell your vinegars through Serenity's catalog, you're going to need to come up with something a little spiffier by way of packaging. Packaging is everything these days."

"It is?"

"Damn right. People will buy anything if it's packaged well. You need more interesting bottles. Attractive labels. A brand name."

"How do you know?" Blade demanded.

"I know it in the same way that you presumably know how to use all that hardware you're wearing. It's what I do. And I'm very good at what I do."

Blade's brow furrowed intently. "You think my vinegars need a brand name, huh?"

"Something simple," Caleb said. "Like 'Blade's

Herbed Vinegars.' And a clever slogan. 'Gives your salads an edge' or something."

Blade stared at him. "You want me to put my name on the bottles?"

"Why not? You're the one who makes the vinegar inside, aren't you?"

"Well, yeah, but I never thought of puttin' my name on these bottles." Blade turned the jar over in his hands. For a moment he seemed utterly fascinated with the notion of his name on a label. Then he scowled. "You really think folks would buy this stuff if it was in a nice bottle?"

"Trust me, packaging is everything."

Blade looked intrigued. "I'll do some thinkin' about this."

"Don't forget what I said about an attractive label," Caleb said.

Blade's face fell. "I'm no graphic artist."

Zone cleared her throat. "I am."

Blade looked at her. "You are?"

"I was before I came here a few months ago. I have a degree in fine arts. I could help you choose the right bottles and maybe design a label for you."

"Good idea," Caleb said. "By the way, can you produce those flower mugs in sufficient quantities to meet the kind of demand we'll get from a catalog mailing?"

Zone's eyes lit up briefly. "I think so. You like my mugs?"

"Yes, I do. More important, I think they'll sell," Caleb told her with grave certainty.

"This is wonderful," Serenity said happily. "We're off and running."

"The next step," Caleb said, "is for everyone in

town who wants to be a part of this venture to bring his or her product in for product evaluation. We'll choose what will go into the first catalog and then we'll see about label designs."

"I can't wait to get to work," Serenity said eagerly. "I'll be with you just as soon as I've finished with George."

Caleb looked at her. "George?"

"The whole-grain sales rep in my office."

"Right. George." Caleb picked up a package of bean soup mix. "Take your time."

Serenity ducked back inside her office. The others exchanged glances.

Blade cleared his throat. "If Serenity says you're okay, Ventress, then I reckon you must be okay."

"I appreciate that, Blade. I'm glad we had this little chat."

"Sort of cleared the air, don't you think?" Blade moved closer and lowered his voice. "I know everyone thinks I'm paranoid, but that don't mean I'm crazy, you know."

"Thanks for clearing up the distinction between the two for me. I was a little worried there for a while."

"I had a reason for figurin' you might be bad news," Blade said out of the corner of his mouth. "Heard a car that night."

Caleb wondered if he had missed an important conversational cue. "A car?"

"Pullin' out of Asterley's drive." Blade swept the grocery aisle with a quick glance, apparently checking for enemies lurking in the granola barrel. "Shortly after midnight. Couldn't identify it on account of the fog."

"I see." Caleb eyed the big man in silence for a few

seconds. "Mind if I ask what you were doing near Asterley's house the night he died?"

"Just regular recon." Blade looked down at the bottle of vinegar in his hand but he didn't appear to see it. He had the air of a man who is looking at something far away or very deep inside himself. "Got to tighten up security when the visibility's bad. That's when they're most likely to launch the first assault."

"I see."

"Reckon I'd better be on my way. Got things to do." Blade set the jar of vinegar back on the shelf. "You really think this vinegar of mine will sell in Serenity's catalog if it has my name on it?"

"Like hotcakes."

"Yeah, well, okay. I could use the money. See you around." Blade strode down the aisle and let himself out the front door.

George the sales rep sauntered out of Serenity's office at that moment. It was clear that he was a new man. His shoulders were squared and there was a definite spring in his step. He caught Caleb's eye and gave him a thumbs-up sign.

"Piece of cake," he said in a conspiratorial aside as he walked past Caleb. "You just gotta know how to handle her. Good luck with your tofu pitch."

"Thanks." Caleb watched George disappear through the front door. Then he turned to look at Serenity, who was lounging in the doorway of her office. He remembered the way she had leaped to his defense when Blade had turned obnoxious a few minutes earlier.

"I hear you're a piece of cake, partner," Caleb said.

"Depends on what you're selling." Serenity grinned. "Partner."

6

DID BLADE HAVE A PARTICULAR REASON FOR PINPOINT-ing you as the advance man for the invasion he's expecting or was he just being his usual suspicious self?" Serenity asked later that evening.

Caleb frowned absently but did not look up from the papers he had spread out on Serenity's living room table. "He said something about having heard a car drive away from Asterley's cabin the night Asterley fell down the stairs."

"Hmmm." Serenity thought about that briefly and then dismissed the problem. "That would have been Jessie, most likely."

"You said she was Asterley's significant other?"

"Occasional significant other. I thought I smelled stale pipe tobacco in Ambrose's cabin that day when I found him. Jessie smokes a pipe. As I recall, there were also two empty coffee mugs on the table."

111

Caleb made a note on the edge of one of the papers. "When we talked to her this morning at Asterley's cabin, she didn't say anything about having been with Asterley the night he died."

Serenity watched Caleb with envious fascination. She didn't know many people who could do two things successfully at the same time. But he obviously had no problem concentrating simultaneously on both his business notes and the topic of Jessie.

"We didn't specifically ask her if she'd been there that night," Serenity reminded him.

"You'd think she'd have mentioned it."

"I don't see why. We only chatted with Jessie for a couple of minutes. She had her mind on a lot of other things."

"Like the fact that she had just inherited a house and a small fortune in photography equipment," Caleb said dryly.

"What in the world are you getting at? I don't see—"

The phone rang, cutting Serenity off. She put down the pen she had been fiddling with and reached for the receiver.

"Hello?"

"Hey, hey, hey, Serenity love. Long time no see. How's my favorite granola pusher?"

"*Lloyd.* I wasn't expecting to hear from you." That was putting it mildly. After the way she had lost her temper the last time she'd seen him six months ago, she hadn't expected to hear from him ever again. Serenity rarely lost her temper, but the rare occasions when she did generally proved memorable. Montrose, full-time musician and part-time operator of Witt's

End's only service station, had once told her it was because of her red hair. "Where are you?"

"Working late in my office here at good old Bullington College. You remember Bullington, don't you, Serenity love? You haven't been gone so long that you've actually forgotten those of us down here at the bottom of the mountain, have you?" Lloyd paused deliberately. "I sure haven't forgotten you."

Serenity's fingers tightened around the phone. Her eyes met Caleb's questioning gaze. "No, I haven't forgotten Bullington."

"Glad to hear it," Lloyd said, relentlessly cheerful, as usual. "I've been making a lot of changes since I became assistant department head. I've even talked the Fordham people into giving me a little honest-to-God grant money. Can you believe it?"

Incredible, Serenity thought. Lloyd was carrying on a perfectly normal conversation. Just as though they were old friends. Just as if he hadn't tried to use her as a research project. Just as if he hadn't once given her reason to think he might give her the real family she dreamed of having someday. "I'm glad for you, Lloyd. Look, I'm very busy at the moment. Was there something you wanted?"

"Thought I'd drive up to Witt's End and pay you a visit soon. It's been what? Six months?"

"Yes. Six months."

"I'm kind of curious to see how things are going for you."

"I'll just bet you are. Anxious to do a follow-up on your research project? Sorry, but I don't have time to fill out a detailed questionnaire at the moment," Serenity said.

"Funny you should mention my little question-naires." Lloyd chuckled engagingly. "I was just going to bring up the subject."

"Oh, no. No. Absolutely not." Serenity flopped back against the sofa cushions in sheer disgust. She was aware that she had Caleb's undivided attention now. He was no longer doing two things at the same time. He was concentrating entirely on her. "We've already been through this. Forget it, Lloyd, I'm not going to play research subject for you again."

"Whoa, there. Hold your horses, Serenity love. Who's talking about using you as a research subject?"

"You are."

"Not true." Lloyd lowered his voice to a warm, persuasive murmur. "Hey, is it so hard to believe that I'd just like to see you again?"

"Yes, frankly, it is. You made it very clear the last time I saw you that you only wanted one kind of relationship with me, the same kind a lab rat has with a scientist."

"Hey, hey, hey, love. Unfair, unfair." Lloyd sounded grievously hurt. "You and I had a modern sort of relationship. We transcended the man-woman thing. We were friends."

"Friends? You don't know the first thing about friendship, Lloyd. Friends don't use each other." Serenity gently hung up the phone.

The silence in the room was palpable. Caleb eyed the phone with a thoughtful expression. "Friend of yours?"

"Not any longer."

The phone rang shrilly. With a groan, Serenity reached for it. "This time tell me what you really want, Lloyd, or I'll unplug this thing."

114

"Listen, this is no bullshit, Serenity. I want to do a full-scale study of Witt's End." Lloyd's voice was crisp and urgent now. All traces of ingratiating charm were gone. "This is very, very important."

Serenity scowled. "A study of Witt's End? Are you crazy? Forget it."

"I'm serious, Serenity. This is mega crucial to my career objectives. I want to come up there and do a thorough analysis of community dynamics in Witt's End. I want to map the entire social structure of that burg. You know, in-depth observations, detailed interviews, that kind of thing. I especially want to see those vision pools you told me about."

"And will there be secretly taped observations and interviews?" Serenity kept her tone deliberately bland.

"Shit, are you going to hold that one little incident against me for all time? Come on, Serenity love, be reasonable. You used to teach this stuff, too, remember? You know how field research works. I wanted pure, unadulterated data. I couldn't let you know what I was doing. It would have influenced the results and conclusions."

"Tell me," Serenity said, "did we get published?"

There was a distinct pause on the other end. "Ah, yeah, we did. This month's *Journal of Social Dynamics*. I called the paper 'Private Codes: Outsiders and the Formation of Communities.'" Lloyd's voice warmed with pride. "I don't mind telling you that article is creating a lot of interest in certain circles. Hey, I'll send you a copy."

"Is my name in it or am I just referred to as research subject A?" Serenity asked.

"I always respect the anonymity of my subjects," Lloyd said gravely.

Serenity didn't know whether to laugh or slam down the receiver. "I ought to sue you, Lloyd. If we had a lawyer here in Witt's End, I might just do it, too. As it is, I can't be bothered. Good-bye."

"Serenity, wait, don't hang up on me again. I'm on bended knee here. I need your help on this thing. None of those weirdos up there in Witt's End will even talk to me unless you tell them that it's okay."

"I'm not going to let you turn Witt's End into a research project."

"Serenity love, I need this study. If I get another paper published this year, I'll be first in line to get the nod for old man Hollings's position as department head."

"Aaaah. I get it."

"What's that supposed to mean?" Lloyd demanded.

"I just wondered what was at stake for you. Now I know. Good night, Lloyd." Serenity hung up the phone again. She leaned over and unplugged the cord from the wall.

Caleb folded his hands behind his head, stretched out his legs and leaned back in his chair. He gazed thoughtfully at the ceiling. "Lloyd?"

"Professor Lloyd Radburn, assistant head of the Department of Sociology at Bullington College. He wants to be named head of the department." Serenity drummed her fingers against the arm of the sofa and studied the notes she had been making earlier. *Verify delivery schedules for all products. Arrange catalog entries. Color or black and white photos in catalog? Cover art? Contact printer in Bullington.*

116

"This Radburn guy wants to study Witt's End?"

"Yes. He thinks our little town is a quaint throw-back, a living example of how the typical frontier community may have functioned."

"Think he's right?"

"Uh-huh." Serenity smiled. "But I certainly don't intend to help him prove it. I've got a business to get off the ground."

Caleb rose to his feet and walked over to the window. He stood looking out into the darkness, his gaze on the glass-walled hot tub room off Serenity's back porch. "Is this Radburn the reason you gave up the academic world and came back here to Witt's End?"

"What?" Serenity looked up from her notes with a frown. "Oh, I see what you're getting at. No, he isn't. I never really left Witt's End. I commuted between here and Bullington most of the time, except for a brief period during my rebellious stage when I lived on campus."

"That didn't work out?"

"Not for long." Serenity smiled wryly. "I didn't really fit in down there in Bullington. At any rate, as soon as I figured out a way to make a living here, I quit my job in the sociology department and opened my grocery store. That was three years ago. Lloyd didn't even work at Bullington when I was there. He got hired by the department about a year ago."

"How did you meet him?"

Serenity wrinkled her nose. "He started showing up around here on weekends early last spring. Hung around the store and Ariadne's café, trying to blend in with the scene. We sort of got to know each other."

Caleb did not turn around. "Sort of?"

Serenity cleared her throat. "You may have noticed that there are not a lot of people my age here in Witt's End. That's one of the things I hope to change around here, by the way. I'd like to see Witt's End attract younger people again, the way it did in the beginning. We need kids and families here. I'm the only person who was actually born and raised here during the past thirty years."

"So Radburn was the first eligible male to hit town in quite a while, is that it?"

"I suppose you could say that." Serenity grew cautious. She had no idea of what was going through Caleb's mind. "He can be very charming company, and he and I had some things in common besides our age."

"Sociology. The world of academia."

"That's right. I was an instructor at Bullington College while I worked on my Ph.D. At any rate, Lloyd heard about Witt's End and got curious. He came up here to take a look around. He decided to study me. Only he forgot to mention that was the real reason for his interest in me."

"When did you find out that you were just a research subject instead of something more to him?"

"I learned the truth the day I accidentally discovered his tape recorder." Serenity smiled ruefully at the memory. "He was dictating into it at the time. Something about the role of myth in the social structure of Witt's End. He'd decided that I had somehow been woven into a local legend that was crucial to the structural dynamic of the community. It was a lot of nonsense, but I suppose it sounded interesting on paper."

"What happened?"

Serenity shrugged. "I hit the roof. Threw his tape recorder on the ground and stomped on it. Told him to get out of town and to stay out. It was really quite a scene, if I do say so myself. I hadn't been that mad in a long time. This is the first time I've heard from him since the showdown."

"When you talked to him on the phone a few minutes ago you didn't sound as though you were still furious. Just a little irritated."

Serenity chuckled. "Well, it has been six months. I've had a chance to calm down. Besides, it's hard to stay mad at someone like Lloyd. I'll admit I was hurt at the time. Mostly my pride, I think. I felt like an idiot for having allowed myself to be used."

"Are you going to let him use you again?" Caleb asked softly.

"No." Serenity tossed her notes onto the table. "Even if I wanted to help him study Witt's End, it would be a wasted effort."

"Why?"

"Do you honestly see anyone around here submitting to a detailed questionnaire and a highly personal interview for the sake of some outsider's sociological research project?"

Caleb was silent for a few seconds while he contemplated that scenario. "Might be interesting to see Blade's reaction to being asked a lot of personal questions about his lifestyle and social interactions."

Serenity grinned briefly. "You've got a point. Maybe I should let Lloyd come up here, after all. He didn't get an opportunity to meet Blade last time. Blade usually sleeps days, you see. I could introduce the two of them and then stand back and watch the explosion."

"But you won't do that, will you?" Caleb asked.

"Nope. I've got more important things to do."

"You're trying to save a town."

"Right. And you said something about helping me, as I recall."

"Serenity?"

There was a new element in his voice. It made her wary. "What is it?"

"Do you know what I'd like to do tonight?"

"No." A rush of excitement whipped through her. The adrenaline made her fingers tremble. What would she say if he asked her to go to bed with him? she wondered frantically. A part of her had been dreading this moment. Another part had been longing for it.

"I'd like to get into your hot tub."

Serenity felt like a balloon that had been stabbed with a pin. Everything went flat. "My hot tub?"

"I've never been in a hot tub."

"You're joking."

He shook his head. "No, I'm not joking."

Serenity was at a loss for words. She had been bathing in hot tubs, after all, ever since she was a youngster. People in Witt's End considered it a routine form of relaxation, akin to meditation. She frequently invited Ariadne and Jessie and some of the other women in town to join her in the hot tub on her back porch.

"I see. Well, you're welcome to use mine, if you like," she finally managed politely.

Caleb turned around. His face was stark and unreadable. "I'd like."

"Uh-huh. Okay, then." Still nonplussed by the

strange request, she got to her feet and walked toward the back door. "I'll show you how to turn it on."

Caleb followed her outside onto the porch. "It's cold out here tonight."

"It will get a lot colder before long." Serenity opened the glass slider of the darkened hot tub room and stepped inside the humid atmosphere. She didn't bother to turn on the lights. There was enough of a glow spilling from the cottage windows to enable her to see what she was doing. "Give me a hand with the cover, will you?"

"All right." Caleb went to work on the fastenings that secured the cover. It didn't take him long to figure out the hooks.

Serenity showed him how to roll back the heavy vinyl sheet and stash it on a nearby bench. Then she switched on the mechanism that caused the hot water to churn and pulse gently in the large, deep tub. She opened a cupboard and removed several thick towels. She stacked them beside the tub.

When everything was ready, she looked at Caleb. She couldn't see his expression clearly in the shadows, but she could tell that he was watching her with the familiar dark intensity that so often characterized him. A new, different chill of tingling sexual awareness shot through her. This time it wasn't just in her imagination; it was coming from him. She felt dangerously energized.

"It's all yours." Serenity said. "Help yourself."

"Will you join me?"

Not a good idea, she thought. Definitely not a good idea at all. She opened her mouth to tell him that she had work to do.

"Why not?" Serenity heard herself say. She could

hardly believe her own words. This was stupid, really stupid. "I could use a little relaxation therapy."

She peeled off the gauzy green dress that she had worn over her knit jumpsuit and hung it neatly from a brass hook. Her fingers went to the zipper of the jumpsuit. She paused, trying to remember where she had stored her old swimsuit. Normally she never used a swimsuit in the hot tub.

Doubt and uncertainty were turning her into a nervous wreck, she realized. When she first met Caleb, she had been so sure, so joyously positive that they were meant to have a relationship. She had looked at him and seen the glimmerings of a shared future, hope for a real family. But his reaction when he'd discovered the existence of the photos Ambrose had taken had changed all that. It had plunged her into this morass of confusion. Normally, she was unselfconscious about her nudity. But not with Caleb. Nothing was clear at all tonight except that the air in the glass-walled room seemed electrically charged.

On the other side of the tub Caleb slowly began to remove his shirt. His strong fingers went methodically from one button to the next. The garment parted down to his waist.

Serenity stopped cold. She was riveted by the sight of the dark, curling hair just barely visible in the shadowed area revealed by Caleb's unbuttoned shirt. She swallowed heavily.

"What's wrong?" Caleb asked.

"I'm . . . not sure I know where my old swimsuit is. And I don't have a man's suit for you to use."

"I didn't think people used suits in hot tubs."

"Ah, well, no, they don't usually. Bathing in a hot

tub is a lot like bathing in a hot springs pool or a Japanese bath."

"Fine. Then we don't need suits." Caleb unbuckled his belt.

Serenity quickly turned her back to him. She kicked off her shoes and finished unzipping her jumpsuit. Until tonight she had never thought of hot tubbing as a sensual experience. But then, she had never climbed into a hot tub with a man who made her insides melt.

Behind her she heard Caleb step into the bubbling tub.

"This feels very good," he said softly.

"It's quite therapeutic. A wonderful form of relaxation." She winced. Her voice sounded too high, even to her own ears.

"I can see why you enjoy it."

Driven by a deep compulsion that she was afraid to name, Serenity turned around very cautiously. Relief was coupled with a measure of undeniable disappointment when she saw that Caleb was safely immersed to his chest in the churning water.

But even though she couldn't see his expression in the shadows, and the darkness certainly guaranteed a high degree of modesty for both of them, it was impossible for her to ignore Caleb's brooding masculinity. Either her imagination was running wild or, as Lloyd would say, she just couldn't seem to transcend the man-woman thing tonight. On the contrary, she had never been so acutely aware of it.

Caleb stretched his arms out along the edge of the tub and relaxed in the churning water. The dim glow from the cottage windows lined his powerfully contoured shoulders, revealing the sleek, muscled strength in him. Serenity could hardly breathe. In spite of the steamy, tropical atmosphere, she couldn't stop shivering. This had definitely not been one of her better ideas.

Turning her back to the tub once more, she took a deep breath, peeled off the jumpsuit and grabbed a towel. In fact, this whole thing hadn't actually been her idea at all, she reminded herself as she secured the towel. Caleb was the one who had suggested that they get into the tub. She wondered if he was having any problem maintaining a gender-neutral attitude or if the excitement was happening only on her side.

In the damp, heated darkness Caleb waited for her. She felt his eyes on her as she walked to the edge of the tub. She knew she was moving with the kind of dainty caution a doe used to approach a waterhole. She felt ridiculous, but was unable to ignore the fact that, while Caleb was merely silhouetted by the light from the windows behind him, she was clearly revealed by the pale glow.

She dipped one toe into the water and froze. She couldn't bring herself to release the towel. She stared helplessly at Caleb's shadowed face, willing him to come to her rescue, to provide a way out of the awkward situation.

As if he could read her mind, Caleb leaned his head back against the edge of the tub and simply closed his eyes.

Serenity breathed a small sigh of relief, unwrapped the towel and slipped into the tub. She sat down quickly on the submerged bench.

Reassured by the knowledge that he couldn't see any more of her beneath the frothing water than she could of him, Serenity racked her brain for polite conversation. She grabbed the first stray thought that popped into her head.

"You handled Blade very well this morning."

"I did, didn't I?" Caleb did not open his eyes. "Considering the fact that I was really pissed off at the time."

Serenity tried and failed to see his expression. "Pissed off?"

"Yeah, pissed off. Can't remember the last time I felt like decking someone."

"Oh." Serenity did not know how to respond to that. "I appreciate the fact that you restrained yourself."

"Think nothing of it. I appreciate your jumping in to defend me. Can't recall the last time someone did that, either."

"Blood in the aisles would not have been good for business."

"You have all the right instincts for a successful entrepreneur." He turned his head slightly. There was just enough light to reveal the amused curve of his mouth. "You know, all in all, this has been a very unusual week for me."

"Is that so?"

"A lot of firsts."

"Firsts?"

"First time that I've ever taken on an off-the-wall consulting job like this one."

"It's not off-the-wall," Serenity said, instantly on the defensive.

"First time that I've ever come close to getting into a brawl with a paranoid lunatic."

"Blade isn't a lunatic. He just functions in two different realities at the same time. It's not uncommon. Zone does that, too."

"First time that I've ever participated in an act of breaking and entering."

"Wait a minute." Serenity was outraged now. "Are you talking about that business in Ambrose's basement this morning? That wasn't breaking and entering. I had a perfect right to search for those negatives."

"First time that I've ever felt jealous of a man I'd never met."

"Jealous?" Serenity was floored by that item on his list of firsts. "Are you talking about Lloyd?"

"Yes."

"Why on earth would you be jealous of him?"

Caleb ignored the question. "First time that I've ever sat in a hot tub."

"You told me that earlier," Serenity said, disgruntled with the change of topic. Had he actually been jealous of Lloyd? she wondered. "It's no big deal. Personally, I sit around in hot tubs all the time."

"Did you ever share your hot tub with Radburn?"

"What? Oh. No, I didn't, not that it's any of your business."

Caleb lifted his lashes and looked at her. "I want you."

Serenity was struck dumb. She could not think of an appropriate response. She couldn't think of *any* response. If only he hadn't turned on her when he'd learned about the photos. If only she could trust him. If only, if only, if only.

"Serenity?" His voice was husky with unmistakable desire.

She moistened her lips with the tip of her tongue,

swallowed a few times to clear her throat and drew a deep breath. "What about the pictures?"

"Forget the damn pictures. They don't matter."

"Caleb, are you sure?" If only she could believe him.

"I'm sure," Caleb said. "The day I kissed you in my office, you told me I'd be sorry for overreacting to those photos." He held out his hand. "You were right."

Serenity contemplated his strong fingers for a long moment. She knew that she had wanted this to happen all along. It was the real reason that she had allowed Caleb back into her life.

But it was too soon. She wasn't certain yet.

Slowly, mesmerized by the knowledge that he wanted her, she lifted her hand out of the water and put it in his.

He wrapped his fingers tightly around hers. Without a word he tugged her toward him through the churning foam. She glided, weightless, straight into his embrace. He settled her against him and brought his mouth down on hers with a driving hunger that swamped her senses.

Serenity savored the hot, male taste of him. His arms were tight around her. She was intensely aware of the hard shape of his thigh under her bottom and the fierce length of his erection lodged against her leg.

"I was a fool to let you walk out of my office that day," Caleb whispered against her lips. "I knew it would be like this between us."

"Yes." She had known it, too. She clung to him now as the urgency within her rose to new levels. She was shaken by the force of the desire she felt. The sheer power of the sensations pouring through her was new to her. It threatened to push her beyond the safe boundaries she knew she should maintain with him.

Caleb's hand moved downward, seeking the curve of her breast beneath the water. He took the soft weight of it in his palm and slid his thumb over one delicate peak. A tight, taut sensation gripped Serenity. She gasped, her head tilting back against his shoulder.

Not yet. Too soon.

Caleb lifted her buoyant body upward just far enough to expose one budding nipple. He lowered his head to it. She shuddered when she felt the edge of his teeth close lightly around her. She clenched her fingers in his hair, turned her head and nipped at his shoulder. Then she kissed his neck. She loved the feel of him under her hands, loved the sense of exultation sweeping through her. Loved the anticipation.

Loved him.

"You taste good," Caleb muttered. "Very, very good. And I've never been so hungry in my life."

He slid his hand down across her stomach to the place where her legs were still pressed close together. When she felt him probe deeper, Serenity slowly parted her thighs. His fingers found her, stroked her, opened her carefully and entered her.

"Caleb."

"So tight." Caleb's voice was raw and gritty with passion. "Tight and hot. You want me."

"Yes." She kissed his throat with a curious desperation that she could not explain.

He withdrew his finger slowly and then thrust it deeply back into her. The edge of his thumb moved against the throbbing little button hidden in the folds of her flesh. He repeated the caress over and over again until Serenity thought she would shatter. She twisted against him, her nails digging into his skin.

"I'm going to go out of my mind," Caleb whispered. He withdrew his hand from between her legs, gathered Serenity against him and made to rise to his feet.

Reality returned in an anguished surge of awareness as the water cascaded off of her. "No, wait," Serenity gasped. She clutched at him and burrowed her face into the curve of his neck. "I'm sorry, I can't. Not yet. It's too soon."

"Too soon?"

"Don't you see? I can't be sure anymore. Everything's confused now. Please, I'm sorry. I can't explain. I just don't think this is the time."

"The time?"

"Oh, damn, this is all my fault. I should never have gotten into this tub. I knew it. I knew it but I couldn't seem to help myself."

Caleb said nothing. He stood waist deep in the churning water and held her clamped in his arms. The muscles in his chest were rigid. His arms and shoulders were tensed for battle or sex. Serenity half expected him to lift his head and howl his anger and frustration to the moon.

But he didn't. Instead he lowered himself slowly back down into the bubbling water and cradled her close. She could feel the enormous control he was exerting over himself. It awed her.

"Caleb, I'm so sorry."

"Hush." He thrust his hand heavily through her wet hair and kissed her roughly on the mouth. "I started this. I'll finish it."

She lifted her head and searched his face, seeking

desperately for some way to explain something that could not be put into words. "This just isn't the right time. Not yet. Not for me."

"I know. You're beautiful. A little weird, but beautiful." There was enough light to see the deeply sensual twist of his lips. He didn't look angry. "My wild, magic princess." His hand slipped down toward her breast. He touched the griffin that hung there. Then his hand went lower, to her waist. "You make me burn."

"Caleb . . ."

"I know. It's too soon for what I want," he whispered. "But is it too soon for this?" He slipped his hand lower still and once again found the warm, wet cleft hidden between her legs.

Serenity flinched and sucked in her breath. "I don't think—"

"I just want to touch you. Can you trust me that much at least?"

"But what about you?" She felt like an idiot.

He laughed softly in the shadows. "You can touch me, too. If you want to touch me, that is."

"I do," she said. "Very much. But Caleb—"

"Trust me tonight." He kissed her throat as he found her softness with his hand. "Give me that much, at least. All I'm going to do is touch you."

"Oh, *Caleb.*" Her small, choked cry was cut off as he stroked her. The unbearably tight, soaring sensation that she had been experiencing a few minutes earlier roared back.

Enthralled by the novelty of the twisting tension building within her, she could only cling to him. Her eyes widened and then squeezed shut as he continued to stroke her intimately.

She knew he was watching her face in the shadows. Serenity could feel the masculine anticipation in him. He was waiting for something to happen. She was waiting also, but she didn't know quite what to expect.

Then she remembered that she was supposed to be touching him, too. She splayed her hands across his chest and slipped them downward across his flat stomach.

"No," he said into her ear. "I've changed my mind. I won't be able to handle this if you do that."

"But I want to touch you."

"Not tonight."

She moaned as he did something incredibly erotic with his hand. And then she stiffened in surprise.

"It's all right. Let it happen. *Trust me.*"

"I don't . . . I can't . . . Oh, my God, I'm going to, I'm really—" Disbelief and then wonder tore through her along with her first climax. Helpless in the storm, she wrapped her arms around his neck and shuddered in his arms.

"Serenity?"

She laughed and then she cried and then she collapsed against his chest in joyous release.

"I'll be damned," Caleb said. "Don't tell me this is another first."

A few minutes later Serenity stirred drowsily. She instinctively snuggled closer to Caleb. The water surged around her. Maybe it was the right time, after all, she thought.

She felt wonderful; very sure of herself. The confusion and qualms had all but vanished in the throes of her orgasm. It was amazing.

Yes, definitely the right time. She wondered why she

hadn't seen that earlier. Things had just been confused for a while.

"Caleb?"

He caught her hand as it strayed across his chest. He held her fingers still, leaned his head back against the edge of the tub and closed his eyes. "I've got a quick question, if you don't mind."

"Umm-hmm?" She wriggled against his leg and began to nibble his earlobe.

"Is this or is this not the first time you've had an orgasm?"

"Is. Nice."

"Very." His smile was sexy and wicked and laced with masculine satisfaction. "Mind telling me why you haven't done it before?"

"Well, I tried. It just didn't work very well."

"I see." He waited.

"Three years ago there was a man. His name was Stewart. Stewart Bartlett. Stop me if you'd rather not hear all this."

"I'm listening."

"Stewart came to Witt's End because he needed this place."

"Why?"

"He needed to heal. A lot of people come here for that reason. They stay for varying lengths of time. I told you, the world needs places like Witt's End."

Caleb opened his eyes and touched her mouth with his fingers. "Was he sick?"

"Yes. Not in his body. In his mind. He'd lost his wife and son in the crash of a small airplane. Stewart was a pilot. He had been at the controls when the plane went down. He walked away from the wreckage without a scratch. And he couldn't forgive himself."

"So he came here to forget? And met you?"

Serenity nodded. "We were very close for a while. Two and a half years, in fact. And then one day he knew that he was going to be all right again. He realized that he could go back to the life that was waiting for him in Seattle. So he left."

"Why didn't he take you with him?"

She smiled gently. "You don't understand. I was never meant to go with him. I always knew that. So did he. Our two and a half years together was a special time for both of us. A time of learning and healing and growing. It was a good time, but it wasn't meant to last. He was from the outside world, you see."

"And during that whole two and a half years with him you never had an orgasm?" Caleb sounded dazed. "That's hard to believe."

"We tried many times," Serenity admitted. She knew she was blushing, and was thankful he couldn't see the color in her cheeks. "But Stewart had a problem."

"A problem?"

"It was all psychological, you understand. Not physical. Caused by his guilt and sorrow, I imagine."

"Hold on a minute here." Caleb narrowed his eyes and studied her intently. "Are you trying to tell me that you spent two and a half years of your life with a man who couldn't get an erection?"

"Sex isn't everything in a relationship," Serenity said severely.

"Yeah, sure, right. Two and a half years with a man who couldn't make love to you properly? Christ, that's incredible." Caleb glowered at her. "So why didn't he do what I just did? Even an impotent man could have managed to give you some satisfaction that way."

Serenity shrugged. "Every time we were together we were both so worried about him that I guess I couldn't relax and enjoy myself. It was no big deal."

"That's a matter of opinion."

She frowned. "It was my relationship and I didn't mind. I was happy."

"Probably because you didn't know what you were missing," Caleb muttered.

"As Quinton says, we are all capable of finding contentment on many different planes of existence. We just have to be open to discovering the peace within ourselves."

"Sure. So what happened to this wonderful relationship that transcended sex?"

"I told you, one day Stewart realized that he was going to be all right. He also knew that his sex life was going to be normal again."

"You mean he was finally able to get an erection, so he split?" Caleb asked dryly.

"That's a rather crude way of putting it, but basically that's what happened. We both realized that he would be leaving Witt's End once he was healed. Stewart was a very kind man and he did what he thought was best."

"Kind? You think he was being *kind?*" Caleb stared at her. "He sounds like a self-centered SOB. He used you to comfort him until he could get a hard-on again and then he left town."

"He didn't think it would be fair to make love to me and then leave for good. I knew it was time to let him go. So that was that."

134

"No offense, Serenity, but between this Bartlett character and what you told me about Radburn, I have to say that you've had some damn strange relationships."

"Speaking of relationships," Serenity said eagerly, "I've been thinking. Maybe I was wrong earlier. Maybe this is the right time for us."

"No. You were right earlier." Caleb exhaled deeply. Then he eased her off his lap and stood up in the tub. Water poured off of his sleek, powerful body as he went up the steps. He reached for a towel.

"Caleb?" She watched the play of light and shadow on his wet, glistening flanks.

He smiled in the shadows. "It's late. I've got to get some sleep tonight. I'm supposed to do product analysis tomorrow, remember?"

"Yes, I know, but I want to explain something."

"There's nothing more to explain. Not tonight. I told you to trust me."

"I know." She watched wistfully as he got dressed. He was lean and hard and so enthrallingly male. She ached just looking at him. "You're out to prove something here, aren't you?"

"Yeah, I guess so."

"I was afraid of that." She got reluctantly out of the tub and picked up a fluffy towel.

Neither of them said another word as they finished getting dressed.

Caleb paused long enough at the front door to kiss Serenity one last time. And then he went out into the night with a flashlight.

She watched through the window for a while, and then she drifted down the hall to her bed.

A few minutes later, hovering on the verge of sleep, she could have sworn that somewhere in the distance a waltz was playing. Montrose, she thought. He often practiced his music late at night. In the vast silence of the mountains the sound carried a long way.

But her last thought was that a waltz was not part of Montrose's usual repertoire.

7

C ALEB WALKED INTO WITT'S END GROCERY ONE MINUTE after Serenity opened the door the following morning. "I've got a favor to ask," he said without preamble.

Serenity was taken aback by the glittering intensity in his shuttered gaze. This certainly solved one small problem, she told herself. She had been wondering all morning what she would say to him when she saw him today. He had taken the matter out of her hands.

"What's the favor?"

He glanced at Zone, who was busily dusting shelves at the other end of the room. Then he looked back at Serenity and lowered his voice. "I have to visit my family this weekend. Tomorrow's my grandfather's eighty-second birthday. I'm expected to be there. I want you to come with me."

"It's very nice of you to invite me," she temporized.

"Will you come?"

She met his eyes and knew she could not refuse. "Where do they live?"

"Ventress Valley. It's a two-hour drive from here."

"Ventress Valley?" Serenity's voice rose. *"Ventress Valley?"* She put her hands on her hips and glared at him. "Is this some kind of grand coincidence in names or are you actually a member of a family that has an entire town named after it?"

"The town was named after my great-grandfather. What's that got to do with anything?"

"Good grief."

His mouth tightened. "What's so strange about it? Aren't there any Witts left here in Witt's End?"

"Heck, no. The original Headcase Witt was a 1960s era dropout, A genuine hippie who tried to establish a commune here. When it didn't work out the way he planned, he went north to Alaska. No one ever heard from him again."

"Ventress Valley wasn't so lucky. The Ventresses stuck around. They owned most of the good farmland in the area."

"Owned? Past tense?"

"For the most part." Caleb braced one hand against the wall and eyed her with grim impatience. "We sold off a lot of the land during the past few years in favor of other investments. My grandfather held on to a few acres. He raises horses. Any other questions?"

"How many acres?" Serenity asked suspiciously.

"Does it matter?"

She pursed her lips and considered that. "I don't know. Are you terribly rich, Caleb? I mean, I know you're successful, but are you a zillionaire or something?"

"We can talk about the state of my finances some other time. Right now I just want a yes or no answer. Will you come with me to Ventress Valley?"

Serenity searched his face. "I don't know. I've spent too much time away from my store lately as it is."

"We'll only be gone overnight. Zone can watch the store."

"Why do you want me to go with you?"

"Because I want you to meet my family. Yes or no?"

She folded her arms across her chest and tapped one toe. "Do you think your family will like me?"

"Who gives a damn what they think? Yes or no?"

"Yes." She threw up her hands in surrender. "Okay. Yes. All right. I'll go with you."

He nodded once, his jaw rigid. "That's settled, then. I'll see you later. I've got a line of people waiting for me over at the Sunflower Café."

"Oh, yes, that's right. Product evaluations." Serenity frowned. "Remember, I want to find space for everyone who would like to be in the catalog."

"I specialize in getting business ventures off the ground, not stroking artistic egos. No one gets in the catalog with a product that doesn't meet standards."

Serenity smiled confidently. "I'm sure everyone's product will meet the requirements. If not, we'll work with the person until it does."

Caleb gave her a laconic glance but he said nothing. He turned around and walked out of the store. The bells clamored loudly as the door closed behind him.

Zone waited until the bells had gone silent. She put down her duster and placed her palms together. "What was that all about, Serenity?"

"Darned if I know."

"Danger," Zone whispered. "Confusion and danger and turmoil."

"Nah. I think he's just in a bad mood because he didn't get laid last night."

"I got the feeling that it's very important to him, Ariadne." Serenity checked the price stickers on several jars of tahini dressing before she began to arrange them on the shelf. "Caleb wants me to go home with him today and I said that I would. We're leaving around ten."

"So he wants you to meet his family." Ariadne Galpin, owner and sole proprietor of the Sunflower Café, wore an expression of profound concern. "Sounds like a very traditional sort of man."

"He is."

"You don't do well with the traditional type, Serenity."

"Caleb's different."

Ariadne pushed one thick, graying braid back over her shoulder and crossed her arms beneath her ample bosom. Everything about Ariadne was broad and ample. Had she lived in more conventional surroundings, she would have been stereotyped as the grandmotherly sort. Here in Witt's End, people thought of her as an earth mother. There wasn't much difference, she had once told Serenity.

"I give up," Ariadne said. "How can he be different and traditional at the same time?"

Serenity shoved the last jar of tahini onto the shelf and straightened. She smiled at Ariadne with all the deep warmth and affection generated by a lifelong bond. Ariadne had been present the day Serenity was born. She, along with the handful of others who had been in Witt's End that day, had helped raise Serenity.

It was Ariadne who had taught Serenity how to cook, how to operate a cash register, and how to keep basic business accounts. It was Ariadne, too, who and been there to advise and instruct Serenity on the mysteries of the transition from girlhood to womanhood.

And it was Ariadne who best understood Serenity's inchoate longing for a real family. She longed to experience for herself the intimate closeness of a mother, father, and child.

"When you meet him, you'll see what I mean," Serenity said.

Ariadne pondered that with elevated brows. "This is serious, isn't it?"

"I hope so." Serenity loved Ariadne like an aunt, but it was hard to talk to her about men. Ariadne was the most asexual human being she had ever met. Apparently, she really had transcended the man-woman thing. "How's the cookbook going?"

Ariadne sighed but she didn't try to pursue the subject of Caleb. "I'm finishing off the bean and pasta dishes. Jessie's completed the illustrations. They're spectacular. The finished manuscript should be ready to go to the printers in another couple of weeks."

"Good." Serenity opened a sack of lentils, hoisted it onto her hip and poured the contents into an open barrel. "That means we'll have copies ready when the first edition of the catalog goes out. We'll be able to advertise it."

"Do you really think this mail order thing is going to work?"

"I'm sure of it." Serenity grinned. "How can it miss? We've got the best start-up consultant in the business on our team."

"I suppose it's much too late to advise you to keep your relationship with him strictly business?"

"Since when has anyone in Witt's End understood the meaning of the words 'strictly business'?"

"I was afraid of that."

Serenity glanced at the clock as she folded the empty sack. "I'd better change for the trip. Time for me to step into the nearest phone booth and emerge as Miss Town and Country."

Two hours later Serenity sat forward in the passenger seat of Caleb's green Jaguar and watched with delight as Ventress Valley came into view. Acres of well-tended farmlands, vineyards, and cattle ranches were spread out across a gently rolling landscape. There were more pickups than sedans on the roads. Tractors rumbled across open fields.

The small town of Ventress Valley consisted of a collection of hardware and feed stores, churches, cafés, and the occasional tavern. The shop windows displayed denim overalls, plaid shirts, and Stetson hats.

"This is where you grew up?" Serenity asked as Caleb drove down the main street. "It looks like something out of a Norman Rockwell painting."

"Rockwell had a convenient way of not showing what really goes on beneath the surface of a small town like this," Caleb said. There was no trace of emotion in his voice. "I used to dream about getting out of this place. I left the summer I graduated from high school."

"Where's your grandfather's house?"

"About two miles on the other side of town."

"You're sure your family is expecting me?" Aware that she had never quite gotten the hang of passing as conventional, Serenity had packed carefully for the trip. She didn't want to embarrass Caleb in front of his relatives.

She was wearing a selection of incredibly dull items from what she thought of as her Miss Town & Country collection. Figuring out how to dress without raising eyebrows in the outside world had been a problem for her until she had hit upon the brilliant notion of buying entire outfits out of catalogs. That way, she assured herself, she couldn't go wrong. Left to her own devices, she tended to run afoul of subtle fashion concepts that she had never fully grasped.

The suits she had worn to Seattle during the weeks she'd been meeting with Caleb had all come from a catalog that claimed to cater to women who preferred the "classic, tailored style." The outfit she had on today was from the same catalog. She felt reasonably confident that she looked suitably normal in it.

For today's journey into the unknown wilds of middle America, Serenity had selected a pair of cuffed, wool gabardine trousers in a subdued camel color. She had paired the pants with a cream silk shirt. Her tasteful gold-toned earrings had been shown on the same page of the catalog as the trousers and shirt, so Serenity knew they were correct.

"I called the house this morning and talked to Dolores," Caleb said. "She'll make sure one of the guest rooms is made up for you."

"Who's Dolores?"

"My grandfather's housekeeper. She and her husband Harry have been with Roland for over fifteen years. Harry takes care of the stables."

Serenity watched, fascinated, as the doors of a quaintly steepled church opened to reveal a wedding party. Bridesmaids dressed in pastel pink spilled out onto the steps. The bride, wearing a traditional veil and a billowing white gown emerged, laughing. The groom, looking a little awkward in his formal attire, grabbed her hand and pulled her toward a gaily decorated car. The guests hurled rice.

"What a pretty sight. Do you know those people over there?" Serenity pointed toward the church.

Caleb glanced briefly at the wedding group. "I don't recognize the bride, but the groom looks like Chuck Jackson. He was a couple of years behind me in high school. He took over his father's feed store after he graduated."

Serenity smiled wistfully. "Did you go through a high school graduation ceremony?"

"Sure." He gave her a surprised look. "Didn't you?"

"Not exactly. I was home-schooled."

Caleb frowned. "By who?"

"By virtually everyone in Witt's End. I learned something from all of them, even Blade. It must have worked, because I breezed through the college entrance exams." Serenity chuckled. "But I wanted a real high school graduation so badly I could taste it. So Witt's End gave me one."

"Just for you?"

"Yep. Ariadne sewed a cap and gown for me. Montrose played the entrance march. Everyone was there. Quinton gave a very inspiring speech about the future of mathematical planes and the universe in general which none of us understood. The best part was that I got all the awards. No competition, you see."

Caleb slanted her a curious glance. "Sounds a little strange."

"Don't laugh. I even got to be valedictorian."

"No kidding."

Serenity slanted him an uncertain glance. "Is something wrong?"

"No."

She sensed that he was lying, but she decided not to pursue it. Her instincts told her that if she pushed for an explanation, he would continue to deny that there was a problem.

Caleb had become more taciturn and remote with every mile they had covered since leaving Witt's End. The closer to Ventress Valley they got, the colder and more withdrawn he became.

Serenity was beginning to wonder if she had made a mistake in agreeing to accompany him on the family visit.

Two nights ago in the hot glow of passion, everything had seemed crystal clear for a time. But today she was forced to acknowledge that her relationship with Caleb was as obscured as ever by a dense fog of emotional confusion.

"I'll bet you've changed your mind about Ventress Valley now that you've been away from it for several years," Serenity said.

"No, as a matter of fact, I haven't. I still hate the place."

She slid a glance toward his granite profile. He looked as if he were preparing to go into battle. "It's your hometown. You were born and raised here. Don't tell me that you don't wax nostalgic about it once in a while."

"It can sink into the darkest part of Hell as far as I'm concerned. I wouldn't miss it for a second."

Serenity was baffled by the sweeping ease with which he consigned his entire hometown to the nether regions. "What, exactly, do you dislike about it so much?"

"Forget it."

"Did something terrible happen to you here?"

"No."

"Then why do you hate the place?"

"Let it go, Serenity." Caleb turned off the main highway onto a narrow, blacktopped road. "I shouldn't have said anything. I don't want to discuss Ventress Valley or my all-American boyhood."

Serenity crossed her arms and sank back into the seat. "Understood. My, this is certainly turning out to be a fun trip. I can't thank you enough for inviting me along. When did you say we could leave?"

Caleb's hands tightened around the steering wheel. "Damn. Look, I didn't mean to snap at you. I don't know why I did that. I never lose my temper."

"Hah. Don't give me that bull. I've seen you lose your temper often enough." She spotted a large, gracious, old-fashioned house in the distance and immediately forgot about the argument she was having with Caleb. "Good grief, is that your home?"

"It's my grandfather's house. I was raised in it. I don't think of it as home."

"You're right. It's more like a mansion. It looks like it should be listed in a historic register."

The house dominated a landscape of wide green

lawns and tall trees. Verandas wrapped around both the upper and lower stories. In the distance sleek horses grazed behind pristine white pasture fences.

"You said that your grandfather breeds horses?" Serenity peered, fascinated, through the windshield.

"Arabians."

"Talk about tradition." She laughed. "Can you ride?"

"Yes."

"I would have been green with envy if I'd known you when I was twelve. That was the year I wanted a pony."

"I take it you didn't get one?"

"No. Julius got me a wonderful dog instead." Serenity smiled. "Look, a genuine barn."

"Stables."

"Stables," Serenity amended. "With hay and everything probably."

"When you've got horses around, you've usually got hay in the vicinity."

"Wow, talk about your classic rural lifestyle. This is incredible. A real slice of Americana. I'll bet everyone here still eats beef. Promise me you'll take me on a complete tour before we leave."

"Why do I get the feeling that this is turning into a sitcom called Serenity Visits Middle America?"

"Don't laugh. Travel is very educational."

Caleb gave her an odd look as he turned the Jaguar into the tree-lined drive. "This is eastern Washington, not Outer Mongolia."

"Both are foreign countries to me," Serenity said simply.

The door of the Ventress home opened just as Caleb brought the Jaguar to a halt in the circular driveway. A woman appeared. She wore an apron over a flower-print dress. Her hair was a froth of graying curls, and her shoes were the sturdy sort favored by people who spent a lot of time on their feet.

"That's Dolores." Caleb opened his door and got out. He lifted a hand in greeting as he walked around to the passenger side of the car.

"About time you got here, young man," Dolores called cheerfully. "Your grandfather was starting to worry."

"I doubt it." Caleb opened Serenity's door. "More likely he was just getting annoyed."

"That, too." Dolores smiled warmly at Serenity. "This must be Miss Makepeace."

"It is. Serenity, this is Dolores."

"How do you do?" Serenity slid quickly out of the Jaguar. "What a beautiful home."

"Thanks. Lord knows I work myself to the bone keeping it that way. Not that I get any thanks for it. Come on in, Miss Makepeace. I'll show you to your room so you can freshen up before you meet the rest of the family."

Caleb lifted his suitcase and Serenity's out of the trunk. "Everyone else is already here?"

"Yes, indeed. Arrived about an hour ago. We've been waiting for you and Miss Makepeace." Dolores smiled at Caleb. "You know your grandfather wouldn't dream of letting things get started until you got here."

"You're lucky to be part of such a close family," Serenity whispered to Caleb as they went up the steps.

"That's us Ventresses for you," Caleb agreed. "Just one big happy family."

* * *

Fifteen minutes later, feeling reasonably refreshed and confident in her Miss Town & Country attire, Serenity walked down a long hall toward the great room at the front of the house. She was carrying the small gift that she had brought for Roland Ventress.

After what seemed an interminable distance, she turned a corner and found herself confronting a group of people who, she guessed, were all Ventresses. Taken as a group, it was easy to see the family resemblance. They were a tall, dark-haired lot who carried themselves with the self-assurance and poise that came naturally to a proud, established clan. She took a deep breath and tried to recall the techniques she had developed for dealing with faculty parties at Bullington College.

"Hello," she said to the room at large.

A hush fell on the small crowd. Everyone turned to look at her.

Caleb was standing at the window talking quietly to a silver-haired man who could only have been his grandfather. He turned his head at once at the sound of her voice. His eyes pinned her across the distance of the room.

"Sir, this is Serenity Makepeace. Serenity, my grandfather, Roland Ventress."

"How do you do, Mr. Ventress?" Serenity smiled as she examined the older man with interest.

Caleb had told her that his grandfather was celebrating his eighty-second birthday, but there was an air of vigor about him that would have done credit to a much younger man. He was almost as tall as Caleb. There was no hint of a stoop to his shoulders from a lifetime of ranch work. His eyes, which were brown instead of gray like Caleb's, were sharp and alert.

"Miss Makepeace." Roland inclined his head in an old-fashioned manner. His voice was laced with an easy western drawl. "Glad you could join us. Allow me to introduce you to my family." He nodded toward a handsome but rather severe-looking middle-aged woman dressed in a navy-blue knit suit and blue and white pumps.

"This is my niece, Phyllis Tarrant."

"How do you do, Miss Makepeace," Phyllis said with cool politeness. She examined Serenity with a vaguely disapproving expression.

Roland indicated the stout man standing next to Phyllis. "Her husband, Howard. He's in real estate."

Serenity nodded politely. "Mr. Tarrant."

Howard bobbed his head and smiled benignly.

"My nephew, Franklin Ventress," Roland continued. "Chairman of the board of the Ventress Valley Bank. His wife, Beverly."

Serenity smiled and then shot a quick, repressive look at Caleb. He had not mentioned that his family was in banking. Caleb lifted one shoulder in a negligent shrug.

"Miss Makepeace. So glad you could come with Caleb," Beverly said with the gracious charm that Serenity had once associated with professional faculty wives.

Franklin, a distinguished-looking man in his fifties, had no doubt been devastatingly attractive in his younger years. He had the dark eyes that characterized most of the family. His once black hair was almost all silver. "Miss Makepeace."

"Mr. Ventress."

Franklin took over the introductions. "Howard and Phyllis's daughter Jessica, and her husband Sam. Sam is a partner in a local law firm. The two youngsters over there are their kids."

Serenity nodded, struggling to keep all the introductions straight. She grinned at the children, who appeared to be five and seven, respectively. They giggled.

Franklin's eyes reflected paternal pride as he nodded toward a handsome man of about thirty. "My own son, Peter. He and his wife Laura, here, operate the Ventress Vineyards Winery. You may have heard of the label. Their cabernets have taken gold medals for the past three years."

"Yes, of course," Serenity lied cheerfully. "Congratulations."

Peter grinned. "Thanks. We're quite pleased. Ventress Vineyards is a relative newcomer to the wine scene, but we feel we've gotten off to a good start."

"Thanks to Caleb." Laura, attractive with tawny hair and blue eyes, smiled. "He oversaw the start-up of our winery. Caleb's very good at that kind of thing."

"Yes, I know," Serenity murmured. She smiled at Laura and the others and mentally added up the total thus far. Real estate, banking, law, a winery, an Arabian stud farm, and a town named after the family. She took another deep breath and hoped her personal version of Miss Town & Country was measuring up.

"Sherry or whiskey, Serenity?" Caleb went to a teak drinks cart and picked up a bottle.

"Sherry, please." She saw that Caleb had whiskey in his own glass. She was suddenly very conscious of the gaily wrapped package in her hand.

"What's that?" Caleb asked as he crossed the room to hand her the glass.

151

"A present for your grandfather." She took a fortifying swallow of the sherry. "You did say this was supposed to be a birthday party, didn't you?"

He frowned. "Yes, but you weren't expected to bring a gift."

"You're supposed to bring gifts when you attend birthday parties. It's traditional. I didn't have much time to make a selection, I'm afraid. I had to grab some things off the shelf at the store."

"It's not important," Caleb said. "You shouldn't have bothered."

Serenity ignored that and turned to smile brightly at Roland. "This is for you, Mr. Ventress. Where shall I put it?"

"Dolores will take it and put it with the others," Phyllis said before Roland could respond.

"No," Roland said. He studied Serenity for a few seconds. "I believe I'll open it now, Miss Makepeace. I reckon I've got a streak of curiosity a mile wide."

"Me, too," Serenity agreed. "I can never wait to open presents." Conscious of Phyllis's annoyed expression, Serenity hurried toward the window where Roland stood. "And please, call me Serenity."

"All right. Serenity." Roland set down his whiskey and turned the package in his hands. "Nice of you to bring this."

"I hope you like it." She watched as he untied the green bow and undid the bright paper to reveal the cardboard box inside.

Roland lifted the lid of the box and examined the assortment of products inside. "What have we got here?"

"It's a collection of items from my store, Witt's End

Grocery," Serenity explained. "A bottle of the best herbed vinegar ever to grace a salad, lemon and orange marmalade from the Sunflower Café, a package of mixed dried beans, and the instructions for a terrific bean chili and some homemade granola. Do you like granola?"

"Don't believe I've ever eaten any."

"This is some of the world's best. Just ask Caleb. He's tried it."

Roland looked speculatively at Caleb. "That right?"

Caleb's mouth curved in the first sign of amusement he had shown since leaving Witt's End. "Be sure to add milk. It's a little dry otherwise."

"For heaven's sake, Caleb." Serenity glared at him. "I'm sure your grandfather knows enough to add milk to his cereal."

Caleb said nothing.

"Thanks, Serenity," Roland said. "I'll look forward to trying the various items. They're all from your store, I believe you said?"

"That's right."

"And where would that be?" Roland asked.

"Witt's End. Ever heard of it?"

"Don't believe so," Roland said.

"I think I have," Jessica said hesitantly. "It's a little town in the Cascades, isn't it?"

Serenity was pleased. "Yes, it is. Have you ever been there?"

"No," Jessica admitted. "We sometimes ski at a resort that's not too far from there, though."

"Has your family lived there very long?" Peter inquired.

"I was born there," Serenity said proudly. "The first

and only person who was ever actually born in Witt's End."

"Is that so?" Roland eyed her closely. "And your father? Did he run this grocery store of yours before you took it over?"

"Oh, no." Serenity took a sip of her sherry. "I opened the store all by myself three years ago."

"What line of work is your father in?" Roland persisted.

It occurred to Serenity that she was being interrogated. She was aware that people in Caleb's world considered such rude questioning normal, but she had grown up with a different set of social rules. In Witt's End, no one asked such personal questions unless invited to do so. Still, *when in Rome,* she reminded herself.

"Julius is into woodworking," she said, not wanting to bog down the conversation with a long explanation of just how Julius's name came to be on her birth certificate.

"And motorcycles," Caleb murmured.

Roland scowled. "Motorcycles? He sells 'em?"

"No, he just likes them," Serenity explained. "He and Bethanne both own Harley-Davidsons. Julius likes to brag that he rode with a wild bunch in his younger days, but just between you and me, I've always taken that story with a grain of salt."

Phyllis stared at her. "How on earth does your father make a living at woodworking?"

Serenity took another sip of sherry and began to relax. These people weren't being deliberately rude, she decided. They were just curious. "Julius and Bethanne follow the craft fair circuit in spring and summer. Several residents of Witt's End do the circuit."

Franklin's hand tightened around his glass. "The craft fair circuit?"

"They sell their creations at various craft fairs up and down the coast," Serenity explained helpfully.

Phyllis pursed her lips. "You mean they sell junky little trinkets at those cheap arts and crafts shows?"

Serenity's determination to be tolerant vanished in the blink of an eye. "Julius and Bethanne are highly skilled artisans. They do not sell junk of any kind."

Jessica reddened. "Mother didn't mean to offend you. She was just a little surprised, that's all."

Phyllis glared at Caleb. "Have you met these people, Caleb?"

"No," Caleb said. "They're out of the country at the moment."

"Out of the country?" Roland's brow furrowed "What are they doing out of the country?"

"They're on their honeymoon, I believe, sir." Caleb looked at Serenity. "Isn't that right?"

"That's right." Serenity recovered her temper. For Caleb's sake, she would be polite. "They got married earlier this month."

Laura looked confused. "I don't understand. Is this a second marriage for one of them?"

"No," Serenity said. "A first for both of them. They've been living together for about fifteen years. Bethanne finally decided that it was time to get married."

There was a short, pregnant pause.

Roland took a deep swallow of his whiskey. "How did you meet my grandson?"

"We met when I hired him as a consultant for my new mail order business," Serenity said. "Isn't that right, Caleb?"

"Yes." Caleb examined the whiskey in his glass. "She can't afford to pay my usual fees, so we've signed what amounts to a partnership agreement. When I get her new catalog business up and running, I'll collect a portion of the profits. Hell of a deal. I couldn't pass it up."

Roland's expression turned fierce. "What the devil do you want with a partnership in a mail order business?"

"I'm diversifying," Caleb said.

Another sharp silence struck the room.

Phyllis put her sherry glass down quite loudly on the polished oak coffee table. "This is preposterous. What is going on here, Caleb? Surely you aren't serious about becoming Miss Makepeace's business partner."

"I'm very serious about it, Aunt Phyllis. I've got a signed contract," Caleb said softly. "It's a very interesting project. Takes up most of my time these days. I'm practically living in Witt's End."

Serenity stared at him. For a second she thought she saw stone-cold anger and an even colder pride in his eyes as he faced his family's combined disapproval and surprise. She had the uneasy impression that invisible battle lines were being drawn.

The expression in Caleb's gaze was quickly veiled, but not before it had ignited a deeply disturbing suspicion in Serenity's mind.

Perhaps Caleb had not brought her here in order to introduce her to his family for the conventional, traditional reasons.

Perhaps he had brought her here in order to use her as a pawn in some unknown game that he was playing with his relatives.

People here in the outside world operated under a different code, she reminded herself. Sometimes the subtleties of those rules escaped her. She had better make it clear to Caleb that she had no intention of allowing herself to be used.

8

T HE CHEAP LITTLE JEWELRY BOX WAS STILL HIDDEN EX-
actly where he had left it the night of his eighteenth
birthday. Caleb pried open the panel in the back of the
bureau and reached inside the small space. His fingers
closed around the case.

He drew it out slowly and examined it in the light of
the bedside lamp. It looked even tackier than he had
remembered. A couple of the fake gems had loosened.
The imitation gilt trim had almost worn off entirely.
The blue vinyl cover had faded and had started to
crack and peel in spots.

Caleb put the jewelry box on the nightstand and sat
down on the bed. He leaned forward, rested his
elbows on his thighs and contemplated the only thing
he possessed that had ever belonged to his mother.

Roland had given the jewelry box to him the day he
turned eighteen. It was the first time Caleb had

realized that his grandfather had allowed anything of Crystal Brooke's to survive.

"It's all in there," Roland had told him. "The whole goddamn story of how she seduced and ruined by son. I kept the clippings for you so that you could see how that bitch very nearly succeeded in destroying this family."

"Why are you giving this to me, sir?" Caleb had stared at the jewelry case and seen a terrible Pandora's box.

"Because it holds the truth. A man has to be able to face the truth without flinching. You're a man now, Caleb."

"Yes, sir." Caleb had taken the jewelry box as if it were made of molten lead. It had burned his hands.

"I've raised horses all my life." Roland had stood at the living room window and gazed out toward the paddock where one of his prized Arabians, a stallion named Windstar, grazed. "If there's one thing I've learned, it's that blood always tells. I've told you that often enough."

Caleb's hands had tightened on the jewelry case until he thought it would shatter. He had heard this lecture often enough in the past. "Yes, sir."

"You've got her blood in you. There's no denying it. The blood of a cheap little hustler, a no-good whore. But you've also got Ventress blood in you, Caleb. The Ventresses are a strong breed. God knows I've done my best to make certain that your Ventress bloodlines are the only ones that show."

Rage had squeezed Caleb's guts, but he kept his face impassive, as always. "I know you have, sir."

"And I think I've succeeded." Roland's voice held

fierce satisfaction. "I know I've been a little hard on you at times, but it was for your own good."

"Yes, sir."

"I'll tell you the truth, Caleb. Part of what happened all those years ago was my own damn fault. Franklin is right when he says that I was too lenient with Gordon when he was growing up. Your father was my only son and I wanted him to have everything. That was a serious error on my part. My leniency weakened his sense of duty and responsibility. It made him vulnerable. When *she* came along, he was easy prey."

"I know. You've told me that, sir."

Roland had made a fist at his side. "But I didn't make the same mistake with you, by God. I've made certain that you learned what it means to be a Ventress, what's expected of you. Now you're off to college. The future of the Ventress family lies in your hands. Don't ever forget that."

"I'll do my best, sir."

Roland had turned around to look at him, his eyes glittering with determination. "Of course you will do your best. A Ventress always does his best. You will be a credit to this family, Caleb."

"Yes, sir."

"And when the time comes," Roland had concluded with quiet vehemence, "you will marry a good woman, a woman who is above reproach, one who will bring strong, clean bloodlines back into this family. You will choose a woman who is the exact opposite of the cheap bitch who bore you. Do you understand that, Caleb?"

"Yes, sir."

A small, scratching sound on the veranda outside

his bedroom broke into Caleb's thoughts. He pushed aside the memories of his eighteenth birthday and rose from the bed.

There was a soft, urgent knock on the French doors just as Caleb reached for the knob.

"Caleb?" Serenity's voice was barely audible. "Are you in there?"

He opened the door and found Serenity, dressed in a bathrobe and slippers, standing outside. She had her hair twisted up into a loose knot on top of her head. The style emphasized the graceful line of her neck. She was hugging herself against the cold.

Caleb felt his insides grow warm and heavy at the sight of her. She was just what he needed to take his mind off the jewelry case. "Fancy meeting you here," he said softly.

"Can I come in? It's freezing out there."

"Be my guest." He held the door open. "I wasn't expecting you."

"I want to talk to you."

Caleb arched one brow as he slowly closed the door. "Something wrong?"

"I don't know. That's what I want you to tell me. I've got a few questions to ask you." Serenity broke off as she caught sight of the jewelry case sitting on the bedside table. "What's that? It looks like a woman's jewelry box."

"It is. It belonged to my mother."

"Really?" Serenity went over to the box and picked it up. "It's beautiful."

"It's just cheap plastic."

"What does that matter?" Serenity examined the box with an air of excited wonder. "Your mother probably used it to hold things that were very impor-

161

tant to her. I imagine it meant a lot to her, and it must mean a lot to you because it's something that belonged to her."

"I'm not the sentimental type."

Her smile was very knowing. "Of course you are. You're a very emotional sort of person. That was one of the things I liked about you right from the start."

"What you liked about me from the beginning was the fact that I could help you get your catalog business going."

She gave him an exasperated look. "What's wrong with you today? You've been in an absolutely lousy mood since we left the mountains."

"Sorry, I don't have much variety when it comes to moods. For the most part, I don't even have moods." Caleb crossed the room and plucked the case from her hand. He opened the nearest bureau drawer and put the jewelry box in it.

"Are you going to take that with you when we leave tomorrow?"

"Why would I want to do that?" Caleb closed the drawer.

"Because it's obviously important to you." Her hand went to the little griffin at her throat. "We all need to keep a few things around us that have a special meaning. No one should try to live in a vacuum, Caleb."

"Forget about the jewelry box. What was your question?"

"Oh, that." She narrowed her eyes. "I want to know why you brought me here."

"Isn't it obvious? You and I are involved. I wanted you to meet the family." He drew a finger down the side of her cheek. "I'm the conventional type, remember?"

The simple act of touching her aroused and warmed him. The gate that had opened deep inside when he had removed the jewelry case from its hiding place closed once more. The old rage was safely trapped behind the iron bars. He had himself back under control.

Caleb knew that Serenity saw the desire in his eyes because she caught her breath and took a step back. He smiled slightly. She couldn't hide her response, he thought. She hadn't had the practice that he'd had at concealing his emotions.

"I'm not sure you brought me here for the sole purpose of meeting your family," she said. "At least, not in the conventional manner."

"No?"

"No. It was almost as if you wanted to make them disapprove of me. And I was trying so hard to fit in, too."

"You did fit in."

"Well, I certainly did my best, but I didn't get much help from you. I didn't like what was going on in that living room tonight, Caleb. It was as if you were deliberately taunting your family."

"Taunting them?"

"Taunting them, baiting them, whatever." Serenity sliced her hand through the air in an impatient gesture. "I got the impression you wanted to provoke them and that you were using me to do it."

"Why would I want to provoke my family?" He moved toward her, and this time he was irritated when she took another step back to avoid him.

163

"I'm not sure." She glared at him as she came up against the wall. "But I've been doing a lot of thinking this evening. I couldn't help remembering how you came totally unglued when you first learned about those pictures Ambrose had taken of me."

"What do those damn pictures have to do with this?" Caleb didn't like the direction of her thoughts. Instinctively he wanted to distract her. He braced his hands against the wall on either side of her head and trapped her.

She lifted her chin. "It occurred to me that your grandfather would probably be even more outraged than you were if he ever found out about those photos. He's from another generation, after all. I'll bet he's even more straitlaced and conventional than you are."

"Don't worry about it. He's not going to find out about those pictures."

"But if he ever did find out, he would be very upset," Serenity insisted. "He might not be able to accept me. He might want you to stop seeing me."

Caleb set his back teeth. "Do you think for one minute that I'd end our relationship because my grandfather didn't approve of you? Understand something here, Serenity. I do a lot for my family, but I don't allow them to interfere in my personal relationships."

"I'm more concerned that you might be throwing your relationship with me in your family's face. I watched you tonight. It was as if you were daring them to disapprove of me."

"The hell with all of them." He captured her mouth and kissed her hard to stop the flow of words.

She didn't fight him, but she didn't respond the way she had the last time, either. She simply waited until he was finished.

When Caleb raised his head, he was breathing hard. "Serenity, this has nothing to do with my grandfather."

"Are you sure of that?"

"Damn sure."

"Because I mean it, Caleb." Her eyes searched his. "I won't let you use me in some private vendetta you may have going with your family."

"I want you," he muttered against her throat. "I brought you here to introduce you to my grandfather. I grew up in a family that values conventional rituals and I'm expected to honor them. But nothing Roland Ventress says or does will influence what happens between you and me. Is that clear?"

She hesitated and then slowly some of the tension went out of her. She smiled tremulously. "Word of honor?"

"Word of honor," Caleb whispered.

The realization that he meant every word of the vow hit him with the force of a tidal wave.

He wanted her more than he had ever wanted anything else in his life. She was one of the few things he had ever wanted just for himself, alone, not because it would please his grandfather or satisfy the old man's unrelenting demands for perfection and success.

Caleb was aware that his desire for Serenity made him potentially vulnerable in a way he had never been. It gave her more power over him than he had ever granted to any other woman. But he was certain he could handle the situation. If there was one thing he had learned growing up in his grandfather's house, it was how to control his emotions.

Furthermore, he had no intention of making the same mistake his father had made. He would not allow a woman, any woman, to destroy his life. Not even Serenity had that much power, Caleb thought.

"Caleb?"

"Kiss me." He caught her head between his hands and set his mouth on hers. This time he coaxed rather than stormed, persuaded rather than invaded.

Serenity opened her mouth and let him inside. She wrapped her arms around his waist and melted against him.

Excitement rushed through Caleb. He slipped his hand inside her robe and found the sweet shape of her breast. She trembled in response. She wanted him. The knowledge set fire to his blood.

Without releasing her mouth, Caleb started to ease Serenity toward the bed. At first she went willingly enough, but after two steps she abruptly dug in her heels.

"No," she whispered, pushing herself out of his grasp. "We can't."

"Why not?" He did not want to argue. All he could think about was getting Serenity into bed. "The other night I got the impression that you'd changed your mind, that you wanted me to make love to you."

She scowled at him while she hastily adjusted her robe. "It's got nothing to do with what I want. At least not tonight. I'm sure it would constitute a terrible breach of your grandfather's notion of good manners. His generation doesn't approve of that kind of thing.

It's only right that we show proper respect for his ways when we're under his roof."

"Damn it, Serenity, I just told you, I don't care what he thinks."

"Yes, I know, but I'm a guest in this household, and I feel I should behave according to your grandfather's rules. He strikes me as a very old-fashioned sort of person. He would probably think it was quite indecent of us to have sex here in your childhood bedroom."

Caleb realized she was very serious. "My grandfather may be in his eighties but he's not senile. I'll give you odds he thinks we're sleeping together."

"That's not the point," she grumbled as she stalked toward the French doors. "The point is, he's the kind of person who would expect his grandson to conduct his love affairs with discretion. That was the way things were done in his day."

"How would you know?"

"Come off it. It's obvious." She paused, one hand on the door knob. "Tell me the truth. Have you ever made love to another woman under this roof?"

Caleb rested his arm on top of the bureau and regarded her in silence for several seconds. He realized he was well and truly pissed. He wanted to take the next step in this relationship. Serenity was deliberately being difficult about it for some reason. If she had been any other woman, he would have suspected that she was playing games with him. But Serenity was Serenity. He could not envision her successfully playing this kind of game.

"No," Caleb said. "I haven't."

"There? You see? Until now, you've felt the need to be discreet while visiting here. Admit it."

Caleb thought about it and then shrugged. "You could say that." There were times when Serenity was too damn perceptive. It was true that on the handful of occasions when he had brought a woman to meet Roland, he had always made it a point to behave with the propriety that he knew was expected of him.

"This is a small town, after all, with small-town values," Serenity said in a lecturing tone. "Your grandfather has lived here all his life. You were raised here. Everyone knows you. It doesn't take a sociologist to figure out that some things never change in small towns."

"If you're so committed to honoring small-town conventions," Caleb said, "why did you come to my room tonight?"

She blushed furiously. "I came down here because I absolutely had to talk to you. I needed to have your word that you weren't using me somehow."

"Serenity—"

"But now that we've had this little chat and I know that you're not playing some weird game with your family, I really have to get back to my room."

"Serenity . . ." Caleb repeated patiently.

"What?" Clutching the lapels of her robe with one hand, she stealthily opened the French doors and peered out into the darkness. It was obvious that she didn't want to be spotted scurrying back to her room.

"I just thought you'd like to know that there haven't been many."

"Many what?" she asked over her shoulder.

"Women. And I have always been extremely discreet."

She grinned. "I know. That's one of the things I like

about you, Caleb. You've got high standards in everything."

"I'm not the only one," he said. "Am I?"

"Nope. I've got my standards, too." She stepped outside into the cold darkness and closed the door very softly.

Caleb walked over to the French doors, opened them soundlessly and watched as Serenity hurried along the veranda to the door of her own room. When she vanished safely inside, he closed his own door again and leaned back against it with a low groan of deeply felt regret.

He considered the condition of his heavily aroused body and decided that he was going to have a very hard time getting to sleep. This was getting to be an unfortunate habit. One of these days he was going to have to get this crazy relationship on track.

He gazed at the bureau where he had hidden Crystal Brooke's plastic jewelry case. Then he crossed the room to open the drawer. He stood looking down at the tacky little box for a long time. Serenity's words echoed in his head. *I imagine it meant a lot to her, and it must mean a lot to you because it's something that belonged to her.*

Serenity was wrong, he thought. The jewelry case meant nothing to him. One of these days he would throw it out.

Caleb hooked one booted foot on the bottom rail of the paddock fence, rested his arms on the top and surveyed the spectacular gray stallion with a horseman's sense of satisfaction.

He had been raised to know good horseflesh when

he saw it, and there was no doubt but that the Arab was a prize. Windsailer was one of the finest studs Roland Ventress had ever owned. The stallion was descended from Windstar, and it showed. There was primitive equine intelligence in the large dark eyes, and grace in every sculpted line of a body that had been bred for endurance and power.

"He's looking good, isn't he?" Roland asked as he walked up to stand beside Caleb.

"Very impressive." Caleb watched Windsailer munch hay.

"Every crop of his foals breeds true," Roland said. "They've all got his looks and his stamina. You can see Windstar in all of them. Blood tells."

"So you've always said."

Roland leaned against the top bar of the paddock fence. "This one's different from the others."

"This season's foals, you mean?"

"I'm not talking about horses," Roland said. "I'm talking about Serenity Makepeace."

Caleb smiled to himself. "Yes, she's different."

"You any more serious about her than you were about the last one?"

"Serious?"

"Goddammit, don't play games with me, boy." Roland narrowed his eyes. "You know what I'm talking about. Are you going to marry this one or not?"

"I'll let you know when I decide," Caleb said politely.

"It's past time you settled down and started a family. Hell, I had a twelve-year-old son when I was your age."

"I'm aware of that, sir."

"Damn, talking to you these days is like talking to a stone wall. Each time I see you it gets worse."

"What do you want me to say?" Caleb asked.

"You know what I want you to say." Roland gripped the paddock rail. "I want to hear you tell me that you're going to marry a good woman and start making babies. I'm not going to be around forever. Before I go to my grave, I want to know that there's going to be another generation of Ventresses."

"My cousins are having babies right and left. There were plenty of Ventresses at your birthday party yesterday."

"It's not the same thing and you damn well know it." Roland seethed with frustration. "I should never have let you set up Ventress Ventures. I should have insisted you come back here to Ventress Valley. Everything started going wrong after you went into business for yourself."

Caleb shrugged. They both knew that Roland had had nothing to say about the establishment of Ventress Ventures. Caleb had made the decision to go into business for himself long before he had even graduated from college. He had known he was never going to live in Ventress Valley.

Ventress Ventures was one of the few things that belonged entirely to him. He ran the business his way and was accountable to no one but himself.

"What do you mean, everything started going wrong?" Caleb asked.

"It was as if you started drifting away from me after that." Roland grimaced, anger and frustration plain in his weathered features. "Hell, I don't know how to explain it. When I look back on it, I realize it started even before you created Ventress Ventures. It started the day you left for college, didn't it?"

"I don't understand what you're talking about," Caleb said. "Are you telling me that I've neglected my responsibilities to the family?"

"No, damn it. You still go through all the right moves, but it's as if you're just pulling strings and pushing buttons these days."

"That's not very specific," Caleb said dryly. "Maybe you'd better clarify things for me. Any complaints about how I've handled the family's investments?"

"Hell, no." Roland shot him a glowering look. "The family's financial picture has never looked better and you know it. The Ventresses have more money today than they've ever had."

"I'm surprised to hear you admit that."

"Why should you be surprised? You did what I expected you to do. It's not just the family that's done all right since you started managing our investments. This whole valley has gotten more prosperous because of the new businesses you've helped get off the ground."

"Then what, exactly, are you complaining about?"

"Don't you get it?" Roland waved a hand to encompass the house and stables. "What's the point of having all this if I can't be certain there'll be another generation of Ventresses? I lost my son because of that slut who stole him away from his people, seduced him into giving up his responsibilities. All I've got left is you."

Caleb looked at his watch. "Dolores will be expecting us for breakfast."

"Breakfast can damn well wait," Roland muttered.

"Something's been bothering me for quite a while, and I think maybe it's time to lay my cards on the table. I got a question to ask you and I want an honest answer. I raised you to be truthful, and to the best of my knowledge, you've never lied to me. Don't start now."

"What's the question?"

"You and I both know that you're the only one who can undo the damage that bitch did all those years ago," Roland said. "You're the only one who can carry my bloodlines on into the future. The question is, are you going to do it?"

"Don't call her a bitch."

Roland looked blank. "What the devil are you talking about?"

Caleb's grip on the paddock rail was so fierce he was surprised that the wood didn't splinter, but he managed to keep his voice very even. For some reason, he recalled the look of wonder on Serenity's face last night when she had examined the jewelry box.

"I said, don't call her a bitch," Caleb repeated quietly. "For better or worse, Crystal Brooke was my mother."

Roland was dumbfounded. "What's this all about? Have you taken leave of your senses? You know what she was. I've told you often enough."

"Yes, you have. And you may be right. But I'm her son and I don't want anyone to call her bitch or slut or whore again."

"Have you gone crazy, boy? What's got into you?"

"Who knows?" Caleb said. "Maybe the bad blood is finally starting to show in me. Excuse me, sir. I'm going to get some breakfast. Got a long drive back to my new consulting project today."

He started walking toward the house.

"Don't you dare turn your back on me, Caleb Ventress," Roland shouted. "I'm the man who took you in and raised you. I gave you a home. Put a roof over your head. Taught you the things a man needs to know. You'll show me some respect, by God."

Caleb stopped. He turned around slowly and looked at the man he had wasted most of his youth trying to please. "Yes, sir."

"What's that supposed to mean?"

"It means you have my respect, sir. You will always have that."

Roland's eyes glittered with frustrated fury. He had demanded an acknowledgment of the respect Caleb owed him, and Caleb had given it to him. It wasn't enough and they both knew it.

There had once been more, Caleb realized. Sometimes he got the uneasy feeling there still was. But Roland had never shown any signs of wanting love from him, and whatever warmth there had been between them had simply withered away.

"Then answer my question," Roland said. "Are you going to give me grandchildren to guarantee a future for this family or not?"

"Haven't I always given you everything you've ever wanted?" Caleb asked softly. "Haven't I always done everything you've ever asked me to do?"

"Then why don't you get on with it," Roland exploded.

"First, I've got to find a woman who will overlook my bad bloodlines."

Serenity stopped in front of the large, glass-fronted display cabinet that stood in the breakfast room. She surveyed the contents with interest. Row after row of gleaming trophies, blue ribbons, merit badges, and plaques lined each shelf. Several were for horsemanship. Some were for Scouting activities. A few honored marksmanship skills. Others were for various academic achievements.

"Good heavens, Dolores, did Caleb actually win all of these?"

"Sure did."

"Amazing." Serenity studied a gleaming trophy at the end of one row. It commemorated the winning of a championship baseball game. Caleb had apparently been the pitcher.

Dolores set glass bowls containing grapefruit at each place on the table. "That boy used to bring home honors and awards and trophies like you wouldn't believe. If he went after something, none of the other kids stood much of a chance."

"I didn't realize Caleb was so competitive."

"If you ask me, he isn't. He prefers to do his own thing, like they used to say. My mother, who worked in this house for thirty years, said she never once saw him take any joy in the winning."

"He certainly did a lot of it. Winning, I mean."

"That's a fact."

"I wonder why he doesn't keep some of these trophies in his office in Seattle?"

"Why would he?" Dolores put down the last of the bowls full of grapefruit. "Everyone knows Caleb didn't win those awards for himself. He won them for his grandfather. Reckon he figured it was only fitting they be kept here in his grandfather's house."

"I think I'm starting to get the picture. Poor Caleb."

Dolores gave her a sharp, knowing look. "You can

say that again. My mother swore there were times she wanted to just weep when Caleb came home with a prize. He never bragged, she said, like boys do. Never talked about it. Never seemed excited. He'd just hand the trophy over to his grandfather and go on to the next goal Mr. Ventress set for him."

"What did his grandfather say when Caleb handed over his awards?" Serenity asked softly.

"When Caleb won, Mr. Ventress made it real clear that the boy was only doing what was expected of him. But lord help the poor lad the few times he didn't take first place." Dolores shook her head. "My mother said she took it upon herself to tell Mr. Ventress that she thought he was riding the boy too hard, but he always told her to mind her own business. Said he wasn't going to make the same mistakes he'd made last time."

Serenity whirled around. "Last time?"

"Expect he meant the mistakes he figured he'd made with his son Gordon," Dolores said quietly. "Sometimes it's harder to forgive yourself than it is someone else. And God knows Ventresses can be as stubborn as mules."

"What mistakes?"

Dolores hesitated. "You'll have to ask Caleb about that. I've already said too much as it is. If you do decide to ask questions, do me a favor."

"What's that?"

"Don't let on I put them in your head."

176

9

W HAT DO YOU THINK OF ARIADNE'S MARMALADE, MR. Ventress?" Serenity asked.

Roland looked at her from the far end of the painfully quiet table. Unlike yesterday's formal celebration, today's gathering was a small one. Only Caleb's aunt, Phyllis, and his uncle, Franklin, had been invited to breakfast this morning. They had done their best to keep the conversation going, but the unrelenting silence between Caleb and his grandfather effectively stifled everyone's best efforts.

"Not bad." Roland took another bite out of the slice of toast he had slathered with the marmalade. "Reminds me of the kind my mother used to make. Good and tart. Not too sweet. Seems like most things these days are too sweet for my taste."

"Isn't that the truth," Phyllis said with a brittle smile. "Take modern breakfast cereals. Most are so sugary, they taste like candy."

Serenity caught Caleb's eye. "That gives me a marketing idea. We'll advertise Ariadne's jams and marmalades as gourmet-style preserves. We'll say they've been especially created for people with sophisticated tastes. What do you think?"

"It has potential." Caleb's tone held all the enthusiasm of a ship's captain for an iceberg. He picked up his coffee cup and took a swallow. "Are you packed and ready to leave?"

"Yes." So much for trying to get that topic off the ground, Serenity thought. She tried another tactic. "Mr. Ventress, I couldn't help but notice those awards behind you in that glass case."

"Caleb won those," Roland said.

"Yes, I know. I saw his name on all the plaques. You must be very proud of him."

Roland scowled. "Caleb knows what's expected of him. Always did."

"I see he was even valedictorian," Serenity continued with determined good cheer. "I was valedictorian of my high school graduation class, too. I also got voted the student most likely to succeed."

Caleb choked slightly on his coffee. He set his cup down quickly.

Serenity frowned in concern. "Are you all right?"

"I'm fine." He got to his feet. "I want to be on the way as soon as possible, Serenity."

She looked up, surprised. "But I thought you were going to give me a tour of the stables. I wanted to look at the horses."

"Some other time. It's a long drive, and the weather report said there might be snow in the mountains this evening."

"Nonsense. It's too early for snow."

Caleb looked at her with hooded eyes. "I'd just as soon not have to stop to put on chains if I can avoid it."

Serenity stifled a small sigh. "I can be ready in five minutes."

"I'll get the luggage." Caleb moved around the long table.

"Need any help?" Franklin asked. "Harry's out back. He can give you a hand."

"I can handle it." Caleb walked toward the door.

Serenity smiled at Roland, whose jaw appeared to have been cast in iron. "Thank you so much for your hospitality, Mr. Ventress. I've certainly enjoyed my stay."

"Thank you for your gift," Roland said. His eyes were on Caleb's back. "I hope you'll be able to visit again sometime."

"I'd like that." Serenity had a sudden thought. "Caleb, don't forget your mother's jewelry case. I think I saw you put it in one of the bureau drawers last night."

The atmosphere in the breakfast room, tense but subdued until now, suddenly took on the aura of impending disaster. Dolores froze, tray in hand, in the kitchen doorway. Phyllis's eyes widened in appalled shock. Franklin looked grimmer than ever. Roland did not move.

It dawned on Serenity that she had just opened her mouth and inserted her foot. That was the problem out here in the outside world, she thought, chagrined. It was too darn easy for someone like her to screw up. She gave Caleb an apologetic look and wondered how to get back out of the hole she had just dug for both of them.

She was grateful to see that Caleb did not appear at all embarrassed by her social gaffe. There was no sign of any emotion on his face. He halted in the doorway and gave her a thoughtful glance. "Thank you for reminding me. I won't forget to pack it."

Phyllis and Franklin exchanged ominous glances.

Roland had a death grip on his butter knife. "Didn't know you still had that old jewelry case. You've never mentioned it. Thought you must have gotten rid of it years ago."

"Good grief, why would Caleb want to do that?" Serenity asked. The damage had been done, she thought. There was no point pretending that she hadn't seen the jewelry box. "He told me it belonged to his mother. It obviously means a great deal to him. He couldn't possibly just throw it away."

Phyllis was the first to recover. "Yes, of course. It's just that we never think of Caleb as the sentimental type. Do we, Franklin?"

"No," Franklin muttered. "We don't."

"That surprises me," Serenity said, relieved that the conversation was beginning to flow normally again. "I realized that Caleb was a very sensitive person the day I met him. I have good instincts for things like that, you know."

"Is that so?" Franklin asked.

"Sure." Serenity chuckled. "It wasn't hard to figure out that deep down Caleb was the caring, sensitive type. How many successful hotshot business consultants would sign on to save a little town like Witt's End? Especially when there's absolutely no guarantee he'll ever see a dime out of the project?"

Everyone stared at her.

"We'll be leaving now," Caleb said from the doorway. Without another word, he walked out of the room.

Precisely fifteen minutes later Caleb turned the key in the Jaguar's ignition. The powerful engine purred to life. Serenity waved to the small group of people on the steps as Caleb drove toward the road. Roland, Phyllis, Franklin, and Dolores lifted their hands in polite, restrained farewells.

Serenity sat back in her seat. "Sorry about that faux pas earlier. I don't know what made me mention your mother's jewelry box in front of the others."

"Forget it."

"I can't believe I did that. I was so careful to make certain that I wasn't seen going to your room last night. I even gave you that big lecture about not offending your grandfather's sense of propriety, remember?"

"I remember."

"Then I go and do something dumb at the breakfast table like blithely reminding you to pack the jewelry case."

"So?"

"So, it's obvious I ruined the good impression I was trying to create." Serenity glowered at him, exasperated. "Now your grandfather and everyone else in the house probably thinks I spent the night with you."

Caleb slid her a brief, unreadable glance. "Is that why you're fretting about it? You think everyone at the table nearly dropped their teeth this morning just because you'd hinted that you'd been in my bedroom?"

"I pride myself on being able to live in two worlds when necessary, but the truth is, I'm not really very good at it. If I spend too long in your world, I invariably mess up." Serenity morosely surveyed her attire. She was wearing the cuffed trousers she'd arrived in yeasterday, together with a shirt and a pullover sweater that she had selected from the same catalog. She was fairly certain that she was appropriately dressed, but clothes did not always make the woman. No one knew that better than she did.

"You didn't mess up," Caleb said quietly. "At least, not in the way that you think you did."

Serenity smiled hopefully. "You don't think your grandfather was seriously offended by the notion that we might have spent the night together while under his roof?"

"I doubt that he even considered that angle. Not after you mentioned the jewelry case."

"What do you mean? It's bound to be the first thing that popped into his mind. His and everyone else's in the room." Serenity rolled her eyes. "You saw the way they all reacted."

"The jewelry case is in that small carryall on the backseat. Unzip the bag and take it out."

"All right, but why?" Serenity unbuckled her seat belt, scrambled to her knees and leaned over the back of the seat. She reached for the carryall.

"I want you to see for yourself why everyone got a little tense when you mentioned it."

Serenity heard the deadly neutral tone in his voice and knew that she had unwittingly ventured again into treacherous terrain. Her hand stilled on the zipper of the carryall. "Caleb, if this is something private that you'd rather not discuss, I certainly understand."

"Get out the jewelry case."

She groaned and finished unzipping the bag. The blue and gold jewelry box was sitting on top of a carefully folded gray sweater. Serenity cautiously lifted it out and closed the carryall.

"What do you want me to do with it?" she asked.

"Open it."

Serenity examined the case. "I'm not sure I should. I get the feeling this doesn't involve me."

"You're wrong," Caleb said quietly. "From now on, it involves you. Open the box and take a look inside."

Serenity's fingers started to tremble. The innocent-looking blue plastic jewelry box suddenly felt like a grenade in her hand. "There's a key to wind up the music box."

"Wind it up if you like."

Serenity did so. When she was finished, she slowly unlatched the clasp and raised the lid. The music started to play.

"A waltz," Serenity whispered.

"What did you say?"

"It plays a waltz." She gazed, fascinated, at the two tiny plastic figures, a man and a woman, that had sprung upright and begun a jerky, clockwork dance.

"Never mind that, take a look at what's inside the compartment."

The compartment of the case was lined with cheap blue velvet. There was a long tear in the satin behind the small mirror on the inside of the lid.

There was no jewelry inside the case. Instead it was filled with old, yellowed newspaper clippings. They looked so fragile that Serenity was afraid to touch them.

"What are these?" she asked.

"My past." Caleb did not look at the open jewelry

case. He kept his eyes riveted to the road. "My grandfather gave that case full of clippings to me the day I turned eighteen. He wanted to make certain I didn't forget my mother."

"That was very thoughtful of him."

Caleb's mouth twisted. "It certainly was."

Serenity carefully unfolded the first of the folded clippings and studied the grainy black-and-white photograph. "This woman was your mother?"

"Yes."

The picture showed a striking platinum blonde dressed in a short, skintight, sequined gown. The dress had a neckline that plunged straight to the navel. The extreme style revealed only the inside curves of her breasts, but it created a sensual illusion that the camera obviously loved. There was a good-natured, provocative quality in the woman's lovely eyes. It was as if she knew men found her sexy and the fact amused her. Beneath the heavy makeup that darkened the full lips and enlarged the eyes it was easy to see the fine bone structure and the glow of youth.

"Caleb, she was lovely," Serenity breathed. "And so glamorous. I think you've got her eyes."

"So I'm told."

Serenity studied the photo with deepening admiration. "Was she a model?"

"Read the articles."

Serenity scanned the headlines on the clippings, most of which were from the *Ventress Valley News*. VENTRESS HIT WITH BLACKMAIL THREAT. VENTRESS ADMITS AFFAIR WITH PORN MODEL. She picked up another article. CENTERFOLD PIN-UP CLAIMS VENTRESS IS FATHER OF HER CHILD. VENTRESS FILES FOR DIVORCE.

"Keep reading," Caleb said quietly. "It's all there.

The blackmail scheme, the affair, the divorce, the accident, everything."

Serenity started to read more quickly, taking in the whole sad tale in one gulp. She paused over the article that related the blackmail scheme. Her stomach tightened. "Someone tried to blackmail your grandfather?"

"The blackmailer sent photos of Crystal Brooke to him. The photos included shots of her posing nude. There were also several pictures of her and my father making love on a beach in Santa Barbara."

"Dear God."

"My grandfather refused to pay the blackmail. The blackmailer sent the pictures to the *Ventress Valley News*. The editor and my grandfather had been quarreling for years. The pictures got published, and the rest, as they say, is history."

"Oh, Caleb, how awful for everyone involved." Serenity stopped reading and carefully refolded the clippings. "No wonder you went bananas when I told you that someone was trying to blackmail me with nude pictures. It was like having your parents' past thrown in your face, wasn't it?"

Caleb slanted her a disgusted look. "I didn't go bananas."

"Yes, you did. Now I know why."

"Damn it, Serenity."

"You're starting to lose your temper," she pointed out. "But I think I prefer that to your zombie mode."

" 'Zombie mode.' What the hell is my zombie mode?"

"It's when you go all cold and expressionless. You're very good at hiding your emotions, aren't you? You must have had a lot of practice."

"I am not an emotional sort of man." Caleb spaced each word very carefully and distinctly.

Serenity gently closed the jewelry box. The waltz stopped. "You don't think your reaction was a highly emotional one?"

"Let's just say the news that there were nude photos of you took me by surprise."

Serenity smiled ruefully. "I'll just bet it did. I'm sorry, Caleb. I shouldn't have called you all those nasty things."

"You mean straitlaced, conventional, arrogant, and inflexible?" Caleb's brows rose slightly. "Don't worry, I've forgotten all about it."

"The same way that I've forgotten that you called me naive and gullible." Serenity traced a line of faded gilt on top of the jewelry case with her fingertip. "I wonder why your grandfather gave you these clippings. He doesn't strike me as a cruel man. Hard and inflexible, perhaps, just like you in some ways, but not cruel."

Caleb smiled without any humor. "I doubt that he considered it a cruel act. He just wanted to make certain I never forgot that there was bad blood in me. He believed it was his duty to remind me that I had to guard against the effects of my mother's genetic influence. He breeds horses, remember? He's a great believer in the power of genes."

Serenity remembered the display cabinet full of honors and awards. "So you spent your childhood trying to prove to him that you weren't tainted with Crystal Brooke's genes."

"For all the good it did."

"Did something happen between you and Roland before you came in to breakfast this morning?"

"We had words."

"Words?"

"He called Crystal Brooke a bitch. It was nothing unusual. Every time he's mentioned her name for the past thirty-four years, he's called her a whore or a bitch or the woman who ruined the family."

"What did you say?"

"I told him not to call her bitch." Caleb flexed his fingers on the wheel. "It was the first time I've ever done that. The first time I've ever told him that I don't want him calling her names."

Serenity reached out and put her hand on his thigh. "You're her son. You have every right to protect her memory. What about your father? Does Roland call him names, too?"

"No. He thinks my father was the victim of a scheming hussy who seduced him from his duty and responsibility. My grandfather blames himself for being too indulgent and too lenient with his son. He thinks that's why my father was vulnerable to some-one like Crystal Brooke."

"So Roland determined not to make the same mistake with you."

"That's about it. My family history in a nutshell."

Serenity cradled the jewelry box in her hands. "At least you have a family history that dates back more than one generation. I never even knew my grandparents. My parents were both left alone in the world at an early age. Julius said my mother once told him that she and my father both grew up in foster homes. I don't really know anything more about them than that, but I've often thought that the fact that they each understood loneliness was probably one of the things that drew them together."

"Maybe it was," Caleb said.

Serenity hesitated. "I wonder what it was that drew your mother and father together?"

"I think it's obvious what drew them together. My mother was a sexy centerfold model who wanted to be a film star, and my father was a wealthy up-and-coming politician. Hell, they were made for each other."

"Don't judge them too harshly, Caleb. After all this time, there's no way of knowing the truth about their feelings for each other. Whatever happened, it was between the two of them. You certainly don't have any responsibility in the matter."

"Don't I? Sometimes it feels as if I've spent my whole life paying for what they did."

"We all have pasts and we all have futures. All we can do is choose to live in one or the other. It doesn't seem to me that there's much point living in the past."

Caleb said nothing.

After a moment Serenity leaned over the backseat to replace the jewelry box in the carryall.

The farewell celebration for Ambrose Asterley proved to be a major social event for Witt's End. At eight o'clock Sunday evening everyone in town poured into the Sunflower Café to drink a toast to Asterley's memory. As soon as Serenity and Caleb arrived, Serenity headed for the kitchen. There she joined Ariadne and a handful of other people who were supervising the food and beverage preparation.

Caleb found himself alone on the fringes of the crowd. He was surprised by the turnout. From what Serenity had told him, he'd assumed that no one except Jessie had been close to Asterley. But there was no shortage of people wanting to say farewell. He wondered privately if the size of the crowd had more to do with the lack of evening entertainment options in Witt's End and the free food than it did with the community's fondness for Asterley.

Whatever the reason, the entire population of the tiny town was present. Caleb knew several of the locals now because he had begun evaluating the products they wanted to sell in Serenity's catalog. He nodded pleasantly at several people as he dunked a wholewheat cracker into a curried yogurt dip. Absently he listened to bits and pieces of the Asterley anecdotes.

"Remember the day Ambrose thought he'd finally got himself a show in a Seattle gallery, and the gallery owner up and croaked before he got his pictures hung?" A man dressed in black leather and chains shook his head mournfully and downed a corn chip smeared with an eggplant and tahini concoction.

"I remember." A woman with short, cropped hair, a plaid shirt, and skintight jeans shook her head sadly. "Jessie said he got drunk and stormed around threatening to destroy everything he'd ever done."

"That was Ambrose for you," Quinton said as he joined the small group near the corn chips. "Things always seemed to go wrong for him. He was forever getting caught between cosmic planes. The mathematics of the universe are like a deck of cards in some ways. That deck was always stacked against poor Ambrose."

"Yeah, a real loser in the karma department, all right," the denim and chain man said. "But he was okay in his own way."

"He wasn't mean-spirited or anything. Just kind of

a loner," a woman dressed in a gown made out of several layers of scarves noted. "The victim of a lot of bad luck. He was a wonderful photographer, you know."

"I know," Quinton said.

"Janine and I keep the photo he took of us together hanging over our bed," the woman with the very short hair confided. A tear trickled down her cheek. "It's beautiful."

Jessie drifted over to the buffet table. "He did have talent," she said quietly to Caleb. "Some of his photos are incredible. Did Serenity ever get around to showing you those shots he took of her?"

"No." Caleb thought of the envelope Serenity had taken from Asterley's files. "She didn't." *A question of trust.*

"You ought to take a look at them," Jessie urged. "They're excellent examples of some of his best work. I'd like to see them hung one of these days. It would be a fitting tribute to Ambrose."

Caleb had a searing mental image of Serenity on public display in an art gallery, her beautiful, graceful body exposed to all and sundry. The cracker he had been holding crumbled between his fingers.

"I don't think Serenity will go for the idea," Caleb said.

Jessie gave him a quizzical look. "Why not?"

"Because I'll raise holy hell if she does." He sought for a logical reason. "Witt's End by Mail doesn't need that kind of publicity."

"I don't see how it would hurt," Jessie said thoughtfully. She started to add another comment but broke off as Blade came up. "Hello, Blade. How are things going? I see Witt's End is still relatively free of an invasion force."

"I'm not so sure about that." Blade's perpetually narrowed eyes swept the room in a professional manner. "I think we've got trouble."

"What makes you think that?" Caleb asked, only mildly interested.

"Zone's acting strange."

"Zone strikes me as the type who always acts strange," Caleb said. "What's new about that?"

"She's nervous. Scared maybe. Keeps talking about danger and turmoil." Blade nodded toward Zone, who was standing by herself near the punch bowl. "I don't like the feel of it."

"Maybe she's just depressed," Caleb said. "This is a wake, after all."

"Don't think it's that." Blade helped himself to a handful of corn chips. "Think it's trouble. Big trouble."

"Have Serenity talk to her," Jessie suggested. "She's closer to Zone than anyone."

"Maybe I'll do that." Blade moved off, crunching corn chips with machinelike precision.

Jessie smiled. "I'm beginning to wonder if Blade and Zone were made for each other. Something about the two of them seems to be clicking. What do you think?"

"I hadn't thought about it," Caleb admitted. "I suppose you could say they both share a common weirdness."

"Everyone in Witt's End is probably weird by your definition," Jessie said. "If you don't approve of weirdness, what are you doing here?"

"You know why I'm here. Business."

"Bullshit," Jessie said. "I'm not an idiot. It's obvious this isn't your kind of consulting gig. You're here because of Serenity, aren't you?"

"She hired me, remember?" Before Caleb could change the topic, someone else changed it for him.

A big, bushy-haired man dressed in a red flannel shirt and a pair of grimy coveralls surged forward with a purposeful air. He halted directly in front of Caleb.

"You Ventress?"

"I don't believe we've met," Caleb said.

"Name's Webster. Missed the product evaluation on Friday. I was busy."

"I see."

"Brought my product with me tonight. Thought maybe you could take a look at it. Tell me whether it's good enough for Serenity's catalog."

"Sure, why not? I'm sure Asterley would understand if we do a little business at his wake."

Webster reached into a voluminous pocket and brought out a palm-sized rock. He displayed it proudly on his dirt-stained hand. "There it is. What d'ya think, Ventress? Sell like crazy, huh?"

Caleb gazed at the rock. It looked like a very ordinary rock. "What, exactly, is it?"

Webster frowned. "It's a rock. What's it look like?"

"A rock." Caleb picked it up. "Interesting."

Webster brightened. "Thought you'd like it. Plenty more where that came from. How many you think I should have on hand when the first catalog goes out? Hundred, maybe?"

"Webster, I've got to be honest with you," Caleb said diplomatically. "I don't really think there's a big market for rocks like this."

Webster scowled. "My rocks are beautiful."

Serenity materialized at Caleb's elbow. She looked anxious. "What a lovely rock, Webster." She gave Caleb a bright smile. "Webster is a connoisseur of rocks. He collects them. I'm sure we'll be able to market them through our catalog."

"I don't think so," Caleb said.

Webster began to look alarmed. "What's wrong with rocks?"

"Please, Caleb," Serenity said. "You're a marketing genius, remember? You can find a way to sell Webster's rocks."

"I'm telling you, there's no demand for ordinary rocks," Caleb said patiently.

Webster snatched his rock out of Caleb's hand. "You want fancier rocks? By God, I'll get 'em for ya. You'll see." He swung around and stomped off through the crowd.

"Now you've hurt his feelings," Serenity complained.

"You're trying to start a business, not a charity," Caleb said. "We are not featuring rocks in the catalog."

Serenity glowered at him and went back to the kitchen.

"She worries about everyone in this town," Jessie said softly. "And I should warn you that we worry about her. You went away with her this weekend."

"I thought this was a town where everyone minded his or her own business," Caleb said dryly.

Jessie's smile was cool. "I've got news for you. This is a small town, and all small towns, even places like Witt's End, share a few common traits."

"I know all about small towns. I grew up in one."

"Then you know that people in small towns talk."

"Yes," Caleb said. "I do. It's called gossip."

The old gossip about his parents had never really died in Ventress Valley. It had been resurrected from time to time while he was growing up.

The tale of how the scion of the town's leading family had been seduced by a centerfold model was never mentioned in Roland's hearing. Caleb, however, had gotten into several fistfights in the schoolyard and out behand a few barns because of the taunts of various classmates who had overheard their parents discussing the past.

Caleb had fought those youthful battles with the same relentlessly focused anger and determination that he used to win prizes and blue ribbons for Roland. His grandfather had noticed the occasional black eye and bloody nose, but he had never asked what the fight had been about. He only wanted to know if Caleb had won.

Jessie studied Caleb closely. "I wasn't talking about gossip. At least not in the way you mean. What I meant was that in a small town people look out for each other. Serenity is one of us. She's got this dream of creating a mail order business, and she seems to think you can help her do it. That's fine as long as she's happy. But if you hurt her or use her, a lot of people are going to get real mad."

"I'll keep that in mind."

"You do that." Jessie turned to walk away.

"Jessie?"

She glanced back at him over her shoulder. "What?"

"I never knew Asterley, but Serenity told me that you and he were more than friends." Caleb met her eyes. "I just wanted you to know that I'm sorry about what happened."

Jessie's gaze softened. "Thanks." She looked out over the room full of surprisingly cheerful mourners. "You know, I really thought he was going to stay sober for a while. When I left him that night he was doing okay. A little depressed, but I didn't think he was feeling bad enough to open a bottle. He stuck to coffee while I was there."

"When did you leave him?" Caleb asked curiously.

"Around eleven. I had cooked dinner for him earlier and we'd talked for a while."

"I'm told he died around midnight. He must have done a lot of hard drinking right after you left."

"When Ambrose got going on the booze, he could really put it away in a hurry." Jessie walked away to join a group of people on the other side of the room.

Caleb started to reach for another corn chip and found the path blocked by Blade, whose eyes were mere slits. Quinton stood to the left of him, looking almost as forbidding as his companion. A man with a balding head and a gray ponytail flanked Blade on the right. He wore a long black cape and a single gold earring.

"This here's Montrose," Blade said without preamble. "Runs the service station. Plays music. You met him yet?"

"Yes," Caleb said. "We've met."

Blade squared his already square shoulders. "The three of us been talking. Decided it was time we had a little chat with you, Ventress."

Caleb glanced at his watch. "You've left it a bit late, haven't you? It's nearly ten o'clock at night. High noon was a long time ago."

Blade scowled. "What the hell are you talking about?"

"Cut the high noon jokes," Montrose said quietly to Caleb. "We're serious."

"Montrose is right," Quinton said. "We'd like you to join us for a private farewell to Ambrose."

"How private?" Caleb asked skeptically.

"Just us and you. Up at the springs."

"Why not?" Caleb said. "You know, considering the fact that I never even met the man, Asterley has certainly had a major impact on my life."

10

A CLOUD OF SILVERY VAPOR HOVERED OVER THE CRYSTAL clear pools. Caleb watched the steam as it swirled gently above the hot spring water. There was something oddly fascinating about the mist's slow dance.

The huge cavern that sheltered the hidden springs was open to the icy night at one end, but the cold outside did not reach very far inside the rocky chamber. It was as though an invisible glass wall sealed the entrance. The heat from the pools transformed the cave into a balmy grotto.

At some point in the history of the springs, an enterprising soul had strung electrical wiring along one stone wall of the cavern. A handful of small bulbs glowed dimly, illuminating the interior in an eerie light. Quinton had shown Caleb the switch that controlled the interior lighting. It was located just outside the entrance.

Caleb and his three companions had the springs to themselves. Styx and Charon were out in the darkness waiting patiently for Blade. Occasionally Caleb saw a gleaming canine eye hovering at the entrance.

"Dogs won't come in here," Blade explained.

"Why not?" Caleb asked.

"Don't know. Just won't."

It was as good an answer as any, Caleb thought. He didn't blame the rottweilers for staying out of the cavern. He had a few doubts about being inside, too, considering the company in which he found himself.

The hike to the caverns had been a cold one lit by a bright, white moon. The path led straight past Serenity's cottage and up into the woods behind it. Once inside the caves, each man had taken a seat leaning against one of the stones around the largest of the pools. Quinton produced a carton of his home-brewed beer and handed the bottles around.

"Here's to Ambrose." Quinton took a swallow from the bottle in his hand. "Good luck to him on his journey into the Big Darkroom."

"Hope he finally went someplace where they appreciate good photographers with unpleasant personalities." Montrose hoisted his bottle in a farewell salute.

"Ambrose," Blade muttered as he downed a swallow. "Knew a guy like him once. He was okay."

Caleb dutifully raised his bottle. He considered and then rejected a comment on the irony of drinking a beer toast to a man who'd died because of a serious drinking problem. He searched for something more appropriate.

"To Ambrose," he finally said. "May he find himself someplace where the light from the National Endowment for the Arts never shines."

Silence descended again.

Blade stared into the depths of the pool. "Supposed to be able to see visions here, you know."

"Yeah?" The beer wasn't bad, Caleb decided, somewhat surprised. He glanced at the label on the bottle in his hand. Old Hogwash.

"That's what they say," Quinton murmured. "Folks here in Witt's End call these springs vision pools. It's an old legend."

"How old?" Caleb asked.

"Dates back to the earliest days of Witt's End," Quinton said.

"No shit." Caleb studied the green rocks beneath the surface of the pool. "That would be all the way back to what? Nineteen sixty-eight or 'sixty-nine?"

"Maybe earlier." Blade's brow furrowed as he gazed intently into the water. "Way I heard it was, you got to spend a long time in here meditatin' and purifyin' your brain first. Then, sometimes, if everything is just right, you get a vision."

"You said this legend dates from the late sixties?" Caleb contemplated the spring. "From what I've heard, visions were fairly common in those ancient golden days of yore, and they weren't usually induced by meditation and purified brains. I think whether or not you had a good vision had more to do with what you'd been smoking."

"One should not scoff at what one does not comprehend," Quinton said. "We cannot perceive all the mathematical planes with the five ordinary senses."

Caleb shrugged. "Maybe you're right."

Silence again.

"I had a vision here once," Montrose said very softly. "Years ago."

"Yeah?" Blade gave him a curious glance. "What was it like?"

"Hard to explain. I remember I'd been giving Serenity violin lessons that afternoon. For some reason I came up here that evening just to think. I used to do that a lot in those days."

"I remember," Quinton said.

"The vision was kind of like a dream except that I knew I was awake and that it wasn't a dream." Montrose rolled his beer bottle between his palms. "It was weird, if you want to know the truth. A real personal thing. I never told anyone about it until now."

"Could you tell if it was a vision of a verifiable mathematical reality?" Quinton asked curiously. "Was there any symbolic logic to it?"

Montrose shook his head. "It was just a vision."

Caleb stretched out his legs and took another swallow of Old Hogwash. "So? What did you see?"

Montrose gazed into the pool. "My old man. He was listening to me practice the piano, telling me how good I was. Same way I'd been telling Serenity how good she was earlier that day. I was just a little kid in the vision. Nine, maybe ten years old, I guess. I remember how great it felt to know that my old man was proud of me. Somehow it made me calmer inside."

The beer tasted warm in Caleb's mouth. "That sounds like a memory, not a real vision."

"Whatever it was, it wasn't a memory," Montrose said. "My old man ran off before I was born. I never even met him."

No one said anything for a moment. They all sat gazing into the crystal pool.

"Maybe you were lucky." Blade gripped his beer bottle fiercely. "I could have done just fine without ever knowing my old man. He liked to hit me and Mom with his belt. Sometimes he used his fists. I wanted to leave home a million times, but I stayed because I figured that as long as he was knockin' me around, he wasn't beatin' up on my mom."

Caleb looked at Blade. "You defended your mother?"

"She wasn't much of a mother, I guess. Kind of weak and pathetic. Never had the guts to leave my dad. Let him kick us around. But she was my mom. Felt like I had to do something, y'know?"

Caleb remembered the confrontation with Roland at the paddock. *Don't call her a bitch.* "Yeah. I know." He watched the water shimmer in the pool. "You ever hit your dad?"

"The day Mom died. Came home from the funeral and told him I was leavin' for good and I wasn't ever comin' back. He took a swing at me. I slammed him into a wall. Knocked him cold. I walked out the door, joined the Marines, and I never saw him again. Heard he died five years ago. Didn't go to the funeral."

Silence descended on the small group once more.

Caleb leaned back against a steam-warmed rock. "This is all very interesting. But did you guys bring me up here just for a little male bonding or was there something more specific that you wanted to say to me?"

"We brought you up here because we wanted to talk to you about Serenity," Quinton said.

"Jessie and Ariadne figure there are some things that need saying," Montrose added. "They decided we're the ones to say them."

Caleb rested his head against the rock. "Talk. I'm listening."

"Don't know if you exactly understand how it is with Serenity and a lot of us here in Witt's End," Blade said. "We're her family. The only one she's got."

"She told me that," Caleb said.

"This town raised her," Quinton explained slowly. "I was here the day her mother arrived, pregnant and all alone in the world. Said her name was Emily Smith and that Serenity's father had been killed in an accident. She didn't have anywhere else to go. No family. No one."

"She wound up here with the rest of us who didn't have anywhere else to go," Montrose said. "Quinton, Ariadne, Julius, Jessie, Blade, and myself were all here then."

"We were here when Serenity was born, too." Quinton rubbed his jaw. "Jesus. I'll never forget the blood. Scared us. We were all so damn young. Didn't know what to do."

Caleb frowned. "Serenity's mother gave birth here? No one took her to a hospital?"

"She went into labor without any warning." Quinton's mouth tightened. "Ariadne said something was wrong. We called the paramedics but it was the middle of winter. The roads were sheets of ice. Took forever for the aid car from Bullington to get here. We didn't dare try to drive her down the mountain ourselves because the bleeding was so bad. Any movement made it worse."

"The medics got here in time, though," Montrose said slowly. "Or so we thought. They got the bleeding stopped and Serenity was safely delivered. Everyone, even the medics, thought Emily was going to make it."

"She was lying on a stretcher," Quinton said. "The medics were getting ready to transport her. She asked to hold her baby for a few minutes and one of the medics put the infant in her arms. Emily kissed her and said she was naming her Serenity. Then she gave the baby to Julius. Probably because he happened to be standing closest to the stretcher."

"She took off her necklace and gave that to Ariadne." Montrose took another sip of beer and stared into the depths of the pool. "Said it had come from Serenity's father and she wanted to be sure it went to Serenity."

"Emily looked at those of us gathered around the stretcher," Blade said. "Begged us to take care of her baby. We thought she meant while she was recovering in the hospital. We said yes. Told her not to worry."

"She died on the way down the mountain," Montrose concluded. "The medics said she went into shock. But we think she just gave up and slipped away. She told us she loved Serenity's father a lot. We all knew how much she missed him."

"It was like she sort of lost the will to live after she did what she had to do." Blade rested his hands on his knees. "Knew a guy like that once. Got shot up on a mission. Realized he'd never make it out alive. But he hung on until he finished the job. Then he let himself die."

"Emily found the strength to survive long enough to get her daughter born and that was the end," Quinton said. "She had nothing left afterward."

"And Witt's End wound up with a baby to raise."

Caleb shook his head in amazement. "I'm surprised the social service agencies let you keep her."

Quinton, Blade, and Montrose exchanged significant looks.

"Well, we sort of made it easy for them to let us keep her," Blade said cautiously. "Ariadne and Jessie said they'd probably try to take her away from us if we didn't do something. Said Serenity would land in a foster home, just like her mother and father had. We figured Emily wouldn't have wanted that."

"Ariadne grew up in foster homes, too," Quinton explained. "She knew the system inside and out. Knew how to handle the bureaucracy and the paperwork. She told us what we had to do to avoid a hassle."

"What did you do?" Caleb asked.

"We lied on the forms at the hospital," Montrose explained. "The men in the group went out into the parking lot. Drew straws. The winner's name went down on Serenity's birth certificate. The hospital didn't have any qualms about sending Serenity home with her father."

"We had to fake Serenity's birth certificate to make sure there wouldn't be any problem keeping Serenity out of *their* hands," Blade said.

Caleb gazed into the shimmering waters of the pool. "Julius Makepeace was the winner, I take it?"

"Yes." Quinton shrugged. "But it didn't really matter. Everyone in Witt's End became a relative of Serenity's that day."

"I see." Caleb studied the label on his bottle of Old Hogwash and wondered why he was suddenly feeling a little light-headed. "Yes, folks, incredible, but true. A fairy princess raised by feral hippies."

"Damn it, this isn't a joke, Ventress." Quinton glowered at him. "And we aren't hippies. Hell, there aren't any hippies left. The last one died years ago."

"I'm not so sure about that," Caleb said. "I think there've always been hippies of one kind or another. They just go under different names with each new generation. Bohemians, beatniks, dropouts, free spirits, freaks, whatever."

"I'm no freak." Blade's expression turned ominous.

"Of course not," Caleb said blandly. "You're obviously as normal as everyone else in this town."

"Damn right," Blade muttered, mollified.

"We took Serenity and raised her as best we could," Montrose said. "We all took turns teaching her stuff. I taught her music and how to change the oil in her car. Jessie taught her art."

"I taught her philosophy and mathematics," Quinton said. "Ariadne taught her how to cook and how to run a small business."

"Julius taught her literature and poetry," Blade said.

Caleb stared at him. "He did?"

"Yeah. Julius likes to read," Blade said. "He also taught her how to drive."

Quinton looked at Caleb. "We all had a hand in her education. We all had something to teach her. But the truth is, she gave us more than we ever gave her."

Caleb smiled faintly. "A sense of purpose? Of meaning in your lives? Something important to do? A feeling of commitment and responsibility?"

Montrose nodded. "Yeah, something like that."

Quinton's mouth curved but he said nothing.

Blade scowled at Caleb. "How'd you know all that?"

"Just a lucky guess." Caleb looked around the circle. "I'm still waiting to hear what you brought me up here to tell me."

"It's simple, Ventress." Montrose took another slug of his beer. "We're all part of Serenity's family so we figure we've got a right to ask some questions."

"About me?"

"Yeah. About you," Blade said. "Seems to us you been payin' a lot of attention to Serenity lately."

Quinton cleared his throat. "It has become clear to us that her relationship with you is far more significant and measurably more intense than the one she had with that idiot of a sociologist six months ago."

"Maybe even more serious than what she had with that guy who came here after he lost his family in a plane crash," Montrose added.

Quinton looked at Caleb. "We therefore feel it is incumbent upon us to make a few inquiries."

"I'll be damned." Caleb settled himself more comfortably against the rock at his back. "Beneath all the picturesque individualism, you guys are as old-fashioned and conservative as a bunch of small-town farmers, aren't you? You brought me up here to ask me what my intentions are."

"Cut the crap," Blade ordered. "Just tell us straight out if you're foolin' around with Serenity or if you're serious about her."

"If I tell you that I'm merely toying with her affections, and have absolutely no serious intentions whatsoever, are you going to tie me hand and foot, weight me down with a chunk of cement, and drop me into one of these pools?"

Blade lifted one heavy shoulder. "Sounds good to me."

"She's one of us," Quinton said quietly. "The first kid ever actually born right here in Witt's End. We don't want her hurt."

"I don't intend to hurt her." Caleb's hand tightened around the beer bottle. "Christ almighty, don't you understand? That's the last thing I want."

The other three contemplated him in silence. Blade and Montrose finished their beer and put the bottles back in the carton.

"What do you want?" Quinton finally asked.

Caleb looked deeply into the pool. "I want her."

It felt good to say the words aloud. For some reason the verbal declaration made him feel more centered, a little more connected to the world.

"Wanting her isn't good enough," Quinton said softly.

Caleb spread the fingers of his left hand on his thigh. "I'll take care of her. I give you my word on it."

No one said anything for a long while after that. Caleb was vaguely aware of the passing of time, but he felt no sense of urgency to leave the warm cavern. He drank his beer slowly and watched the vapor form and dissolve above the hot spring pool.

"Gettin' late," Blade said eventually. "Reckon I'll be on my way. Got to make my rounds." He rose and unbuckled a small flashlight from the array of equipment that decorated his belt. He handed it to Caleb. "Here. You might need this to find your way back down the path."

"Thanks." Caleb thrust the flashlight into the pocket of his jacket.

Quinton and Montrose waited until the hollow echo of Blade's heavy boots on the stone floor faded. Then they, too, got up without a word and walked out of the cave. From the corner of his eye Caleb watched them leave. He stayed where he was. For some reason he didn't feel like joining them.

He could find his way back down the path to Witt's End, he thought. It wouldn't be difficult. He wanted to be by himself for a while.

He closed his eyes and wondered what his relatives would say if they could see him now, sitting alone in a cave warmed by mysterious hot springs.

Time passed. It could have been minutes or hours. Caleb had no way of knowing. He opened his eyes and started to look at his watch. But his attention was captured by the whirling mists above the hot pool.

The vapor appeared denser now than it had earlier. There was more volume to it, a sense of depth and darkness. Caleb studied it with an odd detachment, the way he might have studied a painting. Something about the steam drew his eye down to the water.

The crystal clear waters of the pool slowly began to flow around a central point, becoming a vortex that sank deeper and deeper into the spring.

A hallway took shape within the whirlpool. It had no beginning and no end. There were doors in the walls. Caleb knew that one of them offered escape from the endless hallway. All he had to do was find the right door.

As he gazed, fascinated, into the endless, whirling corridor, he saw the figure of a man running swiftly through it. As the figure moved through the hall, he paused long enough to open each door that he passed. Time after time he found himself looking through a doorway into a featureless gray room. Each time he closed the door and ran on to the next.

Caleb could not see the man's face, but was certain he knew him. He could feel what the figure in the tunnel was feeling. He knew his thoughts, sensed the urgency that drove him. There was a shattering awareness that time was running out. His pulse was pounding and sweat had dampened his clothes.

He was the man running through the endless hallway.

He wanted to stop but he could not. The darkness at the end of the corridor was waiting to claim him. He had to keep moving; he had to keep opening doors, hoping each time that he would find the right one before it was too late.

He had to find her. She held his future in her hands.

Caleb's fingers closed around another doorknob. It was icy cold beneath his fingers. This was the last door.

He opened it.

The room behind the door was not gray like the others. It was bright and white and filled with sunshine.

And she was there.

Relief cascaded over him when he saw that she was waiting for him with the infants cradled in her arms. He walked into the room.

Somewhere in the distance a waltz was playing.

She smiled at him.

He reached for her.

The vision in the pool vanished.

Caleb awoke abruptly. He drew a ragged breath and wiped sweat from his forehead. His pulse thudded heavily, as if he had been running hard for a long distance.

For an instant he couldn't get his bearings. Then he saw the mist rising above the rocky pool. It curled and twisted and dissipated in an endless pattern.

In spite of the warmth created by the springs, a cold shudder went through him. He glanced around the dimly lit cavern and then looked at his watch. With a shock he realized that it was nearly midnight. The others had left over an hour ago.

Caleb got to his feet, aware that his heartbeat was slowing to its normal rate. He walked to the entrance of the cavern and stood looking out into the night. A handful of scattered lights from various cabins sparkled through the trees down below. He knew that the welcoming glow from the nearest windows came from Serenity's cottage at the foot of the path.

He started to reach into the pocket of his jacket for the flashlight Blade had given him. Then he realized he didn't need it. There was enough moonlight to light his way.

It took ten minutes to make his way to Serenity's cottage. The porch light was still on over the front door.

He walked up the steps and knocked. Serenity, bundled up in a robe and slippers, opened the door immediately. Her hair was a frothy tangle of red curls. He knew from the anxious expression in her beautiful eyes that she had been waiting for him.

"Caleb." She smiled tremulously. "I was beginning to get a little worried. Quinton and the others came by over an hour ago to tell me you were alone in the cave. They said you'd probably stop here on your way down."

"The last door," Caleb whispered.

"What?"

"Forget it." He reached for her.

She didn't vanish.

Caleb pulled her into his arms and buried his face in her scented hair. "I want you."

"I know. It's all right, Caleb. I want you, too. You must know that."

He lifted his head and looked down into her brilliant eyes. He was lost in the vision he saw there. "I need you."

She turned her head and kissed his throat. "Yes. I need you, too. It's time."

He swept her up into his arms, kicked the door shut and carried her down the hall to the bedroom. The beaded curtain around her bed glittered in the shadows.

Caleb pushed through the sparkling curtain. It shivered like the water on the surface of a crystal spring. A thousand tiny glass beads clashed and chimed in the darkness.

He fell onto the bed with Serenity in his arms. The force of his need made his hands shake.

Serenity moaned softly. She burrowed against him with a hot, sweet abandon. Caleb's entire body tightened in fierce arousal. The smell of her, spicy and unbearably female, stoked the fires within him. With a groan he thrust his leg between hers and tugged at the sash of her robe.

Beneath the robe Caleb discovered a warm, flannel nightgown. He struggled with it impatiently, shoving the hem up to Serenity's waist. His hand skimmed eagerly over her smooth, soft skin until he found the inviting nest of hair.

She arched against him. "Yes. *Please.*"

"Tell me," Caleb muttered. "Tell me how much you want me."

"I can't. There are no words."

"Then show me." Caleb took her mouth with swift urgency and slipped his fingers into her moist heat. "God, yes. Like that."

He moved his lips to her throat while he fought to lower the zipper of his jeans. Then he fumbled blindly in his pocket for the small foil packet.

It seemed to take forever before he was ready, but in reality it was only a few damp, breathless moments. When he shifted position to settle between Serenity's legs, his foot thrust through the beaded curtain. The glass beads danced.

"Caleb?"

"Right here." He felt the warmth of her soft, inner thighs cradle him. She was wet and ready and reaching for him.

He had never wanted anything this badly in his whole life. He reached down to guide himself to the sultry entrance of her body. He groaned as he thrust slowly and deliberately into her.

She was warm and slick and so snug that he could hardly breathe. *Too tight.*

He heard her catch her breath, felt her stiffen as he sank deeply into her softness. He stopped, shaken.

"My God, Serenity."

"No, don't leave me," she whispered. "It's time. You're the right man."

"Are you all right?" he managed hoarsely.

"Yes. Yes, I'm all right." She wrapped her arms around him and lifted her hips. "It's just that I never dreamed it would be like this."

"Like what?"

"Like finding the other half of myself."

He waged a monumental battle with his self-control, but it slipped from his grasp even as Serenity drew him into her. He held her more tightly than he had ever held anyone or anything else in his life.

Triumph, satisfaction, a feeling of wholeness and a pounding sense of joy raced through him, a fabulous maelstrom of emotions that he could not begin to sort out. He didn't care. He only knew one thing for certain in that gloriously shattering moment, and that was enough for now.

He was alive.

The light moved like a shower of jewels across his face. Caleb sensed the various colors—amber, ruby, emerald, sapphire. It was a strange sensation, not unpleasant, just odd. He waited a moment to see if the feeling would pass. When it didn't, he reluctantly opened his eyes. He found himself lying in a pool of sunlight filtered through the veil of glass beads that formed the curtain around Serenity's bed.

He turned his head and realized that he was alone. The sound of running water told him that Serenity was in the shower. For a moment he lay still, half afraid the memories of the night might dissipate like steam off a hot spring pool.

But a reassuring sense of reality poured in along with the morning sun. He was definitely in Serenity's bed. The warm, rumpled sheets and the satisfaction that permeated his whole body constituted all the proof he needed that he had not been dreaming. He pictured Serenity in the shower and smiled. He sat up and started to thrust aside the covers.

The sight of the three black-and-white glossies scattered across the quilt caused him to go completely still.

For a long moment Caleb gazed at each picture in turn. Ambrose Asterley had done the impossible. He had captured a creature of light and magic on photographic film.

In one of the shots Serenity reclined on a large boulder, looking back over her shoulder at the camera. Her eyes held the innocently sensual curiosity of a woodland nymph. The curve of her hip and thigh echoed the shape of the sun-dappled rock beneath her.

The second pose showed her sitting on the rock, knees drawn up to her chin. There was nothing explicit about the pose, although she was clearly nude. Asterley had obviously been more intrigued by the play of light and shadow on feminine skin than he was with titillating the viewer.

The third shot showed Serenity lying on her stomach, trailing her fingers in a stream. Once again there was an enthralling, earthy innocence about the picture as she gazed into the water. She was not just a woman lying on a rock beside a stream, she was Woman, a gentle goddess secure in the power of her femininity.

Caleb looked at the three pictures and knew that he had just been given a very rare and precious gift.

With a sense of reverence, he gathered the photos together. The beaded curtain clashed and shimmered as he pushed it aside. He laid Serenity's pictures on the bedside table and walked toward the bathroom.

The phone in the living room rang just as he started to open the bathroom door. Caleb hesitated, shrugged, and closed the door again. He scooped up his trousers from the floor where he'd tossed them sometime during the night and went into the front room of the cottage to answer the summons.

"Hello?"

"Caleb, for God's sake, is that you?" Franklin's voice was harsh, almost frantic on the other end of the line. "Your secretary gave me this number this morning. I've been trying to reach you since yesterday."

Caleb went cold. "What's wrong? Has something happened to my grandfather?"

"No, it's not that."

"Then what's the problem?" Something inside Caleb untwisted. *Roland was all right.* Someday, Caleb realized with a strange jolt, he would have to deal with the news of his grandfather's death. *But not today, thank God. Not today.*

He was startled by the force of his reaction. He never allowed himself to think too much about his feelings for the old man, beyond his anger.

"Caleb, I think you should know that yesterday afternoon I paid five thousand dollars for a set of pornographic pictures."

"That's a little steep for porn, Uncle Franklin. Sounds like you got ripped off."

"This is no joke," Franklin whispered in a hoarse, strangled voice. "I paid five thousand dollars to a blackmailer, do you hear me? Five thousand dollars. I got a call after you left Ventress Valley yesterday. I was told I had to come up with the money or photos of your new lady friend would be sent to the papers."

"Serenity?" For an instant Caleb didn't comprehend. Then it hit him. "Shit. Someone sent you the photos?"

"You know about these pictures?"

"Hell, yes."

"She's naked in them, Caleb. She posed nude for these pictures. They're obscene. This is Crystal Brooke all over again. *What have you done?*"

"Calm down, Franklin."

"The man threatened to send these pictures to the *Ventress Valley News.* Just like last time. So I paid him. I had to do it for the sake of the family."

"Calm down, Franklin."

"The family will be humiliated if this gets out. It's all your fault, damn you. In spite of everything Roland did for you, you've shamed him the same way your father did. You've followed in Gordon's footsteps. You've been seduced by a cheap tramp, and now we're all going to pay the price."

~ 11

SERENITY SURVEYED HER FEATURES IN THE STEAM-clouded mirror as she twisted her hair up into a knot on top of her head. She didn't look any different, she thought, astonished and amused. She anchored the curling mass of her hair with a large clip. Several tendrils escaped, but she paid no attention. She leaned over the sink and took a closer look at herself.

Nothing. Nada. Zip. Same old Serenity.

But she knew that she was not the same old Serenity. A glorious satisfaction bubbled up inside her. She had not been wrong about Caleb, after all. No man could have made love the way Caleb had made love last night unless he cared deeply.

She'd seen the truth in his eyes when she opened her door and found him on her front steps. At least she thought she had seen the truth. She had certainly seen something significant in his expression. He had the look of a man who'd had a revelation. The savage need in him had been coupled with another raw emotion so fierce and strong that it could only have been love.

That was why she'd taken the risk of letting him see the photographs. This morning she woke up with the certainty that now Caleb would understand. Now he could look at the pictures with an unbiased eye.

Serenity grinned as she turned away from the mirror. She felt as if she could fly or run a marathon or dance on top of one of the vision pools. No stunning feat seemed beyond her reach today.

She tugged on her robe, slid her feet into slippers, and opened the bathroom door. The sound of Caleb's voice coming from the living room startled her.

"I said I'll take care of it, Franklin."

It was the old Caleb speaking, the one Serenity had met in his Seattle office. Expressionless, detached, all emotion other than an icy, remote calm carefully hidden beneath a layer of steel.

"Don't do anything. Is that clear? Just sit tight. I'll handle this."

A cold wind blew away the warm mists of Serenity's euphoria. She listened as Caleb hung up the phone with far too much care. Her heart sank at the realization that something was terribly wrong. She thought of the photos she had left on the quilt and wondered if she had made a mistake.

Taking a deep breath, she tightened the sash of her robe and made herself go slowly down the hall. She walked into the living room and saw Caleb standing barefoot beside the phone. He had on only his trousers. His face was an emotionless mask.

"Caleb?"

"We've got a problem."

"What kind of problem?"

"I think it's safe to say that Ambrose Asterley was not the one who tried to blackmail you."

Whatever she'd been expecting to hear, that wasn't it. Serenity didn't know whether to be relieved or alarmed. "What are you talking about?"

"Yesterday afternoon, after we left Ventress Valley, Franklin got a call telling him there was a certain set of photos for sale. The caller wanted five thousand dollars for them."

Serenity's stomach plummeted down a very deep mine shaft. "I don't understand."

"No? It's pretty damn obvious to me. Someone you know has those negatives and has decided to use them. Not to get you to stop doing business with me this time, but to extort money out of my family."

"Oh, God." Serenity lowered herself slowly into the overstuffed armchair. She wrapped her arms around her midsection and hugged herself tightly. "I'm sorry. I'm so very sorry."

"Damn it, Serenity, what the hell is going on?" Caleb's voice was dangerously soft.

"I don't know. I wish I did." She looked up in desperate appeal. This was probably not the moment to ask him what he had really thought about those photos, but she couldn't stop herself. She had to know that she'd been right to risk showing them to him this morning. "You've seen those pictures. You don't think they're so very terrible, do you?"

"That's got nothing to do with this. Don't you understand? It doesn't matter what I think." He shoved his fingers through his hair and scowled. His mind was clearly on the latest disaster, not on reassuring her. "What matters is that someone contacted a member of my family knowing full well what would happen. Someone other than Asterley. It couldn't have been him this time because he's dead."

"I don't know what's going on," Serenity whispered. "I can only assume that someone here in Witt's End is violently opposed to my mail order project. Whoever it is must believe that if he can get you to quit as my consultant, my plans will be squelched."

"I think there's more to it than that," Caleb said slowly. "I think there has been all along. But I've been too involved with other things to take a good hard look at the situation."

"What are you saying?"

"Think about it, Serenity. The plain fact is those photos of you have very limited potential as a reason for blackmail."

"I couldn't agree more," she muttered. "I kept telling you they were artistic pictures, not dirty pictures."

"Yeah, well, I think it's safe to say that there are probably any number of families that would just as soon not have one of their own marry someone who had posed for nude photos of any kind."

"I suppose you're right. There are a lot of people out there who don't appreciate fine art."

He ignored that. "I've got a strong hunch, however, that there are relatively few families that would, to use your phrase, go completely bonkers over those photos the way the Ventress family is guaranteed to do." He paused. "The way my uncle is doing now."

Serenity frowned. "I think I'm beginning to see where you're going with this."

"Whoever has those negatives knows a great deal

about me and my family's past. And we now have to deal with the fact that the creep pulling this stunt is not Ambrose Asterley. So much for the theory that he got my name out of the newspapers."

"Perhaps someone found those negatives after Ambrose's death, just as we originally feared." Serenity shivered. "Or maybe the real reason the folder in Ambrose's files was empty except for a few prints is that someone else got there before I did."

"It's also possible that someone else got to them a long time before you went looking for them. Perhaps even before Ambrose died. Someone who knew about my family's past history with blackmail."

"Any way you look at it, it almost had to be someone here in Witt's End," Serenity whispered. "But I don't see how anyone here could know all of those things about your family, let alone actually do something like this. Ambrose was the only possibility."

"And he's dead." Caleb started to prowl the room. "Let's take this from the top. Fact number one: Everyone here in Witt's End knew you had posed for Asterley, right?"

"Yes, I suppose so. No one cared, but I suppose they all knew. It was no secret."

"Fact number two: Nothing happened until after you had met with me several times and had announced that you were going to sign a contract with me."

"Good point," Serenity said. "And don't forget that the first blackmail attempt didn't include a demand for money. The first demand was that I cancel my business arrangements with you."

"And now we have a second demand. This time for

cash. So maybe we've got two different blackmailers. The first one could have been Asterley, just as we concluded the first time we went through this exercise. In which case it looks as if his only goal was to put a halt to your plans."

"And a second blackmailer who knew what Ambrose was doing and who decided, after Ambrose died, that the photos could be used for more profitable purposes." Serenity winced. "Such as extorting money from your family."

Caleb crossed the room to the wood stove, opened the door and began to stoke the embers inside. "Two blackmailers. Both of whom knew about your photos, about your business contract with me, and about my past. One blackmailer apparently wanted only to stop the business arrangements. But the second wanted something more. Money."

"I suppose Ambrose could have told someone else about what he was doing." Serenity chewed thoughtfully on her lower lip. "But the only person he ever really confided in was Jessie. And I *know* Jessie would never try to blackmail anyone."

"Do you know that?" Caleb looked skeptical. "For certain?"

Serenity clasped her hands tightly in her lap. "Of course I do. I've known Jessie all of my life. She's family."

"Serenity, we don't know anything for sure about this mess." Caleb closed the iron door of the stove. "Including how Asterley died."

"What?" Serenity was stunned. "But that's not true. Ambrose got drunk, tripped and fell down his basement stairs."

"Did he?"

"Caleb, what are you saying? That someone might have pushed him?" Serenity was aghast. "But who would have done such a thing?"

"The second blackmailer. The one who wanted to use the photos for more lucrative purposes."

"Oh, no." Serenity shook her head wildly. "No, no, no. Murder? Here in Witt's End? Impossible. You've been spending too much time with Blade. This is starting to sound like one of his conspiracy theories."

"Some people might say Blade was a likely suspect as both blackmailer and murderer."

Serenity flinched. "Absolutely not. I refuse to believe it. Besides, he couldn't have known about your family's past."

"Asterley might have told him. Damn it, Serenity, you're too close to this situation to think logically. You're too emotionally involved."

"And you're not emotionally involved?" she asked, incredulous.

"No. At least not the way you are. I'm in control. I can view this situation much more objectively than you can."

Serenity leaped to her feet. "How can you say that after what happened between us last night?"

He glanced at her, surprised. "That has nothing to do with this."

"Nothing to do with it? It has everything to do with it. I can't believe I'm hearing this." She pointed toward the bedroom. "I was not alone in there last night."

"I'm aware of that."

"And it's your family that's being blackmailed." Serenity folded her arms beneath her breasts and regarded him with grim triumph. "Don't try to tell me you're not emotionally involved right up to your eyebrows."

"Damn it, I'm trying to take an intelligent, logical, pragmatic approach to this problem."

"So take it. But don't try to tell me you're not emotionally involved. And don't try to tell me that one of my friends is a murderer or a blackmailer. Because I refuse to believe it."

Caleb's mouth twisted derisively. "Have you ever met a blackmailer?"

"Well, no," Serenity admitted, annoyed by his condescending tone. "But somehow I think I'd know one if I saw one."

"Yeah? What would he look like?"

"Well, for starters, he'd be a weasely looking character with shifty eyes and very low self-esteem."

"This isn't a joke," Caleb said through set teeth. "Someone is deliberately trying to rake up my past, and that person is using you to do it. He or she may have killed Asterley in order to do it. I want to know what's going on here in quaint, picturesque Witt's End."

Serenity sighed. "I know you want answers. I want them, too."

"We're going to get them."

"How?"

"I think the first step is to take another look through Asterley's files," Caleb said. "Jessie hasn't moved them out of the cabin yet, has she?"

"No. She told me yesterday that she got the photo equipment out, but not the file cabinets. She doesn't have a place to store them. But what would we be looking for in those old files?"

"I'm not sure." The sound of a car in the drive made Caleb glance toward the window. "Who the hell is that at this hour of the morning?"

"I have no idea." Serenity turned and started for the door.

"Hold it." Caleb glowered at her. "What do you think you're doing? You're in your bathrobe."

Serenity glanced down at her attire. "For heaven's sake, I'm perfectly decent."

"No, you're not." His gaze raked her from the top of her tousled head to the toes of her slippered feet. For an instant the icy control vanished from his eyes. In its place was a searing glimpse of remembered passion. "You look like you just got out of bed."

Serenity burned beneath his gaze. She was suddenly breathless. "Not emotionally involved, huh?"

"Go get dressed," he growled. "I'll see who's at the door."

Serenity threw her hands up in the air. "Okay, okay. I'll go get dressed. Are you always like this in the mornings?"

"Only on days when I wake up to discover that someone's trying to blackmail a member of my family and that the lady I'm sleeping with has a habit of answering her front door dressed in her bathrobe."

"You know what your problem is, Caleb?"

"Yeah. I'm old-fashioned, straitlaced, boring, and conventional."

"Wrong on one count," Serenity said. "You're not boring. You're never boring." She hurried down the hall to the bedroom before he could respond.

Outside in the drive a car door slammed. The visitor knocked on the front door of the cottage just as

225

Serenity pulled on a close-fitting purple turtleneck and a pair of green leggings. Caleb's low-voiced greeting held a note of challenge.

"Can I help you?" The words were civil but his tone did not convey any great desire to be of assistance.

"Who the hell are you?" Lloyd Radburn asked, sounding startled.

Just what she needed this morning, Serenity thought as she hastily fastened a tie-dyed, jagged-hemmed skirt around her waist.

"Lloyd?" Serenity yelled down the hall. "Is that you?"

"Sure is, Serenity love," Lloyd called back. "Just thought I'd drop by and see how things were going. Wanted to go over a few of the details of my project with you."

Serenity groaned silently as she walked back down the hall to the living room. She took one look at Caleb's face and knew that things were going to be a bit dicey for the next few minutes. She turned to confront her uninvited guest.

"Hello, Lloyd. This is a surprise. I wasn't expecting you."

"Hey, hey, hey. Great to see you again, Serenity love." Lloyd smiled his engaging grin.

Serenity smiled back, albeit ruefully. Lloyd could be irritating, but it was difficult to get genuinely angry at him for long. He was self-absorbed and no doubt ambitious, but he wasn't cruel or malicious.

There was no denying that he had a certain rugged charm, which would probably stand him in good stead with generations of female undergraduates. He looked more like a dashing foreign correspondent than a professor of sociology. The leather jacket he wore over his khaki shirt had a well-worn look that had been induced by the designer, not by actual hard use in the field. It went well with his low, leather boots and artfully faded jeans. His light brown hair was cut in a windswept style that guaranteed that his forelock would fall rakishly over one dark eye. The hat he had tossed onto a brass hook in the hall was a suede and leather creation that looked as though it had been designed for adventuring in the Outback.

"You're looking terrific, Serenity love." Without any warning, Lloyd swooped down on her, grabbed her around the waist and swung her in a wide arc. "Know something? I've missed you."

"Please put me down, Lloyd."

"It's so damn good to see you again, love. How's my fairy princess?"

"Put her down." Caleb's voice was sharpened steel.

"Sure, sure, in a minute." Lloyd tried to plant a kiss somewhere in the vicinity of Serenity's mouth. He chuckled when she ducked. "Serenity and I are old friends. Isn't that right, love? Haven't seen each other in months."

"For heaven's sake, Lloyd, that's enough." Serenity braced her hands against his shoulders and shoved. "Let me go before I get airsick."

Lloyd roared with laughter and started to whirl her around in another circle.

Caleb's hand clamped down on his shoulder. "Put her down or you're going to swallow every tooth you own."

Lloyd came to an abrupt halt and set Serenity on her feet. He turned to Caleb with a belligerent scowl. "Who's this, Serenity? Some guy who thinks he's your big brother?"

"No," Caleb said very evenly. "I am not her brother."

"He's my consultant," Serenity said hastily. She reached up to refasten one of her hair clips which had come loose.

"Consultant?" Lloyd looked blank. He turned back to Serenity. "What kind of consultant?"

Serenity lifted her chin with grave dignity. "A business consultant. His name is Caleb Ventress. Caleb, this is Lloyd Radburn. He's a professor at Bullington College. I believe I mentioned him to you the other night when he phoned."

"You mentioned him." Caleb eyed Lloyd as if sizing him up for lunch.

Lloyd gave Serenity a disbelieving grin. "Hey, hey, hey, love. Who are you kidding? What the hell do you need with a business consultant? Having trouble counting beans down at the grocery store?"

"If you'll excuse me, I'm going to fix some tea."

"Got any coffee?" Lloyd asked irrepressibly. "I hate tea." He followed Serenity into the kitchen.

"Sorry, no. I don't drink coffee."

"Yeah, that's right. I forgot. Guess I'll settle for tea." Lloyd selected one of the small chairs at the table. He twirled it around, straddled it and rested his arms on the curved wooden back.

Caleb came to stand in the doorway. "Was there something specific you wanted, Radburn?"

Lloyd chuckled. "I just wanted to talk to Serenity."

Serenity filled the teakettle. "If it's about that idiotic idea you had to do a study of Witt's End, forget it, Lloyd. I told you, I'm not going to help you do it."

"Come on, hon. Give me a break." Lloyd's easy-going grin faded. "I told you the other night on the phone, this is important to me. I can get a great paper out of this. Witt's End is pure time warp. The newest incarnation of the classic American frontier town."

"Not quite," Serenity said.

"Sure it is. What's more, it's a perfect subject for me," Lloyd argued. "By rights this town shouldn't have been able to survive this long. Hell, it was founded by social misfits and outcasts and it's been populated with them ever since. You've got everything from ex-cultists to certifiable paranoids living here."

"You are talking about my friends and family," Serenity snapped. "Kindly watch your language."

"Come on, love. You studied this kind of stuff once. You know what I'm talking about. The social dynamics of this place are fascinating. Based on my initial observations six months ago, I've created a theory. Now I want to test that theory."

"What theory?"

"It has to do with the role of legends in small communities, especially small frontier communities. I think local myths are one of the forces that give the social structure substance and make the whole thing work. They unify a community. In a nutshell, my theory states that communities that don't have a few local myths have to invent them in order to survive."

"Sounds interesting," Serenity admitted.

"Sometimes the myths seem mundane, especially to outsiders," Lloyd said. "Just gossip about the neighbors in many cases. Who's sleeping with who. In the old days some of the local legends of a frontier community probably revolved around gunslingers and gamblers and gold strikes. The point is, the community needs those tales in one form or another to help give it cohesion."

Serenity nodded. "I see what you mean."

"Look, I promise I'll tell you all about it later. The thing is, I need your help. I can't do good fieldwork here without you. You know I won't be able to get decent interviews or participant observer responses unless you convince the natives to cooperate."

"Forget it," Serenity said.

"I can't forget it." Some of the upbeat tone went out of Lloyd's voice. It was replaced with grim determination. "I told you the other night, I need this project. I've got a lot riding on this, careerwise."

"Choose some other small town," Serenity said.

"But, Serenity love, Witt's End is unique. And as far as I can tell from the literature search that I did, no one else in the field has even discovered this place, let alone studied it."

Caleb raised one brow. "I think the natives, as you call them, like it that way."

"I'm not going to disturb their precious lifestyle," Lloyd insisted. "Hell, that's the last thing I want to do. But I need to get into the social circle, so to speak. This place functions almost like a tribe, as far as I can tell. That's what gave me the idea about the importance of the local legends."

Serenity glanced at him warily. "Just what local legends are you trying to analyze, Lloyd?"

"The one about the vision pools, or whatever you call them."

"What on earth are you talking about?" Serenity asked coolly.

"Come on, Serenity, don't play dumb with me. This is your old friend, Lloyd, remember?" He grinned. "You told me yourself about the hot springs that are hidden in a cave somewhere around here."

"I may have mentioned them. It's no secret that there are hot springs in this part of the mountains," Serenity said casually. "They've never been commercially developed, however. They're not easily accessible."

"But they're the stuff of local mysticism and legend, aren't they?" Lloyd insisted. "People claim to see visions in them."

"That's nonsense," Serenity said firmly. "I don't know anyone who's ever seen a real vision in the hot springs."

"Hell, I know that no one has ever seen a *real* vision." Lloyd waved that aside. "There is no such thing. The point is, the myth about the pools exists, and that makes them a very interesting element in the local social dynamic."

"Those pools don't have any impact at all on our social structure." Serenity opened a cupboard and took out three mugs. "Lloyd, please try to get this through your thick skull. I'm not going to help you turn Witt's End into a research subject."

"We can talk about it later," Lloyd said easily. He slanted a glance at Caleb and then frowned intently at Serenity. "Tell me again why you need a business consultant? I didn't catch it the first time."

"Probably because I didn't say." Serenity poured hot water over the leaves in the pot. "I'm going to expand my grocery into a mail order business. I think it will be very good for Witt's End. A lot of people here in town have something to market but no practical way of reaching consumers except through craft fairs. When Witt's End by Mail gets going, they'll be able to sell their products through my catalog."

"Are you serious?" Lloyd was clearly horrified.

"You're going to expand Witt's End Grocery into a catalog operation?"

Serenity looked at him. "Yes. That's why I hired Caleb. He specializes in consulting start-up operations."

"Shit." Lloyd stared at her. "It's absolutely out of the question. You can't do it, Serenity."

"I don't see why not," Caleb said from the doorway. "I'm going to help her, and I'm very good at what I do."

Lloyd threw him a disgusted glare. "She can't do it until I've finished my fieldwork here. Don't you understand? If Serenity introduces a major change into the local economy, it will significantly alter the existing social structure. All the basic institutions will change or be modified in some way. It's bound to happen."

"So what?" Caleb said. "It's called progress."

"So, I don't want anything changing here in Witt's End until I've finished my research," Lloyd howled. "How far have these plans gone?"

"We're almost through the initial planning and product evaluation stages." Caleb looked thoughtful. "I've selected the mailing lists. Catalog's going to press next month. I think you could say we're well on our way."

"Christ, you've got to stop right now." Lloyd shot to his feet and turned on Serenity. "You're going to ruin everything."

Serenity finished pouring tea and leaned back against the counter. "Lloyd, let's get something straight here. I've got plans, and I don't intend to put them on hold so that you can study my hometown like a bug on a pin. It would take you weeks, maybe months, to do your interviews and observations. And that's assuming you'd get cooperation from the residents, which you won't."

"I will if you help me," Lloyd said quickly. "They'll listen to you, Serenity. You're the key. I realized that six months ago. If you ask them to cooperate with me, they'll do it."

"But she isn't going to ask them to cooperate," Caleb said. "Are you, Serenity?"

"Nope. I've got more important things to do."

"Your mail order business project can't be more important than my research," Lloyd shouted. "I've got a career riding on this."

"And the financial security and well-being of a lot of people here in Witt's End is riding on my business plans," Serenity retorted. "Go find some other town to study, Lloyd."

"How can you act like this after all we meant to each other?"

Serenity eyed him, exasperated. "I think it's time for a reality check here, Lloyd. We weren't exactly close. You tried to turn me into one of your dippy research projects, and when I realized what you were doing, I told you to get lost. Now you've expanded your scope to include my entire hometown. I'm telling you the same thing now that I told you last time. Get lost."

"Damn it, I'm going to do this study, Serenity."

"Fine. Go ahead and do it. But don't expect me to help."

"I don't believe it. You can't do this to me. I'm going to find a way to get this paper written." Lloyd swung around on his heel and stalked toward the kitchen door.

Caleb politely got out of his way and stood watching impassively as Lloyd grabbed his Outback hat and slammed out of the cottage.

Serenity sipped her tea and listened to the car engine roar to life in the drive. She met Caleb's eyes. "Before we were so rudely interrupted, I believe you were saying something about going through Ambrose's files?"

"Yes, I believe I did bring up the idea." Caleb walked over to the counter and picked up a mug of hot tea. "Care to come along?"

"Wouldn't miss it for the world. When?"

"Tonight. Late."

"Why don't we just ask Jessie's permission to go through Ambrose's things at our leisure?"

"Because as far as I'm concerned, Jessie and everyone else in this town is a blackmail suspect until proven otherwise. But that's only one of the reasons why I don't want to tell anyone about our plans for another serious bout of breaking and entering."

"There's another reason?"

"Yes." Caleb looked at her, his eyes cold and intent. "Think about it logically, Serenity. If someone ever does conclude that Asterley's fall down those stairs was not an accident, guess who would instantly become one of the chief suspects?"

Serenity gave a start. Tea sloshed over the side of the cup, burning her fingers. "Me?"

"Yes. You."

"Oh, my God. I hadn't thought of that."

"You've got a prime motive. Asterley was trying to foil your plans to get rich in the mail order business."

Serenity's eyes widened. "No one would ever believe that. Not for a single moment."

"I'm not taking any chances. We're not telling anyone that we're going to search Asterley's files."

Serenity dropped down onto the chair that Lloyd had just vacated. She realized she was trembling. "This is a bit above and beyond the call of duty, partner."

"All part of the service, partner." Caleb leaned against the counter and cradled his mug in his hands. "I'd like to ask you something."

"What is it?"

"Did you tell Radburn that the legend about the vision pools was nonsense because you were trying to discourage him, or do you really think it is nonsense?"

"Don't be ridiculous," Serenity said. "Of course it's nonsense. Can you imagine any reasonable, intelligent person actually believing that it was possible to have visions in a hot springs pool? Get real."

Serenity finally decided to say something after Zone lost her grip on the sack of pinto beans and sent the contents skittering across the floor. It was the third minor accident Zone had had that morning.

"Zone, are you all right?"

"I'm fine." Zone went behind the counter to fetch a broom. She didn't meet Serenity's questioning eyes. "Just a little clumsy for some reason."

"You're sure?"

"I'm sure."

"You seem a little tense," Serenity said.

"I am not tense," Zone snapped in a very un-Zonelike fashion. She wielded the broom with such force that she managed to knock a carton of rye crackers off a bottom shelf. Beans shot in a variety of directions. Most of them missed the dust bin.

Serenity thoughtfully studied her assistant. Zone had never lost her temper in the four months that she had worked at Witt's End Grocery. Something was very wrong, but good manners as defined in Witt's End inhibited Serenity from pushing the subject.

"All right," Serenity said gently. "I didn't mean to pry. I think I'm the one who's tense. Maybe I'm projecting my mood onto you."

Zone looked up from her sweeping. She searched Serenity's face. "Why are you tense?"

Serenity shuffled a stack of papers. "No particular reason. I was just thinking about all the stuff that I have to do before I can get this mail order business going."

Like prowl through Ambrose's files in the dead of night.

Like hope against hope that the man I love won't turn on me because I'm putting his family through a second generation of blackmail.

Like wonder who among the people I know and trust here in Witt's End hates me.

"It's going to work, Serenity. I know it is."

"I hope so." Serenity smiled briefly. "I thought you were the one predicting danger, turmoil, and confusion."

"I was. I still am." Zone folded both hands on the handle of the broom. The long orange-and-saffron-colored sleeves of her robe drifted down like giant wings. Her eyelashes and brows were a sharp contrast to her shaved head. "But I'm no longer certain of the cause. I assumed at first that it was associated with Caleb, but now I'm wondering if there's someone or something else involved."

"Something else?"

Zone's eyes were troubled. "Serenity, do you mind if I ask you a question?"

"No."

"You've lived here all of your life. Do you believe in the vision pools?"

Serenity stared at her. Then she laughed. "You're the second person to ask me that this morning. Are you serious?"

"Yes."

"Well, you'd know more about visions than I would," Serenity said easily. "I'm just an ordinary, run-of-the-mill shopkeeper. I'm not really into vortices of power and vision pools."

"So you don't believe in them?"

"I'll tell you something, Zone, when I was a teenager I spent several nights in the caves, hoping against hope for a vision. I got nothing, not even a preview of what I'd be getting for my birthday. I tried the experiment once more a year ago, after a friend of mine named Stewart Bartlett left town. I was feeling alone and a little depressed at the time."

"What happened?"

Serenity chuckled. "I guess you could call it a wrong number."

"You actually saw something?"

"I dozed off and my imagination cooked up a little dream for me," Serenity admitted. "But it made no sense. And it was kind of screwed up. It was just a dream."

"You're sure?"

"Positive." Serenity was very concerned now. "Something is wrong, isn't it, Zone? If you decide that you want to talk about it, you know you can trust me."

"I know." Zone clenched her fingers around the broom. "You've been very good to me, Serenity. I don't know what would have become of me if you hadn't given me this job. Four months ago I was truly at my wit's end."

Serenity smiled. "It works both ways, you know. You're very important to me. You're the only person in Witt's End who has a firm grasp on the concept of regular working hours."

"That's probably because I worked regular hours for years until I moved to Witt's End."

Serenity glanced at the ring in Zone's nose. "Hard to imagine you in a conventional job."

"Graphic design isn't exactly a conventional job. Still, I have to admit that I didn't wear a ring in my nose then. And I wore suits instead of these robes. And I was engaged to a stockbroker."

"A stockbroker? I can't see you with a stockbroker. What happened?"

"I realized one day that I was unhappy. I went looking for something else. I started down my own, personal path to enlightenment. It led me here to Witt's End."

"Well, I for one am grateful."

"So am I." Zone went back to sweeping beans. "I've been happy here. I've felt safe."

"Safe?"

"Until this past week," Zone whispered. Without any warning her face crumpled. She started to cry. She dropped the broom and gazed helplessly at Serenity through a veil of tears.

"Zone." Serenity hurried out from behind the counter. She dashed down the aisle, put her arms around her assistant and hugged her close. "What's wrong?"

"I'm so scared, Serenity." Zone wiped her eyes with

the edge of one long saffron sleeve. "I don't know if I'm going out of my mind or if he's really here."

"Who are you talking about?"

"My ex-fiancé." Zone's shoulders shook as she leaned against Serenity. "I saw him last night. At least I think I did. He was outside my cabin staring in at me through the window."

"What happened?"

"I screamed and pulled the curtains. Then I ran through the house checking all the locks. But nothing happened. There was no knock on the door. The phone didn't ring. I felt like a fool, but I spent the night huddled in the closet with the pistol I brought with me from L.A."

"Good grief. How awful. You should have called someone."

"I know it sounds stupid, but I was afraid to leave the closet until dawn. This morning I told myself I'd imagined everything. I made myself go outside. There was no sign of him. Not even a footprint under the window where I thought I saw him."

"It rained last night," Serenity reminded her.

"I know, but I started to wonder if I'd had another terrible vision. I was so careful when I left. He can't possibly know where I am."

"Who?"

"Royce Kincaid. I was so frightened of him. Everyone thought he was such a wonderful catch. The perfect man, they all said. Handsome, successful, intelligent, well-mannered. Perfect. Too perfect. He's a monster, Serenity."

"Did he hurt you?"

Zone nodded and wiped her eyes again. "It started

right after I moved in with him, and it got worse very quickly. He wouldn't let me out of his sight except when I was at work. He accused me of having affairs. He got enraged if I went shopping with some of my friends. He wouldn't let anyone come to see me. I had no family to call, no one to help me."

"What did you do?"

"I packed my bags one day and managed to escape. I went back to my old apartment. He showed up at the door and threatened to kill me. Told me I'd be sorry for leaving him. I believed him, so I ran." Zone dashed tears from her eyes. "I've been running for nearly a year. When I found Witt's End, I thought everything would be all right."

"But you saw him last night?"

"I thought it was him," Zone whispered brokenly. "But now I'm not so certain. This is the second time it's happened."

"When was the first time?"

"The night Ambrose died. I was meditating at the window, letting myself drift with the fog, really becoming one with it. There was a lot of fog that night."

"I remember."

"I thought I saw a glow of light in the mist. Then I could have sworn I saw the silhouette of a man moving through the trees in front of my cottage. I told myself it couldn't be Royce, but I knew it wasn't Blade, either. Something about the shape of him. He wasn't big enough."

"Did you see his face?"

"No. He was all bundled up in a heavy, hooded coat. Before I could decide if I was imagining things, the glow disappeared and so did the man."

"The glow could have been a flashlight reflecting off the fog." An unpleasant chill uncurled within Serenity. "Why didn't you say anything the next day?"

"Because I wasn't even sure if I had actually seen anything." Zone blinked back more tears. "I was in a trance. I thought maybe my imagination had run wild. Ariadne took me to see the vision pools a few weeks ago. She warned me that sometimes you don't always see what you want to see in them."

"Did you have a vision in the caves?"

Zone shook her head quickly. "No. For some reason, I didn't want to even attempt to have a vision there. But this morning I started wondering if maybe the power of the pools extends beyond the caves."

"I think I understand," Serenity said quietly. "You're wondering if you had a pool-induced vision last night, is that it?"

"Maybe the lines of force from the hot springs affect this whole area," Zone said hopefully. "Maybe one can have visions outside the caves."

"No one," Serenity stated categorically, "has ever reported having a vision outside the caves. And I, for one, am extremely skeptical about all tales of visions inside the caves."

"You are?"

"Absolutely. That nonsense about the pools is nothing but an old myth that dates from the very first days of Witt's End. With no disrespect intended toward our illustrious founding fathers, I suspect that on occasion some of them smoked something other than tobacco in those caves."

"If I didn't have a vision, then there are only two other possible explanations." Zone's voice was thin and listless. "The first is that I'm going crazy. The second is that I really did see Royce."

"The third possibility is that you simply have an active imagination, which is only to be expected in a graphic artist," Serenity said.

"I wish I knew what was happening to me."

"One thing's for certain. You can't spend tonight alone. You'll be a nervous wreck." Serenity was about to invite Zone to stay with her when she recalled the unorthodox plans Caleb had made for the evening. It would be difficult to explain to a houseguest why the hostess had to disappear for a couple of hours around midnight. "Let me think."

"I've got the pistol," Zone whispered. "I'll be all right."

"Cold company. You need some human companionship tonight." The door chimes sounded merrily. Serenity glanced toward the door as it opened.

"Serenity?" Ariadne called. "Where are you?"

"Aisle three. Crackers and dried fruit." Serenity stepped into view, one arm still draped protectively around Zone's drooping shoulders. "I'm glad to see you, Ariadne. Zone, here, needs a favor."

"Sure." Ariadne smiled her earth mother smile. "What's up?"

By eleven-thirty that night, Caleb was having second thoughts about taking Serenity with him on the expedition to search Asterley's files.

He'd had such thoughts all day long, but there was no denying they seemed louder and considerably more forceful now that it was time to leave. He'd gone over the logistics of the thing a dozen times since this morning, and he still could not envision any serious risk.

It was highly unlikely that he and Serenity would be seen entering or leaving Asterley's cabin. The fog was back tonight. It would provide a welcome cover from prying eyes.

Welcome cover? Prying Eyes? Searching a dead man's files?

What the hell was going on here? Caleb wondered. Until recently he wasn't the kind of man who got involved in this sort of situation. He didn't accept small-time consulting projects involving tiny grocery stores, either. Nor did he sit around in hot tubs. Or spend the night in a cave. He didn't experience visions while gazing into hot springs pools. And he never, ever made love to women who were potential blackmail targets.

His whole life had been turned upside down lately. He didn't understand how it had happened, but he had a strong hunch that it was far too late to do a 180-degree turn and reverse course.

Furthermore, he had no particular desire to go back to his old life. Things were a little wacky at times in Witt's End, but for some reason he felt good here. He felt as if he had come to the right place.

Caleb reached for the flashlight on the shelf near Serenity's front door. He accidentally caught sight of his own reflection in the mirror. Automatically he started to look away and then he stopped. He could see himself quite clearly in the mirror. His reflection was sharp and clear.

"Caleb?" Serenity fastened her fringed and beaded jacket as she walked into the living room. "I'm ready." She pulled the hood up over her wild, red mane. Got the flashlight?"

"I've got it." He looked at her and knew for certain there was no going back to the man he had once been. "Let's do it."

He opened the door and discovered cold fog swirling on the front steps.

"It's not too bad yet," Serenity observed as she stepped past him. "But I think it's going to get worse. We'd better hurry."

"I don't want to use the flashlight if we can avoid it." Caleb closed the door behind him.

"We won't need it. There's enough moonlight. Besides, I've lived here all my life, remember? I'd know my way around Witt's End blindfolded."

"I'm certainly glad that one of us knows where we're going," Caleb said under his breath. He pulled his collar up against the cold as he followed Serenity down the steps.

For some reason the night reminded him of one long ago, a night from his childhood. The memory of it came back with startling clarity. He had been eleven years old. His grandfather had awakened him to tell him that one of the mares was going to foal and there were complications. Caleb had scrambled out of bed, pulled on his jeans and a sweat shirt, and followed Roland out into the frigid, foggy night.

The mare had, indeed, experienced difficulties. Caleb was afraid that they would lose both her and the foal. But Roland had given calm, clear instructions, and Caleb followed them precisely. Together he and his grandfather had saved the mare and her tiny offspring.

Now, as he walked through the fog beside Serenity, Caleb had a fleeting memory of what he'd felt that night as he stood beside Roland and watched the small foal stagger upright on wobbly legs.

He recalled the sense of relief he had experienced, but most of all he remembered the short-lived sensation of sharing the moment with his grandfather. It was one of the rare times when Roland had seemed genuinely pleased with him. He had grinned and ruffled Caleb's hair with his big, work-worn hand.

"We did it, son. You want to name him?"

"Windstar," Caleb said.

"Windstar it is," Roland agreed. "He's going to be a fine stud. Good blood in him. The best."

Caleb shook off the old memories as Serenity spoke softly beside him.

"I just thought of something," she said. "Jessie told me she locked up Ambrose's cabin. The real estate agent in Bullington has the key. How are we going to get inside?"

"I doubt if that will be much of a problem. No one here in Witt's End seems to be very security conscious. I haven't seen a decent lock on any door yet. Worst possible case is that we'll have to jimmy a window."

Serenity gave him an odd look. "You sound like you've done this kind of thing before."

"I haven't, but I'm a fast learner." In spite of the seriousness of the situation, Caleb was starting to feel an exhilarating sense of excitement. *I'm having an adventure.* He smiled to himself.

"Caleb? Is something wrong?"

"Probably. But I'm not going to worry about it right now." When this was over he was going to make love

246

to Serenity, he thought. The adrenaline flowed like wine through his veins.

"What will we do if we don't find anything useful in Ambrose's files?"

Her question sobered him instantly. "I'm not sure. After we've searched Asterley's records, I'll talk to Franklin. I need to find out everything I can about how he was contacted and what arrangements were made for the payoffs. Maybe we'll get some clues from that."

"I still can't believe that anyone here in Witt's End is involved."

"I don't see how the blackmailer could be anyone except someone from Witt's End," Caleb said. "And after what you told me about Zone's predicament, you'll have to admit that there are a lot of things you don't know about your friends and neighbors."

"You've got a point, I guess." Serenity huddled deeper into the hood of her jacket. "But I've known most of them a lot longer than I've known Zone. She's a newcomer."

"Just because you've known someone a long time doesn't mean you know all their secrets."

"No." She fell silent beside him.

Ten minutes later the darkened bulk of the Asterley cabin materialized in the thickening fog. The trees around it loomed like specters keeping watch at an open grave. Caleb almost groaned aloud. *I'll be damned. I'm developing a vivid imagination.*

He had never allowed himself to be the imaginative type except when it came to business. Outside of business, imagination was a dangerous thing. It fed on emotion.

"Something about this house gives me the creeps

now," Serenity whispered as she studied the cabin. "Every time I come here, I remember finding Ambrose's body at the foot of those basement stairs."

"I'm not surprised. That kind of memory tends to stick with you."

Caleb led the way around to the back porch. He climbed the steps and tried the door. The knob did not turn.

"Is it locked?" Serenity asked softly.

"Yeah." Caleb moved along the porch to the nearest window. He pushed tentatively and felt it give. "Looks like Jessie didn't bother to check the windows when she closed the place."

"Maybe she forgot."

"Either that or the lock is broken." Caleb shoved the window open. A musty smell assailed his nostrils. "It's pretty stale in there."

"I'm not surprised." Serenity watched anxiously as he slipped into the dark interior of the kitchen.

"Okay, your turn." Caleb reached out to help her.

Serenity scrambled over the sill and peered around. "I can't see a thing."

"We'll have to find our way to the basement stairs by touch. I don't want to use the flashlight while we're inside this place. Someone might notice."

"This way, I think." Serenity took a few tentative steps into the inky shadows.

Caleb ran his fingers along the bottom of the window before he followed her. "I was right about the lock. It's broken."

"Probably has been for years. Ambrose was never what you'd call a handyman. Ooooph."

"What's wrong?"

"I've found the basement door. Just walked into it. Good thing it's closed."

"For God's sake be careful. I don't want you taking a header down those stairs."

"Don't worry. Ah, here we go."

The squeak of old hinges told Caleb that Serenity had the door open. He moved toward the sound. His eyes were adjusting to the deeper darkness of the cabin now. He could make out Serenity's shape near the basement entrance. "As I recall, there's a handrail on the left."

"I know. I've already got one hand on it."

Caleb found the rail and the first step. He reached back to pull the door shut. Then he found the light switch on the wall and snapped it on. The stark glow of the bare ceiling bulb lit the room with a gloomy light.

"That's better." Serenity paused briefly on the step below Caleb and then started down into the basement.

Caleb followed. "You said that he filed by date, and within that, by name. We'll start with the most recent years and work back."

"What are we looking for?"

"I don't know. Anything that doesn't look right," Caleb said. He pulled open the first drawer.

Her spirits had been high when they began their venture, but thirty minutes and three drawers later, Serenity was losing hope. She was in the middle of a drawer marked P, and thus far had found nothing unusual.

"These files are incredible," Caleb said as he

opened a drawer marked "T thru V." "I'm starting to change my mind about Asterley. Not only was he a hell of a photographer, he knew how to keep decent files. Do you realize how rare good record keeping is? I can't tell you how many businesses I've seen get into trouble because of lousy filing systems."

Serenity froze. "What did you say?"

"I said Asterley kept excellent records." Caleb frowned intently as he peered into an open file.

"Not that." Serenity was so elated that she lost her place in the row of manila folders. The only examples of Ambrose's work that Caleb had ever seen were the photos that had been taken of her. "What did you mean when you said that he was a hell of a good photographer?"

Caleb didn't look up from his methodical examination of the files. "Judging by those shots he took of you he . . . Damn."

"What's wrong? What did you find?" Serenity glanced over his shoulder.

"I should have started with this drawer. I guess it just seemed too obvious."

Serenity stared at the folder in his hand. The name Ventress was written on the tab. "Uh-oh."

"That sort of sums it up, doesn't it?"

"Ventress isn't a very common name, is it?"

"No." Caleb jerked the folder out of the file and opened it wide. He stared down at the single item filed inside. "Damn it to hell."

"It's a record of sale," Serenity whispered.

"For a set of photos to Franklin Ventress. For the sum of five thousand dollars."

"Good lord." Serenity angled her head to get a better view. "What's the date?"

"The twentieth of October." Caleb glanced at her, his eyes hard. "Just a couple of days before you came to my office to sign that contract and casually mentioned in passing that you were being blackmailed."

"I wasn't casual about it," Serenity said defensively. "I just didn't think it was such a big deal at the time. How was I to know you'd fall out of your tree when you got the news?"

"Let's not start that argument again." Caleb closed the folder. "Come on. We're getting out of here." He shut the drawer and headed toward the stairs.

"Suits me." Serenity slammed her file drawer closed and hurried after him.

At the top of the stairs, Caleb hit the light switch, plunging the basement back into darkness. He opened the door and urged Serenity out into the heavily shadowed kitchen.

She found the way to the open window by touch. When she reached it, Caleb's hands closed around her waist. He hoisted her up and sat her on the sill.

Serenity swung her legs over the edge and landed on the back porch. She brushed her hair out of her eyes and adjusted her hood up over her head as Caleb climbed out through the window. He tucked the file folder inside his jacket and reached for her hand.

"Let's go," he said.

Serenity didn't need any encouragement. She hurried along beside him as they made their way down the steps and into the moonlit fog.

"I don't understand any of this," Serenity said. "Why would there be a record of sale to your uncle that dates back to the twentieth? I thought he told you that he received those photos the day before yesterday."

"Yes." The single word was as sharp and savage as a razor. "That's what he told me."

"But I was the one who got blackmailed first," Serenity continued. It was difficult to think clearly because Caleb was forcing the pace. She was getting breathless. "I received copies of the photos and the threat at the hotel on the morning of the twenty-third. If Franklin had already bought the photos from Ambrose, who sent copies to me?"

"Good question. One of many I intend to ask Franklin."

"You think he's had them all along? But that doesn't make any sense, Caleb."

"I think it does," he said roughly.

"This is no time to go mysterious and enigmatic," Serenity grumbled. "You're not Sherlock Holmes and I'm no Dr. Watson. I want some answers, Caleb."

"So do I. And I'm going to get them."

Serenity abruptly realized that he was furious. The anger in him was all the more dangerous because it was so tightly controlled. She had never seen him like this, not even on the day when she had told him that someone was trying to blackmail her with a set of nude photos.

"Uh, Caleb, I think maybe we should talk about this before you do anything rash."

"Later."

"Sure. Later," Serenity said agreeably. "When we get back to my place, I'll make us a nice cup of tea and we can sit down and discuss this whole thing very carefully before you pick up the phone and call your uncle."

Caleb did not bother to respond. Serenity risked a

sidelong glance, trying to see his expression. It was impossible.

She was contemplating a variety of soothing remarks when a dark, predatory-looking shadow materialized out of the fog directly in front of her. She stifled a small shriek as Caleb drew them both to a sudden halt.

Blade stepped out of the trees, the rottweilers at his heels. "Thought I heard you two," he said so softly the words were almost inaudible.

"We're just out for an evening stroll," Caleb said quietly. "What the hell is your excuse?"

"We got a problem, Ventress," Blade said. "You want to give me a hand?"

"Problem?" Serenity realized she was automatically following Blade's lead and keeping her own voice down. "What kind of problem?"

Blade looked at her. "Don't know how close he is. Probably best to take you home first, then go after him."

"Go after who?" Serenity demanded in a fierce whisper. "If this has anything to do with the big invasion, I vote we postpone the counterattack until tomorrow. It's getting very late."

"We're in a hurry here, Blade," Caleb said impatiently. "What's this all about?"

"I increased the patrols around Zone's place," Blade said. "Heard she was so nervous she was spendin' the night with Adriadne. Just came from my last check. Someone broke in through the window. Trashed the place."

"Oh, my God," Serenity whispered. "Maybe she did see him after all. Maybe he's come after her."

"Who?" Caleb demanded.

"The man she told me about this morning. Her ex-fiancé, Royce Kincaid. She said she was terribly afraid of him. He's one of the reasons she came here to Witt's End. Today she told me she was afraid she'd seen him at her window last night. She told herself it was just her imagination, but she was so scared, Ariadne invited her to spend the night at her place."

"Hell," said Caleb. "If it isn't one thing, it's another." He took her arm and started through the trees. "Let's get Serenity home, Blade. Then we'll go take a look at Zone's cabin."

"Right." Blade turned to lead the way. Styx and Charon moved off on silent paws. The dogs had a distinctly businesslike air about them tonight.

"I'll come with you to Zone's place," Serenity said.

"No, you will not," Caleb said. "I want you where I know you'll be safe and sound. I'm going to have enough to worry about as it is."

"You mean because you're going after a prowler?"

"No, because I'm going to spend what's left of tonight running around out here in the fog with a crazy conspiracy buff who's armed to the teeth."

"Told you before, I ain't crazy," Blade said without any show of annoyance.

"I know you did. I forgot."

Serenity saw the glow of her porch light in the distance. "I'd rather come with you, Caleb."

"It makes a hell of a lot more sense for you to go into the house, pick up the phone, and call Ariadne and Zone. Warn them that there's a possibility of trouble, got that? Make sure they check all the doors and windows."

"Yes, of course." Serenity instantly saw the sensibleness of that suggestion. "Zone has a gun."

"Tell her to barricade herself in a room with Ariadne and her gun. Tell them to stay there until they get the all-clear from one of us. Tell them not to answer the door for any reason. Then start calling everyone else in town. Make sure they're awake and alert."

"I understand."

"Fine." Caleb halted at the bottom of the porch steps. He pulled Serenity close and kissed her with rough urgency. Then he handed her the folder he had taken from Ambrose's files. "Go."

Serenity hurried up the steps. Caleb, Blade, and the dogs waited until she went inside the cottage and closed the door.

She threw back the hood of her jacket and crossed the living room to the phone. She had her hand on the receiver when the silk scarf came from out of nowhere. It looped around her throat before she even realized what was happening. In the next instant it was jerked taut, cutting off her voice, threatening to cut off her breath.

"Not a sound, bitch. Not one, single sound. Or you die."

13

FOR A SHATTERING MOMENT PANIC NEARLY OVER-
whelmed her. Serenity's hand fell away from the
phone. She could feel the scarf circling her throat like
a garrote, but so far it was only a threat. She could still
breathe, still swallow. Barely.

"Who are you?" she whispered. "What do you
want?"

"Never mind that." The intruder's voice sounded
as if it were being filtered through a potato grater.
Everything came out shredded. "Where is she?"

"I don't know who you're talking about." Serenity
remembered the self-defense lessons she had been
taught. Her instructor's words came back to her, just
as if he were standing beside her.

*It all happens first in your head. If you let the fear
and panic take control, it's all over. You're dead meat.
You got to step into another place where you can think
clearly. Just do it.*

"Marion." An uncontrolled rage throbbed deep in the man's voice. "Where is she? Tonight is the night. I'm going to teach her she can't ever leave me. Where is she?"

"I don't know anyone named Marion." Serenity's hand crept up to her throat.

"She calls herself some crazy name now. Zone or something. And don't tell me you don't know where she is. I traced her here. She works for you. Last night I let her see me. Knew it would scare her. Make her think she was going crazy."

"You're Royce Kincaid, aren't you?"

"She told you about me?" He sounded pleased.

"Yes. Said you were mentally ill."

"I'm not sick, damn you," Kincaid hissed. "I'm only doing what I have to do. It's her fault. She made me to this."

"Is that so? She has that much power over you? Are you so weak?"

"Shut up," Kincaid hissed. *"Shut up.* I'm not weak, damn you. And I'm going to prove it."

"She isn't here."

"I know that, bitch. I've already searched the place. I came here after I left her cabin. I thought you might be the one who was hiding her. Where is she?"

"I don't know." Serenity managed to touch the chain at her throat where it dangled beneath the rope of silk. She could feel the shape of the griffin against her skin.

"You know where she is. A small town like this, everyone knows what's going on. Tell me where she is or I'll choke the life out of you." Kincaid tightened the scarf.

Step into another place where you can think clearly.

"Hang on, this really isn't any of my business," Serenity whispered. "This is between the two of you."

"Yes, it is between the two of us. You should never have gotten involved."

"Look, if you'll promise to get out of here right now, I'll tell you where she's hiding."

"Where is she?" Kincaid drew the scarf a little tighter.

"There's a path," Serenity gasped. "It starts behind this cabin and goes up through the forest. You can't miss it if you use a flashlight. Just keep going uphill. There's a special place up there. A safe place."

"There is no safe place for Marion," the man crooned triumphantly. "Or for you, bitch. You tried to help her, didn't you? I'll bet you're the one who talked her into hiding from me."

"Let me go." Serenity had the griffin in her hand.

"I don't think so, bitch. I've got to teach you a lesson, too." He twisted his hands more firmly around the ends of the scarf.

In a situation like that, you only get one chance. Do it right. Don't pull your punches. Go for the eyes, if you can. Even if you miss, you'll make him lose his concentration for a few seconds.

Serenity jerked the griffin hard. The delicate chain snapped, leaving the pendant in her hand. She took a quick step backward and came up hard against Kincaid's body. He grunted in surprise.

Before he could recover, Serenity reached up behind her head and clawed wildly at his face with the metal griffin. She felt the sharp edge of one wing rip soft skin. She raked downward with all her strength.

Kincaid gave a muffled yelp of pain and anger. His

grip on the scarf slackened for an instant as he tried to jerk his face out of reach.

It was all the time Serenity needed. She whirled around and lashed out at his left kneecap with the heel of her right foot.

Kincaid yelped and fell backward, scrabbling for his balance. Serenity knew better than to wait around to see if he was out of commission. *You don't want to get stupid about things at that point. First chance you get, you run.*

Serenity leaped for the door. Behind her a stack of books tumbled off a table and hit the floor as Kincaid staggered to his feet.

"Goddamn you, bitch. I'll kill you. And then I'll kill her."

Serenity got the front door open. *"Caleb!"* she screamed. She dashed across the porch, down the steps and into the fog. *"Blade!* He's here!"

She was aware that Kincaid was not pursuing her, but she didn't stop running. She kept going, straight into the mist.

"Caleb? Where are you? Hurry. Please, hurry."

The dogs found her first. Blinded by the darkness and the fog, Serenity stumbled over Styx before she realized he was directly in front of her. She fell. Styx stood over her and nuzzled her face. Charon came up and looked down at her with obvious canine concern.

"Serenity?" Caleb's voice was fierce. A beam of light sliced through the fog. "Where the hell are you?"

"Over here." She gently pushed Styx and Charon aside and got to her feet. She was trembling.

"Are you all right?" Caleb strode swiftly toward her through the mist, an eerie, faceless figure in the reflected glow cast by the flashlight and the moon.

Serenity ran forward and threw herself into his arms. "I was so scared," she said into his coat. "I've never been so scared in my life."

"What happened?" His arms closed protectively around her.

"He was there, inside the cottage, waiting for me."

"Kincaid?"

"Yes."

His arms tightened around her. "The bastard."

"He tried to kill me. He put a scarf around my neck."

"Jesus," Caleb groaned.

"I got away." Serenity raised her head so quickly she collided with Caleb's jaw. "We've got to find him. I didn't get a chance to warn Zone and Ariadne. *We've got to find him.*"

"We will." Caleb's voice suddenly lacked any trace of emotion.

"Where's Blade?" Serenity glanced around anxiously.

"Right here." Blade's dark bulk appeared between two trees. "I heard what you said. The infiltrator went to your place, huh? Shit. Should of thought of that possibility. You okay?"

"Yes." Serenity realized that her fingers were still clenched around the griffin. Its wings were digging into her palm. "He was trying to choke me from behind. I went for his eye with my necklace. When he let go for a second, I used a flying kick on his kneecap. He went down and I ran."

"Thatagirl" Blade said with unmistakable satisfaction and pride. "Knew you could do it."

"Where the hell did you learn to fight like that?" Caleb asked.

"I taught her," Blade said.

Caleb looked at him. "You did."

"Sure."

"I owe you."

"You don't owe me a damn thing," Blade said. "Serenity's family. Everyone in the family had a hand in raisin' her. We all taught her something."

"I think we'd better discuss this later," Serenity interrupted. "I don't know if Kincaid is still in the house. I also don't know if he's armed. I didn't see a gun, but that doesn't mean he doesn't have one."

"No, it sure don't," Blade said. "First thing we got to do is see if he's still in the cottage." He pulled a small pistol from his web belt and glanced at Caleb. "Meant to ask earlier if you could handle one of these."

Caleb glanced at the pistol. "Yes." He reached out and took the gun from Blade's hand.

Serenity had a sudden recollection of the marksmanship medals she had seen in the glass-fronted cabinet in the Ventress house. A new kind of fear swept through her. "Caleb, please, I don't know—"

"Let's go." Blade motioned to the dogs. Styx and Charon instantly gave him their full attention. He switched off the flashlight and moved silently away through the trees. The dogs fanned out on either side of him.

Caleb turned off his own flashlight and dropped it into his coat pocket. He touched Serenity's cheek with his gloved hand. His face was unreadable in the darkness, but his voice was still curiously even. "Follow us but stay behind me until we find out what's happening."

Serenity nodded, then realized he probably couldn't

see the motion of her head. "All right. Caleb, promise me you'll be careful. Kincaid is mentally unbalanced."

"Believe it or not, I had already figured that out for myself."

Serenity followed Caleb and Blade through the trees to the edge of the clearing that marked her driveway. In the glow of the porch light she could see that the front door was still open, just as she had left it.

Blade gave a signal to the dogs. Styx and Charon bounded forward, sleek and lethal shadows in the fog. Serenity held her breath as the beasts went up the steps and into the cottage.

There was no sound for a few minutes. Then Styx appeared in the doorway. Charon was right behind him. The dogs came back down the steps and trotted across the driveway to where Blade waited in the trees.

"Looks like it's all clear," Blade said. "Bastard's gone."

"He didn't come out this way," Caleb said. "The dogs would have noticed. Must have gone out the back door."

"The caves," Serenity whispered.

Blade and Caleb exchanged glances. Then they both looked at her.

"Why would he go to the caves?" Blade asked.

Serenity stuffed her hands into her pockets. "Because I told him that was where Zone was hiding. Maybe he actually believed me. The man is crazy."

"If he went up that path," Blade said, "we've got him cornered. There's no way down except the way he went up. Unless he goes over a cliff. Let's check it out, Ventress."

"Serenity will have to come with us," Caleb said.

"I'm not taking the chance of leaving her alone in the cottage again."

"Right." Blade glanced at Charon and Styx, who were poised to receive his orders. He said something very quietly to them.

Again the dogs fell in on either side of him. Blade moved off to circle the cottage.

"I don't like this, but I don't see any help for it," Caleb muttered to Serenity. "You stay between Blade and me."

"I'm not going to dash off ahead and play hero, if that's what's worrying you," she retorted. "I've already had enough excitement tonight to last me a lifetime."

"You and me both. When I get my hands on this jerk, I'm going to—"

Blade's voice floated back through the shadows. "Quiet."

Caleb fell silent, but Serenity could feel the simmering rage in him.

Blade used the lights from the cottage to find the path. The moonglow reflecting off the fog provided sufficient illumination to guide the small party up into the woods. They climbed the path in single file with the dogs leading the way.

The tension was thicker than the mist. It seemed to Serenity that the night was imbued with a malevolent quality. The glowing fog creating an alien atmosphere that made the familiar forest appear strange and unnatural. She found herself starting at every small night sound. She took comfort in the knowledge that the dogs would give advance warning of Kincaid's presence.

At the top of the trail, Blade abruptly put out a

hand. Intent on finding her footing, Serenity didn't realize he had halted. She bumped into him. Caleb caught her arm to steady her.

She looked up and saw that both Blade and Caleb were watching the rottweilers. Charon and Styx were standing, stiff and still, a few feet from the cavern entrance.

Far back in the depths of the cavern, a flashlight beam bounced off the rocky walls.

"Goddamn you, Marion, come out." Kincaid's voice rang with a wild, disturbing echo inside the cave. "You can't hide from me. I'll kill you for leaving me. Got to kill you, you bitch."

Blade put his mouth close to Caleb's ear and spoke so softly that Serenity couldn't understand what was being said. She saw Caleb nod once. Then he did something to the pistol in hand. There was a tiny *snick.*

Anxiety made Serenity's fingers tremble as she touched Caleb's arm. She looked at him, silently entreating him to be cautious. He patted her hand absently and then pointed to a rocky outcropping. It was clear he wanted her to stay hidden behind it.

Reluctantly, she followed his silent instructions. Blade gave another hand signal to the dogs. Charon and Styx took up protective positions near her as the men separated and slipped away into the mist.

Serenity realized that she could hardly breathe. She reached into the pocket of her jacket and found the griffin that had saved her life. *Her parents' gift to her.* She held it fast and told herself that Caleb and Blade would be safe.

* * *

The beam of Kincaid's flashlight gyrated erratically around the interior of the cave, bouncing off the stony walls, ceiling, and floor. From the outside it appeared as if a strange, frantic light show was taking place inside.

"I'll kill you for this, you whoring bitch, Marion." Kincaid's voice was becoming increasingly high-pitched. It hovered at the invisible edge of a precipice, almost out of control. "I'll kill you, and when I'm finished with you, I'll go back and get the one who tried to help you. She won't escape me, either. I'll show you both that I'm not weak."

Caleb was aware of a ghostly sense of wrongness as he listened to Kincaid's ranting. He felt the fleeting touch of a sensation that he could only call evil.

Crouching low, he made his way to the left side of the entrance and waited until Blade was in position on the right.

"Too bad we can't use the dogs as a distraction," Blade said. "They could get him in the darkness, no problem. But they won't go inside that cave."

"The lights," Caleb said. "We can use them to shake him up a bit. The switch is out here, remember?"

"Yeah. Hit 'em. See what happens."

Caleb found the metal box beside him and snapped the switch that turned on the row of bulbs that lined one interior wall. The weak lights came on inside the cave.

"What's that?" Kincaid yelled, startled. "Don't come in here, whoever you are." A shot rang out. It sang with warning as it ricocheted off rock. "This is none of your business, whoever you are. This is between Marion and me."

"Put the gun down and come out quietly," Caleb ordered.

"No, I'm not finished with her. Keep away from me or I'll kill you, too. I'm going to kill all of you, starting with that bitch who sent me up here. She lied to me, didn't she? It was all a trick."

"Guy's actin' like he's Looney Tunes," Blade muttered softly.

Not that it took one to know one in this instance, Caleb thought. The diagnosis was obvious. "I don't think we're going to be able to talk him out of there."

"No point. Knew a guy like this once. Probably gonna have to kill him," Blade said matter-of-factly.

"He's not going anywhere. One of us can keep him trapped inside the cave while the other calls the sheriff. The cops are trained to handle this kind of thing. They can talk him out of there."

"Trouble is, no way to know if the sherriff's one of them."

"Blade, this is no time to go into one of your conspiracy theories."

"Ain't no theory. It's a fact. Lay you odds that if we hand Kincaid over to the sheriff, he'll be out on the street in a week. Kincaid's probably one of their best agents. This crazy act of his is a real clever cover. Bet he spent years workin' on it."

"The man's nuttier than a fruitcake, for God's sake. He's guilty of attempted murder. They can't put him back out on the street in a week."

Another shot roared inside the cave.

Blade shrugged. "So maybe they'll make a show of sendin' him to a mental hospital for a few months. Keep him there until things quiet down. Then they'll say he's cured. Turn him loose. First thing he'll do is come after Serenity and Zone."

"Damn," Caleb whispered. "You're severely paranoid, friend, but you're probably right."

"Like I said, knew a guy like him once. He'll want revenge. And he'll just keep comin' back until he gets it or until he's stopped for good."

The notion that Kincaid was an agent for a band of mysterious conspirators might be crazed, but unfortunately the rest of the scenario Blade had just outlined was all too likely to be correct, and Caleb knew it. Anyone who read the newspapers on a regular basis knew it. As long as Kincaid was alive, he was a threat to Serenity and Zone.

Kincaid's gun roared again. The shot whined loudly inside the chamber.

"Don't come in here," Kincaid yelled. "This is between Marion and me."

"How the hell did I get into this one?" Caleb asked the night.

"Just lucky, I guess," Blade said. "Flashlight's stayin' steady now. I can see the beam hittin' the left wall. He must have put it down when we turned on the lights for him. You ready to do it?"

"As ready as I'll ever be." Caleb tried to remember how he had prepared himself before a round in the days when he had won a string of medals for marksmanship. His grandfather's words came back to him as clearly as if Roland was standing beside him.

Clear your mind so you can concentrate. Take a deep breath, let it out halfway. Pull the trigger. Chances are, if you ever have to do it for real, the other guy will be out to kill you, so do it right the first time.

At least it would be self-defense, Caleb thought as another shot rang out from within the cave. Kincaid was doing his damnedest to kill both him and Blade. And if the bastard escaped, he fully intended to go after Serenity and Zone.

He had to be stopped.

"If he's put down the flashlight, he'll panic when the lights go out," Caleb said. "He won't be able to see a thing."

"Good idea. Hit 'em again."

Caleb snapped the light switch again, dousing the glow of the bulbs inside the cave. Kincaid shrieked in fury as he was suddenly enveloped by darkness.

"I can hear him trying to find the flashlight," Blade said. "Got to get him while he's reachin' for it."

Caleb's hand was already on the light switch. He hit it. The cavern's weak bulbs lit up as he ran toward the entrance. He saw Blade's dark form racing to join him.

Kincaid's piercing shriek of undiluted rage shattered the night just as Caleb reached the chamber opening. In the pale glow that lit the inside of the cavern, Kincaid was clearly visible.

He was teetering on the slick, wet edge of the largest of the hot spring pools. He flailed about wildly, trying to maintain his balance on the slippery surface. Even as Caleb watched, he screamed again and plunged head first into the water. The gun clattered against stone. So did Kincaid's head as the man fell.

A sudden, deathly silence seized the interior of the cave.

Blade lowered his gun and looked at Caleb. "He ain't comin' up real fast, is he?"

"No." Caleb slowly lowered his own weapon and walked toward the pool. "He's not."

He reached the water's edge and made himself look down. Kincaid stared back at him from the bottom of the pool, sightless eyes wide, mouth still open in a soundless scream. A dark ribbon of blood seeped from the dead man's head and mingled with the crystal clear waters of the spring. Next to Kincaid's body lay the flashlight.

"Probably panicked and tried to grab it when we turned the lights out," Blade said. "Just like you said he would."

"I think the time has come to call the sheriff."

"Got a better idea," Blade said. "Just dig a hole, dump him in it and cover him up. I know a good place where no one will ever find him."

"We are not going to get in the habit of burying bodies around Witt's End," Caleb said. "Bad for business. Besides, it's never that simple. There are bound to be questions. Better to deal with them now."

Blade looked doubtful. "I dunno. Don't like callin' in the authorities."

"I'll handle them," Caleb said wearily. "I'm good at that kind of thing."

A small sound near the mouth of the cave made him glance in that direction. Serenity stood there, her eyes huge with concern. Caleb decided that having to answer a few questions from the authorities was a small price to pay for the satisfaction of knowing that Kincaid would never again be a threat to her.

"Are you both all right?" Serenity asked.

"Situation's under control," Blade reported.

For the second time that night Serenity ran straight

into Caleb's arms. It was exactly where she was supposed to be, he thought.

"Two accidental deaths in the past week here in a little place like Witt's End seems kind of unusual," Sheriff Banner observed two hours later.

"Hell of a coincidence," Caleb admitted. He watched as Kincaid's body was loaded into the back of the aid car.

"Found out Kincaid had a restraining order issued against him almost a year ago." Banner was a big man who appeared to be addicted to chewing gum. His mouth worked rhythmically as he watched the medics close the ambulance doors. "Looks like he was trying to violate it."

"He was. In the process he nearly killed Serenity Makepeace."

"Nice lady. I always stop by her store when I pass through Witt's End." Banner chewed methodically. "Sells the best granola I ever tasted. You a friend of hers?"

"Yes."

"You're a little different from most of the rest of the folks around here, aren't you?"

"I'm a business consultant. I'm working on a project for Serenity."

"Uh-huh." Banner chewed in silence for a while. "Don't quite understand why Kincaid wound up in that cave."

"Serenity convinced him that was where Marion was hiding. The guy was crazy. He believed her."

"And you and Blade trapped him inside?"

"Right. As I told you, we were going to keep him

pinned down in there while someone called you, but before we could get some assistance, Kincaid slipped and fell into the pool."

"Yeah, I got it all down." Banner popped his gum and patted his notebook. "Sounds real clear-cut to me."

Caleb met Banner's eyes in the glare of the aid car lights. "Have I answered all your questions?"

"Uh-huh. Kincaid was violating a restraining order, trying to find his ex-fiancée. He was armed and dangerous and had already attacked Ms. Makepeace. Went into the caves to look for a lady he called Marion. Didn't know his way around, slipped and fell. Hit his head on a rock in one of the hot springs pools. End of story."

"That about sums it up. If I can be of any further assistance, feel free to call."

"I'll do that." Banner unwrapped a fresh stick of gum. "But I think this'll take care of it. Y'know, I've run into Kincaid's kind before."

"I don't doubt that, given your line of work."

"Real unpleasant types."

"I agree," Caleb said.

"Don't have a real good way of dealing with 'em." Banner frowned as he put the gum into his mouth. "Anyone can see they're crazy as hell, but you can't lock 'em up till they finally kill someone."

"Must be frustrating for law enforcement personnel."

"Damned frustrating." Banner rested his hand on the butt of his revolver and resumed chewing. "But it looks like we won't have that situation with Kincaid. Problem's solved, isn't it?"

"I believe so," Caleb said.

"Just as well." Banner nodded with cool satisfaction. "I've got too many problems as it is. Nice to have one out of the way." He walked off to give final instructions to the medics.

Serenity moved out of the small throng of Witt's Enders who had gathered on the street. She came up to stand beside Caleb as the aid car prepared to follow the sheriff down the mountain road to Bullington.

"Everything okay?" she asked.

Caleb put his arm around her and pulled her close. "Situation's under control, ma'am. But I would like to take this opportunity to inform you that this sort of consulting work isn't covered by my standard contract. I'd appreciate it if you would avoid all similar situations in the future."

"I will, if you will." Serenity pressed her face into his coat and hugged him tightly. "Oh, God, Caleb, I was so scared when I heard those shots in the cave."

"Not any more scared than I was when I found out Kincaid had nearly strangled you. I'm going to have nightmares about that scarf for years to come."

"So will I." Serenity opened her tightly closed fingers and glanced down at the griffin that lay on her palm. "Do you ever have the feeling that there might be something to Quinton's theories about intersecting planes?"

Caleb looked across the street to where Zone stood very close to Blade. Her face was pressed against his shoulder. There was enough light from the lamp over

Witt's End Grocery to see that she had her hand on one of the rottweiler's broad heads.

"Not until tonight," Caleb said.

A long time later Serenity stirred in the depths of her bead-draped bed. The tiny bits of glass shimmered and clashed gently in the darkness. Caleb's leg slid reassuringly over hers.

"Can't sleep?" he asked.

"I woke up again a few minutes ago," she admitted. "I started thinking about something Kincaid said while he had that scarf around my throat."

Caleb's arm tightened protectively around her. "Don't think about it."

She smiled ruefully. "I can't stop thinking about it."

"He's dead, Serenity. He can't hurt you."

"I know. Thanks to you and Blade." She nestled closer against his sleekly muscled body, instinctively seeking the security of his masculine heat. She kissed his shoulder. "But I can't get his words out of my mind."

"Which words?"

"He said that he had deliberately allowed Zone to see him last night. He wanted to terrorize her before he killed her tonight."

"A real son of a bitch."

"Definitely. But what bothers me now is that Zone told me she thought she had also glimpsed him in the fog the night Ambrose died."

"Maybe he'd instituted a campaign of terror," Caleb suggested. "The guy was wacko, Serenity."

"I know, but he was operating under his own

internal logic. He knew who Zone was, where she lived, what he planned to do to her. He took pleasure in telling me all about it. But he only talked about making one appearance at her window."

"He might not have realized that she had seen him the other time," Caleb said. "He could have been prowling around, doing reconnaissance, as Blade would say, before he went in for the kill."

"I suppose so."

"You don't sound convinced."

"The thing that's bothering me is that you can just barely see Ambrose's back porch through the trees from Zone's front window. She told me that she was sitting at that window, meditating, the night Ambrose fell. She thought she saw someone in the fog."

"From all accounts, the fog was fairly thick that night. She might have seen a deer or Blade making his rounds."

"She only got a brief glimpse before whoever it was switched off his flashlight and was swallowed up in the fog. She didn't see him clearly, but she was afraid it was Kincaid."

"We'll never know for certain," Caleb said.

Serenity tried to see his face. "What if it wasn't Kincaid or a deer or Blade? What if it was someone on his or her way to Ambrose's cabin?"

Caleb groaned and pulled her close. "So that's what this is all about. Your imagination has gone into overdrive. Having had a brush with one murderer, you're starting to see them everywhere."

"I'm serious, Caleb."

"So am I." He rolled her onto her back and pushed up the hem of her nightgown.

"Caleb?"

"Let's see if I can give you something else to think about." One hand closed around her hip as his mouth came down on hers.

Serenity put her arms around his neck. He was right, she thought. She needed something else to think about tonight. As usual, Caleb had all the answers.

14

THE PUNGENT AROMA OF FERMENTING GRAIN FILLED THE small brewery room behind the bookshop. Caleb watched with interest as Quinton checked his vats. A new batch of Old Hogwash was being readied for bottling.

"My special winter brew," Quinton explained, peering at a dial. "I only make it once a year, to celebrate the coming of the winter solstice."

"I see," Caleb said.

"Got to keep a close eye on things at this stage." Quinton made a small adjustment to one of the instruments. "Timing and precision is everything in beer, just as it is in the mathematical universe. In the brewing process, one sees a reflection of the interaction of various cosmic vectors. In beer, the forces of destruction, change, and creation are mirrored on a symbolic scale that can be appreciated and comprehended by the human brain."

"I'll drink to that." Caleb braced one hand against the wall, hooked his jacket over his shoulder and glanced at his wristwatch. "Speaking of time, do you want to tell me why you asked me to come in here, Priestly? I assume there was something other than cosmic forces and beer that you wanted to discuss."

"What's your hurry? Going somewhere?"

"As a matter of fact, I am."

Quinton frowned. "You're leaving town?"

"For a while."

"Serenity going with you?"

"No," Caleb said. "She's not."

"You coming back anytime soon?"

"I expect to return tonight. Why?"

"Just wondered." Quinton relaxed and went back to fussing with the brewing equipment. "Well, that's all right, then."

"I'm glad you approve. Now, what was it you wanted?"

"Two things." Quinton fiddled with a valve. "First, I wanted to thank you for what you did last night."

"You mean what Blade and I did, don't you? And we didn't do anything except get lucky when Kincaid slipped and fell into one of the vision pools."

Quinton chuckled. "Right. He fell into the pool."

"It's the truth."

"Hey." Quinton held up a palm. "Whatever you and Blade say happened in that cave, happened. You won't get any argument from me or anyone else in town."

"I'm pleased to hear that, because what Blade and I told you is the truth. Kincaid went for his flashlight, slipped and fell. Pure luck. Good for us, bad for him."

"As to that, who's to say whether it was luck or

something else. Perhaps he was the victim of colliding geometric planes."

"That's certainly one logical explanation," Caleb said.

"But as it happens, I wasn't talking about how Kincaid died, crucial as that particular event was to all of us. I was referring to the aftermath."

Caleb raised his brows. "Aftermath?"

"The way you dealt with Sheriff Banner and all the rest."

"I just answered a few questions."

"You did a lot more than that." Quinton rested an arm on top of one of the small stainless steel vats and stroked his beard. "Things could have gotten confused, what with Blade involved. He doesn't interact well with the official representatives of established authority."

"Somehow, I had gathered that impression."

"The thought of Blade trying to explain last night's events to Sheriff Banner gives one pause."

Caleb thought of how Banner might have responded to Blade's elaborate conspiracy theories. He couldn't help it, he grinned. "Yes, it does. Might have been interesting."

"Might have been an unmitigated disaster for all concerned," Quinton muttered. "At the very least, there would have been a hell of a lot more paperwork. It's not beyond the realm of possibility that someone might have tried to take Blade into custody for questioning or stuff him into a mental institution for observation. He couldn't have handled that."

"No," Caleb agreed. "He wouldn't have done very well in either of those situations."

"What I'm trying to say is, thanks for saving

Serenity and Zone, and thanks for keeping Blade out of trouble." Quinton's teeth showed in his beard. "You're not so bad for a business consultant."

"All part of the service."

"Item two on my agenda today," Quinton continued, "involves politics."

"Personally, I never touch the stuff."

"Neither do I. However, politics is an inescapable fact of life."

"I've never thought of politics as having cosmic implications," Caleb said.

"It does. So do the forces of change. And we've got change coming to Witt's End. A town's like a star. It's got to keep burning at a certain temperature or it dies. This town was dying, taking its time about it, I admit, but definitely dying until Serenity opened her grocery store three years ago."

"That started the process of change?"

"It stopped the decaying process," Quinton said. "Now things are starting to move forward again. This mail order idea of Serenity's may actually give us something resembling a real economy."

"The shining star of Witt's End burns brightly once more."

"And therefore changes," Quinton said. "One can't stop change. The best thing one can do is manage it so that one doesn't get crushed by it."

"What does politics have to do with this?" Caleb asked.

"Politics is how the universe manages change. This town needs someone who can do what you did last night."

"Handle the outside authorities?"

"For starters. I expect there will be more and more

of that kind of work as we here in Witt's End are obliged to deal with the outside world. Bound to get more tourists, for one thing, especially in the summer. Then there will be people from the health department wanting to inspect people's kitchens because of the foodstuff they're selling in the catalog. We'll probably have traffic problems, sewage problems, security problems. You name it."

"Quinton, I'm in a hurry here. Could you get to the point?"

Quinton looked at him. "Point is, Blade isn't the only one around here who doesn't deal well with the outside establishment. Most of us here in Witt's End have a problem with that kind of thing. It's one of the reasons we wound up here. So we took a vote this morning."

Caleb eyed him. "A vote?"

"We all got together first thing at Ariadne's café and talked it over. We voted you in as the first mayor of Witt's End."

Serenity took her customary seat in the window of the Sunshine Café and poured the tea Ariadne had just made. Zone sat on the other side of the table. From this position they could both keep an eye on the front door of Witt's End Grocery. It was only ten o'clock and there was no one in the store at the moment. Serenity had decided that she and Zone needed a chance to talk.

"Here's to a real bonding experience." Serenity raised her mug of tea in a salute. "I, for one, will never wear a scarf again as long as I live."

"I'm so sorry about everything that happened," Zone said for what must have been the hundredth time. "I came here to hide. I never intended for my problems to become a threat to anyone else. I'm just so sorry."

"Stop blaming yourself. It wasn't your fault. At any rate, it's over and everything turned out all right."

"Thanks to Blade and Caleb." Zone shuddered. "And I can't bear to think about what might have happened if you hadn't known those self-defense techniques."

"Quit torturing yourself with what-ifs," Serenity said crisply. "I've got something important to ask you."

"What's that?"

"Now that Kincaid is permanently out of your life, what are you going to do?"

"Do?"

"Are you going back to California?"

Zone looked confused. "Why would I do that?"

"You said that you came to Witt's End to hide from Kincaid. Now that you no longer have to hide, I just wondered if you planned to stay."

"I hadn't thought about leaving," Zone said hesitantly. "Somehow Witt's End feels like where I want to be." She met Serenity's eyes. "Are you trying to tell me that you might not need me at the store? I know you only gave me that job because you felt sorry for me. If it's a question of not being able to pay me the same salary, I could take a cut in my wages."

"Hang on here."

"It doesn't cost much to live in Witt's End. I'm sure that I could get by on less."

"Don't be ridiculous. Getting rid of you is the last thing I want to do. Who else in Witt's End knows how to open a store on time every day?" Serenity chuckled.

"I was panicked at the thought that you might leave and I'd have to hire a new assistant."

Zone smiled tremulously. "I don't plan to go anywhere."

"That's a relief. For the record, I don't plan to cut your wages. If that fancy, high-priced business consultant of mine is a tenth as good as he says he is, I should be able to give you a raise soon."

"Your fancy, high-priced consultant and *partner*," Caleb said dryly, "is even better than he's told you."

"And so refreshingly humble, too." Serenity turned in her seat and saw Caleb standing directly behind her. Something about his newly polished shoes worried her. "Going somewhere?"

"Yes."

A deep sense of unease stirred to life in the pit of Serenity's stomach. "Where?"

"That's what I came to tell you."

Serenity stared at him. "Coming back soon?"

"Tonight."

She let out the breath that she had been holding and managed what she hoped was a bright, breezy smile. "For a minute there I thought maybe you had decided Witt's End was too hard on hotshot business consultants."

"Nothing a good consultant can't handle here." Caleb glanced toward the counter. "I'll explain everything in a minute. First let me get a cup of coffee from Ariadne."

"All right," Serenity said.

"Is this a private conversation?" Zone asked.

Caleb's mouth curved. "If you don't mind."

"No, of course not." Zone got to her feet. "I'll let you two talk. I've got a store to mind."

"Thanks," Caleb said. "I won't be long."

Zone paused and gazed intently up at him. "I want to thank you again for what you did last night."

"Forget it."

"I cannot forget it. Nor do I wish to do so. I asked Blade what happened in that cave. He says Royce slipped and fell."

"That's exactly what happened."

"I understand that you don't wish to burden me with the knowledge that because of me, you and Blade were forced to kill a man. It's kind of you to try to protect me. But as I told Blade, it's not necessary."

"Zone, read my lips: Kincaid slipped and fell."

"As you wish." Zone smiled her solemn smile. "It's clear that you and Blade want to let the matter rest. I will not mention the subject again."

"That's good to know."

"I see now that I misinterpreted the vibrations that I felt emanating from the vision pools. You were not the source of the turmoil and danger that I sensed. You were the counterforce."

"Ah," Caleb said sagely. "That explains it."

"Yes it does," Zone said seriously. "The vibrations I experienced around you were no doubt tuned to the same wavelength as the vibrations of the turmoil and danger that I felt. Naturally your vibrations resonated on the same frequency as the source vibrations."

"Naturally."

"And I accidentally mistook them for the negative energy, rather than the positive," Zone concluded.

"I can certainly understand how someone could make a simple mistake like that," Caleb said.

"Thank you for your graciousness. I shall treasure it as I would the most priceless of gifts. I am forever in your debt." She inclined her neatly shaved head in a graceful bow, turned and floated toward the door of the café.

Caleb watched her leave. Then he looked at Serenity. "Does she really believe all that stuff about vibrations and counterforces or is she just pulling my leg?"

"I don't know," Serenity said honestly. "I've told you, in some ways she's like Blade. They both live on two planes of existence simultaneously, the one we all recognize as real and one that probably exists only in their own heads."

"In other words, they're both weird. Jessie was right. They're probably made for each other. Wait here while I get my coffee."

"Coming right up," Ariadne said as she bustled out from behind the counter. She had a mug in one hand and a handmade almond biscotti in the other. "Here you go."

"Thanks." Caleb hung his jacket over the back of the chair Zone had just vacated. He sat down, pulled the mug toward him and dunked the biscotti into the coffee.

"You're welcome." Ariadne smiled. "And thanks for what you did last night."

"All I did was hang around with Blade while a homicidal maniac fell into one of the vision pools."

"As far as I'm concerned, whatever you say is good enough for me."

Caleb muttered something inaudible around a bite of the biscotti.

"But I wasn't talking about just that," Ariadne said softly. "I wanted to thank you for taking charge afterward. Things could have gotten complicated."

"I'll let you in on a little secret," Caleb said.

"Sheriff Banner didn't want things to get unduly complicated. He ran a check on Kincaid and he knew the guy was a walking time bomb. I got the impression the sheriff was as relieved as everyone else that the bastard took a header into one of the pools."

"Banner is a good man," Ariadne said. "But something tells me that he and Blade would never have understood each other. So thanks for handling everything."

"It's not like I had anything better to do at the time." Caleb paused to eye his half-eaten piece of biscotti with a thoughtful expression. "How long does this stuff keep?"

"You can store biscotti for a month or more," Ariadne said. "It's double-baked over a period of several hours, so it's very dry, like a cracker. I've eaten some that were six months old. You couldn't tell the difference between them and fresh-made."

"I think we can add biscotti to the catalog along with the marmalade and the cookbook," Caleb said.

Ariadne glowed. "I can do several flavors."

"Fine. We'll work on the packaging later. Talk to Zone about the graphics."

"All right. I'll take a look at some of my favorite biscotti recipes. I'll probably need to hire someone part-time to help with the baking."

"And so an economy is born," Caleb murmured.

"What?"

"Nothing. Just an observation on the basic nature of certain cosmic forces."

"Oh." Ariadne went back behind the counter and busied herself amid a pile of cookbooks.

Serenity watched Caleb dunk the last of his biscotti into his coffee. She leaned forward to whisper across the table. "Might as well face it, nobody cares what happened in that cave. They're just grateful you took care of everything, including Blade. Everyone trusts you now. You're one of us."

"Sort of an honorary resident of Witt's End, would you say?"

"You could say that."

Caleb smiled wryly. "Nice to know I belong somewhere."

"So why are you leaving Witt's End today? Are you going to pay a visit to your office in Seattle?"

"No, I talked to Mrs. Hotten this morning. Everything's under control there."

"Where are you going?"

"Ventress Valley. I've been doing some thinking."

"What about?"

"The sales receipt for your photos that we found in Asterley's files."

Serenity groaned. "In the excitement, I'd forgotten all about that."

"I didn't forget about it."

"Obviously." Serenity watched him intently. "All right, tell me what you've been thinking."

Caleb put his hands around his mug and contemplated his coffee. "I'm thinking that maybe my first conclusion was wrong, maybe there weren't two blackmailers. I'm thinking that Franklin was behind this whole thing right from the start. With a little help from Asterley."

"Franklin?" Serenity was stunned. "What do you mean? Why would he do something like this? It makes no sense."

"It all fits, Serenity. Let's assume that receipt we found is telling us the truth. Franklin bought those pictures from Asterley on the twentieth. He sent them to you anonymously a couple of days later in an effort to get you to call off your business deal with me."

"Why would he care about one of your consulting projects?" Serenity asked quickly.

"He wouldn't have given a damn about it if it had been just another project. But if he suspected that I was getting involved with you, and if he knew about those photos, he'd have been worried." Caleb's mouth twisted. "Franklin and Phyllis both share my grandfather's fear that my bad blood will show in the end."

"In other words, they're all afraid that you'll get seduced by a woman with a shady past," Serenity concluded.

"Something like that."

"But how could Franklin have known about me?"

"Good question."

"Well, I guess, in a way, you have met with the fate they feared most, haven't you?" Serenity smiled ruefully. "My past is so clouded, I don't even know what my parents looked like. At least you've got pictures of your mother and father. I don't."

"It must be strange not to know what your parents looked like."

"It is," Serenity whispered. "But I can feel a link with them sometimes. I survived last night because of this." She instinctively touched the griffin that was once more securely hung around her neck. "Their one legacy to me. And because of Blade's self-defense instructions. If it hadn't been for all of them, I would have died."

"Don't remind me," Caleb said grimly.

Serenity lowered her hand. "It's odd, isn't it?"

"What's odd?"

"How connected we all are with each other, even when we think we're alone in the world, even if we don't particularly want to be connected. It's as if, like it or not, we've got bits and pieces of other people stuck to us. Take you and Blade, for example."

Caleb grimaced. "What about Blade and me?"

"The two of you shared an experience in that cave last night that must have left its mark on both of you. No one but you and Blade will ever really know what happened. For the rest of your lives, whenever you think about it, you'll each remember the other because you went through it together."

"Psychically bonded with Blade forever. What an unnerving thought." Caleb loudly set his coffee mug down on the table. "I think we're straying into the metaphysical realm here. That's a bit out of my field. I'm a business consultant, remember?"

"One of the best in the Pacific Northwest. Or so you keep telling me."

"Damn right. And I prefer to operate on one mathematical plane at a time, if you don't mind. Back to Uncle Franklin."

"I'm listening."

"As I started to explain before I was interrupted, my theory is that he got hold of those photos and sent them to you first in hopes that you'd realize the game was over and quietly retreat from the scene. If you didn't quit at that point, if you took the risk of telling me about the photos, he assumed I'd end things."

"But instead of ditching me and my project, you followed me to Witt's End. You informed me that there was no way out of the contract for either of us because you had your precious business standards to uphold."

Caleb raised his brows and took a swallow of coffee. "My theory is that when Uncle Franklin realized that his scheme hadn't worked and that I was still very much involved with you, so involved that I brought you home to meet the family, he panicked and took more drastic action."

"He called you and claimed that he was being blackmailed."

Caleb nodded. "He told me that I had to stop seeing you because someone had threatened to send your pictures to the *Ventress Valley News.*"

"And thereby drag your noble family name through the mud again." Serenity considered that. "It makes sense up to a point. But there are a couple of things that need an explanation here."

"Yes, there are." Caleb leaned back in his chair and contemplated the door of Witt's End Grocery through the café window. "The first big question is, how did my uncle learn that those photos even existed in the first place?"

"Exactly. He's a banker, for heaven's sake. Not the sort to hang around with folks from Witt's End. Who could have told him that the pictures were available and that he could buy them from Ambrose Asterley?"

"Asterley himself, probably," Caleb said. "I still think he must have started all this. But not because he wanted to control the process of change here in Witt's End. He had a much simpler goal. He wanted money. From everything I've heard about your friend Ambrose, he was always trying to talk people into loaning him cash to buy new photo equipment, right?"

"Well, yes," Serenity admitted uneasily. "That's true."

"If we assume that he did know about the old

scandal because of his newspaper addiction, we could also assume that he sent you to me in the first place with the idea of setting up a lucrative blackmail scheme for himself."

"I still find it hard to believe, but I suppose it's possible that Ambrose was so desperate for money that he contacted your uncle after he sent me to see you."

"He told Franklin that the Ventress name was once again being threatened by a scandalous affair, and then offered to sell him pictures of the woman involved. Franklin probably took it from there."

"He bought the photos for five thousand dollars," Serenity said, thinking it through. "He used them first to try to frighten me off. When that didn't work, he went to you and claimed he was being blackmailed."

"There's a certain logic to it," Caleb said.

"The good news is that with your theory, we don't need to worry about the possibility that there's a second blackmailer running around," Serenity said.

"Between Asterley's greed and Uncle Franklin's concern for the family name, the whole thing can be explained."

"Why the missing negatives?" Serenity persisted. "The sale to Franklin was legitimate. Ambrose documented it as if it were a straightforward business arrangement. Ambrose wasn't blackmailing anyone. He had nothing to hide. He had a right to sell those photos."

"Maybe he sold the negatives to Franklin, too. Franklin would certainly have wanted them."

"Maybe. So what are you going to do?" Serenity asked.

Caleb's eyes were as hard to read as a vision pool. "I'm going to go back to Ventress Valley today and verify my theory."

Alarm flashed through Serenity. She forced herself to remain outwardly calm. "Uh, just how do you plan to go about discovering whether or not you're right about the connection between Ambrose and your uncle?"

"I'm going to have a showdown. I intend to get Franklin, Phyllis, and my grandfather in one room together, and then I'm going to confront Franklin. I'm going to force him to admit his role in this."

"Caleb, I'm not sure that's such a good idea."

Caleb looked at her. "Franklin probably thinks that I'll tiptoe around this thing. He's banking that I'll cave in to the so-called blackmail threat for the sake of the family. But he's wrong. I'm going to blow it wide open."

"Your uncle was only trying to protect the family name. Admittedly, he's gone too far, but surely you can understand why he's doing it. I think you should handle this with some delicacy and tact."

"Delicacy and tact?" Caleb's smile was even colder than his eyes. "All of my life I've handled my family that way, and what has it gotten me? I've done all the things that I was supposed to do. I've met every demand, done everything that was asked of me, tried to satisfy everyone. But it's never been enough."

"What do you mean, it's never been enough?"

"No matter what I've done, I've never managed to make up for what my parents did. Every time my grandfather and the others look at me, they don't see me, they see my father's fatal flaw and my mother's

291

bad blood. Every time I look into their eyes, I can see them watching and waiting for the big day when I'll prove that all their suspicions about me are right."

"Oh, Caleb." Serenity reached out to touch his arm.

"The big day has finally arrived." Caleb got to his feet and reached for the jacket he had slung over the back of the chair.

"Wait," Serenity said quickly. "Caleb, I don't want you to do anything rash."

"Rash? That's funny coming from you." Caleb leaned down and kissed her fiercely on her open mouth. When he raised his head, his eyes were gleaming. "You're the one who taught me the meaning of the word."

She grabbed his sleeve as he started to move away. "Listen to me. If you force a confrontation in your present mood, you could tear your family apart."

"Do you think I give a damn?"

"It's your family, Caleb."

"No, it's not. I've never really been a full-fledged member of the Ventress family. What's more, I'm through trying to become one. I put up with a lot from them over the years, done everything they've ever asked of me in hopes of paying off the blackmail debt I inherited from my parents. But you know what they say about blackmail: It never ends. The only way to stop it is to stop payment."

Serenity jumped to her feet. "If you're going to insist on a head-on confrontation with your family, I'd better come with you."

"Forget it. I don't want you involved in this."

"But I am involved."

"You're not coming with me and that's final."

The door of the café opened. Webster, clad in his customary dirt-stained overalls, stood in the entrance. He beamed with triumph as he opened his hand to display a smooth, round, palm-sized rock.

"What d'ya think, Ventress?"

Caleb glanced at the rock. "Webster, I'm in a rush right now. Why don't we discuss this when I get back?"

"This sucker is perfect," Webster said. He gave Caleb a sly look. "And I know where I can get a hundred more just like it. All real beauties like this one."

"Like I said, I'm in a hurry at the moment."

"Take it," Webster urged. "Put it in your pocket. Carry it around for a while. See how it feels."

"All right, all right, give it to me." Caleb grabbed the rock and dropped it into the pocket of his jacket. "Now, would you mind getting out of the way? I've got a long drive ahead."

"Sure thing, Ventress." Webster frowned in concern. "You ain't leavin' for good, are you?"

"I'll be back tonight. We'll discuss the marketing potential of your rock as soon as I've had a chance to take a close look at it."

"Okay." Webster's expression lightened. "Wanted to thank you for what you did last night."

"Forget it. I didn't do anything."

"Sure." Webster winked knowingly. "Whatever you say, Ventress."

Caleb ignored him. He went through the door and strode swiftly along the wooden sidewalk to where his Jaguar was parked.

Serenity grabbed her coat. "Excuse me, Webster."

293

"Huh? Oh, sorry. Didn't mean to get in your way." Webster stood aside as Serenity slipped past him. "Ventress is gonna like that rock. You'll see."

"I'm sure he will." Serenity paused briefly to glance back at Ariadne. "Tell Zone I'm going out of town with Caleb. I'll be back tonight."

"I'll tell her," Ariadne said.

Serenity whirled around, raced through the door and ran toward the Jaguar. Caleb was already behind the wheel. He switched on the engine just as she reached the car.

Serenity yanked open the door and hurtled into the passenger seat.

"What the hell do you think you're doing?" Caleb asked.

"I'm coming with you." Serenity buckled her seat belt.

"No, you're not."

"You can't leave me behind." Serenity sat back in the seat and locked her door. "You're my business partner, remember? I never abandon a business partner. I've got certain standards to maintain."

"Damn," Caleb said.

He snapped the Jaguar into gear and pulled out onto the road.

15

T EN MILES DOWN THE MOUNTAIN CALEB FINALLY SPOKE
again. "This isn't going to be pleasant, Serenity."

"I know."

"I won't allow you to interfere."

"I won't interfere."

"The fact that you're along isn't going to change the
way I deal with the situation."

"I understand."

"You can't talk me out of doing this my way."

"I realize that."

"It's not too late. I can turn around and take you
back to Witt's End."

Serenity put her hand on the long, taut muscle of his
upper thigh. "You're not going into this alone. Remember what I said earlier about everyone having bits
and pieces of other people stuck to them?"

"I remember."

295

"Don't look now, but you've got a whole lot of me stuck to you. And I don't come unstuck very easily."

Caleb couldn't think of anything to say to that. She was right, more right than she could possibly know. With every passing day and night, he was increasingly aware of just how much of her had stuck to him, of how much she had become a permanent part of him, a vital, necessary part.

Caleb glanced into the rearview mirror and saw his own reflection. The image was solid and real and alive. He definitely looked pissed off, he thought, but he looked solid and real. Alive. He could touch things. He could make a difference. And things, *people,* could touch him.

"Darn," Serenity muttered.

"What's wrong? Change your mind about coming with me?"

"No, that's not the problem."

"What is the problem?"

She plucked at the long, loose batik printed shirt she was wearing over a matching pair of flowing, wide-legged pants. An elaborately studded belt with a massive buckle marked the waistline of the outfit. "I didn't get a chance to step into a phone booth and change into Miss Town and Country."

"Don't worry about it." Caleb glanced at her wild, red curls and smiled. "You look fine the way you are."

"Do you really think so?"

"Believe me, you've never looked better. Except maybe in those shots Asterley took of you."

Serenity's head came around with a swiftness that betrayed her startled surprise. "You never really told me what you thought of those photos."

Caleb recalled the juxtaposition of innocence and ancient, womanly wisdom that Asterley had captured so vividly in the pictures of Serenity. "You were right about them. They're works of art. Asterley made you look like some sort of mythical woodland goddess. Elemental. A force of nature. Beautiful."

"I'm glad you liked them." Serenity sounded relieved. "I was a little worried about your reaction. You didn't say much after you saw them."

"I got distracted by Franklin's phone call, as I recall, and what with one thing and another, never got back to the subject. Those shots of you are stunning."

"Thanks."

Out of the corner of his eye he saw her mouth start to curve in a pleased smile. "And when this is all over," Caleb added very deliberately, "I intend to make certain that I have the negatives and every single print of those photos in my possession."

Her eyes widened. "Why?"

"Those pictures are going to become a part of my personal collection of photographic art."

"I didn't know you had a personal collection of photographic art."

"I didn't until quite recently."

For some reason, Ventress Valley did not look nearly as picturesque and charming to Serenity this time as it had the last. Perhaps it was the gray light filtering through the leaden clouds, which created the sullen atmosphere. Then again, she thought, maybe it was her own uneasy mood that transformed the landscape from a quaint slice of Americana to a scene imbued with brooding menace.

Whatever the cause, there was no denying that today the fields on the outskirts of town looked empty and forlorn now that the harvest was nearly completed. The shops along the main street of Ventress Valley appeared subdued rather than bustling. There was no colorful wedding party in front of the church to add a note of optimism.

"Are you certain you want to go through with this?" Serenity tensed in her seat as Caleb turned the Jaguar down the long drive that led to his grandfather's house.

"I'm certain."

"Maybe you should consider a different approach to the problem. Confrontations are always nasty."

"I warned you this wouldn't be pleasant. I offered to take you back to Witt's End."

Serenity gave up the last ditch effort to change Caleb's mind. She had known all along that she could do nothing to stop what was about to happen. All she could do was be there with him when he ripped apart the fabric of his past.

The door of the big house opened as Caleb brought the Jaguar to a halt and switched off the ignition. Dolores came out onto the wide porch. Surprise and pleasure lit her features. She hurried down the steps as Caleb and Serenity got out of the car.

"Caleb, what are you doing here? We weren't expecting you." Dolores smiled at Serenity. "Nice to see you again, Miss Makepeace. I'll have your room ready in no time."

"Don't bother." Caleb closed his car door. "We won't be staying long."

Dolores's smile turned questioning. "What do you mean? You just got here. Surely you'll stay the night."

"No," Caleb said. "We won't be able to do that. I'm sorry, Dolores."

The last of Dolores's smile vanished. "Something's wrong, isn't it?"

"It's a family matter." Caleb's voice was as bleak and cold as the steel-colored clouds. "Is my grandfather home?"

"He's in the stables with Harry."

"Will you please call Uncle Franklin and Aunt Phyllis for me? Tell them they're needed immediately here at the house."

"Of course." Dolores cast another quick, anxious glance at Serenity. "Franklin will be in his office at the bank. He doesn't like to be disturbed at work."

"Tell him this is family business," Caleb said. "Tell him that I said he'd better come here or I'll hold this conversation in his office."

"Oh, dear." Dolores twisted her hands in her apron.

Serenity huddled deeper into her jacket. The warm lining didn't offer much protection against the chill in the air.

Roland came around the corner of the house at that moment. He looked startled at the sight of the small group standing near the Jaguar. His eyes went straight to Caleb.

Serenity could have sworn that something warm and welcoming moved in the depths of the old man's gaze, something that might have been hope. It was hidden almost immediately behind a cool, unreadable mask not unlike the one Caleb had learned to wear so well. *Bits and pieces of other people.*

"Weren't expecting you, son. Miss Makepeace." Roland nodded politely at Serenity and then looked at Caleb again. "What the devil is this all about?"

"It's about the past," Caleb said. "And the future. Let's go inside and wait for Franklin and Phyllis."

It was worse than Serenity had anticipated. The atmosphere in the living room was heavier than the air outside. It held more tension, too. She watched Caleb pace back and forth like a caged lion in front of the windows. There was so much dangerous energy emanating from him that she half expected a bolt of lightning to explode in his immediate vicinity.

He commanded the attention of everyone in the room. Roland watched him the way an aging monarch watches the young warrior who will replace him. His grip on the arms of his leather chair betrayed his tension.

Phyllis, her mouth pinched in a disapproving line, sat primly on the sofa. Her back was as straight as an iron bar and just about as flexible. Franklin sat beside her, his brows knitted in a scowl. He looked angry but wary.

"I think we've had enough dramatics," Roland said. "Tell us what's going on here."

"What is going on here," Caleb said, "is a dose of blackmail."

Phyllis gasped in dismay. Her hand went to her throat. Roland stared uncomprehendingly at his grandson.

Franklin's jaw sagged in stunned amazement. He had to make several attempts before he managed to speak. "You *fool*. What do you think you're doing, Caleb?"

Caleb came to a halt near the window and looked at him. "I'm doing the same thing Roland did thirty-four years ago when he was hit with a blackmail threat. I'm refusing to pay the price. I'm here to make a formal announcement of that fact to everyone involved so that there will be no misunderstanding."

"Blackmail." Roland appeared more confused than outraged. "What the devil are you talking about?"

Caleb did not take his eyes off Franklin. "Why don't you tell him, Uncle?"

"I don't know what you mean," Franklin blustered.

"All right, if you won't do it, I will." Caleb switched his focus to his grandfather. "Franklin called me yesterday and told me that he was the victim of an extortion threat."

Roland froze in his chair. "On what grounds?"

"The usual." Caleb's smile was fleeting and cold. "Pictures. In this case of Serenity."

"What the hell?" Roland stared at Serenity.

"Miss Makepeace?" Phyllis glanced quickly at Serenity and then pinned Caleb with a scandalized gaze. "Are you telling us that there are dirty pictures of Miss Makepeace floating around?"

"They aren't dirty," Caleb said. "They're works of art created by a gifted photographer. And as far as I know, they've only floated as far as Franklin, who, it turns out, was not actually being blackmailed. Just the opposite."

"The opposite?" Phyllis frowned.

"That's right," Caleb said. "He's the blackmailer."

"Me? A blackmailer?" Franklin shot to his feet, his face reddening with fury. "This is an outrage. How dare you accuse me of blackmail? I'm the one who's being blackmailed with those filthy pictures."

"Christ. Blackmail." Roland leaned his head back against his chair and closed his eyes. "Not again."

Franklin rounded on him. "Roland, listen to me.

The note said that if I didn't pay ten thousand dollars, the photos of Miss Makepeace would be sent to the *Ventress Valley News.* Just like last time."

"Damn it to hell." Roland opened his eyes. His expression was savage. "Goddamn it to hell."

"The only thing I could do was call Caleb and tell him what had happened," Franklin said desperately. "I wasn't blackmailing him, for God's sake. I was the victim. All of us were potential victims. It's Miss Makepeace's fault. She brought this disaster down on us."

"Oh, my God," Phyllis looked faint. "Roland's right. This is just like the last time."

Franklin swung around to face her. "Except that I was the one who received the photos this time. Naturally, I did my best to protect the family. I called Caleb at once and told him exactly what sort of woman he had gotten himself involved with. I expected him to handle the problem with discretion."

"But several days before that you sent the photos to Serenity, didn't you?" Caleb asked with lethal softness. "And in the accompanying note you told her that if she didn't call off her business arrangement with Ventress Ventures immediately, you would send the pictures on to me. You thought she'd cave in to your threat, didn't you? You thought she'd back out of the deal."

"I don't know what you're talking about," Franklin said.

Caleb ignored the interruption. "Instead, she came to me and told me about the pictures and the blackmail threat. You hadn't counted on that, had you? Or if you did take that possibility into consideration, you probably assumed that I'd be so disgusted by the knowledge that Serenity had posed nude that I'd end my relationship with her."

"Posed nude?" Phyllis's tone rose to a horrified shriek. "Miss Makepeace, have you no shame?"

"I did it for art," Serenity mumbled. Speaking of art, she thought, the scene was becoming distinctly surreal.

"Art? Don't you dare try to excuse such filth as art. I know your sort," Phyllis retorted. "You're part of that immoral, left-wing artistic crowd, aren't you? The sort that takes our hard-earned tax money and uses it to fund obscene photographs and foul-mouthed plays."

Serenity felt as if she had slipped into the Twilight Zone. "I assure you, poor Ambrose never got a dime from the National Endowment for the Arts, if that's what's worrying you."

"To think that our government has sunk to the level of funding nude photography with that national endowment thing," Phyllis continued. "It's unconscionable."

"That's enough, Aunt Phyllis," Caleb warned.

"I'll say it is," she snapped. "Franklin is right, this is outrageous."

"Of course it is," Franklin declared. "I won't tolerate it."

"That's my line," Caleb said. "That's why I'm here today. To tell you that I won't tolerate any more blackmail."

"Goddamn it," Franklin roared, "you can't prove that I tried to blackmail anyone."

Roland shot Serenity a speculative glance and then gave Caleb a sharp look. "Well? Can you prove what you're saying, Caleb?"

Caleb pulled the folded record of sale from the pocket of his shirt. "I got this from Ambrose Asterley's files. It says he sold a set of photos of Serenity Makepeace to Franklin Ventress. You'll notice the date on the receipt. The transaction took place on the twentieth of October, ten days ago. But Franklin only got around to calling me about this yesterday."

"You're lying," Franklin hissed.

"No." Caleb's gaze glittered briefly. "I don't lie, and whatever else he may believe about me, I think Grandfather knows that much. I have never lied to him."

Roland looked troubled but he said nothing.

"Damn it, why would this Asterley person give you a receipt for a bunch of pictures that he supposedly sold to me?" Franklin asked swiftly.

"He didn't have much choice," Caleb said. "Ambrose Asterley died a few days ago. I found this record in his files after his death."

"Impossible. Let me see that." Franklin charged across the room and grabbed the incriminating slip of paper out of Caleb's hand. He stared at it in dismay for a long time. Then his shoulders slumped. His whole body seemed to deflate. When he raised his head, he looked defeated.

"Franklin?" Phyllis spoke sharply. "What is it? What's going on?"

"I don't understand," Franklin muttered. "I just don't understand. It's not possible. I did everything I was told to do each time."

Caleb plucked the receipt from his hand. "What don't you understand, Franklin?"

"There wasn't supposed to be any record of this. He

told me there wouldn't be any way to trace the sale."
Franklin rubbed the bridge of his nose. He appeared
dazed. "On both occasions, I carried out his instructions to the letter."

"What instructions?" Serenity asked.

"I parked my car in the Ventress Valley Mall
parking lot." Franklin stared out the window at the
gray sky. "Left the door unlocked, the money in the
glove compartment. I went into the mall for fifteen
minutes. I never saw him, but when I returned to the
car, the money was gone."

"And the photos were in the glove compartment?"
Caleb asked.

"Yes. The first time. I paid five thousand for them."

"And on the second occasion?"

Franklin looked haunted. "He called again on Sunday. Said it wasn't over. Said he still had the negatives
and that he'd send prints to the *Ventress Valley News* if
I didn't pay him five thousand dollars."

"Then you admit you purchased those pictures?"
Roland asked roughly.

Franklin's head came up proudly. His shoulders
straightened. "Yes, I admit it. As soon as I knew those
photos existed, I realized it was my duty to get hold of
them. I had to see just what sort of woman had gotten
her greedy little claws into Caleb."

"And once you did have the pictures in hand, you
tried to threaten Serenity, didn't you?" Caleb asked.
"You sent copies of the photos to her and warned her
that if she didn't end her business relationship with
me, you'd send the pictures directly to me."

"I hoped she would have enough sense of shame to
end the relationship on her own." Franklin gave
Serenity a furious glance. "I suppose I should have

known better. Any woman whose moral standards are so low that she has no compunction about posing nude, wouldn't care who saw the pictures, I suppose."

"Don't worry about Serenity's moral standards," Caleb said. "I guarantee you that they're a lot higher than yours are."

"How can you say such a thing about a member of your own family?" Phyllis demanded.

"On my scale, blackmailers rank a lot lower than photographers' models," Caleb said.

"Really," Phyllis grumbled. "I don't see that Franklin was actually blackmailing anyone."

"I was only doing what I had to do to save you from her." Franklin stared at Caleb. "Don't you understand? I had a duty to this family. I could not allow you to repeat the mistakes of the past. I simply could not allow it. We all suffered too much the last time. I couldn't let you follow in your father's footsteps."

A sudden hush gripped the room. The dreadful words had finally been spoken aloud. Serenity knew they had all been waiting for them.

"No, I guess you couldn't allow that to happen, could you?" Caleb said quietly. "Not after you and my grandfather and Aunt Phyllis had worked so hard over the years to make sure that I didn't repeat my father's mistakes."

Serenity looked at Roland's stark face and felt colder than ever. She could see the pain in him very clearly now. Every word that was being spoken was a knife thrust that cut to the bone.

"We did our best," Phyllis said grandly. She narrowed her eyes at Serenity. "Apparently we failed."

Serenity stirred. "I think you're all overlooking one

major fact that makes this situation different from what happened in the past."

"And what would that be?" Phyllis asked disdainfully.

"Caleb isn't married to another woman, as his father was when the original scandal broke," Serenity pointed out gently. "You may not approve of his involvement with me, but you can't claim that he's repeating his father's sins. He's not committing adultery. He's not betraying a wife."

"He's betraying his family, just as his father did." Phyllis's voice shook with indignation.

"There may not be an innocent wife involved this time, but that makes no difference." Franklin gave Caleb a fulminating look. "The end result will be the same. You'll embarrass this entire family. You'll humiliate all of us again, just as Gordon did. This is a small town. Everyone will know."

Phyllis lifted her chin. "Perhaps that is precisely what Caleb wants."

Roland stared at her. "What the hell are you saying?"

"That perhaps that's what this affair is all about," Phyllis snapped. "It occurs to me that by taking up with a woman like Miss Makepeace, your grandson has found a very effective way to punish all of us."

"Punish us for what?" Roland demanded. "I took him in and raised him. I gave him a home. Made him my heir. What more could I have done for him?"

"Yes, I know, Roland. You did everything you could for him. We all did. One would think he would be grateful." Phyllis gave Caleb a gimlet-eyed look. "But it appears that gratitude is not what he feels for us. I've suspected as much for years."

Roland's hand curved into a fist on the arm of the chair. His gaze was riveted on Caleb. "Is that why you're doing this? Are you trying to punish us for some reason? Is this your notion of vengeance? For God's sake, why?"

"I didn't get involved with Serenity because I wanted revenge on you," Caleb said evenly. "I got involved with her because I wanted her."

"You sound just like your father," Roland shot back. "You even look like he did that day when he told me he wanted Crystal Brooke. How dare you do this to me?"

Serenity raised her hand before Caleb could lash back. "I would just like to point out once again that this scene, however unpleasant, is not, I repeat not, a replay of what happened thirty-four years ago. Things will turn out differently this time if you handle them differently. There is no need to replay the past."

Phyllis glowered at her. "As you yourself noted earlier, Miss Makepeace, the only thing that's different this time is that Caleb isn't married."

"It seems to me that's a major difference," Serenity said. "It also raises a very interesting question." She turned toward Roland. "I'm curious. Had there been problems between Caleb's father and his wife? Or did the affair with Crystal Brooke just come out of the blue?"

"Problems?" Roland beetled his brows. "They'd only been married a couple of years. All young couples have problems. Moving out West was an adjustment for Patricia. We all knew that. What's that got to do with it?"

"I just wondered if perhaps your son got involved

with Crystal Brooke because his marriage was in trouble," Serenity said.

"It was an excuse." Roland's fist slammed down on the arm of the chair. "Nothing more than a trumped-up excuse for satisfying his own selfish lust for that slut."

Caleb went dangerously still. "I warned you not to call her those names."

"Bah, I don't care if she was your mother," Roland said. "She was no good and that's a fact. And I don't care what Gordon said, I never believed for one minute that Patricia was having an affair."

"Patricia?" Serenity repeated quickly. "Was that the name of Gordon's wife?"

"A fine young woman." Roland's eyes were piercing.

"A beautiful young woman," Franklin murmured. "Refined, elegant, well-mannered."

"She was a Clarewood," Phyllis chimed in with obvious satisfaction. "One of the New England Clarewoods, you know. Old money. Ancestors back to the *Mayflower*. Gordon met her when he went back East to visit friends from college. After the scandal broke, she returned to her family. She remarried. A senator, I believe."

"We never heard from her again after she left Ventress Valley," Franklin said in a distant voice.

Caleb paid no heed to Phyllis and Franklin. His entire attention was on his grandfather. "My father claimed Patricia was having an affair?"

"It was a lie," Roland said bluntly. "He made up the accusation to justify his own actions."

"Lies, nothing but shameful lies," Franklin echoed fiercely.

Serenity tilted her head to one side and considered that. "Are you sure?"

"Of course I'm sure," Roland insisted. "Good lord, Ventress Valley is small now, but it was even smaller thirty-four years ago. It would have been impossible for the wife of Gordon Ventress to have an affair for long without someone in the family knowing about it."

"And even if it was true, even if Patricia had an affair, it changes nothing, *nothing!*" Franklin roared. "That's the important thing here. Gordon had no right to subject this family to the shame and humiliation he brought upon it, no matter what the provocation. There was no excuse for it."

Roland peered at Caleb. "Franklin is right. I don't for one moment believe that Patricia was having an affair, but even if she was, it does not excuse Gordon's irresponsibility."

Franklin gave Caleb a seething look. "Your father was spoiled and overindulged from the day he was born. Gordon could do no wrong in Roland's eyes. Roland insisted on giving him everything. All the while I was growing up I had to watch my cousin being raised as if he were someone special, a young prince just waiting to be crowned king of the Ventress clan. All I got were the leavings."

"That's enough, Franklin," Phyllis said firmly. "What's past is past. We all know what came of overindulging Gordon. The important thing here is that nothing excuses his actions." She glowered at Caleb. "Nor yours, you ungrateful wretch. When I think of all we've done for you, I could just weep."

A sense of desperation welled up in Serenity. She met Caleb's eyes. "We'll never know the truth," she said. "In a way, it's really none of our business, is it? Whatever happened between your father and Patricia is in the past, and it will have to stay there. All we're concerned with here is the future."

"What about the future of this family?" Roland demanded.

Franklin's mouth was a thin line. "It's obvious your grandson doesn't care about that."

"I always knew it would come to this," Phyllis muttered. "From the earliest days I could see that Caleb was never really a part of this family. I knew he only tolerated us so that he could take advantage of Roland's money and position. I sensed he never cared about any of us no matter how much we did for him."

Roland's jaw was rigid. "This has gone far enough, Caleb. You're acting the way Gordon acted that day when he told me that he was going to marry Crystal Brooke. And I'll tell you now exactly what I told him then."

"What's that?" Caleb asked.

"If you go through with this shameful marriage, I'll cut you out of my will. I swear to God, I will. You'll never get one penny of the Ventress money."

Serenity noticed that Phyllis and Franklin looked stunned by the threat.

Caleb smiled wearily. "Do you really think I give a damn about being disinherited? Want to know the truth? It will be one hell of a relief."

"Relief?" Franklin's mouth fell open.

"It will set me free," Caleb said.

"How can you say that?" Phyllis gasped. "Think of what you'll be losing."

Caleb flicked her a brief, disinterested glance. "I don't need my grandfather's money. My private income from Ventress Ventures last year nearly equaled that of the family's total income. If I choose, it can go even higher next year." His mouth was a bleak line. "Trust me, Aunt Phyllis, money is the least of my problems."

"I don't believe this," Franklin whispered. "You can't possibly mean it. After all Roland has done for you? After what this family has done for you? You'd walk away from a fortune without a backward glance?"

"As I see it, the only thing I'm walking away from is thirty-four years of blackmail payments. Like I said, it will be a relief."

"Blackmail?" Roland surged to his feet. "What the devil is that supposed to mean?"

Caleb braced his legs slightly apart and confronted Roland. "All of my life I've paid for what my parents did. I've never been allowed to forget for one damn moment that I was the cause of all the scandal and tragedy that this family endured."

"Now just one goddamn minute—" Roland snarled.

"It has always been made clear to me that if I hadn't existed, things would have turned out differently. Perhaps Crystal Brooke could have been bought off. Perhaps my father would have eventually come to his senses and come home to his wife. Who knows? But things didn't turn out right because I was born."

"You've got it all wrong," Roland whispered.

"Have I? How many times have you told me that you were afraid of making the same mistakes with me that you'd made with my father? How many times did you say that I had to be better at everything than my father had been? That I had to prove that I wasn't tainted with my mother's bad blood?"

"You don't understand," Roland said fiercely.

"How often did you lecture me on my duties and responsibilities to the family? *How many times have you called my mother a slut?"*

"Crystal Brooke was a slut," Franklin raged. "She ruined everything."

Caleb ignored him. He kept his attention on Roland. "I've spent my whole life trying to give you what you wanted. But it was never enough, was it? I could never win enough ball games for you. I could never collect enough trophies to satisfy you. I could never make enough money for the family."

"Now see here," Roland thundered, "if I was a little hard on you, it was for your own good."

"No, it was for your own good," Caleb said. "You tried to use me to undue the mistakes of the past. You made me pay for them. That's blackmail. And the one sure thing about blackmail is that it never ends. But I can choose to stop paying it. And that's what I'm going to do."

Roland's mouth worked. He turned away from Caleb and leveled his finger at Serenity. "So help me, if you leave this house to go off with that woman, you'll never be welcome here again."

"I haven't been welcome here since the day I arrived," Caleb said softly. "I was allowed to stay on sufferance. You had to make do with me because I was all you had left."

"Damn you, you sound just like your father," Roland said.

"Bad blood always tells, doesn't it?" Caleb held out his hand to Serenity. "Let's get out of here, Serenity."

Tears stung Serenity's eyes. It was like being on board the *Titanic,* knowing what was going to happen but being unable to stop the impending disaster. Slowly she put her hand in Caleb's.

He strode toward the door, hauling her along in his wake.

"She's done this to you." Franklin was almost hopping up and down in his agitation. "It's all her fault."

"I'm sorry," Serenity whispered.

"I'm not," Caleb said. He nodded brusquely at Dolores, who had appeared in the doorway. "Goodbye, Dolores."

"Please don't do this, Caleb," Dolores begged.

"I have to do it," Caleb said. He paused to glance back at Roland. "You shouldn't have pushed me. I'd probably have gone on paying the blackmail forever, you know. I'd have continued to do my best to give you everything you wanted. But you made one mistake. You tried to come between me and the one thing I want."

Roland gazed at Caleb with white-hot fury burning in his eyes. "Go on, get out of here. Take your little slut and don't ever come back."

Caleb turned without a word and started through the door into the hall. Serenity tugged sharply on his hand and frantically dug in her heels.

"Wait," she said. She looked back at Roland. "It doesn't have to end like this. This isn't the past. You can make it end differently this time."

"Come on, Serenity," Caleb muttered. He yanked her forward into the hall.

"Just a second." She clawed frantically at the edge of the doorway, her eyes still locked with Roland's. "Come for dinner on Thursday. Day after tomorrow. Please. I'll make vegetable curry. You'll love it."

"Serenity, for crying out loud." Caleb pulled hard on her wrist and managed to break her death grip on the doorjamb.

"Witt's End," Serenity called as Caleb dragged her down the hall. "An hour's drive. Once you get there, just ask anyone where I live. If it snows, stop in Bullington. We'll drive down the mountain and get you. I've got chains."

"Damn it, Serenity, shut up." Caleb had the front door open now.

"We'll be expecting you, Mr. Ventress," Serenity yelled. "Six o'clock. Come early, if you like. You can stay the night. I've got room."

Caleb yanked her out onto the porch.

"Christ." He slammed the front door shut and started down the steps to the Jaguar. "What the hell do you think you're doing?"

"Trying to change the past."

"Forget it. Some people don't want the past changed."

16

T HE SOFT STRAINS OF A WALTZ INVADED SERENITY'S troubled dreams. The music seemed closer than it ever had before.

She cuddled the infants in her arms and soothed them gently while she waited for the door of the sunlit white room to open.

Serenity awoke with a start to find herself alone in the bed. She raised herself on one elbow. A glance at the clock on the table told her it was three in the morning. She frowned. The distant waltz continued to play even though the dream had vanished.

Serenity pushed the covers aside and got out of bed. The beaded curtain shuddered, creating a symphony of crickets and bells. She slid her feet into her slippers and reached for her robe. The tinny notes of the waltz grew louder as she went down the short hall to the living room. The cottage was chilly. There was very little heat from the banked fires of the wood stove.

The soft glow of a lamp greeted her as she came to a halt in the arched entrance to the main room. Caleb was seated on the sofa, dressed only in a pair of jeans. His hair was tousled from an obviously restless sleep. His feet were bare, in spite of the cold.

He sat leaning forward, his elbows resting on his knees. Crystal Brooke's jewelry box was open on the coffee table in front of him. He was absorbed by the jerky movements of the tiny dancers.

"I didn't mean to wake you," Caleb said without taking his eyes off the jewelry box.

"It's all right. I wasn't sleeping very well, anyway." Serenity padded softly into the room and sat down beside him on the sofa.

"That's my fault, too. I shouldn't have subjected you to that scene at my grandfather's house."

"I was the one who insisted on accompanying you."

Caleb stared at the tiny dancers. "He won't come for dinner on Thursday, you know."

"If he doesn't, I'll invite him again for Sunday."

"You're wasting your time."

"Maybe. Maybe not." Serenity tucked her hands into the sleeves of her robe and leaned forward to study the jewelry box. The newspaper clippings tucked inside the main compartment were still neatly folded. "What are you thinking about?"

"Something Franklin said today."

"He said a lot of things today. He certainly seems to think he has a duty to keep the past fresh and alive. What a sad, bitter man."

"Sad and bitter?"

"That's the way he strikes me," Serenity said. "There was a strange look in his eyes today when he talked about your father and about Patricia."

"I think Franklin was always envious of my father. He's certainly told me often enough what a beautiful woman Patricia Clarewood was. A perfect lady, as Aunt Phyllis likes to remind me. She always referred to her as the woman who should have been my mother."

"A woman who may have been having an affair behind your father's back," Serenity mused.

"Roland and Franklin are right. Even if Patricia was involved with another man, that's no excuse for my father's actions. He should have divorced Patricia before he got Crystal Brooke pregnant."

"Well, as I said earlier today, that's in the past. Let it stay there, Caleb."

"I've tried." Caleb stared down at the tiny waltzing figures as the music came to a halt. "But for some reason the past has come back to haunt me."

"Because of me." Serenity sighed heavily. "If it hadn't been for me, that terrible scene between you and your family today would never have taken place."

"That's not true." Caleb turned his head to look at her. His eyes were brilliant. "Don't ever say that again. I've been living with ghosts since the day Roland took me to Ventress Valley. I'd grown so accustomed to living with them that I was starting to become one myself."

Serenity stared at him. "Oh, *Caleb*. What do you mean?"

"Forget it." Caleb picked up the jewelry case and rewound the music box. "It doesn't matter any longer."

"But it does matter." She put her hand on his arm. "Do you still feel like you're turning into a ghost?"

"No." He set the jewelry case back down on the table. The little figures began to jiggle as the waltz started. "I feel very much alive these days." He smiled faintly. "I haven't felt this alive in years. And it's all because of you."

He reached for Serenity and pulled her into his arms. The explosive passion in him inundated her. She was caught up by the tide of masculine energy and power. It swept her away on a great wave of surging excitement.

"Caleb."

"You can't even imagine how good this feels. How good my name sounds when you say it like that." Caleb fell back against the sofa cushions, taking Serenity with him. "How good it is to want a woman as much as I want you."

"I'm glad you want me." Serenity sprawled across his bare chest and twisted her hands in his hair. The urgency in him unlocked a tumultuous need deep within her. She was hot and breathless with it.

Caleb kissed her hungrily on the mouth. The kiss grew deeper, until she was shuddering in response. Then his lips slid down to her throat. He yanked at the sash of her robe. When the garment fell open, he slid his hands inside, pushed the hem of her nightgown to her waist and cupped her buttocks. His fingers sank eagerly into her skin, squeezing gently.

Serenity sucked in her breath. She felt his leg shift beneath her. He raised his knee. The rough fabric of his jeans slid along the inside of her thighs, burning her skin, opening her to his touch. The bulge of his confined erection throbbed against her belly.

"You're so wet, I can feel the dampness right

through my jeans," Caleb muttered. "I want you now. Before I lose my mind."

She smiled down at him.

He sat up abruptly, picked her up in his arms and rolled to his feet beside the sofa. Serenity kissed his shoulder and threaded her fingers through the hair on his chest.

Caleb rounded the arm of the sofa and took two strides toward the hall. He stopped, groaning. "Hell, I'm not going to make it as far as the bedroom."

He set Serenity on her feet. She could barely stand. She braced herself against the back of the sofa, a hand on either side of herself, seeking support. Metal scraped on metal, the sound of a zipper being lowered.

She pushed hair out of her eyes and was instantly riveted by the sight of Caleb's heavily aroused body. He already had the foil packet open. In a matter of seconds he was ready for her.

"I want to be inside you." His voice was a harsh whisper. His gaze was stark with sensual hunger.

He crowded close, moving between her legs. He wrapped his hands around her waist and lifted her. Serenity gasped and clutched the back of the sofa more tightly. He held her eyes in an unbreakable bond as he drove himself deeply into her.

Serenity arched and cried out softly as he became a part of her. Her head fell back. He kissed her throat, tightened his grip on her hips and began to move within her. The urgency in him fueled her own need. She felt the fantastic curling sensation grip her lower body. Instinctively she clenched herself around him. Her nails dug into the fabric of the sofa.

"Put your legs around me," Caleb muttered against her throat. "Hold on tight. Yes. Just like that. Like that, oh, God, *yes."* He shifted one hand to the small, throbbing bud between her legs.

She screamed softly as the small convulsions began.

Caleb went rigid as his climax tore through him an instant later. Serenity felt his body shudder again and again.

Somewhere in the distance she heard the strains of a waltz.

Closer now. So very close.

A long time later Caleb stirred on the sofa. He frowned, aware that the room had grown colder. He ought to get up and stoke the wood stove, he thought. Better yet, he probably should get Serenity and himself into bed beneath a pile of quilts. They were both going to freeze if they stayed here on the sofa much longer.

He felt her wriggle on top of him. One sleek leg slipped between his thighs. A plump little nipple moved against his chest. Caleb smiled. On second thought, he decided, there wasn't much chance of either of them freezing. The heat that they generated together was enough to power a large chunk of the Northwest in the middle of winter.

Damn, but he felt good after making love to Serenity. There was nothing else in the world that felt as good as this.

"Caleb?"

"Yeah?" He speared his fingers into her sexy hair.

She raised her head and looked down at him with her unsettling, fairy eyes. "You never got around to telling me what you were thinking about earlier. Something to do with Franklin. What was it that got you out of bed in the first place?"

Caleb remembered the jewelry box on the coffee table. He turned his head on the cushion to stare at it. The music had stopped several minutes ago. The dancers hovered motionless above the old clippings that held the ghosts of his past.

Disturbing thoughts trickled back into his head, driving out the sultry satisfaction that had held him in temporary thrall.

"I couldn't sleep because I kept thinking about something that Franklin said. About the two transactions he said he'd had with Asterley."

"What about them?"

"He claimed that on both occasions he had followed instructions to the letter." Reluctantly Caleb eased the soft, inviting warmth of Serenity aside. He tucked her snugly into her robe and sat up beside her. "He drove his car to a mall, parked, and went inside."

"And left the money in the glove compartment." Serenity tightened her sash. "I suppose it's possible Ambrose drove to the Ventress Valley Mall on two occasions and arranged to collect blackmail money, but I just can't bring myself to believe he did something like that."

Caleb said nothing for a moment. Then he stood and went over to the wood stove. He opened the glass door and tossed a piece of wood inside. He walked back to the sofa, sat down, and contemplated the jewelry box again.

"I can believe he did it once," Caleb finally said softly. "But not twice."

"I don't understand."

Caleb picked up the jewelry box and gazed into the little mirror that was glued to the torn blue satin inside the lid. "If we're to believe Uncle Franklin—a dicey proposition, at best, given his recent track record—he had dealings with Asterley on two occasions."

"So?"

"So, if he told me the truth the morning that he called me here, the second demand from the blackmailer came after Asterley died."

"Good grief. You're right."

"According to Franklin, someone collected money from the glove compartment of his car long after Asterley took the fall down those stairs."

Serenity sat very still, her hands fisted in the ends of the robe's sash. "There do seem to be a lot of ghosts floating around these days."

"I've started to notice that myself."

"As you said, we can't be certain that Franklin was telling the truth about being blackmailed, let alone the timing of the second five-thousand-dollar payoff," Serenity said cautiously.

"No," Caleb agreed. "He could have been lying about that. But he had already confessed to paying five thousand dollars for the pictures in the first place. Why lie about the second transaction?"

"For some reason," Serenity said, "I didn't get the impression Franklin was lying about either transaction. But you know him far better than I do. What do you think?"

Caleb met her eyes in the small mirror. "I didn't stop to think about it at the time. There were other things going on."

Serenity shivered. "That's true."

"At that moment during our confrontation, Franklin was completely preoccupied with the fact that the whole thing was starting to unravel on him. He'd been caught in one lie and he had nothing to gain by continuing to embroider the story. What would have been the point?"

Serenity nodded. "He felt he was justified in his actions, anyway. After all, the photos existed. True, his clever little scheme to blackmail me had fallen apart, but everyone in the family was still nicely shocked by those pictures. He'd accomplished all he could have hoped to accomplish."

"Two blackmail transactions, one before Asterley's death and one afterward." The possibilities spun relentlessly through Caleb's head. "Two blackmailers or one?"

Serenity frowned. "You think that someone other than Ambrose was behind this whole thing right from the start?"

"It's possible."

"That makes more sense to me. Ambrose just wasn't the blackmailing type. A mooch, yes, but not a blackmailer."

"We're back to our earlier conclusion," Caleb said. "Someone else besides Asterley knew about those photos, about me and about my past."

"What worries me the most is that your uncle seemed convinced that he was dealing with Ambrose Asterley both times. And Ambrose was the only one who could have had the pictures."

"All right, so the blackmailer somehow got hold of the photos and posed as Ambrose. Franklin never actually met him in person, remember? He wouldn't have recognized Asterley even if he had." Caleb thought about it. "We're talking about a man, though.

We know that much. Franklin said it was a man's voice on the phone."

"I'm not sure about that. Some women have deep voices."

"Jessie, for instance."

Serenity shook her head quickly. "No, I just can't believe she would do something like that."

Caleb's brows rose. "Face it, Serenity, you aren't going to be able to believe that any of your friends here in Witt's End are guilty."

"True."

"Jessie knew Asterley better than anyone, according to you and everyone else around here. He left everything to her. As his only close friend and heir, she had access to his files before and after his death."

"I just can't imagine Jessie resorting to blackmail. She's one of the few people in Witt's End who makes a decent living from her art."

"If Asterley sold the first set of pictures for cash for photo equipment, he might have confided in Jessie," Caleb said. "After he died, she may have seen the potential of the situation and decided to pick up where he had left off."

"No."

Caleb looked at her. "Then you think of someone else here in Witt's End who meets the criteria. Who else would have had access to both the pictures of you and the information about my past?"

Serenity's eyes were very steady. "Why does it have to be someone here in Witt's End?"

The question rendered Caleb momentarily silent. "Because it all started here in Witt's End," he said finally. "The logic is inescapable. It began when Asterley sent you to hire me as a consultant."

"That doesn't mean it emanated from Witt's End," she insisted.

"It's the only reasonable explanation." He switched his gaze to the jewelry box. "For some reason, I keep thinking there's an answer here somewhere. It always comes back to this."

"The jewelry box?"

"It's all I've got of hers." Caleb reached slowly into the box and pulled out the stack of tattered clippings. "Maybe there's something in these. A name. Another direction we can try."

"I'll take half and you take the other half." Serenity removed a portion of the clippings from his hand. "We'll compile a list of every name that cropped up in the old scandal. Who knows? Maybe something will ring a bell with one of us."

"All right." Caleb got up to hunt for a pen and a pad of paper. When he found them, he put them down on the coffee table. Then he went into the kitchen and poured two small glasses of brandy.

He didn't know about Serenity, but he had a feeling he was going to need a little fortification for what lay ahead.

Half an hour later the list was finished. It wasn't a long one and most of the names on it were familiar to Caleb. They included those of his own family; Gordon's wife, Patricia; a handful of people from Ventress Valley; and one or two minor political figures who had been important at the time but who had long since died.

Serenity studied the list. "Everyone on this list would have known about your past, but there's no one on here who could have known about me and the photos that Ambrose took."

"We can't be certain. I'll have to hire a private detective to check out some of these names," Caleb said.

Serenity looked up uneasily. "If you send an investigator into Ventress Valley to ask questions about the old scandal, you're really going to cause a commotion."

"Do you think I give a damn?" Caleb frowned at the torn satin that lined the lid of the jewelry box. "All I care about now are answers. I'm going to get them."

"I understand," Serenity said softly. "I just wish there was some other way to go about it. There's been so much damage done already."

"You know, there's something strange about this thing." Caleb picked up the jewelry box. "I'm going to tear it apart."

"I can see that. You know something, Caleb? I think blood does tell. Once you start down a certain path, you're every bit as stubborn as your grandfather."

He glanced at her. "I'm not talking about tearing apart the past, I mean this jewelry box."

"The jewelry box?"

"There's something odd about the way the lining is torn. It's too neat. As if it were sliced with a razor or a knife. The other holes are from wear."

Serenity studied the slit in the faded blue satin. "Do you really think that tear is different?"

"Yes."

Caleb took hold of one corner of the small mirror. He ripped it off the inside of the lid with a single tug. A large scrap of thin blue satin came with it.

A black and white photograph that had been hidden behind the satin fell out. It landed, faceup, on the ring drawer.

Caleb found himself staring at a picture of three people. One of them was Crystal Brooke. She was dressed in a demure, high-necked dress that was three decades out of fashion. A wide-brimmed hat was tilted at a stylish angle on her platinum-blond hair. She was smiling down at the infant she held in her arms.

Gordon Ventress stood behind her, his hand resting tenderly on her shoulder. He looked out at the camera with the unmistakable grin of a proud father.

"Caleb." Serenity leaned close, her eyes alight with wonder. "It's a family portrait. Of you and your parents."

Caleb couldn't think of anything intelligent to say. Nor could he take his eyes off the photograph. "Looks like it."

"A real family portrait." Serenity laughed with delight. "This is absolutely fabulous. How lucky you are to have a picture of all three of you together. Look how happy your parents are. They're both glowing. It's obvious they loved each other and you very much."

Caleb realized that his vision was blurring as he stared at the photo. Irritated, he blinked rapidly a few times and his normally excellent eyesight was restored. "I wonder why it was stuck behind the satin."

Serenity lifted one shoulder in a small shrug. "I wouldn't be surprised if your mother put it there as a keepsake and then forgot about it."

"My grandfather must not have seen it when he put

the clippings in the box. If he'd found it, he would have destroyed it."

"You don't know that for certain," Serenity said gently. "In any event, there's no point rehashing what Roland might have done thirty-four years ago."

Caleb forced back the rush of indecipherable emotions that threatened to swamp him. This business of letting himself feel stuff again was all well and good once in a while, but it could be a damned nuisance at other times. His calm, methodical, logical approach to important things tended to get muddled up when he allowed the emotional side of his nature to take over.

He schooled himself to think clearly and logically. "The picture is interesting, but it's not exactly a major clue."

"I suppose you're right."

"Serenity?" Caleb tucked the photo into the jewelry box and closed the lid.

"Yes?"

He took a deep breath and felt the blood pulse slowly, heavily, in his veins. "Will you marry me?"

Her lips parted on a soundless exclamation. She seemed to be having trouble with her throat. "Marry you?" Her voice was higher than usual. "Why on earth do you want to marry me?"

He looked at her. "Probably because I'm a conventional, straitlaced, old-fashioned kind of guy."

"Oh."

"What's the matter, Serenity?"

"Nothing," she said quickly. "You've just taken me by surprise, that's all. I hadn't realized you were thinking about . . . about marriage."

"No? What have you been thinking about?"

"I don't know." She swallowed. "I mean, why marriage at this point?"

"I told you why."

"You're conventional, straitlaced, and old-fashioned." Her anxious eyes searched his. "But I'm not. Conventional, straitlaced, and old-fashioned, that is. Here in Witt's End, we do things differently."

"Is that right?"

"Yes, well, I mean, just look around." She gestured wildly with one hand. "Julius and Bethanne just got married last month. They've been living together for years. Jessie and Ambrose never got married. My own parents weren't married."

"And neither were mine, remember? I'd just as soon not repeat that particular part of the past."

"Caleb, there's no rush. I'm not pregnant. We haven't really had a chance to get to know each other."

He felt himself grow cold inside. She was trying to edge away from him. Trying to put some distance between them. Maybe she didn't want him as much as he wanted her. He forced back the surge of despair.

"I can guarantee you that you know me better than anyone else on the face of the planet." He kept his voice calm with a supreme effort of will.

She faced him with a strange, expectant expression in her peacock eyes. "Caleb, do you love me?"

The question made him stop breathing for a good three or four seconds. She had a right to an answer, he thought. But he didn't have one for her. Desperation seized him. He couldn't lose her because of a few simple words.

Give her the words. They're only words.

She was the most important thing in his life. If he lost her, he would lose part of himself, the part that had learned to feel again.

It was hopeless. He would kill for her, but he couldn't lie to her. *It wouldn't be any good if he lied.*

"I don't know," Caleb said starkly. He was starting to dematerialize again. He could actually feel it happening right there on the sofa.

Serenity watched him. She looked like a creature of moonlight and magic who had been accidentally trapped in the harsh glare of the sun. She blinked once, twice, and then she smiled her fey smile.

"No, I don't suppose you do know if you love me," she said. "When was the last time someone told you that you were loved?"

"I can't remember." Why didn't she just answer his question? All he wanted was a simple answer. "What the hell does that have to do with this?"

"Everything, I think. But it's not important now." Serenity touched his cheek. "I love you, Caleb. But I can't leave Witt's End. Do you understand that? There are things I have to do here."

"I won't ask you to leave Witt's End."

"But you can't stay here forever," she said sadly. "I've known that from the beginning."

"You're wrong. I can stay here as long as I want. Hell, that's the least of the problems. I can run Ventress Ventures from here."

"You can?"

"This is the age of computers and fax machines, remember?" he said impatiently. "I can set up shop anywhere."

"But would you want to stay here?" she asked.

"Are you crazy?" he whispered. "Why would I want to leave? This is the one place on earth where I've ever felt completely alive."

"Caleb." She threw herself into his arms and hugged him fiercely. "Yes. Yes, I'll marry you, if that's what you want."

He could breathe again. He crushed her so tightly against him that she gave a tiny squeak that was half laughter and half protest.

"Sorry," he muttered into her hair. He loosened his grip slightly, but not much. The warmth and scent of her caused a welter of indefinable emotions to sweep through him. He didn't care what the sensations were or whether or not they were affecting his logic. The important thing was that they were there and they were strong and he could feel them.

He was no ghost.

He was alive. He had a future.

He had Serenity.

17

 Y OU'RE GOING TO MARRY HIM?" ZONE DROPPED THE LID
on a large barrel of whole wheat flour back into place
and swung sharply around. Her orange and saffron
robes flared wide, echoing her agitation. "Serenity,
what are you talking about? Why would you want to
marry Caleb?"

"Because I love him." Serenity dusted off a row of
jars containing blackstrap molasses. "And he loves
me. He just doesn't know it yet."

"If he doesn't know it, don't you think it might be a
bit premature to marry him?"

"Probably." Serenity moved down the aisle to wield
her duster over an array of noodle packages. "But I
don't think I can wait."

Zone stared at her. "Are you pregnant?"

"No."

"Then why can't you wait?"

"It's a little hard to explain, Zone." *Even to herself.*

She knew she was taking a risk by trying to second-guess Caleb's true feelings.

Unfortunately, it had become very clear that Caleb himself wasn't very good at identifying and dealing with his own emotions. She suspected that he had spent too many years learning to distance himself from his own needs in an effort to satisfy his family's endless demands, too many years fulfilling his responsibilities to the name of Ventress. He didn't fully comprehend the nature of his responsibility to himself.

The years spent paying for the sins of his parents had left him with a bone-deep distrust of his own desire to love and be loved. She didn't think he even comprehended the real meaning of the word, at least not in the same way that she understood it.

But Caleb's failure to define love properly did not mean that he didn't have a hidden talent for it, Serenity thought optimistically. She had sensed it in him from the first. It was, after all, one of the things that had drawn her to him at the start of their relationship.

This morning she was still convinced that she was right about his ability to love. In the past few days she had seen the banked fires in his eyes, felt the gentleness in his touch, caught glimpses of the deepest reaches of his soul.

Surely a man with such depths had to be capable of giving and receiving love.

Last night she had concluded that the real problem was that Caleb's working definition of love was an extremely narrow one. A person learned about love, after all, from example.

Until she had come along, Serenity realized, the only kind of love Caleb had ever known was the kind that came with strings attached.

It was no wonder he didn't recognize his true feelings for her, Serenity thought as she took another swipe with the duster. For Caleb, the word *love* had a lot of harsh definitions. Most of them had to do with icy concepts of duty and responsibility. The negative, underlying message that Caleb had always received from his family had been that if he repeated his father's mistakes, he would be unworthy of love.

The meaning of love for Caleb was all tied up with the necessity to prove himself over and over again to a family that never quite trusted him. Or forgave him for the past.

But he felt something else for her, something that he didn't yet understand because it wasn't icy and stark and unforgiving like the concept of duty. It was something for which he did not yet have a clear definition, let alone a name.

At least, she hoped that was true. Because if it wasn't, if she was deluding herself, she was going to pay a terrible price.

That fact left her faced with a dangerous choice. She either took a chance that she was right about Caleb's feelings for her or else she let her own chance at love slip away.

"Serenity, perhaps you should meditate on this decision a little longer," Zone said gently. "Ariadne says that Caleb is different from the other men you've known."

"That's true." Totally different from any man she had ever known, she thought with a small smile.

"Serenity?" Zone stared at her. "Is something wrong?"

"No. I was just wondering if I should order another batch of Luther's homemade salsa. We're running low. Caleb says it's going to be a big seller in the catalog, by the way."

Zone sighed. "Please don't misunderstand. I know Caleb has got wonderful plans for your mail order business. And I am personally, very, very grateful to him. He and Blade together probably saved my life. But I'm just not certain Caleb's the right soul mate for you. Even though I like him, I still sense danger in his vicinity."

"I thought you'd decided you'd gotten his vibrations mixed up with Royce Kincaid's."

Zone frowned thoughtfully. "It's true that I did, but I have that all sorted out now and things still don't feel quite right. I detect more darkness in Caleb's aura."

"I'll bear that in mind."

The phone rang before Zone could continue. Relieved at the excuse to end the conversation, Serenity put down her duster and hurried to answer the summons.

She dodged behind the counter, rounded the corner of the office doorway and grabbed the receiver. "Witt's End Grocery."

"I wish to speak to Miss Serenity Makepeace."

There was no mistaking Phyllis's perpetually disapproving tone. Serenity was not in a mood to deal with her. She was, in fact, thoroughly annoyed with the entire Ventress clan today.

Last night she had come to the stunning realization that she may have been the first person in history who had actually said the words "I love you" out loud to Caleb. If it was true, the Ventresses had a lot to answer for as far as she was concerned.

"This is Serenity. What can I do for you, Mrs. Tarrant?"

"I do not appreciate the fact that I am forced to make this call, Miss Makepeace."

"Well, I'm not real thrilled with having to take it, either, so let's get it over with."

"Very well, I shall be blunt. I suspect that is the only approach your sort understands. Franklin and I have talked it over. How much do you want?"

Serenity caught her breath. Then she forced a lightness that she was far from feeling into her voice. "How much? Oh, dear. Are you selling something, Mrs. Tarrant? Door-to-door cosmetics, perhaps? I really don't use very much of that kind of stuff, but I suppose I could buy some hand cream or something."

"Your sarcasm serves no purpose except to waste time. You may as well be as straightforward with me as I am being with you. Just tell me how much money it will take to get you to leave all of us alone."

"I'm not interested in all of you, only in Caleb." She probably shouldn't be baiting Phyllis like this, Serenity chided herself. But it was difficult to be polite under the circumstances.

"I am only too well aware of your mercenary interest in Caleb, Miss Makepeace." Phyllis's voice sharpened with tension and anger. "But your so-called 'interest' in him is tearing this family apart."

"I'm not sure that the glue that holds your family together is very strong in the first place. Raising a boy with the notion that he has to pay for the mistakes of his parents is not a good way of making him feel loved and wanted. It's also not a smart way of ensuring that he develops any real affection for his family."

"Damn you," Phyllis snapped. "The private affairs of the Ventress family are none of your concern. We did our best for that ungrateful boy in spite of what his father did to the family."

"And you never let Caleb forget it for one minute, did you?"

"Caleb was strong-willed, even as a youngster. He needed to be reminded frequently that he must not make the terrible mistake his father made."

"Fat lot of good it did to keep drumming that into him."

"I am hoping that Caleb's lapse in judgment regarding you, Miss Makepeace, is merely temporary. I do not wish to discuss it further. Now then, as I said, Franklin and I have discussed the issue of money. Franklin has already paid a total of ten thousand dollars to keep your pictures out of the public eye. We are willing to make it worth your while to disappear from Caleb's life."

"First blackmail threats and now an offer to buy me off. I'm not sure what to say. I have to tell you, Mrs. Tarrant, where I come from, people don't do things like that. It's considered tacky. Good-bye."

Serenity slammed down the phone, cutting off Phyllis's outraged yelp. She sat on the edge of the desk, fuming, for several seconds. Then she grabbed the receiver again and dialed information.

"What city?" the operator asked.

"Ventress Valley. I want the number for the home of Roland Ventress." Serenity waited, afraid that she would be told that the number was unlisted.

It wasn't. She grabbed a pen, jotted it down, then dialed it swiftly.

"Ventress residence."

"Dolores, is that you? It's me, Serenity Makepeace."

"Miss Makepeace." Dolores sounded startled and anxious. "Good heavens, I wasn't expecting to hear from you. I thought it might be Mrs. Tarrant again. Has anything else gone wrong? I've been so worried. It's been pretty dreadful around here."

Serenity clutched the receiver. "I was calling to see if by any chance Mr. Ventress has made plans to come to dinner tomorrow night."

There was a short, depressing pause. Dolores sighed. "No, I'm afraid not. At least, he hasn't said anything to me about it."

"I want you to give him a message, Dolores. Tell him that we're still expecting him. Tell him that he has the power to change the future just by showing up here for dinner tomorrow night. Tell him . . . oh, heck, I don't know what else to tell him."

"I wish I could do something to help, Miss Makepeace. This is just so unfortunate. Mr. Ventress is a fine man, but he and his grandson are both too proud for their own good."

"Too proud." Serenity slid off the desk and stood beside it, thinking swiftly. "That's it. The one thing the Ventresses have in common is that stubborn pride of theirs."

"That's a fact."

"Listen, Dolores, tell Mr. Ventress that Phyllis and Franklin have tried to buy me off and it won't work. Tell him that if he wants to deal with me, he'll have to do it face-to-face over dinner tomorrow night. Tell him he can't hide behind his niece and nephew."

"Mr. Ventress would never hide behind Mrs. Tarrant and her brother," Dolores said loyally.

"That's not the way it looks to me," Serenity said. "I got the distinct impression that he's using them to do his dirty work. Tell him that, Dolores. If he wants to convince me otherwise, he'll have to come here to Witt's End and face me like a man."

Dolores sighed. "I see what you're trying to do, but it'll never work."

"It's worth a try. Give Mr. Ventress the message. Oh, and Dolores . . .?"

"Yes?"

"It's a long drive for a man his age. Do you think—"

"Don't worry," Dolores said. "If this works, Harry will drive Mr. Ventress to Witt's End."

"And leave him here overnight?" Serenity added persuasively.

Dolores hesitated. "I think that can be arranged."

"Good-bye, Dolores. And thanks."

"Good luck, Miss Makepeace. Lord knows, we're all going to need it."

Serenity heard the grocery's door bells chime as she replaced the receiver. She ignored them while she contemplated her desperate scheme. There was no denying that her ploy to get Roland to Witt's End was based on a rather lame dare. It didn't stand much chance of working unless Roland just happened to be looking for an excuse to come to dinner in the first place.

Serenity recalled the well-concealed warmth that she had glimpsed once or twice in Roland's eyes when he had looked at Caleb. She could only hope that she had not misread his true feelings toward his grandson.

A movement in the office doorway interrupted her thoughts. She turned around to see a familiar figure attired in a leather jacket, jeans, boots, and Outback hat.

"Oh, no," she muttered. "Please. Not now."

"Hey, hey, hey, Serenity love. How's my little redheaded Titania today?" Lloyd swooped through the doorway, grabbed Serenity and enveloped her in a bear hug.

Serenity braced herself against his chest and shoved herself back out of his arms. "What are you doing here, Lloyd?"

"Had a couple more thoughts on how to handle my study of Witt's End. Wanted to go over them with you. I think we can work out a compromise vis-à-vis the mail order catalog project. If you'll just put your plans on hold for a few months, I can get my interviews and observations done."

"I can't talk to you about your study now, Lloyd, I'm very busy at the moment."

"This won't take long, love." Lloyd threw himself down into a chair and propped his boots on her desk. He took off his hat and tossed it onto the desk beside his boots. "All I'm asking is that you listen to my plans."

"I'm going to have to ask you to leave, Lloyd. I've got too much to do and I have no intention of changing my plans so that you can pursue your stupid study."

"Listen, Serenity, I've got it figured out. All you have to do is delay your catalog project until next summer."

"I'm not going to delay it one minute."

Lloyd's grin vanished. "Serenity, I've got a career riding on this study."

"The future of Witt's End is riding on my mail order catalog plans."

"Bullshit." Lloyd's eyes narrowed. "This is personal, isn't it? It's got nothing to do with the future of Witt's End. You're trying to punish me for what happened six months ago. I never realized you were so vindictive, love."

Serenity ran her fingers through her hair. "Believe me, I'm not trying to get even for what happened."

"I don't believe you." Lloyd smiled with understanding. "You were hurt."

Serenity glared at him, exasperated. "I was pissed off. Look, we've both agreed that we're not exactly meant for each other."

"Okay, maybe we weren't meant to hear wedding bells, but we can be colleagues."

"Colleagues?" Serenity repeated very sweetly. "The way we were colleagues on that paper you published?"

Lloyd's teeth flashed in another disarming grin. "Hey, hey hey. Tell you what. We'll do this study of Witt's End together. I'll put your name on the paper as co-author. How does that grab you?"

"It doesn't. Even if I was inclined to help you, Lloyd, I have to be honest and say up front that I don't believe for one minute that you'd put my name alongside yours on any paper you got published."

"Well, truth is, a grocery store owner wouldn't have much credibility with the editor of a major academic journal, but I'll acknowledge your assistance in the notes. How's that?"

"Gee, Lloyd, that's a really dazzling prospect." Serenity drummed her fingers on the back of her chair. "If I had publishing ambitions, that is. Which I don't. And if I was willing to postpone my plans for Witt's End, which I'm not. All things considered, I'm not going to be able to be of much assistance to you."

"You don't mean that." Lloyd gave her his most winning smile, mouth curved with just the right laconic twist, eyes lit with an intimate, knowing gleam. "You'll do it for me, love. For old times' sake."

She batted her lashes. "Old times' sake? You've got to be kidding."

Lloyd's smile tightened. "Serenity, I'm going to level with you. I've got too much riding on a study of Witt's End to let you get in my way. One way or another, I'm going to get a paper out of this dipshit little town."

"So do your study. I'm not stopping you."

"Damn it, I need the cooperation of the natives, and we both know I won't get it unless you talk them into giving it to me."

Zone floated into the doorway and cleared her throat gently. She put her palms together and looked straight at Serenity. "Your fiancé is here."

Serenity gazed blankly at her. "My what?"

Lloyd was a bit faster on the uptake.

"Fiancé." His booted feet came down off her desk and hit the floor with a crash. "What the hell are you talking about? Serenity, you're not thinking of getting married, are you? You can't possibly be engaged. You can't do this to me."

"Fiancé?" Serenity repeated slowly. "I never thought of it quite like that."

"You'll have to excuse her, Radburn." Caleb eased Zone out of the doorway so that he could fill the opening himself. He did a thorough job of it. "Serenity's still getting accustomed to the idea. Marriage is kind of a novel concept around here."

Lloyd gaped at Caleb and then rounded on Serenity. "Is this guy serious?"

"About getting married?" Serenity glanced at Caleb. The dangerous expression in his eyes made her distinctly uneasy. "Uh, yes. Yes, as a matter of fact, he is."

Caleb braced one hand against the doorjamb. "Real serious."

"You can't do this to me!" Lloyd howled.

Serenity blushed furiously. She was not accustomed to being argued over by two virile males. It was rather flattering. "Lloyd, don't you think you're overreacting just a tad?"

"Overreacting?" Lloyd echoed in thundering disbelief. *"Overreacting?*

"As in going bonkers," Caleb clarified. "Falling out of your tree. Going nutso."

Serenity shushed him with a repressive little movement of her hand. She smiled gently at Lloyd. "I didn't realize you felt that strongly about our relationship, Lloyd. I'm touched. But we both know that we would never have made a success of a long-term, committed relationship, even if we didn't have that unpleasant business of six months ago between us."

"Damn it, I'm not talking about our relationship," Lloyd shouted, "I'm talking about my fieldwork. My paper. My career, for crying out loud. You can't get married, Serenity."

"I can't?"

"She can't?" Caleb asked with one dangerously arched brow.

"It will ruin everything." Lloyd looked acutely desperate now. "It will cause even more damage to the existing social structure of Witt's End than your mail order catalog business."

"I don't believe this," Caleb muttered.

"I don't see how my marriage will destroy the world as we know it in Witt's End," Serenity said stiffly.

"Don't you understand?" Lloyd yelped. "Getting married is too damn normal for you."

Serenity blinked. "Too normal?"

Lloyd began to pace the tiny office. "I've explained to you that the beauty of Witt's End is that it functions very much like a frontier town, complete with its own legends and customs. And you're the most important part of the local scene. You're the heart and soul of Witt's End, a legend that's being created even as we speak. Don't you get it?"

"No, I don't." Serenity scowled. "Lloyd, you're getting carried away with your academic analogies."

"The hell I am. You're the magic princess of Witt's End," Lloyd insisted. "The fairy in their midst, the sacrificial maiden."

"Sacrificial maiden?" Serenity stared at him.

"As far as the locals are concerned, you came to them from out of nowhere. Your origins are cloaked in mystery, just like the origins of any good myth."

"For heaven's sake, Lloyd, that's ridiculous."

"Think about it," Lloyd urged. "It's so damn primitive, it's incredible. You were seen as someone special, someone important, right from the start. You were raised by the tribal elders. Educated in the ways of the community's arcane lore."

"Arcane lore." Serenity couldn't believe her ears.

"Initiated into ancient mysteries . . ." Lloyd continued.

Serenity held up a hand to stop him. "Hold it right there. This nonsense has something to do with your curiosity about those hot springs, doesn't it? How many times have I told you, there's nothing to that old legend about vision pools."

Lloyd was undaunted. "You've grown up with a sense of duty and responsibility toward this community. Witt's End saved you, gave you everything it had. And in turn you're trying to save it. You're willing to sacrifice yourself for Witt's End. Talk about a myth that's woven into the very fabric of the community. It's perfect. Absolutely perfect."

Serenity eyed him uneasily. "Lloyd, I think you're cracking up. Maybe the pressure of trying to make department head is getting to you."

"No, I'm on to something here." He slapped her desk with his palm. "I've felt it all along. It's dynamite. I recognized your unique role in this culture immediately."

"You mean my role as sacrificial maiden and magic princess?" Serenity asked politely. "Gosh, Lloyd, I wish you'd mentioned it to me earlier. I could have sent off for a mail order tiara."

"This isn't a joke," Lloyd said through gritted teeth. "You're critical to this culture. You have to maintain your role in it, at least until I finish my study. You have to keep yourself pure and undefiled, like any good sacrificial maiden."

"I'm afraid it's a little too late for Serenity to play Vestal Virgin," Caleb said softly.

Lloyd glared at him. Then he turned to Serenity. He jerked a thumb toward Caleb. "Don't tell me you're sleeping with Ventress, here. I don't believe it."

Serenity's cheeks burned. "I have absolutely no intention of discussing my sex life with you."

"You're going to ruin everything," Lloyd hissed. "Damn it, why the hell do you think I didn't take you to bed, myself? Why do you think I broke off our relationship when I realized things might get too serious? The last thing I wanted to do was disrupt the social dynamic around here by seducing you."

Serenity could feel herself turning a brilliant shade of red. She had never been so mortified in her life. "I see."

"It's bad enough if you're sleeping with him," Lloyd said urgently. "But you absolutely cannot ruin all of my hard work and plans by marrying an outsider like Ventress."

Caleb's brows rose. "Think of it as a fairy-tale marriage, Radburn. Local princess gets prince."

"Yes," Zone exclaimed suddenly, startling everyone in the office. Her voice rang with excitement. "Yes, that's the explanation for everything. I understand it all now."

Serenity, Caleb, and Lloyd turned to stare at her.

"It has become clear to me at last." Zone's eyes shone with something that closely resembled transcendental wonder. "The wedding of Caleb and Serenity is a cosmic event. Caleb is the mysterious intruder who has come to claim the sacrificial maiden of Witt's End."

"Told you so," Caleb said.

Zone's robes fluttered as she raised her hands above

her head. "It will be a marriage of yin and yang, a soaring, metaphysical connection between male and female, a celebration of the renewal of the life force."

"Zone, I don't really think this is the time or the place for this kind of thing," Serenity said.

Zone ignored her. "I knew from the beginning that Caleb's presence here in Witt's End meant that some strong forces had been set in motion. I sensed it but I did not fully comprehend the meaning of the dark, dangerous aura that surrounds Caleb. Especially when it did not fade after the events involving Royce Kincaid."

"And now you've got my dark aura figured out?" Caleb asked with grave interest.

"Yes," Zone said. "It is the aura of raw power under the control of your masculine will. Only a man capable of channeling such power is suited to bond with Serenity, for she is a woman of equal feminine power. This marriage is fated to change the destiny of Witt's End."

"Wait a second," Lloyd said. "I'm trying to tell you that I don't want Witt's End to change. At least not until I've had a chance to immortalize it in my study."

Caleb's smile was laced with cheerful malice. "Sorry about that, Radburn. But you know what they say, you can't halt progress."

Lloyd glared at him. "You're not going to be reasonable about this, are you?"

"Nope," Caleb assured him, "I'm not. Us mysterious intruders with dark auras aren't noted for being reasonable. Not when we're bent on claiming sacrificial maidens, at any rate."

"Son of a bitch." Lloyd stalked toward the door.

"You business types have no respect for intellectual research."

"And no particular desire to help you get that promotion to department head, either." Caleb politely stood aside as Lloyd brushed past him.

Lloyd did not bother to respond. He continued out through the front of the store. He slammed the door so violently that one small bell fell to the floor with a pathetic little tinkle.

Serenity, Caleb, and Zone looked at each other.

Zone smiled serenly and slipped her hands inside the sleeves of her robe. "If you'll excuse me, I'll go finish pricing the new supply of yogurt."

Serenity watched Zone move off out of earshot. Then she spun her chair around and collapsed into it with a shudder. "What a ridiculous scene."

"I don't know about that," Caleb said thoughtfully. "It had its moments. And Zone's assessment of our wedding plans was nothing short of brilliant."

Serenity glowered at him. "A marriage of yin and yang? A soaring, metaphysical connection between male and female? A celebration of the renewal of the life force?"

"Yeah," Caleb said. "And the sex isn't bad, either."

Serenity raised her eyes to the ceiling. "I do so admire a man who doesn't fall prey to his baser instincts and the lure of lust in the dust, a man whose goals and motivations spring from the metaphysical realm rather than the mundane physical world, a man who takes a cosmic view of male-female relationships."

"How about a man who can put two and two together?" Caleb removed the photograph of his parents and himself from his pocket and tossed it down onto the desk in front of her.

Serenity glanced at the little family portrait. "What do you mean?"

"Turn it over."

Serenity picked up the photograph and looked at the reverse side. It had been stamped with the date and the name of the studio.

ASTERLEY AND FIREBRACE. PHOTOGRAPHERS TO THE STARS.

Serenity's eyes widened. "Oh, my God. Asterley and Gallagher *Firebrace?* Ambrose and that photographer who tried to rip off some of his equipment after he died were partners at the time this picture was taken?"

"I should have figured out the connection right from the start."

Serenity glanced up and saw the self-recrimination in his eyes. "Yes, I know. You're usually good at that kind of thing." She smiled gently. "Don't be too hard on yourself, Caleb. This is family stuff. Sometimes we don't always think too logically when it comes to dealing with family relationships."

"I've never had that problem myself."

"Is that right?" Serenity murmured under her breath. She nibbled thoughtfully on her lip as she studied the information on the back of the photograph. "It looks like Ambrose might have actually met your parents. And you. Weird, huh?"

"It definitely explains a few things. Like how he knew about the old scandal."

"He probably kept track of you over the years because he had once photographed your family. He was always so obsessive with details. When I told him

350

I was going to hire a hotshot business consultant, he naturally thought of you."

"Apparently so." Caleb picked up the photograph and tapped it gently against his palm. "And according to this, he wasn't the only one who knew a lot about me and my family."

"Gallagher Firebrace might have known your parents, too."

"If Firebrace was Asterley's partner in the old days, he would definitely have known about the scandal."

"And Ambrose kept in touch with him over the years. Borrowed money from him. There's no telling how much he might have told him about my plans."

"I think it's time I looked up Gallagher Firebrace and paid him a visit."

"You think he might be the blackmailer, don't you?" Serenity asked.

"I think it's a damn good possibility."

"I'm going to Seattle with you."

"No," Caleb said.

"What makes you think that you can stop a cosmic force like me?"

18

Aʀᴇ ʏᴏᴜ sᴜʀᴇ ᴛʜɪs ɪs ᴛʜᴇ ʀɪɢʜᴛ ᴀᴅᴅʀᴇss?" Sᴇʀᴇɴɪᴛʏ
came to a halt on the sidewalk and surveyed the sign
in the window of the small, run-down photography
studio.

Caleb pulled a slip of paper out of the pocket of his
jacket and consulted the address that he had gotten
out of the Seattle phone book. "First Avenue. Yeah,
this is it."

He glanced at the neon sign that had captured
Serenity's attention. In a garish shade of orange it
proclaimed: FIREBRACE PHOTOGRAPHY—PASSPORTS AND
I.D. PHOTOS—NO WAITING. The *No* portion of the sign
had burned out, leaving the impression that one could
expect to wait indefinitely.

He probably shouldn't have allowed Serenity to
come with him, he thought. On the other hand, how
dangerous could this confrontation be? Firebrace was,

in all probability, the blackmailer, but the photographer would know as well as he that there was no proof to link him to the crime.

"It doesn't look like Gallagher Firebrace has been wildly successful in his chosen field," Serenity remarked.

"At least he seems to be making a living at it, which is more than Asterley did." Caleb winced as a horn blared behind him. The familiar sounds of hissing air brakes and roaring engines annoyed him today for some reason. He had only been away from the city for a short while, but apparently he had already grown accustomed to the tranquil atmosphere of Witt's End.

"The place looks closed," Serenity said. "Maybe we should have called first."

"I didn't want to give Firebrace a chance to work on his answers before I asked my questions." Caleb studied the dust-shrouded windows. There was no sign of life behind the glass, but there was no Closed sign hanging in the door window, either.

He wrapped his fingers around the doorknob and twisted. The door opened with a squeak, revealing the empty front portion of the shop.

A scattering of faded examples of badge photos and identification pictures adorned the walls. There were two metal folding chairs and an ashtray filled with cold cigarette butts in the waiting area. The pattern on the linoleum was obscured by years of wear. A small notice on the glass countertop read: *Will Return in Five Minutes.*

"Anybody here?" Caleb called.

There was no response.

"Maybe he's in the back," Serenity suggested. "He

might be working in his darkroom or taking photographs of a client."

"More likely he saw us coming and decided to keep out of sight."

Caleb went around behind the counter. He pushed open the swinging door that separated the front portion of the shop from the studio.

He went through the doorway and came to an abrupt halt when he saw what was waiting for him.

He was standing in a black-and-white wonderland filled with giant images of Crystal Brooke's vivid face.

The enlarged photos of his mother were everywhere in the studio. Her mischievous, laughing eyes looked down on him from the ceiling and confronted him from all four walls of the room. Her sultry lips, parted in a timeless, provocative smile, filled vast stretches of space. Her platinum hair spilled across the floor in waves beneath his feet.

The camera had caught a variety of luminously lit expressions from seductive to serene to humorous. They were all brilliant portraits, not of a particular person, but of an archetypal woman-goddess, and they were all focused entirely on Crystal's face. None of them showed her in the nude.

Caleb studied them intently. He had seen work this fine somewhere else, he realized. And recently.

Serenity came through the door behind Caleb. She stopped in amazement. "What in the world?"

"It's a little strange, isn't it?" Caleb tore his eyes away from the myriad images of Crystal Brooke and examined the rest of the room. There was no trace of color anywhere in the studio. Everything, from the black metal tripods, cameras, and lighting equipment to the sheets of white gauze used as backdrop material was either black or white.

"It's like walking straight into an old photograph," Serenity whispered. "Caleb, I don't like this."

He glanced back at her over his shoulder. Serenity was standing nervously amid a jungle of lights mounted on tall, spindly tripods. She had insisted on wearing one of her town-and-country outfits today, a beige and tan pantsuit that did nothing for her. But, as always, her own, naturally vibrant features more than compensated for the drab clothing.

Her hair was a radiant cloud of fire against the eerie black-and-white room. Her peacock eyes had never looked more intensely green. They were also very wide as she met Caleb's gaze.

"Wait outside if it makes you uneasy," Caleb said. "I want to look around."

"I think we should both get out of here. Right now. Please, Caleb."

"Just give me a minute." Caleb saw a row of black cabinets at the rear of the studio. Thinking of the interesting information he had discovered in Asterley's files, he started forward.

"Caleb, wait. There's something very wrong about all this," Serenity said anxiously. "I really think we should leave."

"Too late, I'm afraid, Miss Makepeace." Gallagher Firebrace spoke from the doorway behind her. "Much too late. But then, maybe it always was."

"Oh, my God," Serenity whispered.

Caleb turned. Firebrace smiled his crooked smile and pointed the barrel of a gun at Caleb's midsection. "I didn't think you'd figure it out. At least not for a long time. What gave you the lead?"

"A photograph," Caleb said. "A picture of my parents taken shortly after I was born. It had 'Asterley and Firebrace Studios' stamped on the back."

"A photograph." Firebrace grimaced. "How appropriate. So you put it all together and came looking for me."

"Not all of it." Caleb glanced at the gun. "If I'd figured out all of it, I wouldn't have brought Serenity with me today."

"An unfortunate mistake as far as Miss Makepeace is concerned."

"Wait a second," Serenity said tightly. "What's going on here?"

"Don't you get it, Serenity?" Caleb asked. "Firebrace is not just a blackmailer. He's a murderer."

"Murderer?" Serenity stared at him in amazement. "But no one's been killed."

Caleb kept his eyes on Firebrace. "Ambrose Asterley was killed, wasn't he, Firebrace?"

"Ambrose?" Serenity's hand went to her throat. "Oh, no, not Ambrose." She turned accusing eyes on Firebrace. "You killed him?"

"It was an accident," Firebrace snapped. "I never meant for him to die."

"Accident?" Serenity breathed. "I don't understand."

Firebrace gave her a brief, impatient glance before returning his attention to Caleb. "He caught me that night when I broke into his cabin the second time. I thought he'd gone to bed drunk, you see, like the first time. But he hadn't. After his girlfriend left, he just sat there in his living room with the lights turned out. He heard me come through the window, I guess. It was almost as if he'd been waiting for me."

"Maybe he was waiting for you," Caleb said casually. "Maybe he had a hunch you'd be back. After all, you'd already broken into his files a few days earlier, hadn't you?

Firebrace's thin mouth tightened into an even narrower line. "The first time I went in to get the pictures of Miss Makepeace. He never heard a sound that time. Passed out in the bedroom."

"You returned the second time in order to put a receipt into the files, didn't you?" Caleb asked. "A receipt that showed the photos of Serenity had been sold to Franklin Ventress. You wanted to cover yourself just in case someone came looking for the blackmailer."

Serenity was outraged. "You deliberately tried to make Ambrose look like a blackmailer?"

"It seemed the logical thing to do," Firebrace said. "Just in case anyone ever came looking."

Caleb watched his face. "Too bad you hadn't thought of that little touch the first time around. Because things went wrong when you went back the next time, didn't they, Firebrace?"

Firebrace's fingers tightened on the gun. "Ambrose heard me come through the kitchen window. He caught me. Demanded to know what was going on. I told him the whole story, tried to reason with him. I offered to cut him in on the deal, but he went into a rage. He came at me like a wild man. Said Serenity was a friend of his."

"I knew Ambrose would never have blackmailed me," Serenity said.

Firebrace didn't appear to hear her. He had an odd look in his eyes. "I ducked to the side but Ambrose just kept going. Straight through the open basement door. Straight down the stairs. I never meant for it to happen that way."

"You bastard," Serenity whispered.

"I realized afterward that I had to make it look like the accident it was," Firebrace said quickly.

Caleb shoved his hands into the pocket of his jacket. His fingers touched the palm-sized rock Webster had given him. It was still right where he had left it. He'd forgotten to take it out of the pocket.

"You wanted it to look like an accident," Caleb said, "because you didn't want anyone asking questions that might lead to an investigation or an autopsy. An autopsy would have shown that Asterley was not intoxicated when he fell."

"I got a bottle from his kitchen stash," Firebrace said. "I knew him well enough to know that he always kept a bottle around, even when he was on the wagon. I poured the whiskey over him."

"Just another little added touch," Serenity said angrily. "Like sticking the receipt into his files. I suppose it must be instinctive for a photographer to keep fiddling with his subject, trying to get everything perfect before the final shot. Why did you take the risk of showing up in Witt's End the morning after I found Ambrose?"

"That's easy," Caleb said. "He wanted to do a little more fussing with the scene, didn't you, Firebrace? You couldn't resist checking the details. You wanted to make certain that you hadn't left any evidence behind."

"Once I knew Ambrose's body had been discovered, I thought it was safe to go back," Firebrace explained. "After all, what could be more natural than for an old friend to stop by after hearing of the tragedy?"

Caleb eyed him thoughtfully. "And who would notice, after all, if you helped yourself to a couple of cameras or some lighting equipment. Just a few mementos of your old friend and partner."

"Well, why not?" Firebrace's smile was bitter. "Ambrose sure as hell didn't need the gear any longer. Some of that equipment was worth a small fortune."

"There's one thing I don't understand," Serenity said. "How did you know that I'd gone to see Caleb about my plans for expanding my business?"

Firebrace shrugged. "Ambrose called me up a couple of weeks after you went to see Ventress the first time. He tried to hit me up for a few bucks. It was a regular routine with him, you know."

"I know," Serenity said softly.

"As usual, I told him I didn't have a dime to spare," Firebrace said. "Then, out of the clear blue sky, he started talking about the old days. Said something about life being weird and how what goes around, comes around. He said that he'd just sent a friend to see Crystal Brooke's son. Asked me if I remembered Crystal."

Caleb glanced around the walls of the studio. "Obviously you did."

The gun jerked in Firebrace's hand. "Ambrose was having one of his good days. He wanted to talk. He told me all about Miss Makepeace's plans for Witt's End."

"Did you know about the pictures he'd taken of me?" Serenity asked.

"Sure." Firebrace made a face. "He'd bragged about them last spring after he'd finished the shoot. He said at the time that it was some of the finest work he'd ever done."

"When he told you that I was going to see Caleb, you remembered the old scandal, didn't you?" Serenity said. "You knew what you could do with those photos. You realized that if you could convince the Ventresses that I was involved with Caleb, you could capitalize on their fear of a new scandal."

Firebrace rocked on his heels. "Very clever, Miss Makepeace. You're right. I knew all about the Ventresses. I had a good idea of how they'd react to the news that the heir apparent to the family fortune was following in his father's footsteps. All I had to do was make it appear that Caleb was romantically involved with you. That was easy to do."

Serenity frowned. "How did you do that? Caleb and I weren't really involved in anything but a business arrangement at that point."

"I took a few shots of you and Ventress leaving his office here in Seattle together. One of you and him going into a restaurant. Franklin Ventress's imagination did the rest." Firebrace chuckled humorlessly. "Imagine my surprise when I discovered later that you and Ventress actually were involved."

"You were too smart to go to my grandfather with your demands," Caleb said. "You knew how he'd respond to a blackmail threat."

"Hell, yes, I knew." Frustrated anger flashed in Firebrace's eyes. "He'd refused to pay thirty-four years ago when I'd sent him the pictures of Crystal and Gordon Ventress. But I knew there were other members of the family who weren't so stubborn and who would do anything to keep the precious family name from being dragged through the *Ventress Valley News* again."

Serenity drew a deep breath. "You were the one who tried to blackmail Roland Ventress all those years ago?"

"Everything went wrong that time," Firebrace said in a strange, faraway voice. Then his eyes hardened. "But I made up for it this time. I planned things more carefully. I contacted the banker in the family, not the old man. I knew Franklin Ventress would be an easier target. I was sure he'd pay."

"What made you think you knew him so well?" Caleb asked, suddenly and deeply curious about the answer.

"Crystal told me about him," Firebrace said impatiently.

"What did she tell you about him?"

"Just what your father had told her. Franklin was having an affair with Gordon's wife. I knew he had hated Gordon Ventress with a passion. I took a chance that he probably also hated Gordon's son and would give anything to see him ruined in the old man's eyes."

"Damn," Caleb said under his breath as the missing pieces of the puzzle fell into place. "So Franklin came across with the first five thousand without even batting an eye, didn't he?"

"He wanted the pictures. He wanted them real bad."

"Too bad you didn't take that one payment and run."

"It was only five thousand," Firebrace said, looking genuinely offended. "I couldn't stop there. I figured someone in the family would pay again to keep the pictures out of the papers."

"You were greedy," Caleb mused. "And you still had the negatives, after all. Why not go back just once more?"

"I planned to go back several more times," Firebrace said. "As often as I could, in fact. But then Ambrose broke his neck in that fall and destroyed my plans."

"Because with him dead, you no longer had any protection," Caleb said. "Continuing the blackmail scheme would be a lot more risky without a fall guy to take the rap. Sooner or later someone might start an investigation. The trail might lead to you. Still, you had to go back just once before you packed it in, didn't you? It was just too much money to throw away."

Serenity studied Firebrace as if he were a member of the rodent family. "You couldn't resist contacting Franklin with another demand a few days after Ambrose died, could you?"

"It was worth the risk. I'd only gotten one payment out of him. I knew those pictures were worth at last another five grand to the Ventresses. It was unlikely that Franklin Ventress would ever find out precisely when Ambrose died," Firebrace said.

"Or even that he was dead?" Serenity asked.

Firebrace scowled. "Why would anyone tell him something like that? Asterley's death certainly wasn't significant enough to make the *Ventress Valley News*. Besides, Franklin Ventress was the last person who would start asking questions. All he cared about was his own revenge on Gordon's son."

"But why did Franklin hate Gordon so much?" Serenity asked softly. "Was it just because Gordon was Roland's heir?"

"That was probably part of it." Firebrace sounded irritated. "But not all of it. According to Crystal, it was mostly because of Patricia Ventress."

"Patricia?"

"Don't you get it?" Firebrace said. "He loved her. Really loved her. And she left him because of the scandal. He never saw her again."

"It fits," Caleb said slowly.

"Crystal understood." Firebrace narrowed his eyes. "She knew how much Franklin cared about Patricia. She said he'd seduced Patricia in the beginning because he was envious of Gordon and wanted to take something that belonged to his cousin. But in the end Franklin fell in love with Patricia."

"Franklin blamed my father for the humiliation Patricia endured." Caleb thought quickly. "Franklin could never forgive him because the scandal cost him the woman he loved."

"He could never forgive you, either," Serenity whispered. "He had to punish you for daring to get involved with a woman who reminded him of Crystal Brooke."

"Yes."

"Franklin paid for those photos the first time because he wanted ammunition to use against Caleb," Serenity said slowly. "But why was he willing to pay the second blackmail demand?"

"Because he was a Ventress," Firebrace said with a

grim laugh. "Damn family is so proud it makes me sick."

Caleb fingered the stone in his pocket. "You're right. Franklin has the Ventress pride. He didn't want another scandal to hit the local papers any more than anyone else in the family would have wanted it. He knew my grandfather wouldn't pay blackmail so he had no choice but to do it himself."

"He was caught in his own trap," Serenity said.

"Exactly," Caleb said. Out of the corner of his eye he saw Serenity watching him, saw her gaze dip briefly to where his hand disappeared into his pocket. He hoped she realized that he still had Webster's latest discovery, but he couldn't take the risk of looking directly at her to see if she understood the significance of that fact. He kept his attention on Firebrace.

"You seem to know a great deal about my family," Caleb said.

"I learned everything I needed to know about your whole damned family over three decades ago," Firebrace said. "Nothing has changed. You Ventresses still think you're more important than the rest of us. You think you can have anything you want just for the taking."

"You wanted my mother, didn't you?" Caleb said softly. "You wanted Crystal Brooke for yourself."

Firebrace flinched as if he had been struck. "She was mine." He blinked several times. "Your father stole her from me. He seduced her with his money and his fancy family name and his big-time political connections. Promised her the world. And she believed him, the little fool. She believed he would marry her."

"And in the end, that's exactly what he planned to do, wasn't it?" Caleb said.

"She tried to treat me like a friend," Firebrace said fiercely. "She didn't understand that she belonged to me. She wouldn't allow anyone else to photograph her except me, you know. She trusted me to make her look like a goddess. And I did." He flung out a hand to indicate the photographs laminated to the walls, ceiling, and floor. "Take a good look. I made Crystal Brooke unforgettably beautiful."

"I think she was already beautiful to begin with," Serenity said crisply. "Furthermore, if you cared so much about her all those years ago, why did you try to blackmail the Ventresses? You must have known how much damage you would create."

"It was for her own good," Firebrace insisted. "I thought that once the Ventresses realized what was going on between her and Gordon, they'd put pressure on the bastard to end the relationship. But it didn't work. Roland Ventress wouldn't even pay for the pictures. So I sent the photos to the editor of the *Ventress Valley News*. I thought the resulting scandal would force Crystal and Gordon apart."

"Instead, my father walked away from his family, his political career, and my grandfather's money," Caleb said. "He announced he was going to get a divorce and marry Crystal."

"Before I could think of another way to stop the marriage, it was too late. Crystal and Ventress had both been killed in that crash." Firebrace's voice rose to a keening wail. "You were the only one left alive. It wasn't supposed to end that way. As far as I'm concerned, the Ventresses killed Crystal just as surely as if they'd put a gun to her head and pulled the trigger. After everything I did for her, she was gone forever."

"Just what did you do for her?" Caleb asked softly. "You certainly weren't the one who took these pictures of her, were you?"

Firebrace's face contorted with fury. "I was her photographer. I made her a goddess. If she hadn't thrown herself away on that son of a bitch who was your father, she'd have become a brilliant film star."

"Not because of your photography," Caleb said. "This is Ambrose Asterley's work, isn't it?"

"That's a lie," Firebrace shouted. "A damned lie."

"I don't think so," Caleb said with growing certainty. "I've seen work that resembles this quite recently. There's something about the play of light on the face, the way she looks into the camera, the otherworldly feeling of the picture. Asterley captured those same elements in the pictures that he took of Serenity."

"No," Firebrace yelled. "These aren't Ambrose's pictures. Ambrose was a failure."

"He may have been a commercial failure because of his drinking problem, but the man knew how to handle a camera." Caleb curved his fingers more tightly around Webster's rock. "And as his business partner, you ripped him off on a regular basis, didn't you? You must have really panicked when he finally gave up and headed for Witt's End. You knew you'd never survive without his talent."

"That's not true, damn you," Firebrace shouted. "You don't understand. I was the one with the talent." He raised the gun a notch and bared his teeth. He braced himself to pull the trigger.

Caleb risked a quick glance at Serenity. And in that

instant he knew that she had already read his mind. She had one hand wrapped around a tripod.

With a swift, violent movement, Serenity sent the metal stand crashing into the forest of lamps and cameras. The domino effect took hold. Expensive equipment began to topple to the floor.

"My cameras!" Firebrace screamed. He took his gaze off Caleb and instinctively turned toward the scene of the disaster.

Caleb knew it was the only chance he would get. He pulled Webster's rock out of his pocket and hurled it at Firebrace's head.

The small missile struck its target with a dull thud. Firebrace jerked, dropped the gun and crumpled to the floor without a sound.

Several more tripods holding lights and cameras fell with a thundering clatter. The crash of metal and glass seemed to go on forever before a stark silence fell on the black-and-white room.

Serenity looked at Firebrace's motionless body for a shocked instant. She whirled and ran toward Caleb. He opened his arms and caught her close.

"I was right," she whispered against his jacket. "You did have Webster's rock in your pocket."

"You mean I had Webster's unique, one-of-a-kind, hand-selected, genuine Witt's End paperweight in my pocket," Caleb said. "Remind me to make room for his innovative new product in the catalog. No home should be without one."

Serenity made an odd sound and clung even more tightly to Caleb. "Webster will be thrilled."

Firebrace groaned.

Caleb released Serenity and walked across the room to where the photographer lay on the floor. Firebrace's lashes fluttered and then opened. He looked up with a dazed expression.

"You'd better find a phone and call 911," Caleb said to Serenity.

"I think I saw a phone out on the counter." She started toward the swinging door. "This is going to be a real mess to explain to the cops."

"I'll take care of it."

"Yes, I know," Serenity said softly. "You're good at that kind of thing." She went through the door.

"It wasn't supposed to end like this," Firebrace muttered thickly. He gazed up at the picture of Crystal Brooke on the ceiling. "She wasn't supposed to be in the car."

A chill went through Caleb. He went down on one knee beside Firebrace. "Who wasn't supposed to be in the car?"

"Crystal." Firebrace stared blindly at the huge photo of Crystal's face. "I loved her. I didn't want her to die. Only Ventress was supposed to be in the car when the brakes failed. Only Ventress and the baby."

"You son of a bitch," Caleb whispered. "You killed them both, didn't you?"

"Cost me a thousand dollars to bribe the mechanic. But it didn't work. She died, too." Firebrace's eyes filled with tears as he gazed up at Crystal Brooke's face. "Why doesn't anything ever go right for me?"

Caleb waited until much later that evening to make the call to Franklin.

"Just tell me one thing." Caleb tightened his grip around the hotel room phone. "Why did you do it?"

"You don't understand," Franklin said in a defeated voice. "Gordon always got the best of everything. He even got Patricia. But she didn't love him. She never loved him. She married him for his money. Her family insisted on it. The Clarewood fortune had all but disappeared because of a series of bad investments."

"So she married my father?"

"She called him a rude, unsophisticated cowboy," Franklin said. "She told me she couldn't stand to get into the same bed with him. She hated his hands on her. She hated Ventress Valley just as much as she hated Gordon."

"She turned to you for consolation, didn't she?" Caleb leaned forward and rested his elbows on his knees. He was aware of Serenity watching him quietly from the other side of the room. "And you encouraged her."

"I loved her," Franklin said fiercely. "I admit that at first I wanted her just because she belonged to Gordon. But I fell in love with her. I thought, after the scandal broke, that we would marry."

"Instead, she went back to Boston."

"It was Gordon's fault," Franklin whispered. "Everything was his fault. Patricia had to leave after he died. She said that if she married me, Roland would turn on me. She said he would blame me for seducing her. Accuse me of causing problems in her marriage. She said he would cut me off from the Ventress money."

"And you knew that was probably exactly what would have happened, didn't you?"

"Roland went a little crazy after Gordon died. He would have vented his rage on any available target. We knew that. Patricia didn't want me to suffer, she said. Said it would be better if we never saw each other again."

"You kept quiet about your affair with Patricia and she left town."

"Patricia was right. It was for the best. There's no telling what Roland would have done if he'd discovered our affair. But I did love her. You've got to understand that."

"Not enough to risk my grandfather's anger."

"For God's sake, I couldn't. There was too much money involved. And the family name. Gordon had already done enough damage. I had a duty to avoid any more scandal."

"You did your duty, is that it? You stayed in Ventress Valley, married, and raised a family. And prospered. And nursed your grudge. And then one day you got a phone call telling you that history was about to repeat itself."

"I did what I had to do. It was my duty to prevent you from humiliating all of us the way your father had. I did it for the sake of the family."

"I don't think that was why you did it at all, Franklin." Caleb met Serenity's gentle, sympathetic eyes. "I think you did it because you wanted plain, old-fashioned revenge."

"What the hell do you mean by that?"

"I wasn't Gordon, the cousin you had resented all of your life, but I was his son. That was close enough, wasn't it? You transferred your resentment of my father to me. And when you got the call telling you that there were nude photos of a woman with whom I was having an affair, you jumped at the opportunity to avenge yourself on me."

"No, it wasn't like that."

"I think it was exactly like that," Caleb said wearily. "You wanted to make certain that I didn't find what my father found for a while, what you yourself had never found."

"What was that, damn you?"

"Happiness."

19

"I'VE BEEN THINKING," SERENITY SAID THE FOLLOWING EVE-ning as she went about preparing dinner. "That man Zone thought she saw in the fog the night Ambrose died must have been Firebrace. We assumed it was Royce Kincaid come to terrorize her, but Kincaid himself said he'd only appeared once at her window."

"You're right." Caleb concentrated on the bottle of wine he was in the process of opening. "It was probably Firebrace. Based on what he told the cops, the timing fits. And the car that Blade heard driving down the road shortly after midnight must have been his."

"Jessie told us she had left around eleven." Serenity selected a knife from the kitchen drawer and went to work on a pile of vegetables for the curry dish she had planned. She only bothered with the elaborate dish, which required a wide variety of exotic spices, on occasions when she was expecting company.

372

The rice was cooking in the steamer, and a row of small condiment bowls containing chopped peanuts, raisins, chutney, chives, candied ginger, and coconut sat ready on the counter. She had made Caleb stop at a wine shop to select a couple of bottles of expensive chardonnay before they drove back to Witt's End this morning. They had spent the night in Seattle because the interview with the police took most of the afternoon.

Serenity surreptitiously glanced at the clock for the fifth time in the past twenty minutes. Dinner would be ready in half an hour, and there was still no sign of Roland Ventress. She was trying to maintain an outwardly calm facade, but her insides were starting to twist themselves into knots. She had been so certain he would come.

Caleb was in his full stoic mode, acting as if nothing at all was out of the ordinary. He was calm, cool, and in control, as usual. He was not sneaking glances at his watch, as far as Serenity could tell. He hadn't mentioned the possibility of his grandfather arriving for dinner. It was as if he didn't even recall that the invitation had been issued.

But then, Caleb's expectations had been much lower from the start, Serenity reminded herself. Close to zero, most likely. He had never believed that his grandfather would come.

She, however, had convinced herself that Roland would take advantage of the excuse she'd provided him to salvage his relationship with his grandson. She was counting on Roland being too smart to repeat the errors of the past.

The table had not yet been set. Serenity dreaded doing so because then she would be forced to make the decision regarding the number of plates. She could not bring herself to put out only two plates tonight. But she also knew that it would be far worse to set the table for three and have one place setting remain unused. It would be like having a ghost for dinner.

"Are you going to tell your grandfather about what really happened to your parents?" Serenity asked as she attacked a potato with her knife.

"Most of it. He deserves to know the truth."

Serenity looked up as Caleb poured the wine into two glasses. His face was carved in stone, his eyes unreadable. He was waiting, too, she suddenly realized—listening for the sound of a car in the drive; wondering if there would be a knock on the door.

Waiting, but expecting nothing. He was good at this kind of thing, she thought. But then, he'd had a lot of practice.

"What about Franklin's role in things all those years ago?" Serenity asked quietly. "Are you going to tell Roland about that, too?"

Caleb hesitated. "Probably not. What would be the point? Franklin's got a wife and a son. Grandchildren. They'd all be hurt if the past got thrown in their faces at this stage. And they don't need to know how loyal he still is to his romanticized version of his affair with Patricia."

"I wonder why your father never told Roland the name of the man who was having an affair with Patricia."

Caleb was quiet for a moment. "He probably figured he was already doing enough damage to the family. There was no need to do more by naming Franklin as Patricia's lover. It wouldn't make any difference, anyway."

"And being a Ventress, he was probably too proud to bother trying to justify his affair with Crystal," Serenity said.

"Probably."

"So he protected Franklin, and that no doubt made Franklin even more resentful," Serenity said.

"Why?"

"It would have made Franklin feel weak. What a mess. He had always resented Gordon, but after Patricia left Ventress Valley because of the scandal, and Franklin saw his own happiness forever doomed, at least to his way of thinking, his bitterness grew worse."

"He blamed the fact that she left on my father."

"The bottom line," Serenity said, "is that she probably didn't love him at all. She was unhappy with your father, feeling trapped three thousand miles from the life she knew, so she turned to Franklin for comfort and consolation. But she didn't really love him."

"No."

"And deep down Franklin must have known that."

"Just one more reason why he could never forgive my father."

"Or you," Serenity said.

"Or me," Caleb agreed. "But then, that's no big deal. No one else in the family ever forgave me, either."

Serenity slanted him a quick glance. His face was still expressionless. "I suppose Franklin reacted so strongly to news of my pictures because he desperately wanted to believe you were Gordon all over again. He wanted to think you were doing what your father had done, that you'd gotten yourself involved with some-

"I'm not sure." Caleb started to dress. "But it looks like we'd better take a look. The last time Blade discovered a point man for an invasion force, things got real serious." He hesitated. "Want to come along?"

"Hell, why not? Seems to be my night for doing a lot of crazy things."

"Ain't crazy, sir," Blade said stiffly. "Folks say I'm paranoid, but I know I ain't crazy."

Roland shrugged into his shirt. "I wasn't referring to you, soldier." He scanned Blade's array of implements. "You got any extra firepower you can loan me for the mission? I didn't come prepared."

Blade eyed him. "You got some experience in this kind of thing, sir?"

"Been a rancher all my life. Spent a few years in the Marine Corps."

Blade beamed with satisfaction. "Reckon you're the one who taught Caleb here how to handle a weapon."

Roland flicked a hooded glance at Caleb. "Reckon I was."

"Here you go, sir." Blade removed a revolver from his belt and handed it to Roland.

Roland examined the gun for a few seconds. "Nice."

"I keep all my equipment in good shape," Blade said. "Man's only as good as his equipment."

"Ain't that the truth," Roland agreed.

Caleb swore softly and raised a hand for attention. "Hold on a minute here. Nobody goes off half cocked. We will all proceed to Asterley's cabin in an orderly fashion, and we will find out precisely what is going on there. But no one, I repeat, *no one,* is to open fire on one who would shame the family. It justified all his bitterness. Verified his belief that you and Gordon were both unworthy of being Ventress heirs."

"I suppose so."

Serenity sought for a way to change the subject. "Lucky for us you were a championship player on your high school baseball team." She recalled the rows of trophies in the glass cabinet in his grandfather's house. "You saved our lives with your pitching skills. You must have had a heck of a coach."

"My grandfather was my first coach," Caleb said without inflection.

Serenity stopped chopping vegetables. "Really? Roland taught you to pitch a baseball?"

Caleb picked up his wineglass and looked at her. "You know how you keep saying that we all have bits and pieces of other people stuck to us?"

Serenity touched the griffin that hung on the chain around her throat. "What about it?"

"I think I'm beginning to see what you mean."

"Caleb—"

"He's not coming tonight, Serenity. I told you that he wouldn't be here. I wish you hadn't gotten your hopes raised."

"If he doesn't come tonight, he'll come this weekend. I know he will."

Caleb shook his head once, with grave certainty. "No."

"I can't believe he would be so rigid and unbending and so stupidly stubborn."

"He's a Ventress," Caleb said.

"Okay, I'll admit it appears that a talent for that kind of thing does run in your family. I still can't believe he won't have the sense to do what he can to change the past."

"Some people don't want the past changed. Take Franklin, for example."

The sound of an engine in the driveway shocked Serenity into silence. Her eyes locked with Caleb's.

"Someone else," Caleb said gently. "Montrose or Ariadne."

"No, I don't think so." Serenity flung down the towel and raced for the door.

A blast of cold air hit her like a wave as she stepped out onto the front porch. The glare of headlights blinded her. She put up a hand to shield her eyes so that she could see who was getting out of the car.

Caleb emerged from the cottage and casually put one hand on her shoulder.

The car door on the passenger side slammed shut with an air of decisive finality. A tall, broad-shouldered figure stalked forward to stand silhouetted in the lights. It was impossible to see his face against the blinding glare, but Serenity had no doubts as to the visitor's identity.

"I'm so glad you could make it, Mr. Ventress," she said as she went down the steps. "You're just in time for dinner."

Roland swung around as the car started to back out of the drive. "Where the hell do you think you're going, Harry?"

"Be back later, boss," Harry called cheerfully as he gunned the engine.

"Much later," Serenity murmured. "Come inside, Mr. Ventress. We have a lot to talk about."

* * *

As it happened, they didn't have a lot to discuss. By the time the meal was concluded, Serenity was getting desperate. Her hopes, which had soared so high a short while earlier, were having trouble even staying aloft now. Roland and his grandson were indeed having dinner together, but they seemed to have nothing to say to each other.

"More curry, Mr. Ventress?" she asked.

Roland looked at her. "No, thank you. I've had enough."

Serenity gave Caleb a beseeching look. "What about you, Caleb?"

"No, thanks."

"Well, then, I'll get the dessert." She jumped to her feet and began to clear the table. "I hope everyone likes lemon pie."

"Fine with me," Roland said.

"Tea, anyone?" Serenity offered.

"No thank you," Roland said.

"No thanks," Caleb muttered.

"Coffee?" Serenity prodded.

"No thank you."

"No thanks."

Serenity started to panic. She had exhausted all the usual sources of dinner conversation. The weather, including the possibility of snow, had been the liveliest topic so far. It had lasted for nearly five whole minutes. Roland had shown a brief interest in the curry ingredients, but that subject, too, had quickly waned, as had a short chat about the state of the mountain roads.

She was a desperate woman, Serenity decided as she sliced into the lemon pie. Desperate measures were called for if the evening was to be salvaged. Something had to be done to break the ice. She glanced out the window as she carried the plates of pie back to the table. The darkened bulk of the glass-walled hot tub room loomed in the shadows.

Perhaps it was easier to melt ice than to break it.

"I have a terrific idea," Serenity said as she set the pie in front of Caleb and his grandfather. "Why don't you two try out the hot tub after dinner?"

Caleb choked on a forkful of pie. "The hot tub?"

Roland looked thoughtful. "Do you know, I've never been in a hot tub."

"I'm sure you'll enjoy it. Very relaxing," Serenity said brightly. She ignored Caleb's strange expression. "You two will have to go in alone, however."

"Damn right," Caleb said. "You sure as hell aren't going in unless you can dig up a swimsuit."

"I've got one somewhere," Serenity murmured. "But I'm not going to go look for it. I plan to stay out of hot tubs for a while."

Caleb scowled. "Why?"

"For the same reason that I won't be drinking any alcohol for the next several months," Serenity said serenely. "I'm in training."

Roland beetled his bushy gray brows. "In training for what?"

"To have a baby."

Caleb's chair toppled over with a crash as he got to his feet. "You're *what?*"

"Getting in training to have a baby," Serenity said patiently. "It's time."

"You're going to marry her, then?" Roland eyed Caleb from the other side of the bubbling hot tub. The lights were off inside the glass-walled room, but there was sufficient glow from the cottage windows to reveal his glowering expression.

"As soon as possible." Caleb stretched his arms out along the rim of the tub and settled back. A brief memory of his first experience in this room flitted through his mind. He remembered the first time he had touched Serenity's lovely breasts, the enthralling way she had caught her breath and clung to him as the gentle convulsions of her first orgasm shook her. He smiled to himself.

"Just as well, I guess," Roland grumbled. "Especially if she's serious about having a baby."

"I take it that the notion of me marrying Serenity is preferable to the thought of the Ventresses being forced to endure the embarrassment of having another bastard in the family?"

"I never thought of you as a bastard," Roland muttered.

"No?" Caleb looked at him with cool disbelief. "How did you think of me?"

"As my grandson," Roland said quietly. "The only one I had. You were all that remained to me of Gordon."

Caleb exhaled slowly. "Bits and pieces of other people."

"What?"

"Nothing. It's not important. Just something Serenity keeps saying."

"She's an unusual young woman."

Caleb watched the hot water churn. "Yes, she is."

"Did you know that she contacted Dolores yesterday morning?"

"No."

"Sent word that Phyllis and Franklin had tried to buy her off."

Caleb frowned. "I didn't know about that."

"She told Dolores that she wouldn't deal with them. Said if anyone was going to try to buy her off, it would have to be me. And I'd have to come here tonight to do it."

Anger sliced through Caleb. "I didn't hear about any of this."

"Expect she didn't intend for you to hear about it." Roland paused thoughtfully. "I knew what she was up to right away, of course. Knew she was trying to force me to make the first move."

"Is that why you came here tonight?" Caleb asked. He should have known. He should have guessed that Roland was here only because he'd thought he might be able to buy off Serenity.

"No," Roland said. "There's not enough money in the world to buy off a woman like her. I knew that from the start."

The warmth of the hot water seeped slowly back into Caleb, driving out the cold in his guts. "But you came anyway."

"Figured I had nothing to lose by accepting a dinner invitation," Roland said. "Hell, maybe she'll be good for all of us. God knows it probably pays to get fresh bloodlines into a family now and then, just like it does in horses."

"There is that." Caleb kept his tone neutral, but he was secretly stunned by the massive olive branch Roland had just offered. "There's something I need to tell you."

"About what?"

"The past. It's a long story."

"I don't think it's a good idea to talk about the past anymore," Roland said. "Let's just let it rest in peace."

"We've never been very good at letting it rest in peace, have we?"

"No, I guess not."

"Maybe we can after I tell you what happened yesterday in Seattle." Caleb wondered where to begin. Then he recalled the family portrait of himself and his parents. "First, there's a picture I think you should see."

"A picture of what?"

"Me and my parents."

Roland seemed to sink deeper into the frothy water. "Didn't know there were any pictures of you with them."

"There is. One. It was hidden in my mother's jewelry case. And it led me to some answers to a lot of questions that should have been asked a long time ago."

"All right," Roland said. He sounded as if he was bracing himself for battle. "Tell me what you found."

Something made Caleb glance out into the night at that moment. Shadows moved in the darkness. Two massive canine heads appeared at the glass walls of the hot tub room. They were followed by a large, familiar figure draped in great quantities of lethal-looking hardware.

"Hell," Caleb said. "Not now."

Blade made a fist with his gloved hand and pounded softly on the glass. "Got to talk to you," he mouthed.

Roland straightened abruptly in the tub and stared

at the figure on the other side of the window. "Who the devil is that?"

"His name is Blade." Caleb climbed out of the hot tub and reached for a towel. "Don't worry. He's a friend."

"Looks like something out of a goddamn war movie."

"Yeah." Caleb opened the door. Cold air, dogs, and Blade moved into the steamy room.

"You got visitors," Blade said. He stared at Roland.

"As a matter of fact, we do," Caleb said. "My grandfather. So unless this is something really urgent, Blade, I'd like to suggest that you come back some other time."

"It's urgent, all right." Blade turned back to face him. "Invasion's started."

"Again?" Caleb asked.

"What invasion?" Roland demanded. He stood up in the hot tub and grabbed a towel.

"Don't ask." Caleb waved his grandfather into silence. "Okay, Blade, let's take this from the top. What makes you think the invasion has begun?"

"Someone's nosing around Asterley's cabin."

"Asterley's cabin? Are you sure?"

"Probably the point man. More'n likely the rest of the commando team is on hold at the bottom of the mountain, waiting to see if this guy can secure a fire base. Stop him and we got a chance of nipping the invasion in the bud." Blade indicated the clothes that Caleb had left on a hook. "Better get dressed. Ain't got much time."

Roland scowled in the shadows. "Would someone mind telling me just what in blazes is going on here?"

anything or anyone unless I give the command. Understood?"

Blade snapped to attention. "You're in charge around here, Mr. Mayor."

Roland's brows rose. "Mr. Mayor?"

"Remind me to tell you about my budding career in local politics," Caleb said.

"Politics."

The back door of the cottage opened at that moment. Serenity appeared. She hovered anxiously on the threshold for a minute, peering into the glass-walled hot tub room. Then she hurried across the porch and slid the glass door open.

"What is going on out here? *Blade."* She glared at him in the shadows. "What on earth are you doing here?"

"Got trouble, Serenity," Blade said. "Invasion's started. Got to neutralize the point man before he signals the others with an all-clear."

"Oh, no, not tonight," Serenity wailed. "Couldn't you halt the invasion some other night? I've got a houseguest this evening."

"Sorry," Blade said. "They picked the time. Not us."

Serenity turned to Caleb. "Can't you do something about this?"

"Don't worry." Caleb put one foot on the bench and leaned over to tie his boot laces. "I'm good at this kind of thing."

For some reason, Caleb was genuinely surprised to see the flashlight beam sweep past the kitchen windows of Asterley's cabin. "I'll be damned. Someone is in there."

"Told you so." Blade's voice was a gravelly whisper. It emanated from the vicinity of a huge fir tree. Charon and Styx waited eagerly in the shadows beside him.

Roland came to a halt next to Caleb and studied the darkened cabin. "There's someone in there, all right."

"I can see that." Caleb braced himself against the biting cold and tried to think quickly. So much for the theory that this was a simple fantasy born of Blade's chronic paranoia. There was definitely an intruder in the Asterley cabin. He wondered who would want to prowl around in there at this time of night.

Then he recalled the file cabinets in the basement. Nearly four decades of photographs were stored in the downstairs room that Jessie had not yet cleared out. There was no way of knowing what Asterley had photographed over the years. The files had contained fodder for Firebrace's blackmail scheme. They might very well contain other pictures that someone else would consider devastating. Maybe others had learned of Asterley's death and had come to search through his files for dangerous pictures.

"Point man, all right," Blade said. "No doubt about it."

"Looks like you got yourself a burglar in there, Mayor," Roland said quietly. There was an underlying current of excitement in his voice.

"Or just a transient who decided to bed down in an empty cabin for the night," Caleb said, trying to maintain his role as the rational one in the group.

"Wouldn't think you'd get many transients here in Witt's End," Roland observed. "Especially at this time of year. Too damn cold."

"We get all kinds here." Caleb listened to the

sentence as it echoed in his mind. *We get all kinds here.*

We.

For the first time he realized he had started to think of this bizarre community as home. Home was where a man settled down. Got married. Raised a family of his own.

I'm in training to have a baby. It's time.

"Well, son? What do you think?" Roland asked.

"I think it's time," Caleb said softly.

Blade stirred amid the branches of his tree. "Want me to send the dogs in first?"

"No," Caleb said. "Not until we know what's going on. The last thing we need is a lawsuit filed against us for a malicious dog attack."

"Won't be no lawsuit if we get rid of the body," Blade said helpfully.

"You're right," Caleb said, trying to be patient. "But it'll be a lot cleaner if we handle this one officially, the way we did the last one."

Roland's head swiveled around in the shadows. "What last one?"

"It's a long story," Caleb said. "I'll tell you about it later. Right now we've got other things to do. Follow me, gentlemen."

"We going to break down the door?" Blade asked.

"Not right away." Caleb led the way through the trees, circling the cabin. "First we're going to see if there's a car parked in the driveway."

"Good idea." Roland held the revolver pointed toward the ground as he fell into step beside Caleb.

"There's a car in the drive," Blade said. "Saw it earlier. Guy came in undercover."

Caleb saw the familiar silhouette of a sports car as

soon as he rounded the corner of the cabin. In the shadows it was impossible to discern the color, but he was fairly certain it would prove to be red.

"Forget the invasion." Caleb came to a halt. "That's Radburn's car."

"The professor?" Blade sounded disappointed. "The one who's been botherin' Serenity?"

"I'm afraid so," Caleb said. "I wouldn't be surprised to find out that Jessie's real estate agent rented the cabin to Radburn. Looks like he's decided to take an aggressive approach to his research."

"Does this mean the excitement is over for the night?" Roland asked. He sounded almost disappointed.

Caleb smiled slowly. "Not necessarily. Blade, why don't you take the dogs and go knock on the front door?"

Blade's teeth flashed briefly. "I get it. You want me to be the welcoming committee, is that it?"

"Something like that," Caleb agreed. "Don't forget to warn him that he's living in a high-risk zone. Could be an invasion any day."

"I'll tell him all about it," Blade said. He motioned to Styx and Charon, who fell in happily at his heels.

Roland watched Blade and the dogs head toward the front door of the cabin. "This should be interesting."

"It usually is," Caleb said.

Caleb was still laughing half an hour later when he walked into the warmth of the cottage. Roland followed him through the door, chuckling. Serenity eyed both men warily as she closed the door.

"What's going on here?" she demanded. "Where's Blade? What happened?"

"Don't worry," Caleb said. He shrugged out of his jacket and hung it on a brass hook. "Situation's under control. The invasion has been put off indefinitely."

Roland grinned as he took off his jacket. "Your friend Blade is back out on regular sentry duty."

"But what have you been doing?" Serenity hastened after Caleb and Roland as they crossed the room to warm themselves near the wood stove.

"Performing my mayoral duties. I and my companions have been busy welcoming a new citizen to Witt's End." Caleb held his hands out to the heat. He caught his grandfather's amused gaze and winked.

"What new citizen?" Serenity asked.

"Lloyd Radburn, distinguished professor of Sociology." Caleb grinned. "Jessie's real estate agent rented him the Asterley cabin."

"Oh, no." Serenity looked thoroughly disgusted. "I was so hoping he'd give up his stupid research project."

"He's probably considering doing just that about now," Roland said with suspicious blandness.

Serenity frowned. "Wait a minute. What have you two been up to out there? I hope you haven't done anything that's going to cause trouble."

"We haven't done a damn thing except welcome the guy to town," Caleb said.

Serenity put her hands on her hips and regarded both men with narrowed eyes. "And just how did you go about doing that?"

"We sent Blade to the front door to tell him about the possibility of an impending invasion," Roland explained. "Caleb said that it was only fair to warn the man about the risks of living here."

"You sent Blade in?" Serenity looked startled. "But Lloyd has never met him. He wouldn't understand. You know how alarming Blade can be on first sight. I hope you went to the door, too, in order to sort of explain Blade to Lloyd."

Caleb smiled at Roland across the wood stove. "Damn. We didn't think of that, did we?"

"Nope, sure didn't. Don't exactly know how you'd go about explaining your friend Blade, anyway. Kind of unique."

"You don't explain Blade, you experience him." Caleb headed for the kitchen. "I believe the news that we're not going to be invaded tonight calls for a beer. Want one, Roland?"

"Why not. Not every night a man gets to celebrate an invasion that's been called off."

Serenity's smiling eyes met Caleb's as he opened the refrigerator. "You two can sit out here all night, drink Old Hogwash and tell each other how you stopped the invasion of Witt's End. As for me, I'm going to bed. I need my sleep."

"Yeah, I know." Caleb picked up two bottles of Old Hogwash and closed the refrigerator door. "You're in training."

"That's right. Good night, gentlemen." Serenity smiled serenely at both men and went down the hall to the bedroom.

A heady rush of emotion filled Caleb as he watched her disappear. He turned his head and saw Roland regarding him with a peculiar expression.

"She'll make an interesting granddaughter-in-law,

all right," Roland said as Caleb handed him one of the bottles of Old Hogwash. "But promise me one thing."

"What's that?"

"Try to keep those photos Asterley took of her out of the *Ventress Valley News*, will you? I'm not sure your hometown is capable of appreciating that sort of fine art."

Caleb thought of the negatives he had found in Firebrace's desk drawer a couple of minutes before the Seattle police had answered the 911 summons. "Don't worry. I think I can promise you that those pictures are going to stay in my private collection. There's only one person who may still have copies, and I believe we can get hold of those."

"Who's that?"

"Franklin."

"I'll get them back from Franklin," Roland said grimly.

Caleb took a swallow of Old Hogwash and considered how to say what had to be said. "There's a couple of things you should know about the past."

Roland sighed and sat down in the overstuffed armchair. "I'm listening."

The gentle clink of beads awoke Serenity an hour and a half later. She stirred amid the covers as Caleb parted the curtain and got into bed. He reached out to pull her into his arms.

She touched his face gently. "How did it go?"

Caleb threaded his fingers through her hair and leaned over to nuzzle her ear. "How did what go?"

"Your talk with Roland."

"Fine. He's bedded down on the sofa." Caleb kissed her throat.

Serenity tried to evade his mouth. "Did you tell him everything? About how your parents died? About Firebrace?"

"Uh-huh." Caleb eased his leg higher between her thighs.

"Did you tell him about Franklin's affair with Patricia?"

"No. Like I said earlier, there's not much point."

"Well?"

"Well, what?"

"Well, how did he take all your news?" Serenity asked, exasperated.

"He took it," Caleb said. "As he himself reminded me, he's eighty-two years old. He's had a lot of experience at taking whatever life hands him."

Serenity thought about that. "And he's capable of changing, Caleb. He's proven that."

"Yeah." Caleb moved his hand up along her leg to the top of her thigh.

"For your sake."

"Yeah." He squeezed gently.

"He didn't come here tonight because I coerced him into it, you know. He came because of you."

"I know." Caleb pulled her down across his chest.

"He came here because he wanted to do things differently this time," Serenity said earnestly. "Because he didn't want to repeat the mistakes of the past."

"If you say so." He curved his hand around the back of her head and pulled her mouth to his.

"And you care for him," Serenity mumbled against his lips.

"He's my grandfather. I'm his grandson. We didn't get all mushy about it. We just decided that we both have a hell of a lot of bits and pieces of each other stuck to us."

"Caleb, I'm sure that what you feel for your grandfather is a genuine filial love," Serenity said. "And he loves you like a son. I can tell."

"Is that right?"

"I'm sure of it."

"You're entitled to your opinion. Now, if you don't mind, I'd like to change the subject."

"What do you want to talk about?"

"Your training schedule." He brushed his mouth lightly across hers and then he kissed the line of her jaw.

"Oh, that." Serenity smiled in the shadows. "I want to do the best possible job on this baby. After all, it will be the first baby born in Witt's End since I arrived."

"I can understand your desire to do your best. Rest assured that you have obtained the best possible consulting assistance on this project."

"That's nice to know."

Caleb framed her face between his palms and looked up at her with disturbingly serious eyes. "I should warn you that I haven't had much experience with babies and all the stuff that goes with them."

"Don't worry about it," Serenity whispered. "Something tells me you'll be very good at that kind of thing."

The loud knock on the front door brought Caleb abruptly awake. He turned on his side, untangled his legs from Serenity's and sat up in bed. The cold light of morning was seeping through the window.

Whoever was at the front door pounded again, more heavily this time.

"Someone's at the door," Serenity mumbled from beneath a pillow.

"No kidding." Caleb shoved aside the covers. "Whoever he is, he hasn't got long to live."

Serenity gave a muffled laugh. "It's probably Harry come to collect your grandfather and take him home. He'll be nervous enough as it is, don't terrorize him."

"He didn't have to arrive at the crack of dawn." Caleb yanked on his jeans and stalked down the hall toward the living room. He heard the front door open before he reached it.

"Good morning," Roland drawled politely. "Bit early to come calling, isn't it?"

"Who the hell are you?" a deep, gruff voice demanded.

"Name's Ventress. Who are you?"

"You're Ventress?" The bearlike voice rose on a note of patent disbelief. "Ariadne told me you were in your thirties. Some kind of hotshot business consultant or something."

"I'm Caleb Ventress," Caleb said stonily as he rounded the corner.

"Is that a fact?" The huge man in the doorway glared at him from beneath a jutting browline that would have done justice to a Neanderthal. The gold earring he wore gleamed evilly. He flicked another glance at Roland, who was holding the door open. "Just how many Ventresses are there around here?"

"Two." Caleb swept the visitor with a quick, assessing glance.

The big man not only sounded like a bear, he looked like one. He had massive shoulders, a thick beard, and broad, heavy features. His dark brown eyes glittered ominously. He was dressed in faded jeans, leather boots, and a black leather jacket trimmed with silver studs. He wore a bandanna tied around his receding gray hair in a fashion favored by motorcycle outlaws and pirates.

"Well, well, well." The man looked Caleb up and down with a blunt, appraising expression. "So you're the one."

"Looks like it. Who are you?" Caleb asked.

"Name's Julius Makepeace, son." White teeth flashed in the middle of a brushy beard. "Let's hope we get along real good. From what I hear, I'm the closest thing you've got to a future father-in-law."

20

NINE AND A HALF MONTHS LATER, SHORTLY AFTER NOON on a bright summer day, Serenity abruptly realized that something was happening inside her. She looked up from the glowing review of the Ambrose Asterley Retrospective exhibit that had appeared in yesterday's edition of the *Seattle Times*.

"I think you'd better go find Caleb," she said to Zone.

Zone did not lift her gaze from a stack of order forms that had arrived in the morning mail. The second edition of the Witt's End by Mail catalog had gone out and business was brisk. "The mayor and his grandfather are inspecting the warehouse. The big storm last night did some damage, apparently. A tree was blown down across the roof."

A warehouse had become a necessity within three months of the publication of the first edition of Witt's

End by Mail. The orders had come in swiftly and steadily. Caleb's major concern, in fact, had been finding ways to stabilize and control the growth of the business.

Serenity put her hand to her lower back and winced. "Please go find Caleb and tell him it's time."

"Time for what?" Zone looked up with a quizzical expression. Then her eyes widened. "Oh, my goodness. Time? You mean it's *your* time?"

"Yes." Serenity caught her breath.

Zone leaped to her feet. "You aren't due for another two weeks."

"I think you'd better hurry."

"Stay right where you are." Zone's saffron and orange robes formed wings in the air as she rushed for the door. "Don't move. I'll get Caleb and the others."

"Don't worry," Serenity whispered aloud to the empty office. "I'm not going anywhere."

Zone was right about one thing, she thought. It was too soon. Two weeks too soon. And it was all happening too fast. According to her doctor, she was supposed to have plenty of warning. Plenty of time to make the drive down the mountain to Bullington Memorial Hospital.

Belatedly she realized that she should have paid more attention to the ache in her lower back that had awakened her this morning. She was so accustomed to the general discomforts of her pregnancy these days that she hadn't given the new pains much thought.

She glanced at the clock and realized with a shock that she might have been in labor for several hours and only just now realized it.

Serenity hauled herself to her feet and then promptly collapsed back into the chair again as a strong contraction seized her. She tried to remember the birthing mantras Zone had drilled into her.

The bells in the outer room clashed violently as the door was thrown open.

"Serenity?" Caleb shouted. "Where are you?"

"In here." She smiled weakly as he appeared in the doorway. Roland, Ariadne, Zone, Julius, and Montrose were right behind him. She heard footsteps pounding outside on the wooden sidewalk as others got the word. "I hope you're good at this kind of thing, because I don't think there's going to be time to get down the mountain."

"Can't get down the mountain," Montrose said, looking close to panic. "There's a tree down because of last night's big storm. Road crew from Bullington hasn't gotten to it yet."

"Call the aid car," Caleb said. "Tell them you'll meet them at the downed tree. You can pick the medics up there and bring them here to Witt's End."

"Right." Montrose spun around and grabbed one of the three new telephones that had been installed to handle Witt's End by Mail business.

Julius loomed in the doorway behind Caleb. He had a stark, oddly stricken expression on his face. "Goddamn it, no. It can't happen here like it did last time." He grabbed Caleb's arm. "We've got to get her to the hospital, man."

"We will." Caleb went toward Serenity.

Serenity sucked in her breath on another contraction.

"Damn." Jessie appeared in the doorway. She stared at Serenity. "We've got to do something."

"Please." Ariadne gave Serenity a beseeching look. "You've got to hold on until we can get you to the hospital. We can't take any chances."

Caleb leaned down and scooped Serenity up out of the chair. Cradling her in his arms, he turned toward the door. "Get out of the way."

Everyone moved aside.

From the security of Caleb's arms, Serenity looked at the sea of anxious faces that surrounded her. She knew that everyone in the room was recalling the circumstances of her mother's death. They needed reassurance more than she did.

"It's all right," she said. "This isn't going to be like last time. I've been in training." Another wave of pain swept through her. She turned her face into Caleb's shoulder. "Take me home, please. This baby is going to be born in aisle three between granola and salsa if you don't hurry."

"Hang on," Serenity," Caleb said fiercely. "You're going to be all right."

"I know. That's what I'm trying to tell you." Serenity tried unsuccessfully to choke back a strangled cry as another wave of pain crashed through her.

Caleb strode toward the door with Serenity in his arms.

"Don't worry, folks," Roland said very calmly from somewhere nearby. "Caleb and I have delivered more than one baby together. We can handle this."

"Those were foals we delivered," Caleb said roughly. "Not babies."

"Not that much difference," Roland said gently. "Nature does all the work. You'll see."

* * *

Sunlight, warm and golden, poured into the white room. Serenity held the infants cradled in her arms and watched the closed door. Soon it would open and he would come to her.

Little Gordon Trevor Ventress stirred. She glanced down and smiled. "Don't worry, your daddy will be here soon. He'll take us home." Tiny Emily Crystal Ventress waved a tiny hand.

The twins had been born, safe and sound and without complications, in their parents' bed in Witt's End. Their father had caught them both in his arms.

The drama had no sooner concluded than word had come that the road had finally been cleared. The aid car arrived a short while later. The medics took Serenity and the babies to Bullington Memorial for a routine medical examination.

Mother and babies had been pronounced fit and healthy by a cheerful doctor who had praised everyone concerned. Serenity, Gordon Trevor, and Emily Crystal had spent the night in the hospital. Now it was time to go home.

Serenity crooned to the infants while she gazed in wonder at the hospital room. She had awakened this morning with a curious sensation of déjà vu. It hadn't taken her long to recognize her surroundings. A stark white room, golden sunlight, and a closed door. It was straight out of the vision she'd had last year in the pool cave.

"Impossible," she whispered to Gordon and Emily. "Sheerest coincidence."

She could have sworn that she heard a waltz playing.

The door opened.

A man walked into the white, sunlit room.

He smiled at her.

"Damn," Serenity said. "Wrong man."

"Hey, hey, hey, Serenity. How's the new mother?" Lloyd Radburn bounced cheerfully over to the bed. He was grinning hugely. In his hand were two rolled-up copies of what appeared to be an academic journal. There was a pink bow tied around one and a blue bow tied around the other.

She smiled. "Hi, Lloyd. What have you got there?"

"This?" Lloyd held up the journal. "Just a little present for the kids. An advance copy of the next quarterly issue of the *Journal of Social Dynamics*. My article is in it. Thought maybe it would make a good souvenir for the twins."

"Why, thank you, Lloyd. That was very thoughtful of you."

"Think nothing of it. It got me the promotion. You are looking at the new head of the Department of Sociology at Bullington College."

"Congratulations."

"Hey, couldn't have done it without you." Lloyd chuckled as he looked down at the infants in her arms. "The paper didn't turn out quite the way I had anticipated, but the editor said it was a unique piece of work. I, of course, agreed."

"What's the title of your paper?"

"'From Outsiders to Entrepreneurs: The Effects of a Small Business Enterprise on the Social Structure of a Typical Frontier Town.'"

"That sounds impressive."

"Thank you. I thought so, too." Lloyd tried and failed to appear modest. "Got to admit, I owe you,

Serenity love. If you hadn't told the good people of Witt's End that it was okay to cooperate with me, I wouldn't have gotten anywhere with that paper."

"I'll show your article to little Gordon and Emily as soon as they're able to read," Serenity promised.

"Great. Say, uh, I've been thinking, Serenity . . ."

Serenity looked up and saw the familiar gleam in his eyes. She groaned. "No, absolutely not. I told everyone to cooperate once in order to get rid of you. Don't expect any help on another study. I've got too much else to do these days."

"But this study will have more of an anthropological orientation," Lloyd said persuasively. "I'm thinking of calling it 'Visions, Traditions and Change: The Development and Modification of a Legend in a Typical Frontier Community.'"

"Forget it."

"But it's perfect, Serenity. Especially now with little Gordon and Emily, here. Big finish for a living legend."

"What living legend?"

"You."

"Lloyd, I'm warning you, I have absolutely no intention of helping you do another sociological study of Witt's End. Is that clear?"

"Sure, hey, no need to worry about it right now," Lloyd assured her. "You've got other things to think about at the moment. I understand that."

"I'm glad you do." Serenity frowned. "Lloyd, do you hear a waltz?"

"Someone's got a radio on down at the nurse's station." Lloyd leaned forward get a better look at Emily Crystal.

The door of the white, sunlit room opened.

Caleb came into the room.

He smiled at her.

For an instant time stood still.

"Right man," Serenity whispered. "We've been waiting for you."

"Hey, hey, hey." Lloyd stuck out his hand to Caleb. "Congratulations, Mr. Mayor. Kids look just like you."

Caleb glowered at Lloyd but allowed his hand to be shaken. "What are you doing here, Radburn? Thought we'd seen the last of you after you finished your research project."

"Just came to pay my respects to the new arrivals," Lloyd said.

"Fine. If you don't mind, I'd like to take my family home."

"No problem." Lloyd sauntered toward the door. "See you all later."

"Not if I can help it." When he left, Caleb smiled at Serenity. "Ready?"

She cradled Gordon Trevor and Emily Crystal close. "We're all ready."

"The nurse said she'd be along in a minute with a wheelchair." Caleb touched his son's tiny hand. Quiet amazement warmed his eyes.

"I don't need a wheelchair."

"They won't let you walk out of here under your own steam." Caleb grinned as he admired Emily Crystal. "Incredible, aren't they?"

"Yes, they are. Where's your grandfather?"

"Waiting outside along with everyone else."

"Good grief, *everyone's* out there in the waiting room?"

"Just about."

"Who's running the store? Who's responding to the new catalog orders that will be in the mail? Who's handling the phones to take complaints and check on order problems?"

"Relax. We left someone behind to handle the phones," Caleb said.

"Who?"

"Blade."

"Oh, no." Serenity panicked. "We've got to get back to Witt's End immediately. Blade will assume that anyone who calls in to place an order is secretly planning an invasion."

"I'm just kidding. Don't worry. The situation's under control. Zone's with him." Caleb met her eyes. "Before we leave, I want to give you this." He held out a package he had brought with him.

"Oh, Caleb. Thank you."

Caleb picked up Gordon Trevor and held him while Serenity cradled Emily Crystal in one arm and removed the brown paper from around the gift with her free hand. She found herself looking down at two volumes bound in fading imitation leather.

"What on earth? High school yearbooks." Serenity looked up. "I don't understand. Are they yours?"

"No." Caleb watched her intently. "They're from your parents' high schools."

"My *parents.*" Serenity could hardly breathe.

"It took a private investigator several months to trace the schools and then locate yearbooks from the right years. He sent them to me in yesterday's mail. What with one thing and another, I didn't have a chance to give them to you."

Serenity's mouth was so dry she could hardly speak. "My parents are in here?"

"I marked the pages." Caleb smiled. "Take a look."

Serenity slowly opened the first volume. Her gaze went instantly to the face of a young woman. A senior. The photo revealed a gentle-looking creature whose eyes held both wariness and hope.

Serenity stared at the picture for a long, long time. *Her mother.*

"You have her eyes. Take a look at the other one," Caleb prompted after a minute.

Serenity's fingers were trembling so badly she could hardly get the second volume open. When she finally managed it, she found herself gazing down at a color photo of a young man, a senior. *Trevor Jones.* The shadows in his eyes betrayed a cloudy past, but there was resilience, strength, and determination in his face.

Serenity touched the picture of her father with a sense of wonder. "He had red hair."

Caleb looked at the cloud of fiery hair that framed Serenity's features. "You didn't think it came out of nowhere, did you?"

"Bits and pieces of other people," Serenity whispered. Her eyes misted over. "Caleb you have given me a wonderful gift."

"It's nothing compared to what you've given me," Caleb said. "I love you, Serenity."

She looked up at him and saw the sure and certain knowledge in his eyes. "I always knew you'd be good at that kind of thing."

The door opened at that moment. A smiling nurse entered the room with a wheelchair. She looked at Serenity. "Ready to go home?"

"Yes," Serenity said. "We are."

Caleb paused briefly to glance around the sunlit

white room before he followed his family out into the hall. He frowned thoughtfully. "You know, there's something familiar about this place."

Serenity laughed. Joy welled up inside her, crystal clear water bubbling forth from a fathomless spring. "I know exactly what you mean."